THE FAERIE KING

THE FAERIE KING

STRANGER MAGICS,
BOOK TWO

ASH FITZSIMMONS

Print Edition ISBN: 978-1-949861-00-6

Cover design by BespokeBookCovers.com

www.ashfitzsimmons.com

CHAPTER 1

Hindsight is a smug bastard.

In retrospect, I see the contours of the puzzle, the sequential effect of each decision on the next like a chain of poor choices. But there's no known method of scrying the future via enchantment, and that September, I saw only progress ahead. I'd survived my first six months as king of a faerie court that vacillated between indifferent and sullen toward me, I'd reconnected with the woman I adored, and I'd begun to adapt to the rhythms of governing the peculiar sort of asylum I'd inherited. My guards did my bidding, my daughter's bind—and rewritten memory—appeared to be holding together...what more could I have wanted? True, I grumbled at the petty annoyances of court life and the constant complaints of my temperamental people, but I reassured myself that I'd bring their squabbles and griping under control. Another six months, I mused, and I'd have the court running like a fine pocket watch.

In truth, it was as if I were hiking toward a lovely range of mountains in the distance, thinking I'd never have a problem more challenging than the occasional blister, and unaware that one of those snow-capped mountains was an active volcano days away from explosion.

Had I known the lurking danger, I wouldn't have rested until I'd ground it beneath my heel and burned the remains. But my foresight is no keener than a mortal's, and so I slept the comfortable, self-congratulatory sleep of a fool.

But then came the phone call in the wee hours, the beginning of the chaos of that autumn. I woke to see the aggravating little device sitting on the bedside table inches from my face, blinking its red notification light and blasting its snippet of fugue, and I made the mistake of flipping it open, holding it to my ear, and mumbling, "Yes?"

"Hey, Colin," said the soft voice on the other end— Joey, I realized, trying to sound confident but barely disguising the tension in his whisper. "Sorry to bother you, but, uh…do dragons exist?"

The list of activities in which I enjoy partaking at two in the morning is short, and most of the items comprising it are some variant of "sleep" or "drink heavily." Skulking around a tent on bare feet, holding my breath so as not to disturb a feeding dragon, is most definitely not on that list. But there I was, all the same: rumpled T-shirt and sweatpants, bed-mussed hair, and lurking backup with a twitchy sword hand—who, incidentally, was the reason I was wandering around the godforsaken backcountry of Faerie in the deep predawn in the first place.

The dragon, nearly eye-deep in Joey's ruined food bag, was too preoccupied with its prize to notice me as I crept closer, but still, I took my time, trying not to startle it. I was no expert on dragons—though I knew enough to understand that they were best left unprovoked, mind you—and until that night, I had yet to see one in the flesh. In the light of the blue flame I kept half-shielded in my hand, I could make out something black and scaly with a pair of folded wings, roughly the size of a Shetland pony, and with the table manners of a boar. It rooted, swallowed, and belched intermittently, and as it was fixated on its meal, it was oblivious to my dash behind a tree near its right flank.

I leaned against the trunk, trying to formulate a plan,

and silently berated myself. It was a dragon. Just a stupid little dragon. A hatchling, obviously, judging by the shell fragments in the weeds. Probably couldn't even fly yet. Nothing to worry about. I could take it, easily.

And yet…

I cut my eyes back to Joey, who had slipped out of his tent to watch. He quietly unsheathed his sword and pointed it at the dragon, but I shook my head. There was no need to risk injury to him, no matter how loudly the small, dogged part of my mind that believed in the buddy system was begging me to set aside my pride and remember that I'd never actually fought a dragon before. Plenty of faeries, scores of wizards, and a troll or two, yes, but never an opponent that scored a bingo in my internal game of *Should I Run Now?* The sad truth of the matter was that I wanted Joey beside me—and if I were honest with myself, a tiny part of me wanted him there for the same reason that when faced with an angry bear, one desires nothing more than a paraplegic companion.

Fortunately for my continued ability to look myself in the mirror, I pushed those thoughts aside. Joey was quick and reasonably skilled with a sword, but in the end, all he was holding was a pointy stick. I could take on a dragon by myself, especially a damn *hatchling*, but that knowledge did nothing to silence the voice that continued to remind me, with increasing fervor, that there's a certain risk inherent in maintaining proximity to a giant lizard with correspondingly large teeth.

"Damn it, Coileán," I muttered to the night, "pull yourself together."

The frantic little internal voice was joined by a second one, which nagged instead of shouted but was no less irritating. I didn't have to do this, it whispered. I could have sent someone else to take care of the problem. Hell, I could have just yanked Joey back through the rift to my bedroom and returned him to clean up what was left of his camp in the morning. But any of those options would have resulted in a certain loss of face, and I'd maintained hold of my mother's vacated throne for a mere six months. I couldn't afford to look weak.

And there was the matter of Joey to consider. I couldn't, in good conscience, let anything happen to the kid. He had balls of titanium to be exploring the realm on his own, and he had been calling daily with his findings, trying to help me get the lay of the land as I dealt with matters closer to home. But Joey had made camp late that evening, and he must have either missed the egg or mistaken it for a boulder in the dark. I couldn't be too angry with him for camping by a nest—he'd been in the realm barely a season, after all, and that night was the first time he'd called me with an emergency.

I glanced around the tree again, but the dragon was too busy trying to bite through a tin of SpaghettiOs to pay me any heed. As it fumbled with the can in the darkness, I played through possible scenarios. The best option, I mused, would be to run out, stun it, and if necessary, dispatch it...or I could stun it, give Joey time to pack his gear, and take us out of there before the beast recovered...

I was still mulling over strategy when I noticed that Joey had left the shelter of the tent and was crawling through the low grass on his elbows toward the dragon, sword in his right fist, flashlight in his left. I froze, trying to add this new variable to my computations, but before I could push Joey out of danger, the dragon pulled its nose from his shredded knapsack and turned its oversized head toward the light on the ground.

Joey lay still, poised to spring, and I readied a ball of fire in my fist.

To my surprise, the dragon flopped to its belly and fixated on Joey. It inched forward hesitantly, and when he held his ground, the dragon let loose a psychic outburst of rapturous joy: *MAMA!*

By the time Joey scrambled to his feet and sheathed his blade, the dragon was upon him. It knocked him to his back and nuzzled him in the gut with the force of a prizefighter's first-round blow. Extinguishing the fireball for safety, I ran from my hiding place before my resident quasi-knight could be crushed under three hundred pounds of excited lizard. "No sudden moves!" I yelled. "Just stay still, I'm coming!"

The dragon continued to rub its face against Joey like an oversized kitten, and he awkwardly reached up to pat its snout. "What's it doing?" he asked, keeping his eyes on the dragon and his voice calm.

I crouched at his side and lit my flame once more, but I stayed out of the preoccupied dragon's line of sight. "That's a hatchling," I said. "You're looking at a newborn."

Joey's dark eyes widened. "*Newborn?*"

"Shell fragments twenty feet behind me. It probably hatched while you were sleeping." I slid aside a pace, giving the dragon's flailing tail a wider berth. "No sign of the mother or the rest of the clutch, so we're in luck."

He continued to rub the hatchling's nose, eliciting from the beast a sound somewhere between a purr and a growl, with overtones of garbage disposal. "So what do we do?"

"I don't know, man, you seem to have this well in hand—"

"*Colin.*"

"I'm serious." The dragon's pleased rumble increased in volume as Joey's hand moved toward its horn buds. "You've heard of imprinting?"

"Like…birds?" he asked, raising his voice to be heard over the hatchling.

"Exactly." I stood and took in the scene—the dragon wasn't crushing Joey, but it had him pinned. "I'd guess that this one hatched late. Mom and the others must have moved on. Wait there, I'll check."

A quick jog back to the nest site told me all I needed to know, and I rejoined Joey after a moment. "Yeah, this was a late hatch. The fresh fragments are still damp, but the shells around them are bone-dry. This one's a few days behind, maybe a week." I paused and peered at his inscrutable expression. "Are you hurt? I could blast it now, but I'd rather get you out from underneath first, just in case."

Joey kept rubbing the dragon. "Don't leave me, okay? You ran off, there."

His voice was steady, but his eyes betrayed his fear, and I kicked myself. Joey was resourceful and surprisingly tough for a seminary dropout—and that still left him grossly outclassed by everything around him. Sure, the steel he carried would do decent damage against any faerie, but dragons weren't native to the realm, and as this one was making perfectly clear by its proximity to Joey's sword, it was insensitive to iron. Unless he could skewer it, he was defenseless, and given that there was a mass of very happy dragon between his free hand and his sheathed sword, the odds of skewering seemed slim.

"I'm not going anywhere," I reassured him, crouching beside him again. "I'm not leaving you, Joey. Stay calm, all right?"

A degree of tension left his face as he nodded. "Okay. So you're telling me we've got an abandoned baby, yeah? Can we get it back to its mother?"

The dragon closed its red eyes and snuggled against Joey's T-shirt, pressing the air from his lungs with its bulk.

"Bad idea," I said. "Those things grow incredibly fast. If its siblings have a week on it—"

"It'll never catch up?" he gasped.

"It'll never get the chance. Mom will reject it, siblings will eat it. Cannibalism isn't unheard of among dragons. Kinder to put it down now."

Joey's hand continued to stroke the cuddling hatchling. "It thinks I'm its mom."

"Well, yes, it saw you first and imprinted—"

His voice was strained. "Colin, *it thinks I'm its mom.*"

That reaction gave me pause. My plan had been to stun

and run, but Joey—who, I reminded myself, had grown up with a horse under him and didn't automatically expect every animal he encountered to try to bite his head off—was, dare I say it, bonding with the thing crushing his ribcage with its love. I mean, true, the thing in question was a massive lizard—low-scoring in terms of cute and fuzzy—but it was still a hatchling, and it had thrown itself at Joey. A lucky choice, all things considered. Sure, Joey had faced down two faerie queens with an augmented nail gun, but he was, at heart, somewhat tender.

The look he was giving me at that moment could only be interpreted as a modified version of *Can I keep it?*

I sighed and rubbed the corners of my eyes. "It's going to *grow*."

"It's all alone, and I think it's hungry," he protested between shallow breaths.

I began to counter that, but I realized it was a lost cause and began to draw upon the magic around me. The dragon, which had fallen asleep on top of Joey, levitated with my enchantment, and I pulled Joey to his feet before moving underneath the hatchling for a closer inspection. "Female. Definitely female."

"Good to know," he said, brushing wet grass off his back.

"Females go into heat."

"Been there, handled that."

I tried another tactic. "She's going to be enormous, kid. Two hundred feet, easily."

He didn't flinch. "I'm guessing there's somewhere around here that she could be housed, hmm?"

"I…suppose I could work something up," I reluctantly admitted.

"And fed?"

"Sheep are easy."

I dropped the dragon back onto the grass, and Joey folded his arms. "She's telepathic?"

"It's a dragon thing. They're intelligent, but their

mouths aren't formed for speech. Hey, did I mention the fire breathing? Because that could turn into an adorable little fire-breathing bundle of trouble."

"And I can't just leave her," he murmured, kneeling beside the beast's head and resuming his horn rub. "She'll starve." He looked up at me and frowned. "Can she understand us?"

"No," I replied, squatting on the other side of the dragon. "And I'm going to assume that you haven't been hiding telepathy from me, yes?" He grunted, and I rested my free hand on the dragon's head. "This should work, but I make no guarantees."

As the new enchantment hit it, the creature's eyes flew open—in shock, I hoped, not pain—and Joey made shushing noises until its eyes focused on him. "It's okay, little girl, you're safe," he soothed in his drawled version of Fae, stroking her face.

The dragon, to whom everything was still new, seemed nonplussed by his words. *Mama?*

Joey paused, then slowly exhaled. "I'm sorry, girl, but your mama's not here. She's gone. I don't know where she is."

I didn't know it was possible to read anguish in a dragon's face.

Mama? she asked again. The thought was tinged with panic, and her eyes bored into Joey's, as if waiting for an explanation that made sense.

"Don't you worry," he assured the hatchling, and wrapped his arms around her head and neck. "I'm going to take care of you. You can come home with me, and I'll get you a nice bed—"

The dragon's rumbling stomach silenced him, and she whimpered.

"It's okay, you're hungry," he said, trying to console her. "We'll fix that." He looked at me expectantly, and a dead, skinned sheep appeared at his feet.

"Pre-cooked," I said, watching him examine the corpse.

"See if she'll take it."

The dragon looked around at the sudden smell of charred meat, then spied the sheep in the dirt and dove for it. Joey jumped back in time to avoid the juice splatter as the dragon attacked its meal with inch-long teeth, and I shrugged. "And that answers that."

He stayed within the dragon's sight as she ate. When the sheep was little more than bones, she wiped her face on the damp grass, burped, and rubbed up against him. *Mama?*

"Joey?" he suggested.

The dragon looked at him and snorted contentedly. *Joey.*

My lord? Are you...well?"

I groaned, rolled over, and found a dark blob blocking the sunlight that was streaming annoyingly through the windows to the left of my bed. Two blinks resolved the blob into Valerius, the captain of my guard, who was staring down at me with concern. "I'm fine," I muttered, darkening the windows to near-opacity. "Long night. What time—"

"About an hour after dawn, my lord."

I ran back the clock. "Then I went to sleep an hour ago. Is anything pressing?"

He offered a one-shouldered shrug. "Nothing that can't be rescheduled. Your brother—"

"Which one?" I mumbled through a yawn, pushing the blankets back.

Valerius had the grace to say nothing about the grass clinging to my feet or littering the bed. "Lord Doran, my lord. He sent a messenger to beg an audience."

"He can rot." I scratched my ribs, felt something askance, and plucked a leaf off my shirt. "Anything else?"

"Not yet, to my knowledge. I could check," he offered, but I waved it away.

"Save it. I'll eat first. Bathe, maybe." I caught a whiff of my shirt. "No, bathe first. Definitely a bath. Hold down the fort, will you?" I said, heading for the door.

"Consider it…held?"

I looked back at Valerius, whose smooth, glamourless face belied his youth in Rome—a senator's faerie bastard who had made his way over the border long before my time. That was the extent of what he'd told me of his history before Faerie—he hadn't even offered me his full name—but I did him the courtesy of not prying. I knew too well the parts of my own past best left unvisited. "Idiomatic. Just make sure no one sneaks in to stab me, hmm?"

That earned a smirk in reply. "Of course. Would you like assistance, my lord?"

"How many times have we been over this? Remind me."

He held his hands up in placation. "I assume nothing."

"I'm not my mother, Captain," I said, opening the bathroom door. "And should I ever feel the need for an audience in the bath, I'll give you fair warning and ample time to have my head examined, understood?"

He chuckled softly, and when I left the door open a crack, he took up a position beside it. "A question, my lord?"

I paused with my hand over the giant Jacuzzi I'd installed. After years of living in my bookstore apartment, it was extremely satisfying to be in sole possession of a tub large enough to host Olympic events. "Go ahead," I called back to him across the echoing bathroom, willing several thousand gallons of hot water into existence.

Valerius hesitated. "I couldn't help but notice the new, uh…barn."

"I can move it if it's troubling you."

"No, no, nothing of the sort," he hastened to assure me. I could almost see him cringing in expectation of the blow to come. "I…was wondering about its purpose…"

He let the question die, and I stripped off my soiled T-shirt. "Joey acquired a pet last night. He needed somewhere to house it."

"A pet, my lord?"

"Of the draconic variety."

My bodyguard swore softly. "May I ask *why*, my lord?"

I glanced in the mirror, which was beginning to fog over, and rubbed at a streak of soot under my eye. Small wonder Valerius had been concerned—I looked like shit, and Mother had never appeared with so much as a hair out of place. "Abandoned hatchling. She bonded with him, so what was I supposed to do?"

"Kill it?"

"Joey would never have forgiven me. So we came back here last night, and I put up the barn. And the sheep pen."

"I was about to ask, my lord."

"Hatchling needs to eat. Joey butchered and roasted a few before she settled down."

"Hence the fire pit?"

"Hence the fire pit." I shucked off my pants and sank into the tub. "When I left them, he was sleeping with her. He's probably still out there if you want to shake some sense into him."

"Perhaps later." The door creaked, and I assumed Valerius had leaned toward the slight opening to be better heard. "My lord, uh…will you grant me one more question?"

I closed my eyes as my muscles unkinked. "Sure."

He hesitated again, and I waited through a solid minute of awkward silence before telling him, "No, he's not my lover. Or, to be clear, my plaything."

The relief in Valerius's voice at being saved the asking was unmistakable. "Then what *is* the mortal doing here, my lord? If I may enquire."

It was my turn to puzzle out a response. "I like him," I finally replied. "I can't shake the feeling that I may have ruined his life, and for that, at least, he's my responsibility.

And he's been mapping the woods for me, you know…"

Valerius cleared his throat. "I mean this in the best possible way, my lord, but are you quite sure you're fae?"

I reached for the shampoo. "Realm seems to think so."

"And the realm accepts your, um…guest?"

The question caught me off-guard, and I left the bottle where it sat. "Yes. Shouldn't it?"

"Perhaps. The queen…"

His sudden quiet told me enough. "Go on."

He coughed. "Some changelings couldn't stay long. The realm wouldn't accept them, and the queen—"

"The nagging, I know. You should hear it bitch when Toula pops by." I grabbed the shampoo and tried to rub the smells of wood smoke and roasted mutton out of my hair. "Any commonality among the rejected?"

"None that I know, my lord."

"Well, the realm seems to tolerate Joey for now." I held my breath and ducked beneath the surface, letting the jets rinse the lather away, then popped back up and wiped my eyes. "Valerius?"

"Still here," he called through the door.

"You've never spoken to me of Mother before."

His boots shuffled against the stone in the other room. "I did not wish to cause offense, my lord."

"You served her well. And willingly."

He paused for the space of a long breath. "I did."

"And now you serve me."

"I do," he replied without hesitation.

"Why?"

"My lord?"

I sniffed the ends of my hair, still picked up hints of campfire, and shampooed again. The exercise was unnecessary—I could have simply willed myself clean—but what's life without little pleasures? "You were under no obligation to keep your position," I told him. "I mean, you were there—"

"I saw what she did to Lord Robin," he murmured,

almost inaudible with the distance between us. "And Lady Moyna. And the child's mother. And…others."

I put the bottle down. "And?"

"And Joey is an excellent shot."

"That he is," I said, and ducked under again.

Valerius had the decency to wait until I'd broken the surface once more before continuing the conversation. "Is he going to be staying here now, my lord?"

"Joey?" My hair passed the sniff test, and I drained the tub and began to dry off. "I would assume so, given the dragon. Why?"

"The sword he carries—"

"Is for his protection," I interrupted, "and I won't hear anything about it. Hell, if the kid wants to wear maille, I won't stop him."

"I wasn't suggesting disarming him," Valerius replied— again, too quickly to hide his unease, and I wondered what Mother had been in the habit of doing when her guards displeased her. "How adept is he?"

I gave it a moment's thought. "Passable, though I understand his martial training was at the hands of actors."

Valerius groaned. "I could work with him."

I tried to imagine Joey—who, on his best day, was still a twenty-five-year-old kid—squaring off against a guy who'd been armed and fighting long before Caesar set off on his French vacation. "Promise me you won't kill him."

"Or seriously maim him, my lord."

"That, too." I willed my hair dry as a set of clothes appeared. "Ask him. He might want a challenge."

"Aside from the dragon, you mean?"

"Eh, kid's good with animals." I straightened my robe, wiped the mirror clear, and made a face at my improved reflection. "But if Joey sets the lawn on fire, do me a favor and put it out, won't you?"

Once decent and fed, I wandered down the rose-hedged

avenue behind the palace to survey the work I'd thrown together in the dark. The barn was rough, yes, and of a style more properly belonging in a pasture than squatting in my pleasure gardens like the world's shabbiest folly, but at least the framing seemed level, and the containment measures around the rudimentary fire pit appeared to have done their job. The place could use a good paint job, I decided as I pushed open the narrow side door, and maybe some nice stonework to match the vaguely gothic palace beside it—there was no reason *not* to class the place up, now that I could see what I was doing—but first, I needed to check on Joey.

He still lay where I had left him, spooning behind the snoring hatchling on the straw pile he had requested. The charred carcasses of two sheep had been stacked in the far corner of the room beside the remains of Joey's camping gear. I took a closer look at the bones and discovered, with some unease, that the dragon had bitten through the skulls.

When I straightened and turned around, I saw that Joey was watching me from his makeshift bed. Raising his finger to his lips, he gingerly slipped away from his sleeping charge, who had begun to run in her sleep. He cocked his head toward the open door, and I followed him out to the sheep pen, where a dozen pairs of bored brown eyes stared as we leaned against the wooden fence.

Joey frowned, counted the sheep, and gave me a strange look. "I thought we started with twelve last night."

"We did."

"There are still twelve in there."

"Those aren't ordinary sheep. Watch," I instructed, pointing to a fat specimen a few yards into the enclosure, who bleated on cue before splitting down the middle. As the head and hind parts walked away from each other, each quickly regenerated its missing half, and the two sheep turned their attention to the grass, unfazed.

Joey's frown deepened. "The sheep are *budding*."

"Slowly. I can speed up the process when little Smaug's

appetite grows. And it will. Have I mentioned that? Giant lizard—"

"Several times." He smirked and propped his dirt-caked hiking boot on the lowest rail, then ran one hand over the three-day blond growth on his chin masquerading as a beard, giving him the air of a rancher straight out of, oh, Boston. "And her name is *not* Smaug."

"She could be," I replied, mimicking his pose.

"Says the guy who's looking very Rivendell today."

I pushed up my robe's embroidered sleeves. "Just giving it a try. This is, apparently, on trend right now."

"Said who? Peter Jackson?"

"Yeah, you're right." The robe melted into well-worn jeans and a gray Oxford, and Joey grunted. "Testing the waters, you know. I've worn worse."

His eyebrow rose. "Oh?"

"You have no idea what used to pass for underwear."

"Duly noted." Joey bit at a hangnail, gave his filthy knuckles a quick glance, and turned his attention back to the sheep, nonplussed by matters of hygiene. "I've been trying to decide what to call her, now that you mention it."

I tried to judge the size of the bags beneath his eyes, then adjusted the strength of the coffee before it appeared in my hands. "Thoughts?" I asked, passing him the thermos.

He accepted it with a nod and swigged. "Well," he said after running the back of his hand over his mouth, "I don't want anything that screams, 'I am the Demon Lizard, Destroyer of Worlds,' so I was thinking of something a little girlier. Maybe Stella, maybe Aurora."

Honestly, I tried not to laugh—Joey seemed so serious about the matter—but I couldn't hold it back. "Come on, kid, you're one leaping dolphin away from a Lisa Frank poster," I said when the fit had passed. "Would you like some glitter? I could make the sheep pink for you."

He scowled and drank again. "Okay, plan B: Georgina. Call her Georgie."

I produced a slightly weaker carafe for myself and contemplated his choice. "Naming a dragon for Saint George, eh? Cheeky."

Joey snorted into his coffee. "Try me, man. I've got a saint for all occasions."

We stood in silence at the fence, drinking and watching the sheep graze until one paused, let out a quick bleat, and split in two. "That's fucking creepy, Colin," said Joey.

"It's a regenerating flock," I protested. "And it doesn't hurt them, you know." Joey regarded me skeptically over his thermos, and I sighed. "Look, you come up with a better idea at three a.m., and then we'll talk."

Joey's retort was silenced by the tramping of boots that had become far too familiar to me, and I turned from my mutant flock to see Valerius tromping through the dirt with his fingers firmly digging into my brother's shoulder. "Problem?" I asked, and sipped my coffee, fairly confident that I was going to need it.

Valerius grimaced. "Your pardon, my lord, but Lord Doran wouldn't be denied."

I nodded, and he released Doran, who rubbed his bruising shoulder through his robe, a confection of green silk and gold thread that put my discarded garb to shame. "You're early," I said. "Coffee?"

He glowered, then inspected his shoes—also silk, I noticed, and now mud-caked. Joey had to slaughter the sheep somewhere, and I had washed the area down instead of creating new dirt. My creativity is at its ebb before breakfast.

"I requested a meeting," Doran began, simultaneously drying the ground beneath him and producing a clean pair of slippers. "You would insult me, Coileán?"

"I don't build my schedule around your whims," I replied, "and it was a busy night. This isn't a convenient time."

His eyes—Mother's eyes, large and dark brown—glittered. "My quarrel with Syral—"

"Can wait. And I'm going to tell you both what I told you last time: you're fighting over a stupid acre. Split the hill and get on with it."

His face began to flush. "Mother gave me—"

"And Syral says Mother gave it to her. Mother isn't here with the truth, so I'm settling this my way."

Doran massaged his shoulder again, and his voice was harder when he spoke. "No, she isn't here, is she?"

I saw Valerius tense, then cut my eyes to Joey, who was unarmed but for a carafe. His coolness was glacial, however, and when I followed the direction of his gaze back to the barn, I understood why.

"No, Mother isn't here any longer," I told Doran, and pointed over his shoulder. "But *I* am, and I'm slightly busy with *that* right now, so why don't you get out of the way?"

He turned, then jumped back, straight into the unhardened mud. "What is—"

"That's Georgie," Joey drawled. "And you're standing between her and her breakfast. Come here, sweetie!" he called, waving to the groggy dragonet. "The food's this way!"

Georgie happily trotted over, splashing Doran and Valerius with muck as she passed, and my brother, walking stiffly in his filthy clothes, ripped open a gate home and disappeared without another word. Valerius ambled over and took up Joey's spot on the fence as Joey, coffee forgotten, began to chase the suddenly spooked flock around the pen.

"I should have taken out their self-preservation instinct, too," I muttered.

"It's good for him," Valerius replied, wiping mud from his face as he watched the sheep enter their third circuit. "Entertaining, at least."

One of the flock paused and bleated, and Joey leapt upon it as it split, then dragged the regenerating halves out of the pen by their legs. "Somebody want to get me a damn axe?" he called, straining as the sheep regrew.

Valerius glanced at me, and I waved a finger. The sheep dropped dead at Joey's feet, and with a nod of acknowledgement, he dragged the corpses toward the fire pit with Georgie at his heels.

"She'll learn to hunt on her own before long," I said, topping up my coffee.

"Undoubtedly. It's what they do best." Valerius hesitated, then produced a clay tankard and sipped when I showed no sign of objection. "A word of counsel, my lord?"

I studied him only a moment before deciding that one did not simply turn down advice from a man more than twice one's age. "Please. But I'm not getting rid of the dragon unless Joey tires of her."

"I recognize a futile endeavor," he replied. "No, a word concerning your siblings."

"I *can't* get rid of them."

His mouth twitched in the ghost of a smile. "Let them put on airs, my lord. Take their grievances seriously. The queen…" He mulled over his thoughts. "'Coddled' isn't the right word, but you see the idea."

"I think you're looking for 'spoiled,' Captain."

"Perhaps." He drank deeply and watched a sheep bud. "That really is revolting, my lord."

"Yeah? Then I'm holding court here from now on. Between the mud and the flock, I'll shave hours off my work day." When he hid his amusement again, I added, "You and Joey should get along well. You can bond over my attempts at animal husbandry."

"We'll have much to discuss. But I meant what I said about the high lords and ladies," he continued, sobering. "Lord Doran is…temperamental."

"Full-blooded, you mean."

"As is Lady Syral."

"And the others. I get it." I shook my head and returned to the coffee's comforting embrace. "You don't reason with insanity. You merely placate it."

"Precisely."

I slouched and looked Valerius in the eye. "How *did* you survive all those years with Mother, anyway?"

He blinked slowly and drank. "The first lesson is silent obedience."

"I see. I, uh…I'd appreciate a bit of feedback. On occasion."

Valerius cocked his tankard. "The second lesson is observation."

The sheep continued to graze, even as Georgie's hungry squawks echoed over the yard.

"I need eyes, Captain. And the wisdom to know what they're seeing," I said quietly.

"I know," he began, but turned in alarm as the fabric of the realm ripped open behind us. Faerie itself began to shout its displeasure in my head, and when I dropped my coffee and wheeled about, I found a slim woman, her hair styled into blue-tipped black spikes, stepping through in three-inch black heels—and then sinking into the mud.

"Aw, for crying out loud," Toula muttered as she pulled her feet free, then absently waved her shoes clean. "What sort of operation are you running now, Gramps?"

I grinned and pushed the realm's warning to the back of my mind, and Valerius relaxed his stance. "Good morning to you, too. What's the occasion?"

She spread her arms, showing off a tailored black pantsuit and a heavy, braided silver necklace. "Greg asked me to aim for professional. I told him you didn't care what I wore."

"True, but make me happier and leave the jewelry home next time, all right?"

Toula touched her neck, realized what was there, and rolled her eyes as the necklace vanished. "Forgot. Still friends?"

"I don't suppose I'm going to be free of you either way," I replied.

She smiled in quiet triumph. "Anyway, this is official,"

she continued, primly picking her way across the hardened mud. "Greg wants to see you if you're available. Little issue's come up, and I think you'll be interested."

I pointed to my discarded coffee. "Will there be Irish?"

"If you ask nicely, I'm sure. And what's with the sheep?"

Georgie screeched again, and Toula cringed in surprise as she looked around for the source of the noise. "Joey adopted a baby dragon," I explained, heading for the open rift.

"He did *what?*"

"Tell you later. Your boss is waiting," I reminded her, and Toula, with a little salute to Valerius, closed the gate behind us.

CHAPTER 2

It always struck me as odd that the most powerful wizard in the world kept his office in a windowless room deep within a repurposed missile silo buried in the middle of nowhere, Montana. Oh, Greg had decorated the place—or more likely, Missy, his long-suffering wife, had decorated the place—with warm paneling, two decently plush green leather sofas, and a well-stocked wet bar (all surveyed by Missy's large bridal portrait, a deterrent should her husband get a peculiar thirst), but still, I couldn't shake the feeling that the grand magus could have at least made an attempt at posh.

Then again, I had largely based my office on Greg's, so I had no room to complain.

"Afternoon," he said, turning from the bar with a bottle of bourbon in his hand as I stepped through the gate. "A little something for your trouble?"

"Morning, actually," I replied, momentarily thrown at hearing English again after ten days straight in Faerie. "And sure, why not?"

He passed over the bottle and a highball glass, and I poured more than would be considered wise in most social situations. "Toula said you had something interesting on your hands," I continued, glancing at her as she flopped onto a sofa and propped her heels on the coffee table.

Greg slipped his thick glasses off and slowly wiped the lenses on his wash-faded blue polo. "That I do. Drink up, old timer. You may need it."

I knocked back half the full glass and winced at the

burn. "Sounds reassuring. Care for one yourself?" I added, tilting my drink.

He shook his head and cut his eyes to Missy's portrait, and I nodded. Greg Harrison might have been grand magus, seventy-eight, and perfectly able to regulate his own alcohol intake, but Missy took no chances. Or, for that matter, prisoners.

"There's someone I'd like you to meet," said Greg, waving toward the sofas. I accepted a seat beside Toula, warming the rest of my breakfast libation between my palms, and he walked off toward the door. "Nothing to worry about, no tricks," he assured me over his shoulder. "I only wanted to get everyone situated first." He touched the knob, then paused, looked back, and peered at my glass. "Might want to finish that."

My stomach began to clench. "Just what do you have living down here, anyway?" I said, trying and failing at levity.

Greg's mouth tightened. "You'll see momentarily. Chug."

If anyone else had been that insistent, I would have suspected a trap, but Greg had grown up into a halfway decent fellow, and I tasted nothing odd about the bourbon. And so I did as he suggested, then put the empty glass on the coffee table, creating a coaster as I did to avoid incurring the wrath of Missy. "Edge is off," I announced. "Hit me."

He opened the door and stuck his head into the hallway. "Mr. Carver? You can come in now, son."

Given Greg's behavior to that point, I had braced myself for something gruesome, perhaps something with tentacles, but the boy who walked through the door nearly knocked me out of my seat.

He seemed ordinary enough. Perhaps an inch above five and a half feet, skinny in the manner of growing boys whose bones and bulk failed to plan ahead and coordinate. His light blond hair was slightly golden even under Greg's artificial lights, and his face was pale—not sickly, but the color of a creature long accustomed to shaded places. But his eyes, dark as polished oak…

Mother's had never held that look of warring distress and terror, but in all other respects, his eyes were hers.

Or Áedán's. Or Doran's.

I thought I might be gawking at a ghost until he shuffled his feet and hugged his scrawny chest, casting his gaze on the carpet to dodge my stare.

Shaking my head and closing my eyes, I undid the bourbon's pleasant effect and looked up again to find him still slinking against the wall, miserable but not a mirage. "What—"

"Lord Coileán," Greg interrupted before I could begin to babble, "allow me to present Aiden Carver."

The boy flinched at his name, and I realized after a few seconds that my mouth was agape. I snapped it closed, forced myself to blink, and said, "I'm sorry, Greg, *what* did you call him?"

"Aiden Carver," he repeated, puzzled by my reaction. "Is that—"

"Nothing. Thinking of someone I used to know." I pushed myself off the sofa and slowly crossed the room toward the boy, who remained frozen near the door. His expression was even clearer at close range, confusion and misery under a generous layer of fear, and I pushed my own shock aside. "Aiden," I murmured, and waited in silence until he looked at me. "You're in no danger. Whatever they've said, I'm not going to hurt you."

He nodded and chewed his lip.

I looked back at Greg and Toula, who had risen and joined him. "You think…"

Greg hesitated. "We're not a hundred percent certain, but that's the working hypothesis. Based on what his father said—"

"Come on, he's the spitting image of Titania," Toula cut in. "But we needed you here to confirm or deny."

I shrugged. "Aside from stealing Olive, I have no idea what she was up to in the last...how old are you, Aiden?"

"Fifteen," he mumbled.

"Sixteen years," I finished, folding my arms. "Unless you were planning on taking cheek swabs."

"There's a quicker route," she said with a little smirk. "Painless, and much faster than going on *Maury*. I just need you for comparison."

The boy looked like he wanted to sink into the wall, and my gut, now bereft of the calming booze, tightened again. "Details."

Toula rolled her eyes. "I'm not going to hurt you, you big baby. It's only a little aural comparison. Highly technical spellcraft, you wouldn't understand."

I let the jab slide. "What do you mean, aural comparison?"

She sighed and returned to the sofa. "In other words, looking at the signature of the energetic field you're putting off," she explained, sounding bored. "We've been tweaking it for years, but it's tightened up nicely. It's easiest with half-breeds—"

"Skip the lecture. *Details*," I said, taking the seat beside her.

"I'm getting there," she snapped, crossing her long legs. "In brief, an individual's aural signature is distinctive—it's the combination of his parents' signatures, and he shares it with all of his full siblings. Follow me?"

I waved her on, and she closed her eyes and began to mutter under her breath. Twenty seconds later, a glowing orb manifested in front of her face, and she opened her eyes with a satisfied nod. "Right. This is mine," she said, setting it on a slow revolution. "What do you see?"

I studied the hollow sphere, trying to make sense of its colorful latticework. Red and green swirls roped around the circumference and entangled themselves with each other, but I could find nothing familiar in their twining. "I see a mess, frankly," I confessed.

"That's because you're looking for meaning in the patterns. The patterns *are* the meaning. Here."

She whispered something unintelligible, but that was nothing new; most of Toula's incantations were nonsensical and variable, the mark of a wizard who didn't need the crutch of mangled Latin to work her will. Or in her case, I suppose, the mark of a master so comfortable with spellcraft and flush with the power to enchant that the two melded into a hybrid all Toula's own. In any case, she had no need of a wand, but I knew without doubt that I couldn't replicate the spell she was obviously weaving.

As Toula continued to whisper, the sphere divided down the center and flattened, and the swirls split themselves by color, red to her left and green to her right. When they had settled, she pointed to the modified lattices. "I color-code for convenience. Red marks fae lines, green marks wizard, and blue marks anything mundane. The division's pretty clear with my signature, see?" She flipped her finger back and forth between the two unreadable patches of glowing tendrils. "That's Mab's signature, and that's my father's. Classic witch-blood division."

I caught Aiden's questioning look but turned my attention to Toula's work. The red side burned brighter than the green—her mother *was* one of the Three, after all—but the Pavli side of the equation wasn't exactly dim. "So what you're suggesting," I said, "is that, were we to have another of Mab's children here and compare his signature to yours—"

"The red parts would match," she finished.

I didn't need to ask whether she had actually made the comparison. Even if we had known where to find Mab's people, Toula had no interest in seeking out her siblings. "And how would that meeting go?" she had asked when I broached the subject for the first and only time. "Assuming that I run into a half-breed who isn't entirely psychotic and doesn't try to kill me on sight. 'Yeah, I met

Mom once, just a few minutes before I let my good buddy Colin kill her. She seemed bitchy. Oh, and I should probably mention that my father was a mass murderer. So, where are we doing Thanksgiving this year?'"

I wasn't sure whether I would consider Toula my good buddy, but there wasn't a more apt term to describe our relationship, especially in light of our matricidal tit for tat. And so, not wanting to push her, I had let the matter of her potential family drop. I had enough familial mess to deal with myself, anyway: five younger, fully fae brothers and sisters I barely knew, none of whom was happy to have me around. I couldn't exactly recommend connecting with one's siblings to Toula when all I wanted to do most days was banish my family to the mortal realm and make them Oberon's problem.

But the boy…

While Toula had been demonstrating, Greg had led Aiden to the sofa facing us, and now the boy sat stiffly on the edge of the cushion, hands locked in his lap, eyes unsettled. As he stared at Toula's dissected signature, she waved it into the empty space to the left of her head and leaned toward him. "I promise you, dude, it doesn't hurt. Here, we'll make Colin go next, eh?"

With that, she turned to me and resumed her mumbling. Before I could protest, I felt a warm tingle above my skin—a unique sensation akin to comfortable pins and needles—and within seconds, a red and blue sphere appeared before me. "Huh," I muttered, watching it turn. "All right, I'll give you that, it's painless."

"Told you," she replied, and with a flick of her fingers, my sphere began to unravel and split. "Okay, here we go," she said, pointing to the bright red lattice. "Titania. This other bit," she continued, gesturing toward the faint blue lattice beyond it, "is from your father, who was definitely normal."

"That's debatable," I muttered, but quieted as she stacked Mab's and my mother's signatures together. "Not a match," I said. "Not even close."

"I'm the control, then," said Toula, and grinned across the table at Aiden. "Your turn!"

He remained stoically frozen as she worked the spell, then blinked as his signature appeared. "Okay," Toula continued, rotating the orb, "you're definitely a witch-blood." He flinched, but she continued as if she'd not seen it. "And when we pull this apart, like so…"

The red and green split as before, and Aiden's linked fingers whitened.

Toula gave him her best reassuring smile, then pulled Aiden's signature and mine together for comparison.

The fae lattices overlapped perfectly.

"Well, that's pretty clear," said Toula, and patted my shoulder. "Meet your kid brother."

Aiden looked sick, and Greg cut his eyes between the two of us, waiting for a reaction while Toula broke the spell. After a long moment of awkward silence, I cleared my throat. "Could we have a moment alone, please?"

Greg nodded and stood, and Toula gave me a warning look as she followed him into the hallway. When the door latched behind them, I sighed and regarded the boy—my little brother, apparently—across the coffee table. "So."

"So," he whispered.

I rose and headed for the bar. "I don't know about you, but I could do with another drink. What's your poison?"

When I looked back at the sofa, Aiden's brow was furrowed. "I'm *fifteen*."

"It won't kill you. Come on, surely you've sneaked something before."

He hesitated, then slinked toward the bar and scanned the bottles on display. "I had a Mike's once. That was okay."

"I think Greg's more of a whisky man. No matter." A cold bottle appeared at Aiden's elbow, and he cautiously picked it up. "Should be close, at least. I'm not one for lemonade, to be honest."

He popped the cap off, sniffed the clear liquid, and took a tentative sip. "Little sweeter than I remember. It's not bad," he rushed to add, then drank again.

"We won't tell your parents." I poured myself a fresh triple and headed back to the sofa. Aiden lingered by the bar, clutching his bottle, and I pointed to his vacated seat. "Come on, sit down. I won't bite."

He shuffled back to his cushion and perched on the edge once more, as if poised to run.

I produced another coaster and put my drink on the table beside my empty glass, then folded my arms and leaned back into the sofa. "Witch-blood, huh?"

His head bobbed a micrometer in either direction.

"They just told you, didn't they?"

Aiden nodded again, this time with emphasis.

"Shit." His eyes widened, and I shook my head. "You're fifteen, and you're only now learning this? What did they do, say you were a foundling?"

He drank slowly, collecting his thoughts, then stared at the table. "They told me I was a dud," he mumbled. "It happens. And my sister's really strong, so I…" The color rose in his face. "You know, I guess I thought we balanced each other out. Hel got all the power, and I got…this." The bottle stayed upraised for a long swig. "She's probably going to be grand magus someday. Hel, I mean. My older sister. Well, I mean, she's my only sister, but she's older, and—"

"Moon and stars," I sighed, "big sis is on track for Greg's job, and you're the witch-blood in the middle of the silo. That's…fucking awful, kid. I'm sorry."

Aiden seemed shocked but collected himself quickly. "It's not so bad…"

I waited until his voice trailed off into silence. "Did they even teach you the first thing about magic?"

"No point in teaching me." He shrugged. "Can't do anything with it."

"Can you sense it?"

"I see it. Doesn't change anything."

"Well, you've got one on me," I replied. "I smell it. Far less precise, from what I've heard. Of course, I take it that your reality looks rather like a light show, so maybe I got the better deal after all."

"I'm used to it," said Aiden, lifting his drink again. "But like I said, it doesn't matter—I can't *do* anything. I'm a dud." He paused, then amended, "Witch-blood, I guess."

"And how's that working out for you? Dud among wizards, how does that work?"

He stared at the coffee table so long that I started to apologize for the unintended offense, but he cut me off before I could begin. "This place is a nightmare," he said softly, finally meeting my eyes. "Some of the guys my age...they're real assholes. Chase me, beat me up...I don't know how many times they've broken something. Mom keeps putting me back together." His jaw clenched until he fought down the tears. "Mom and Dad pulled me out of school last year when Hel went off to college. No one there to protect me anymore, see?" He drank long and deeply. "So I've been teaching myself. Passed all the exit tests in April. I graduated, so I've been looking at college courses online. Mom says I'm too young to go away, and there isn't a good community college near here..."

While he finished his drink, I said, "Your mom's good to you?"

"Can't complain," he agreed. "Dad...he's disappointed, you know, that I'm...that I'm the way I am. But Mom doesn't care." Aiden frowned at the table as a second bottle appeared beside his empty first, but he picked it up and started over without protest. "But she's not really my mom, I guess. Not if...if I'm—"

"She's the best mother you'll ever have," I interrupted, "and just because she isn't your blood doesn't make her any less your mother. Understand?" He nodded slowly, and I leaned toward him and lowered my voice. "Aiden, our mother...well, she didn't raise me, either. If there's anything redeeming about me, the thanks go to my surrogate." My hand sought and closed around my glass, and I made up for lost time. "She was one of the most wonderful people I've ever known. Mother, on the other hand, was cruel and cold, and she never, *ever* forgot a slight."

He drank again, matching me. "I heard you killed her."

"That was mostly Toula. And then I killed *her* mother, so we're even." I paused, trying to judge his mood. "If you wanted to meet Mother, I'm sorry. I can tell you about her—"

"The grand magus said she dumped me upstairs when I was a few days old," he murmured. "I don't think she really missed me, do you?"

"Could have been worse." His eyebrows rose in challenge, and I shrugged. "I know a witch-blood whose father tried to kill him."

Aiden sat silently for a few seconds, then mumbled, "Might have been better that way."

"Hey, now. *Hey*." I rose and stepped around the table to join Aiden on his sofa. "Don't say that, kid. There's no reason that—"

His eyes had begun to fill. "I can't do *anything*. I can't go to college because I'm too young, and I can't do one damn thing with magic. I mean, come on, I failed at card tricks. *Card tricks*."

"That's sleight of hand, not magic."

"Same result." He sniffed and rubbed at his eyes, flushing again. "Dad ignores me, Hel's on the other side of the country, I don't have any friends here—"

"Want to live with me?"

His mouth opened and closed a few times, and I hastened on. "I can't guarantee it's perfectly safe, but anyone who touched you would answer to me, and I, uh...I can do some rather unpleasant things. Let's leave it at that." I tried to puzzle out his enigmatic expression. "The reason I offer—it's not just because of your…*problems*…down here. There's, well…Faerie has this effect on people. Some of the, um…" Aiden's face remained a mask, and I bit the bullet. "All right, it's no secret that changelings have been taken in the past. I don't agree with it, but I can't change history. Yes?"

He nodded.

"Some of them…*many* of them…when they'd been around long enough, they started showing rudimentary magical talent. I can't guarantee anything," I cautioned, "but if you came over and stuck around for a while, something latent might be triggered. I'm not saying it would be magus-level ability, but…well, maybe you could throw away your trick deck."

Aiden's face practically glowed as a wide smile broke across it. "*Really*? I could do magic?"

"Again, I can't make any promises," I said, reluctant to dampen his sudden joy, "but it's entirely possible. Probably likely, too, since you're predisposed toward it. And I've got plenty of space," I went on. "Wouldn't be breathing down your neck or anything. As I said, it's not completely safe, but then again—"

He grabbed my forearms and stared at me with a fervor bordering on manic. "I'll do anything. *Anything*. If there's any chance it'll work…anything. Really. Name it."

I carefully freed myself, taking caution to avoid Aiden's steel wristwatch, and picked up my drink. "Okay, first ground rule: get that word out of your vocabulary."

"Huh?"

"*Anything*. Tempt the wrong person with terms like that, and I won't be able to save you." I paused and drank, letting that soak in, and when Aiden was suitably chastised, I patted his shoulder. "This isn't a bargaining situation, anyway. Faerie's your birthright, kid—come and go as you please. Well," I amended, "by which I mean I'll open gates for you whenever you like. I'm not trying to hold you prisoner, if that thought had crossed your mind."

His brows knit in confusion. "What do you mean, it's

my birthright?"

"Aiden," I replied, speaking slowly, "I realize this is all new to you, but you're Titania's son and my brother. Why *wouldn't* it be your birthright?"

He spread his arms, encompassing Greg's desk and wet bar. "Arcanum?"

"Hate to break this to you, but you're never going to be Arcanum. They don't take witch-bloods, or else Toula would be on the Inner Council by now."

"Toula *Pavli*?"

"Point taken," I muttered. "But you, now—you're a high lord of Faerie, Aiden. I have no right to keep you out of the realm."

He exploded in a fit of laughter, but I heard the edge of hysteria in his gasps, and so I waited and drank as he worked it out of his system. A few minutes later, when the worst had subsided into tears, he hiccupped and shook his head. "You're nuts."

"You're tipsy," I countered. "Parents lock the liquor cabinet, do they?"

"I'm fine," he said, wiping his face dry. "But there's no way in hell that I'm a lord of anything."

I rolled my eyes and leaned back into the soft cushions—surely another of Missy's ideas. "Some lords earn their titles by being ridiculously talented and doing massive favors for people in power. And then there are the high lords and ladies, Titania's and Oberon's children…and mine, I suppose," I mumbled. "Look, it doesn't matter that you can't enchant your way out of a paper bag—the title is hereditary. Trust me, Greg's well aware of that," I added, and finished my whisky.

He was still processing when I put my empty glass down. "So…let me get this straight," he said. "I'm—"

"Lord Aiden. Assumedly Mother's youngest, but I'll ask around," I replied, watching his face work. "And I also assume that, at least nominally, you're affiliated with my court, but if you'd rather hang around Oberon, I can't stop you. He's down in Florida, pretending he's Jimmy Buffett or something. I can only hope that's a phase."

My brother stared at me then as if seeing me clearly for the first time. "You're really Lord Coileán?" he murmured.

"I am."

"*The* Lord Coileán? The Ironhand?"

I shrugged to hide my discomfort. "I also answer to 'Colin,' 'Hey, You,' and, just for Toula, 'Gramps.' She's a real charmer, that one."

But Aiden wasn't to be deterred. "There's a file on you here. It's massive. I…may or may not have hacked into the restricted materials when the archivists started digitizing the library." He bit his lip. "Do me a favor and don't tell, okay? Dad would kill me if he knew."

"Secret's safe," I replied, and crossed my arms. "As for that file, the Arcanum and I go way back. Half of what you saw is probably wrong, and the rest is surely littered with exaggerations. And whatever they've said about me, remember that the Arcanum isn't filled with angels. They hunted me first."

His eyes fixed on mine. "And…you're my big brother?"

"Half brother, if you want to be technical about it, but yeah."

He said nothing, and I listened to the fluorescents buzz for a few minutes until Aiden finally whispered, "Cool."

CHAPTER 3

Greg stepped to the wall just in time to avoid being bowled over as Aiden ran toward the elevators. "Scared him off that quickly, did you?" he asked, catching his breath. "Fleeing in terror after, what, ten minutes?"

"He's going home to pack," I replied, lingering at his side as Toula strolled over. "I'm getting him out of here, Greg."

I had expected a bit of blow-back, maybe a halfhearted protest, or possibly exhortations to the effect that he was the grand magus, damn it, and I couldn't just waltz in and do as I pleased, but Greg merely nodded. "That's probably for the best." He glanced at me over his glasses, rubbed his chin, and cocked his finger as he wandered off in the direction Aiden had run. "Walk with me. You need the full story before you thrust yourself into this."

Toula caught my querying look and shrugged, then followed her boss. "This a private meeting, guys?"

He stopped and turned, then considered her for a moment before muttering, "I suppose you'd hear this soon enough."

"No doubt," she said cheerily. "So save us all the time, eh? What's up with the kid?"

Greg walked in silence down the long hallway of closed doors, wincing each time he put his weight on his left leg. The thick beige carpeting muffled the tell-tale syncopation of his limp, but it was obvious that he was in pain. I touched his shoulder and concentrated for a beat, and Greg looked back, startled. "What—"

"Temporary. I can fix the symptoms, but the underlying arthritis…"

He shook his head as I let the thought end unspoken. "Best not tempt me. And let me know in advance the next time you do that, huh?" he said, but tested his bad leg and grunted. "Thanks, though."

"So what do I need to know about Aiden?"

We continued past the twin elevators, and Greg sighed to himself as we turned the corner toward the stairwell. "I just told him, you know. Did he mention that?"

I slowed to keep pace with him, and Toula stayed a step behind us, soundless even in her pumps. "Why the hell did you wait so long?" I asked, not bothering to hide my indignation. "That's unfair—"

"It wasn't about fairness. First"—he depressed the steel bar to unlatch the stairwell door and held it open—"I didn't think he was safe while Titania lived. And before you protest, I was down the hall when Rick Matherson's father came to kill him," he murmured. "Popped in here like our defenses didn't exist. We've since beefed them up," he added, giving me a steady look as we trooped downstairs, "but I really didn't want to test them against *her.*"

"Understood, but—"

"You didn't let me finish," he interrupted, leaning on the handrail despite the enchantment on his joints. "Secondly, it's tough for witch-bloods down here, especially when their conception was, to be delicate, non-consensual. The Council has always known about Aiden— just as they knew about you, Toula," he said over his shoulder. "Necessity and all. But there was no need to let Aiden's peers know where he came from."

"Difficult to hide a baby," I said, stepping carefully to avoid an unbalanced grasp at the railing. The gray paint would do nothing to shield me from the metal beneath, and I had left my gloves at home. "How did you explain that one?"

Greg paused on the landing to rest. "Rachel and Howard had been trying for years to give their daughter a sibling. They claimed it was a surprise labor, and no one asked too many questions."

"Indigestion gone wrong?" said Toula with a smirk.

"A home birth, what a shock, bullshit and nonsense," Greg replied. "At least Aiden looks enough like them to pass for Rachel's. I don't think his sister knows the truth yet, to be honest. No reason to upset her." He pulled a floral handkerchief out of his pocket and coughed phlegm, then folded it away and resumed our downward march. "Someone left him in the gravel when he wasn't more than a day or two old. Little guy might have died of exposure if one of the watchmen hadn't gone up to check on a tripped ward. Stray cow," he explained offhand. "Cold spring night, as I recall. Poor bastard almost had a heart attack when Aiden cried."

The air in the stairwell began to grow musty as we descended. "How did you determine his father?" I asked.

Greg waited until we reached another landing, then leaned against the wall as his mouth tightened. "Howard suspected it, and that little spell you saw upstairs confirmed it. Aiden's his, no question about that."

"So...this Howard—"

"Carver. Howard Carver."

"So Howard...what? Had a fling with Mother? And his wife...Rebecca, was it?"

"Rachel," said Greg.

"Rachel Voss," Toula muttered behind me.

Greg flicked her a look of impatience. "The former Ms. Voss, yes. And no, it wasn't a fling." He stuffed his hands into his khakis and looked me in the eye. "Howard had a younger sister, Ella. Pretty little thing. They were orphaned young, and he just about raised her. She didn't have any great gift for magic, and she eventually moved out to Seattle to find herself." He shrugged. "Someone found her first."

It didn't take a genius to know where this story was going. "Changeling?"

He nodded curtly. "The Carvers didn't know she was missing until she'd been gone two weeks, and then Howard tracked her movements and figured out what had happened. And *then* he managed to open a gate into Faerie so he could go after her."

"He did *what*?"

"Believe me, I know." Greg shook his head and sighed. "Stupid, *stupid* move, but that boy loved his sister, and nothing in heaven or hell was going to stop him from bringing her home." He blinked slowly. "Of course, by the time he got into Faerie, Ella was already dead."

I tasted bile at the back of my throat. "What happened?"

"Don't know. She did something to set Titania off, I guess, but long story short, the queen didn't take too kindly to Howard barging in. Probably his saving grace was that she thought he was handsome."

Greg paused, waiting for my reaction, but all I could do was nod. "That...doesn't surprise me at all."

He glanced around, and, satisfied that we were the only three on the stairs, continued in a near-whisper. "He claims she pinned him down and...well, had her way, then threw him out with Ella's body. And since he was happily married with a three-year-old at that time, I tend to believe him."

I rubbed my face, if only to relieve the pressure of Greg's eyes on me. "And he's been living with a daily reminder of that for the last fifteen years."

"Exactly. It took Rachel threatening to leave him before he agreed to raise Aiden. Heck," Greg muttered, "*Rachel's* the one who named him. She was so thrilled to have another baby, she didn't give a damn where he'd come from."

So that answered that—Mother hadn't begun recycling names. Still, the coincidence bothered me, especially given

Áedán and Aiden's physical likeness. "That's why you lied to him?"

"For his safety and Howard's dignity," said Greg. "And I'll ask you not to repeat any of this to Aiden—I gave him the simplified version of the truth." My expression shifted, and he held up his hands. "Someday, someday. But not now. The boy's just fifteen, and I think he's had quite enough for one day, don't you?"

We climbed down another flight of stairs, and Greg patted the thick steel door. "The Carvers are right down this hall. We should have given Aiden a decent head start by now…"

He opened the door on a brawl.

Well, that's not entirely accurate. Calling something a brawl suggests that all participants are engaged in the melee. What we found on the other side of the door was a knot of half a dozen teenage boys beating Aiden as if they had no dearer desire than to reduce him to his component atoms. I couldn't make out much—Aiden had partly covered his face and crouched into a groaning ball—but I recognized the unnatural bend of his arm and the copious bleeding that could only signal a broken nose.

"Don't kill them," Greg rushed as we realized what we were seeing. "If you kill them—"

I was too furious to answer, and the force building inside of me needed an outlet or six. Before Greg could get another word out, I flung the boys into the walls with a satisfying shower of plaster and pinned them above the ground. Toula ran to where Aiden crouched and began assessing the damage, but I had eyes only for the boys, who ceased fighting their unseen binds as soon as they spotted Greg—all, that is, but their leader, a dark-haired kid with an angelic face and blood on his fingers.

"Want to tell me what's going on?" I asked, reaching up to grab his throat. "Or do I have to squeeze it out of you?"

With a little pressure, the kid went limp, and a dark

spot began to spread on his trousers. I watched his eyes until the sullenness turned to terror, then stepped away and slowly, deliberately, cracked my knuckles. "How is he, Toula?" I asked, not taking my eyes off my target.

"Nose is a goner," she replied. "Compound fracture in his right arm, if I had to guess, and plenty of bruising. Wouldn't be surprised if he has internal damage. Hang on, bud," she murmured, "I'm going to dull the pain, just bear with me."

I kept my face still, but the tremor in my fists belied my mask of controlled calm. "Six on one? Was he carrying a rocket launcher that I missed?" I asked, scanning the boys' colorless faces. "Someone, please explain this to me."

Greg's hand landed on my shoulder, and he cleared his throat. "These young men are all sons and grandsons of Council magi," he said quietly. "And they've been warned about this sort of behavior."

I pulled away and stared at him, aghast. "This has happened before?"

"First time in a few months," said Aiden, letting Toula pull him to his feet. He held a corner of his ripped shirt to his nose with his good hand, slowing the flow that had already stained the carpet. "I don't go out much these days," he mumbled, his words distorted by his battered nose.

I had heard Aiden earlier, but I hadn't appreciated the extent of the beatings he had described, and now I dearly wanted to hurt the boys I was holding in place. Every instinct screamed at me to kill them painfully, but I fought down the rage and, with a final glower at Greg, dropped them to the floor. The boys scrambled up into a defensive knot, and I pointed at their leader. "Touch Aiden again, and *he* won't be able to save you," I told him, cocking my head toward Greg. "And if you think I give a damn about your families, you're bigger idiots than you seem."

"Go home, all of you," Greg barked. "I'll deal with you later."

The boys sprinted off, followed quickly by the sound of slamming doors. When the last footsteps had died away, Greg contemplated the bloodstained floor. "My hands are tied," he muttered. "They're little shits, but they're well-connected little shits. I can't just beat sense into them."

"Look what they did!" Toula shouted, keeping Aiden upright as he groaned. "If we hadn't gotten here—"

His eyes flicked up and down again. "He's had it worse. But as I was saying, their folks are Council. If I were to punish them, especially for something done to *Aiden*—"

"He's had it worse?" Toula echoed.

I waited in silence until Greg looked up. "You let them beat him until he pulled out of school," I said through gritted teeth. "He's defenseless, and you let them—"

"They didn't use wands this time," Aiden mumbled, then hissed as he shifted his weight. "I'm okay. Mom knows how everything fits back together."

I looked from my little brother, whose eyes were turning black, to the grand magus, whose dark skin hid any embarrassment he might have felt. "You disappoint me."

"You don't understand the situation," Greg countered.

"I understand well enough. And I thought you were better than this."

With that, I turned to Aiden and Toula, then carefully pulled him from her shoulder and into the air. "Less stress on you," I said before he could panic. "Point the way home, and I'll float you in the right direction."

The Arcanum's living quarters had all the cheer and character of a retirement home for nuclear submariners. From the outside, the Carvers' apartment was identical in appearance to its neighbors: another gray, windowless door set into a white wall. Someone had placed a floral-print welcome mat over the hallway carpeting, which, thanks to the complete lack of sun in the silo, was still as colorful as the day it was purchased. In other words, the setup was as depressing as a birthday party for a pediatric hospice patient.

"Let me go in first," said Aiden, holding on to Toula's arms to steady himself as I lowered him to his feet. He grimaced on landing, but the kid surprised me with his stoicism in the face of injuries warranting an ambulance. As if sensing my bemusement, he shrugged his uninjured shoulder and mumbled, "Nothing Mom hasn't seen before, but she'll panic less if she doesn't have to perform for an audience."

And so we held back and waited as Aiden limped into his family's apartment. "Mom?" he called, leaving the door ajar. "Are you home?"

"In here," a female voice began, followed by a sharp gasp. "Oh, good God, *Aiden!*"

Toula rolled her eyes and leaned against the wall with her sinewy arms folded. "I could have fixed him," she whispered.

"I don't doubt that," Greg replied in kind, giving me a wider than usual berth as he joined her. "But Rachel's had some practice at this." He caught my glare and muttered, "Don't look at me like I'm some sort of monster, Coileán. His hide isn't the only one I've got to consider."

"Your own?" I replied, pulling up a patch of wall on the other side of the door.

"I don't expect you to understand, seeing as you're new to this game," he retorted, "but sometimes, the job calls for tough decisions. Sometimes, you get to choose between two bad options. And sometimes, the lesser of two evils is turning a blind eye when a little boy crawls home with fractures in both arms and legs." I continued to stare, but he didn't look away. "You think I'm proud of that choice? Shit, you know me better than that."

"I thought I did."

He rubbed his face and exhaled softly. "I'm responsible for several hundred souls here," he said. "Several thousand more worldwide, many of whom would like to see me out of a job. Some of them want to see the Arcanum disbanded. Hell, some of my strongest critics are on the Council. And the only thing that's going to keep this derelict afloat is a succession plan everyone can get behind." Greg nodded to the open door and lowered his voice. "Helen Carver is the strongest wizard I've seen in three generations, but she ain't ready for this job yet. I'm keeping the seat warm for her. Got to hold on for a few more years, see? Keep everyone happy long enough to get her in."

I waited as Aiden failed to stifle a cry in the apartment. "And if the only way to get her in is to sacrifice him?"

"As I said, two bad options. If there's one thing I've learned in this job, it's that magic can't fix everything." Greg flinched while Aiden screamed, then shook his head as if banishing the sound. "The problem with you," he resumed, watching over his glasses as I glowered, "is that you've been Batman too long."

"Say *what?*" Toula interjected.

Greg shot her a reproving look, and she fell silent. "Batman," he said, "only worries about fighting criminals—whom he wants, when he wants. He doesn't follow rules, doesn't take orders. Lone vigilante. Now, he's pretty damn effective, but he's still working solo.

"Me, I'm the mayor of Gotham. I've got to keep the lights on, the water running, the schools open, the trash collected, *and* the criminals behind bars, and oh yeah, if I fail at any of those, I'll get voted out. All it takes is a 'no confidence' vote from the Council, and I'm retired." His mouth tightened into a scowl. "And on top of that, I've got a loose cannon in black running around my city, doing untold millions in property damage and dropping lunatics on my doorstep. So give me a break," he said, raising his voice a notch as Aiden yelped. "Batman gets to think about heroics. I've got to keep Gotham from eating itself alive."

"By letting a pack of thugs torture my brother?"

His face was impassive. "You may think I'm a stupid child, but believe me, I know too well what's hiding behind the curtain. And you will, too, if you don't already," he added with a little smirk. "You want to rule, you prepare to make exceptions to every principle you hold dear. Maybe not where *your* brother is concerned," he said, pushing himself off the wall, "but you'll do it to someone else's. Wait here, I'll see if he's back in one piece."

I lurked outside the door and listened as Greg stepped into the apartment. "Rachel?" he called. "Where are you?"

"Grand Magus?" came the female voice I'd heard before, but its tone had shifted toward wary—and, if I wasn't mistaken, angry. "Den. Watch your step, I'm reshelving."

"How is he?"

"Did you see them do this?"

Definitely angry. I cut my eyes to Toula, who made a face.

Greg hesitated. "I…saw something, yes."

"*Something?*"

"Mom," Aiden began, but she cut him off almost immediately.

"Go lie down, sweetie. Let that arm harden. Mom needs to have a little talk with the grand magus, okay?"

"But Mom, I—"

"*Now*. And as for you, Grand Magus—"

"Dang it, Mom, *listen to me!*"

Greg and Rachel fell silent for a long moment. Facing me across the door, Toula whistled softly. "He's in for it now."

As if on cue, Rachel asked in a voice far too low to bode anything pleasant, "Yes, Aiden?"

"Mom, I…I'm leaving. I just came by to get my stuff. They jumped me on the way."

"What are you…" she started to say, then paused. "No. No, Greg, you didn't…"

"Rachel," he soothed, "let's talk about this—"

"*What did you tell him?*" she yelled. "What have you *done*, you son of a bitch?"

"And that's my cue," I muttered, nudging the door open with my loafer.

The tableau inside the apartment suggested imminent violence: the pale boy standing in the hallway, whole again but sweating; the white-haired old man, his thin hands raised in protection; and the furious blue-eyed blonde standing between them in the midst of haphazard towers of books, her right fist curled around a well-worn oak wand, her left thrust back as if to push Aiden from danger. All three turned my way when I cleared my throat, and I stuffed my hands into my pockets. "Sorry to interrupt. Aiden, do you need help?"

Rachel bared her teeth, then executed a maneuver I had, to that point, seen only in cats: a snarling leap at my face. I threw up a shield an instant before her wand began to spark, and the thin jet of fire shooting out the end split and rebounded toward her oriental rug, burning twin oblongs on impact. She screeched and waved harder, but my shield held, and I waited in safety as she tried to kick, claw, and incinerate her way through the invisible wall.

"Can we talk about this?" I asked over her war cries.

Rachel shouted nearly unintelligibly, though I thought I recognized a few choice terms in her response. As I held my ground, she advanced on my shield, transitioning from ineffective fire attacks to pure force. She was trying to push me backward, I realized as my neck began to tingle. A quick glance over my shoulder confirmed what I suspected: I had angled myself in the kitchen doorway—and directly behind me was the Carvers' stainless-steel refrigerator.

"Rachel," I tried again, attempting to project calmness, "I don't want to disarm you, but I will if you don't drop the damn stick."

She flashed her clenched teeth and shoved against my shield with renewed strength. "You're not taking my son!"

"I'm not *taking* him. I invited him, and he accepted. This is an agreement, not an abduction." I stepped away from the fridge, slowly driving Rachel back toward her books. "Forty-eight hours. Give us two days, and let's see how he gets along. If he doesn't like it, he comes back here. If he likes it, he still comes back to check in. Sound fair?"

"Rot in hell!" she panted.

I sighed. "I'm offering Aiden the possibility of unlocking magical talent. You're offering him an isolated bedroom and a good chance of a beating if he steps outside, am I right?" Something flickered across her face, and I pressed harder. "How many times has he come home with a broken arm? Broken leg?"

"Burns," Aiden supplied. "Fire burns, acid burns. Grit embedded in my skin from a sandstorm. I've almost drowned six times. Peed blood for a week before Mom realized that my kidney was busted. I've lost track of my nose jobs, and let's not even start counting my teeth."

"I'm not the enemy," I told her. "I only want to help him."

"You're a monster," she spat, then stepped backward into a tower of books and began to tumble.

I remotely broke her fall before she slammed into the coffee table, and she shrieked until she realized that she was no longer about to make impact with something harder than her head. Another little tug pulled her upright, and I released the enchantment before she had time to fully comprehend the situation. "Watch your step."

"Don't you *ever* do—"

"The alternative was stitches, and that's messy." I waited until she had checked herself for broken bits, then destroyed my shield, letting her watch the haze between us disappear. "Now, *I'm* the monster? Your child is abused, and all you do is stand by and clean up the blood?"

Her face flushed, though with anger or shame, I couldn't tell. "I've told the grand magus for years—"

"And he did nothing. Why didn't you run? Get your kids and drive? Hell, woman," I said, folding my arms, "there are wizards all over this damn country. No one's going to come for you in the night if you leave the silo."

"It's not that simple," she mumbled.

I let her stew for a moment in silence. "No, it isn't," I said, "because you've got your daughter's future to think of. She needed to be here, and you couldn't leave her for Aiden." She wasn't squirming yet, but her tight shoulders betrayed her unease. "And you couldn't pack a—what, a five-year-old? Six?—off to boarding school, could you? Send him to relatives elsewhere? No," I murmured, watching Rachel's face flame, "I'm guessing you're both old Arcanum, wizards up and down those family trees. No one wants to deal with a dud, right? A mongrel even less—"

"Stop it."

"So you let Big Sis watch out for him, maybe give her a little kiddie combat practice, but if she fails, eh, it doesn't matter, these things happen," I continued, ignoring her growing distress. "And when she leaves and little Aiden's all alone against a pack of sadistic teenage wizards, well, you lock him in his room until he's old enough to run away and never look back. Is that right?"

By the look on her face, I guessed that if not for Greg's presence, Rachel would have renewed her efforts to kill me.

"Mom," Aiden said quietly, "I haven't seen the sun since April."

She turned to him and grabbed his uninjured hand. "Sweetheart, you listen to me. Go pick a school. *Anywhere*. Dad and I will sign the papers, put you on a plane…if you want to transfer to MIT next year, we'll take care of it—"

"Mom…"

"But you can't go with *him*," she continued in a desperate rush. "They're dangerous, and they lie, and…and it'll break your father's heart," she begged, squeezing him until he flinched. "You can't do that to him, Aiden. Whatever they told you, you can't hurt your dad like that."

He took a deep breath, but he didn't drop her stare. "And what about me?"

"You can go study your computers!" she cried. "Robotics! What you've always wanted—"

"I've always wanted to be a fucking *wizard*!"

"Aiden Theodore Carver!" she cried, recoiling. "Language!"

He pulled free of her grip and shook his head. "Coileán says there's a chance. I'm going to try."

"And I'll vouch for his safety."

We turned to find Toula standing in the foyer behind me, looking almost professional in her suit. "I promise, Rachel," she continued, stepping out of the shadows, "nothing's going to happen to him. I can get to him. Trust me—"

The crazed sparkle had returned to her eye. "Trust *you*?" she laughed. "I'm supposed to trust *you*, Pavli?"

Toula waited until Rachel's laughter died, then pushed me aside, strode through the book stalagmites, and grabbed her by the blouse. "Yeah," she growled, "you trust me. Because I've been where that poor bastard's been, and I know what a hellhole this place can be for those of us who don't *quite* measure up." She shoved Rachel back and brushed her hands off. "He'll be safe. I'll keep an eye on him."

Her tirade had done nothing to lessen Rachel's scorn. "And what's a little witch going to do against a faerie, hmm? Tell him who your daddy was and hope he runs in terror?"

Toula glanced at me, then back at Rachel's mocking smirk. "I'm not a witch," she said in a voice that was equal parts soft and dangerous. "I'm witch-blooded fae." A white corona burst into flame around her body, and Rachel fell backward in alarm. "Emphasis, it appears, on fae," Toula added, smirking in turn. "And believe me,

Voss, I remember my childhood here *very* clearly."

Rachel's pale eyes nearly bulged. "You…" she began, floundering, and then her slipped gear righted itself. "We were kids. Our parents said—"

"Your parents told you to lock a child half your age in a storage closet overnight?"

"We thought the Grahams would find you!"

"Like they ever looked for me!" Toula clenched her fists, but the flames subsided. "Now, here's how this is going to go. Aiden's going to pack whatever he wants— and we're going to help with the schlepping," she told him, indicating herself and me, "because you don't need to put any stress on that arm until it's solidified. Seriously, man, no heavy lifting. And when he's packed," she said to Rachel, "he's out of here, at least for the next two days. Got it?"

Rachel looked up at Greg from the rug. "Do something."

"What would you like me to do?" he replied, showing his empty palms.

"You're the grand magus!"

"And *he's* a faerie king," he said, cocking his thumb toward me, "who did me a favor by not blasting six magi's children into ash. My hands are tied, Rachel. I'm sorry."

As if finally realizing that she was outgunned, Rachel's shoulders sagged, and she dropped her wand. "Monsters," she whispered, glaring at Toula and me in turn. "Thugs and monsters. That's all you are. Stealing a child…"

I glanced at Aiden, who still lingered in the hall, and nodded.

"I, uh…" he said, looking away from his fallen mother, "I'll be in my room, then."

CHAPTER 4

An hour later in Aiden's bedroom, surrounded by hastily taped boxes of electronic components and one small duffel bag of clothing, Toula and I said our farewells. "Let me know if there's a problem," she insisted for the fifth time. "If Faerie doesn't work out, I've still got my place in Butlerville…"

I followed her offer with our shared thought. "Or Meggy."

"Hey, what's one more teenager, huh?" she said, trying to laugh it off. "Maybe Olive needs a friend."

Aiden looked up from tallying his boxes and frowned. "Who's Meggy?"

Toula arched a neat eyebrow, but I brushed her off. "My girlfriend," I told Aiden, adding, "who is also the mother of my daughter," before Toula could jump in.

"Got it," he replied, bending back to his work. "Baby mama."

"I truly loathe that term," I muttered, glaring at Toula's grin. "Anyway, Meggy and Olive live in Virginia. If we need a third option, I could ask if she wouldn't mind letting you stay. The apartment would be cramped, but I suppose I could modify the attic without attracting too much attention…"

"Or ask your neighbor to take him in," said Toula.

"Mrs. Cooper is a lovely lady, but you're out of your mind."

Again, Aiden paused in his packing. "Wait, you have a daughter?"

"Long story," I sighed. "Though, given how long I've been hanging around, it's surprising that I've only the one. She's about your age," I added. "Sixteen last March."

Aiden shook his head and picked up his discarded roll of tape. "Okay, so I've got a niece, too. And she's older than me. Fantastic."

"Join the club," I said, perching on the sliver of his bed not covered in debris. "I'm not Mother's eldest, you know—not even close. I was just the eldest left standing when she dropped. I mean, I've heard of maybe eighty-odd older siblings, and that's not to say there weren't more."

He dropped his tape and gaped. "*Eighty?*"

"Shit happens. Feuds start. Fights get out of hand. Someone gets in the way of the wrong wizard. And Mother had a penchant for disposing of the ones who particularly annoyed her."

"Tink," Toula muttered, flipping and catching a dried Sharpie.

"The last she killed was Robin," I told him, "and you'll hear about him if you stick around. But to go back to the main point, I've got plenty of nieces and nephews who predate me—most in Faerie, some still in this realm. Look," I said, shrugging, "you're not going to see the sort of neat generational divides you're used to here in a family like ours. Not when you've got centuries between children. Hell," I muttered, "the next one down from me is Doran, and he's a bit over five hundred, if I'm remembering correctly. I only really met most of my surviving five siblings in the last few months," I told him, watching his eyes widen, "and some of the details blend. But there's Doran at five and change, and Syral's about thirty years younger—they're at each other's throat at the moment—Huc's a little over four hundred, Ji's maybe three and a half, and Nanine's…not quite three hundred yet, but I'm not sure how far away she is, to be frank. And then there's you." Aiden looked back at me mutely, and I rubbed my arm. "Too much at once?"

"Just…" He stared into the corner for a moment, deep in thought, then resumed attacking the box with tape. "Let me focus on the fact that I've got six half siblings I've never met, and I'll get over the age thing eventually." He leaned over the box to pull it closed, then cut his eyes back to me. "But before I let this go…"

"Eight hundred and twelve, give or take."

"*Seriously?*"

"We stop aging. Aiden, I…I know this must be terribly strange for you…"

He pulled a fresh strip of tape off the roll and sealed the carton. "What about me? I'm half fae, right? What does that mean, practically speaking?"

Toula made a face behind him, and I chose my words carefully. "Well…I'm only half, and you see the result. My—*our*," I amended, "siblings are fully fae, and there's no physical difference between us. The blood's strong."

"So I—"

I hurried to cut him off before his hopes could rise. "A wizard cross screws everything up, most of the time. Toula's the one big exception." She seemed almost sheepish when he turned to look up at her. "No one truly knows why everything falls apart for witch-bloods," I said apologetically. "It just does. You can't really use magic, you're mortal…but on the positive side," I continued, pointing to the boxes, "you obviously don't have any problem with iron. Not judging by the tools in here, at least."

"Doesn't seem like a fair tradeoff," he mumbled, moving to the next box.

"It's not. Magic doesn't make allowances for fairness." I stood and held the carton together while he picked at the tape. "I'd fix things for you if I could, but I don't have that kind of power. No one does. I'm sorry, but I don't know—"

He ripped the end loose and began sealing. "You're

trying to help me," he said, focusing on his work. "And you're getting me out of here. So thanks anyway." Aiden let Toula move the box onto a pile, then frowned at me again. "You said they're fully fae, right? Our siblings?"

"That's right."

"What are they like?"

"Honestly? I think they're assholes, but they'd probably say the same about me."

Aiden nodded. "Figures."

I opened a gate from Aiden's room into one of the many vacant guest suites that littered my inherited palace, and his belongings flew along behind us and stacked themselves against a bare stone wall. As he blinked in the sudden brightness of midmorning, I touched his forehead. "One last thing," I said, and willed what should have been his native tongue upon him.

Aiden jerked, startled, then cocked his head as I pulled away. "What was that about?"

"Do you understand me?" I asked in Fae.

"Sure, why wouldn't..." He left the thought unfinished as he heard himself processing unfamiliar words. "What did—"

"A small mental manipulation. This is the common tongue around here—no sense in making you learn it the hard way, is there?"

"Huh."

He scowled at the floor, and I offered, "You'll adjust in a few minutes. Trust me on this."

"This...you've done this before?"

"Mother did it to me, and I've picked up a few tongues along the way. That odd feeling, like you know you're hearing nonsense but it makes sense? It passes."

I wanted to be reassuring, non-threatening, but I hadn't the faintest idea what I should say to put Aiden's mind at ease. I'd had little recent experience with teenage boys, certainly none with boys cloistered for their own protection—hell, I barely remembered fifteen, but I suspected that even if I had, my fifteen and his would have little commonality. There were hormones, as I recalled, my voice played pranks on me, and I kept having to lengthen my clothing during a massive growth spurt, but other than that...

Aiden stepped cautiously over the flagstones and watched the shadows like a rabbit, preparing himself for attack even as he investigated the largely empty room. Good strategy if one were dropped into the middle of the Serengeti at midnight, I thought, but a poor way to fight through life. I had been there—I recognized his expression, watching for movement, listening for a breath out of place—but I had also been able to defend myself, even as a young man on the run from the Arcanum. Aiden had no such skill, and there was nothing I could do to improve the situation, not unless something in the realm got into his system.

I didn't have the heart at that moment to tell my little brother that it might be decades before he could work a basic glamour.

"It's utilitarian, I know," I said, wincing as he jumped at my voice. "But there's no point in spending time on design when most guests change their rooms on arrival." I patted one of the bed's thick mahogany posts and shrugged. "If you'll tell me what to do, we can give this place a bit more personality."

"It's nice," said Aiden noncommittally, running one hand over the brocade coverlet.

I snorted. "It looks like it belongs in a museum. Give me a starting point, or I'm going lacy."

The corner of his mouth twitched in an uncertain smile. "That's low."

"Think of it as motivation. So." I considered the bed for a moment, then watched as the posts melded into a low headboard and footboard and the frame widened.

"Better? Worse?"

He joined me at the foot and drummed his fingers on his arm. "Could it be pine instead?"

The wood lightened to pale honey. "Like that?"

Aiden looked up at me in disbelief. "You don't even need a wand."

"It's a glorified stick to me. Does absolutely nothing." I squinted at the bedding—something of Mother's design, I guessed—and ended up with navy cotton. "Yes? And as for wands, not all wizards use them. Greg keeps his around as a formality, you know."

"Yeah," Aiden pointed out, "but he's really *good* at magic. My parents use them. Hel took hers to college with her. Told her roommate it was a Harry Potter replica," he added, grinning.

"*Conjurus homeworkus* or something?"

"Maybe. She *did* get Dean's List twice last year." He tentatively patted the new blanket, then flopped onto the mattress. "Not bad."

"Any changes?"

He tucked his hands behind his head. "What about a waterbed?"

"Unless you like midnight seasickness, I strongly discourage it." I sat next to him, contemplated the rest of the room, and whipped up a dresser and wardrobe. "What do you need in terms of desk space?" I asked, throwing a thick rug on the floor.

Aiden sat up and glanced at his boxes. "Ideally or bare minimum?"

I had to choke back laughter, the question was so absurd, but composed myself before Aiden could become concerned. "Listen," I said, gripping his shoulders, "I understand that there are certain limitations on what you can do when you're living with the Mole People, but you're out of the silo. This is Faerie. The laws of physics are more like defaults." I nodded to the boxes and said, "If you need more room, I can always adjust the walls. Get it?"

"Really?"

His surprise threw me off. "You were serious when you said they taught you nothing about magic?"

Aiden's cheeks colored, and I released him. "I mean, I've picked up a little," he said, rubbing the back of his neck, "but for most of it, why bother? It's not like anyone was going to give me a wand."

"It's just a stick, Aiden."

"I know," he mumbled, staring at his fists. "Just a stick. Wouldn't work for me, either."

Before his misery could reassert itself, I wrapped the open wall with a seamless wooden bench, threw in a rolling chair for good measure, and slid off the bed. "That's a start. You can give me your specs once you've unpacked. Come on, there's someone I want you to meet."

He dutifully followed me across the room. "Sibling?"

"Better. Tell me," I said, opening the door, "what are your thoughts on lizards?"

"They're okay, I guess," he replied, puzzled. "Why?"

"Got a baby dragon out back."

Halfway down the hall, I realized that Aiden was no longer at my heels, and I turned to find him standing in the middle of the runner. "Something I said?" I called.

"You have a dragon."

"Newborn, really. The guy who's working with her probably wouldn't mind if you wanted to hang out."

"Dragon."

"Just a little one, nothing to be too concerned about yet. Are you—"

"Man, you've got a friggin' *dragon*?" he shouted, and ran toward me as the paralysis snapped.

"**B**efore you say anything, my lord, he won't let me help."

Valerius loitered in the narrow doorway of the barn, watching Joey shovel what looked to be fifty-odd pounds of manure. "Where did he find the tools?" I asked.

"He let me do that much," my guard replied, "but no more. Said he needed the exercise." He slowly shook his head as Joey grunted in time with his scooping. "How long, do you suppose, before he gives in and lets someone dispose of the...*soil*...properly?"

A pair of sheep bleated behind me, and I surveyed the makeshift pasture, which was filling faster than Georgie could empty it. "He's wary of my brilliant solutions. Give him time."

Valerius began to protest but let it go when Aiden, who had lagged to gawk when we passed the barn's open door, ran up and panted, "There's something wrong with those sheep."

"They're budding, I'm aware of it," I said with a sigh. "It's under control."

Aiden appeared unconvinced. "Council tried that once with our cattle. The herd grew exponentially, and then they had to cull. Ever eaten hamburger for a month straight?"

"There are worse fates, you know." I looked back at Valerius, about to suggest that he dispose of the dragon's waste and give Joey a set of weights, but he had taken a step away from the door and stared at Aiden as if he were seeing an apparition. "Something wrong?"

He swallowed hard, then pointed at the boy. "My lord...who..."

"This is, uh...my brother, Aiden," I said, choosing my words carefully, "who has been Arcanum-reared to this point. Greg wanted to introduce us."

I had expected that this would end the matter—Valerius had been around long enough to know what I meant without forcing me to say "witch-blood"—but his tanned face drained of color as I spoke. "I know, I know," I hastened to add, "he looks like—"

The captain dropped to his knees in the mud. "Forgive me, my lord, I couldn't do it," he said in a rush. "She ordered me, but I couldn't, he was so small, I left him, and I shouldn't have, but I never thought—"

I grabbed his shoulders and pulled him back to his feet, shocked to feel him quaking in my grip. "Calm down. What are you talking about?"

Valerius took a deep breath, avoiding Aiden's questioning frown. "The queen ordered me to dispose of him," he said quietly. "When it was obvious that he was a...an ordinary mongrel. She wanted him dead, but she was busy—Lady Moyna's nurse had brought her to court, and the queen—"

My stomach very much wanted to liberate itself from the shackles of my body at that moment, and I forced myself not to look at Aiden. "Mother told you to kill him?"

He nodded as his jaw clenched. "I tried, my lord. But he was only two days old..." His eyes unfocused, as if he were watching something replay in the space behind me. "I killed hundreds for her without hesitation, but I...never a child, she'd always personally killed the ones she didn't want. When she ordered...I couldn't do it."

"Captain—"

His expression was equal parts fear and desperation. "I knew how to find you—I thought of bringing him to you—but with the way the queen watched you, I knew she'd find out. So I brought him to...to his father. I'd seen where his father came from when he opened a gate here, and I backtracked. Left the boy asleep outside. I...didn't know if anyone would find him in time."

I finally gave in and turned to my brother. Aiden looked stricken, and Valerius had tensed for the abuse to come. I wasn't sure which to address first, but I decided on the one less likely to require therapy. "Valerius," I murmured, waiting until his eyes darted back to mine, "you did the right thing."

His shoulders remained taut, but his wariness faded by a degree. "My lord?"

"She told you to kill him. You avoided infanticide. If I'm not mistaken, most would find that commendable."

"She *ordered*—"

"I don't care what she ordered. And should I order you to do something similarly asinine, I would hope you'd have the good sense to thwart me. Yes?"

He nodded, seemingly stunned to still be breathing. "You're not…angry?"

I looked again at Aiden, who was fighting tears and trying not to show it. "You saved him from certain death. I believe we owe you thanks, Captain."

Valerius's face twitched. "But the shame…"

He let the thought hang, and I released him. "If there's any shame to be felt, it's Mother's. Aiden isn't responsible for his condition."

"I fear your other siblings will disagree, my lord." He hesitated, then said, "Two of Lord Doran's have been mongrels. He…disposed of both. Quickly."

Aiden's jaw had begun to quiver, and he abruptly turned away to watch the sheep spawn.

"The boy is under my protection," I told Valerius in a low voice. "Should you see Doran, and should he express any sentiments that strike you as alarming, I would ask that you convey to him my sincere promise that I will make him beg for death if he harms Aiden. This extends to harm by proxy. Is that clear?"

"Yes." His breathing steadied, and with a glance, the mud cleaned itself from his soaked leggings. "Perhaps it would be wise to assign the boy a guard, should I not be present to convey your displeasure."

"We'll talk of this later," I said, watching Aiden hunch over the fence. "If you would…"

He retreated into the barn without a word, and I joined Aiden by the yard, which was already showing signs of overgrazing. "I'm sorry," I began. "I didn't know. I'd have prepared you otherwise, but—"

"Please don't make me go home," he whispered, and looked up from the flock with watery eyes. "Anywhere else. Just don't make me go back there, okay? I can't take another five months underground."

"No one's making you go anywhere."

"But he said—"

I squeezed his shoulder, staying well away from the recently knit bones. "What Doran did to his children was out of my control. I won't let him hurt you."

Aiden's hands clenched and unclenched on the top rail as he mumbled, "I don't want to be a problem."

"Who said you were a problem?"

He cocked his head back toward the barn. "Something about shame? Look, it's okay, it's nothing new. I've been a dud all my life, remember?" He shrugged, feigning nonchalance. "If I need to go, that's fine, I understand— but I'd really appreciate it if you'd drop me a few states away from home."

I climbed the rails and took a seat atop the fence, and after a trio of surprised sheep became six, Aiden joined me. "It's no sin to be hurt," I said, watching the new ewes turn to the grass with gusto. "Or scared...lonely...lost..." One sheep wandered close, and I nudged it away with my toe. "Aiden," I said, tracking the redirected animal as it explored an untrampled bit of green, "I'm not going to sit here and pretend to know what you're feeling. I could look," I allowed, "but I'd rather not. You're entitled to your privacy."

The sheep chewed slowly, mindlessly, and stared at a fencepost.

"If you're angry at Mother," I continued, "I *do* know that feeling. Hated her for years. She murdered my surrogate mother to spite me, she killed the nephew I half-raised in front of my face, and then she imprisoned me for an entirely justifiable homicide. Once she finally let me go, she sent me old changelings to deal with in order to torture me—most of those that didn't want a mercy kill wanted to go back to Faerie, and I couldn't send them here. She did that for *centuries*." I hesitated, trying to read his inscrutable face. "And a few months before your time, she kidnapped the daughter I didn't know I had, only to drop her at my feet last spring as part of a plan to drag me home. Backfired horribly, but that's beside the point. Anyway, what I'm trying to say is that if you feel like punching something, I understand."

Aiden gave no sign that he had heard me. I was on the cusp of looking into his thoughts, privacy be damned, when he muttered, "I just want to belong somewhere for once."

"I know that feeling, too," I replied, catching his look of skepticism. "Hey, you saw Toula's little trick—I'm only half fae, remember? Didn't always fit in here, and I had Arcanum hitmen on my back over there. There's no good middle ground."

He picked at a splinter in the rail. "At least you weren't the biggest disappointment in your dad's life, right?"

I laughed softly. "My dad was a *monk*, okay? I might not have been a disappointment, but I was one hell of a surprise." Aiden snorted, and I threw up my hands. "Didn't even like women. He had no idea he'd been with one until I wandered over."

"Then how—"

"Glamour, wielded properly, is an amazing thing, and let's leave that there. But no, the poor son of a bitch always thought he'd broken his vows with a man, and then, 'Surprise! Hi, Dad!'" My brother smirked as I waved at thin air, and I shrugged. "Well, it wasn't *quite* like that, but you see the picture. We met, had a chat, and he died shortly thereafter. At least you have a father."

Aiden looked back at the flock, his mouth a tight line. "I'm pretty sure he hates me."

"You're fifteen. Everyone hates teenagers."

He sneaked a look at my expression from the corner of his eye, and then, apparently satisfied with what he saw, socked me in the arm.

The blow caught me off guard, and I rocked on the fence, saving myself from a fall into the mud in time to see

Aiden flash a quick grin.

I tried to remember the last time I'd actually liked a member of my family and extrapolate from that relationship what the proper response should be. Finding myself going back centuries, however, I instead settled for punching Aiden in turn. "This is how you treat your elders?" I asked as his smile widened. "Trying to beat them into submission?"

"Yeah, you've seen my mad attack skills."

"You know," I offered, "if you want, I could teach you to not punch like a girl. No magic necessary." I turned at the sound of approaching boots and added, "And when you're finished with that, Joey will teach you the basics of stabbing things for fun and profit."

Joey held up his empty palms, which now bore bright red stripes. "Blisters first, then swordplay, and Val wants to kick my ass."

My eyebrows shot up. "'*Val*'? You got away with that? And I realize church Latin is a disaster, but you do know he pronounces his name with a W, right?"

"He didn't strike me dead, did he? Hi, there!" Joey extended his raw hand to Aiden and smiled. "Heard there was a newcomer out here. I'm still pretty new, too," he added, leaning conspiratorially toward my brother, "but at least I know where the bathrooms are, eh? And I see Colin's breaking you in gently with the most screwed-up livestock management system in the universe."

Aiden met his handshake and chuckled. "It's pretty weird."

"You hang around this guy long enough, and that becomes the norm. So," he said, leaning on the fence between us, "by any chance, do you like dragons?"

His face lit up. "I saw it when I came by, but it was dark in the barn—"

"Her, not it," Joey corrected. "Her name's Georgie, and she's expecting you. Also, she's telepathic, so think happy thoughts." With that, he tugged Aiden off the railing and pushed him toward the barn. "Go on, go say hi. I'll be along in a minute, okay?"

Aiden gave me a last uncertain look, and when I waved him on, he dashed toward the open doors, splashing mud with each footfall. I slid off the fence and shook my head, then muttered, "Thank you."

"I got the quick version from Val, and Georgie filled in a few gaps. She said something didn't feel right, so she helped herself. Guess someone's going to have to talk to her about minding her own business eventually." He folded his bare arms against the breeze, protecting what his T-shirt failed to cover. The sleeves had grown tighter, I noted—Joey had changed in more ways than one in the months since he abandoned seminary.

"He's had a rough time of it," I said, keeping my voice too low for Aiden to hear.

"Staying here for a while?" Joey asked.

"That was the plan."

He nodded. "You all right?"

"Who, me? Why?"

"I don't know, Greg just sprung a kid brother on you. That would throw me for a loop."

"It's…sinking in," I replied, glancing at the barn. "And now it looks like I've got a bright, awkward, magically inept teenager on my hands. What do I need to know?"

"What do you mean, what do you need to know?" he echoed.

"You're only ten years his senior, yes? Anything pertinent?"

Joey thought for a moment, then nodded again. "He can't legally drink."

"*That* is the best advice you can give me?"

"Not necessarily the best," he said with a wry smile, "but for you, I'd say it's pertinent."

CHAPTER 5

Meggy would have understood if I'd cancelled our date, but Joey was more perceptive than he realized—I needed a moment of normalcy, and that season, normalcy meant Meggy. Joey assured me that life would continue in my absence, and as for Aiden, he was too absorbed with Georgie, who had flopped onto her back for a belly scratch, to be bothered by my departure. "I'll keep an eye on him," Joey quietly assured me at the barn door, "and *he'll* keep an eye on everything else," he added, tilting his chin toward Valerius, who lurked in the far corner of the barn, watching uncertainly as the hatchling's forked tongue lolled. "What could possibly go wrong?"

"Please don't tempt fate while I'm away," I muttered as a mirror appeared. My wardrobe was appropriate—and after a once-over, mud-free again—but re-creating the face I used each time I visited Meggy required a bit of work. Applying the glamour took no effort, but getting the details right necessitated a certain degree of skill. I had been lazy in the beginning, slapping together something vaguely late-thirties to match Meggy's assumed face, but after a few weeks, one of her regular customers had asked when I'd had work done. I'd weaseled out of an answer by blaming the lighting, but I'd taken greater care since then, though my appearance was only the minor half of the glamour. Far more important was the enchantment that my modified features made believable: no one in Rigby, save my former neighbor and my bartender, recognized me as the young man who had formerly run Ex Libris. For

Meggy's sake, the glamour couldn't be allowed to fail.

Much of magical practice is physical, the art of effecting change on the world through the judicious use of a force unseen, unfelt, unquantifiable, and unwieldable to all but a tiny percentage of mortals—and even then, the freakish few often require something like a wand to channel and amplify the little ability they possess. But even with their limitations, they do get by, and a well-trained wizard with a fair amount of talent can be a powerful opponent. (Not for me, of course—not in a few centuries, and certainly not since Mother's demise—but there was a time when I preferred running to taking my chances with a pack of Arcanum assassins.) A strong wizard can hurl his opponent across a room, bury him in an avalanche of bricks pulled from midair, and cap off the rout with a lightning bolt from the blue if he's feeling particularly peeved. Even a middling wizard should be able to play with fire, temporarily levitate, and shield a shot. Physical magic takes discipline to master, but it's not an impossible task.

It is, however, exceedingly rare to find a wizard who excels at mental manipulation, the subtler and more delicate work of fucking with others' heads. Here, at least, is where a hefty dose of fae blood confers a significant advantage—we're innate masters of glamour, a skill most wizards will never learn. If I wish to walk about appearing as anything other than a pale twenty-something with unruly hair, all I need do is create the appropriate glamour—taller, older, balder, female—and under most circumstances, the illusion is indistinguishable from reality. The bags under my eyes, the beard I'll never be able to grow—they're real to sight and touch, and, conveniently enough in this age, glamour extends to cameras. Physically, though, I've done nothing. Once the illusion drops, my face remains my face, largely unchanged since, oh, about a decade after a certain charter was signed at Runnymede.

Personal glamour isn't the extent of mental magic,

however, and I've had plenty of time to hone my skills. In Meggy's case, that meant shoring up my cover story with the aforementioned enchantment, which gave me a clean slate even among people whose faces I'd known for years. Sure, they remembered the guy who'd sold used paperback romances and slunk into Slim's on a nightly basis, but they couldn't recognize me as the same person, albeit slightly aged.

The enchantment helped keep awkward questions to a minimum for Meggy—she'd told her new neighbors that she'd been given the bookstore by a cousin, and having said cousin show up and behave with more than familial affection would have proven problematic. More importantly, though, the enchantment helped keep our daughter's true memories safely locked up, which was the only way she would ever have consented to live with her mother. When I bound the girl who had been molded into Moyna into the girl who could have been Olive, I had effectively erased myself from her past, giving her a doting, if dead, father and a childhood spent happily with Meggy. Moyna knew me and despised me, but to Olive, I was merely an annoyance that had come with the move to Rigby, and I intended to keep it that way. Meggy had lost her child once—I wasn't going to put the stability of the bind in jeopardy by dropping my illusions around Olive.

And so, once I was confident that no one in coastal Virginia would give me a second look, I produced a pair of leather gloves, ignored the realm's wordless displeasure at my imminent departure, and opened a gate to the back of my old building, where my appearance was less likely to be noticed. After closing the gate behind me, I straightened my shirt, ran a hand over my hair once more for good measure, and carefully started up the fire escape to the second-floor apartment. Night was falling, and a false step would mean tumbling straight into the metal stairs—and I didn't need the tingling in my sheathed hands to remind myself of the staircase's composition. Extended iron- and silver-free periods in Faerie had begun to spoil me, but as a side effect, my metallic warning system hadn't been so sensitive in ages.

When I sidestepped the last of Meggy's potted ferns and reached the top landing, I rapped on the kitchen door and waited, momentarily wondering if I should have had flowers at the ready before I spotted Olive's silhouette against the semi-sheer curtains. She flipped the latch and cracked the door open, then gave me a disdainful once-over before flouncing back the way she'd come.

"Hello to you, too," I called after her. "Is your mother home?"

"Downstairs!" she yelled, and slammed her bedroom door.

With Olive obviously in no mood for social niceties, I let myself out of the apartment via the inner staircase and wandered down to the bookstore on the ground floor. A quick survey of the room revealed Meggy behind the old wooden counter, resting her folded forearms on the worn oak as a younger brunette in a black hood began to pick at a cloth-wrapped package. Meggy brushed a red curl from her eyes and held out her hand in offer, but the brunette shook her head and continued her slow work.

"Open late again?" I asked from the stairway.

Meggy beamed. "Hey, stranger," she called back. "Come on down, I want a second opinion."

The brunette—who was wearing not a sweatshirt, as I had first imagined, but a floor-skimming cloak—frowned and paused in her unwrapping, but Meggy motioned her on. "An expert," she said, nodding toward me. "If you have what you claim to have, he'll know."

The girl's fingernails were lacquered the color of old blood, and her cloak was clasped about her throat with a silver broach formed into a Celtic knot. A witch, I surmised, a nervous witch with a treasure wrapped in oilcloth, afraid someone was going to take her toy away.

I held up my hands to show her I was unarmed. "Been

in this business a while," I said, making my way past an overflowing rack of cookbooks, "and I've seen just about everything. What did you find?"

"I didn't *find* anything," she snapped, bending back to her task. "I inherited it. It's legitimate, I'm not a thief."

"No one said you were," Meggy soothed. "It helps if we know the provenance and history of these things. Makes them more easily sold." The girl looked up at her blankly, and Meggy explained, "Easier to check for residual spells if you know who last had it."

"My grandmother," she muttered, and finally exposed the brown leather beneath the wrappings. "She bought it because it looked good on a shelf. Never made it work."

Meggy inspected the book without touching it, then produced a pair of white gloves from beneath the counter and slipped them on. Next came a set of green foam wedges—softer than the counter, and far easier on the book's binding—and a light-up magnifying glass. With practiced care, Meggy extracted the volume from its bindings and peered at the embossed spine. "Okay, at least the spelling's right," she murmured, then placed the book on the blocks and carefully opened it to the front matter.

"What are we dealing with?" I asked, switching my gloves for Meggy's spare cotton pair.

"It's a Roux," she replied, peering at the script through the lit glass. "*Aegis.* And if my Latin is up to snuff, this is, as promised"—she glanced up at the waiting witch—"his treatise on wardwork."

"First edition," the witch replied. "Perfect condition, as I said—"

"Good old Déodat," I interrupted, sliding next to Meggy. "Prominent in the late fifteenth century, head of an Arcanum splinter faction, executed by the grand magus as a witch—so inconvenient when your primary rival is also a bishop, isn't it?" I leafed through the first few pages, then looked across the counter at Meggy's eager seller. "First edition, you say?"

"Says so right at the bottom," she pointed out, jabbing her uncovered finger at the bottom of the book. Meggy flinched, and I blocked the witch's hand before it could reach the paper.

"It's in good condition," I said, gently pushing her back, "but it won't be if you keep getting oil all over it. And yes, this is a first *printing*." Her brows knit, and I pressed on. "Déodat Roux was widely reviled by the Arcanum, and not only because he wanted to overthrow the king. It wasn't until after the Revolution that any French wizard bothered giving his work proper consideration. As it turns out, once you get past the politics, the heresy, and the *slight* twinge of, for lack of a better term, magical racism, Roux was a brilliant theoretical wizard. This work," I said, closing the book, "was one of his finest, and still a foundational text. Which you would know, were you Arcanum."

The witch's lips tightened to white, and she drew herself to her full height. "At least I have the gift. You people resell greatness, unable to ever reach it yourselves. Scavengers, really," she said with a little sneer. "Picking at the leavings of the dead."

I leaned on the counter and rested my chin in my hand. "Do tell."

She took the bait. "All this power, right here," she said, tapping the cover, "and to you, it's just another book. Sure, you know your history," she added, smirking, "but what's that compared to the power to change the universe? The sheer, boundless power to—"

"To do nothing. You're obviously a witch, you can't work the most basic spell in that book, and you're probably broke, which is why you're trying to pawn it off." I met Meggy's eyes, which implored me to cut it out, and forced myself to be civil. "Yes, you have a first-run Roux on your hands," I told the witch. "One copy of about two thousand, most of which are in the private collections of Arcanum-affiliated wizards. There's a market for this book."

"I sold one three years ago for five thousand dollars," Meggy added. "The leather's a little worn on this one, but the paper appears intact. I'll give you four and a half."

The witch's cheeks blazed. "That's robbery! A first-edition Roux is worth half a million, easily!"

"A first-edition would be extraordinary," I agreed, cutting her rant down before it could flower. "But this book is only from the first printing." I leaned toward her and permitted myself a trace of a smile. "As I said, Roux wasn't a popular fellow. He wrote *Aegis*, and he made a copy for his second in command, Pons Charron—a handwritten copy. The two are nearly identical: red ink on mid-grade vellum, written in Latin, bound in white lambskin. They're indistinguishable but for a few strike-outs in the original, which, if I'm not mistaken, is still kept at the Arcanum outpost in Glastonbury. The Charron copy made its way into the hands of Pons's granddaughter, Gabrielle…" I paused, looking for a sign of recognition on the witch's face, and found nothing. "Who renounced her grandfather's beliefs and became grand magus. She gave the book to the Arcanum collection to keep it away from suggestible practitioners, not realizing the extent of Roux's genius."

The witch seemed to deflate before my eyes.

"A first-edition *Potestas et Sententia*, of which there are five copies, went for nearly ten million dollars—in 1903." I let that sink in, then said, "You can't put a dollar value on *Aegis*, though, because if you have a copy to sell, you've stolen it from the Arcanum, and you're about to be able to discuss Roux's theories with him in person, if you know what I mean. But fortunately for you, this is only from the first printing, and Ms. Horn is willing to deal. I'd take it, were I you."

She hesitated, giving the book a final stare, then nodded. "Yeah, sure. Fine. I'll sell it."

Meggy opened the locked drawer in the counter that

had served as my cashbox, briefly glanced my way, and dropped a quick wink as several neat stacks of twenties filled the empty space. "Here," she told the witch, pulling bundles free, "all cash, so you won't have to worry about bad checks. We're square."

The witch riffled through the bills, and then, satisfied as to their authenticity, stuffed them into an oddly mundane messenger bag hidden under her cloak.

"And here's your receipt," Meggy added, scratching out the transaction details on a slip of paper. "Thanks for coming by."

This, too, was crumpled into the bag, and then, with a last baleful look in my direction, the wizard let herself out into the night, cloak swishing in her wake.

When the doorbell tinkled her departure, Meggy exhaled and pulled off her gloves. "First-edition *Aegis*, my ass. I knew it couldn't be, but I couldn't tell over the phone whether she was ignorant or a con artist."

"I never knew you read Roux," I replied, tossing my borrowed gloves onto the counter beside her pair.

"I haven't. But if you're going to deal in magical books, you've got to learn your subject." My eyebrows rose, and Meggy grinned. "Toula gave me the hot list years ago. What about you, stalking the Arcanum's collection?"

"Nothing so sinister. I…may or may not have drunk Déodat under the table at a little inn near Avignon every night one summer," I replied. "Not a bad sort when the wine was flowing."

"Déodat Roux?" she asked incredulously. "*The* Déodat Roux?"

"We both had scores to settle with the Arcanum," I explained, slipping my leather gloves back on, "and he thought an alliance could be mutually beneficial. I wasn't about to jump on *that* crazy train, but I wasn't above passing on what I knew—and he kept the wine flowing."

She began to reply, floundered speechlessly, and then shook her head. "Jesus, Colin, what do I do with that?"

I met her waiting lips.

When we broke apart, she gave me her best look of prolonged suffering. "And it's so bad for business when you provoke my customers."

We kissed again with new intensity, my hands tangled in Meggy's hair, the small of her back pressed against the counter, and all about us the teasing ghost of the jasmine perfume she favored. I was about to shuck off my gloves again and begin exploring the regions beneath her deep-necked T-shirt when she pulled back and murmured, "Olive's upstairs."

"She's in her room," I said, surprised at the growl in my voice. "Door closed. Won't notice."

Meggy nuzzled the side of my neck and whispered, "Her friends are coming over."

I sighed, forcing the frustration down. "Later?"

"Later." She slid away from the counter and straightened her shirt, once more Olive's socially appropriate mother. "Where did you want to go for dinner?"

I cut my eyes pointedly to the wide oak counter, which had of late seen a type of use never attempted during my tenure in the building.

She snorted and smoothed her hair. "Yeah, that's not dinner. Szechuan Garden?"

Rigby's sole attempt at international cuisine was mediocre on its best night, but chopsticks eliminated the need for gloves at the table, a perk we both appreciated after too many meals spent lying about eczema flare-ups and a mistrust of all silverware not cleaned at home. "Sounds good," I said. "You're driving?"

Before she could respond, the doorbell jangled, and four girls in short skirts and midriff-baring attempts at shirts trooped into the store in a perky clump. "Hi, there," Meggy called across the shop, stepping out from behind the counter. "Olive's upstairs, if you want to get her."

The pack thinned into a single-file line as they quickly

threaded their way through the aisles and up the stairs, and I winced as the apartment door slammed. "Quite the conversationalists," I muttered, looking to the ceiling at the sound of squealed greetings overhead.

"Friends from camp," Meggy replied, tidying a shelf of special orders, a few hardbacks in library binding and a selection of bagged books of older vintage.

The *special* special orders, the stock Toula had retrieved from Meggy's old house and delivered to her new place, were stored in a locked room in the dark recesses of the shop, protected by wards of my creation. On separate occasions, Toula and I had tried to teach Meggy the art of ward building, but Meggy was young and new to her power, and her attempts fell apart. My style of construction was still too technical for her to master, while the technique Toula used was too close to spellcraft to work properly. She had been practicing, but until she could create a ward she trusted, she allowed me to protect the books for her.

I couldn't tell how far she had progressed, though. Meggy learned primarily from Toula, who had been unknowingly working her own blend of magics for years. Toula had a wizard's discipline and a faerie's strength—a strength amplified by her father's unusual ability—and she proved an apt teacher, even if, as she admitted to me, half of the things she produced were the result of intuition and luck. Still, even if she was winging it, Toula had proven herself formidable, and I rested more easily knowing that she paid Meggy regular visits.

There was much I could have taught Meggy and saved Toula the trial and error, but Meggy and I had agreed it would be better if I left her instruction to another. I had been her friend, her employer—and now that the truth was out in the open between us, I was free to be her lover without guilt. Complicating a relationship that was already complicated would have been awkward at best, and certainly mood killing. Meggy wanted to be with me, but on her terms, which meant coming together as equals. And so I held back, letting Toula guide her and correct her missteps.

I also refrained from evident displays of magic around her—why, I couldn't say, but something cautioned me to go slowly. Meggy was learning about her abilities, but when we were together, she seldom mentioned them, and she never spoke of Faerie. Granted, her only stay in the realm had been ten days of slow torture and the shock of her life, but she avoided the subject, asking for no details of where I went when I left her.

There was no sense in pushing Meggy. I reasoned that she would come around in time, that her curiosity would get the better of her, that she would come over and see she had nothing to fear with Mother gone. She was, I had realized, still in denial to a degree: able to accept her newfound power, happy to have Olive and me back in her life, but unwilling to process the news that she had joined the ranks of the half fae. The latter could, in some way, have been due to the minor fact that her father threw a fatal bind on her at the time of conception and never looked back, or it could have been due to the years she had spent sourcing books for wizards, who seldom spoke well of anything out of Faerie. In any case, the last thing Meggy wanted to discuss was my new status as the only active monarch in the realm, and so we avoided the topic, talking instead of the book trade, summer on the Atlantic coast, and our child's first foray into public education.

As Meggy finished her cleanup, the upstairs door opened again, and the girls marched back down from the apartment with Olive in the lead. I looked up at the noise and stopped cold at my daughter's change of wardrobe. "Hang on, Olive," I said, sliding over the counter. "Where are you going?"

Her friends slowed, but Olive tugged the nearest along. "That's just my mom's weird boyfriend. Ignore him."

"Olive Marie Horn," Meggy snapped, and the girl

reluctantly paused. "Colin asked you a question. There's no need to be rude."

She heaved an award-caliber sigh and turned back to me with her hand on her largely exposed hip. "What?"

"Where are you going?" I asked again, trying not to stare at her skirt. I'd seen hand towels that afforded greater coverage. "Dressed like…that?"

Her eyes, pale blue and now fringed by spider lashes and glitter, narrowed in challenge. "Like *what*?"

"Like you come with a price tag," I retorted, briefly wondering where she had procured see-through platform heels in Rigby. "I'm being honest, Olive—you look like a prostitute."

She snorted her disdain. "Asshole."

"*Olive!*"

"*Mother!*" she mimicked, and absently pushed her blonde locks over her bare shoulder. "We're going to a party. You don't want everyone to think I'm a loser, do you?"

"They're going to think you're for *rent*," I protested.

Meggy silenced me with a pointed look. "Sweetie, unless this is a costume party, there's no need for you to go out dressed like a stripper."

"I look *cute*!" she argued, stamping her foot as both hands went to her hips. "And all the guys are going to be there, and you want me to look like a freak…" The tears came on cue, dramatic sobs that stopped just short of turning into an ugly cry, and Olive's posse closed in around her.

"Really, Ms. Horn," one of them whined, "Olive looks great! She's *so* on trend."

Olive wiped her eyes, avoiding her lacquered lashes. "You used to be cool, Mom," she said, sniveling for effect. "What happened? Why are you being so *mean*?"

Meggy surveyed the pack of girls for a long moment, then closed her eyes and sighed. "Okay," she murmured. "Go to your party. But if you get there and want to change clothes, I'm not coming to bail you out. Understood?"

The tears dried instantly, and Olive flashed a smile of faux gratitude. "Thanks, Mom, you're the best," she replied, and breezed out into the night.

When the ersatz streetwalkers were gone, I muttered, "What the hell, Meggy? She can't go around like—"

"The first rule of parenting is to choose your battles," she said, cutting me off mid-protest. "I'm not going to fight her over a miniskirt." She stuffed her hands into her pockets and stared out the plate-glass window, watching Olive until she rounded the corner, heading toward the beach.

The silence hung between us, but it confirmed what I had begun to fear. "She's fighting you, isn't she?"

"Not always," Meggy said quietly, staring into the night. "But it's getting worse."

I joined her at the window. "Is she remembering—"

"No, not like that. Not that she's shown me, anyway." Meggy's shoulders tightened as she spoke. "It's the false memories, I think—she has this great picture of the two of us living together happily, and our current reality doesn't live up to that past. Then again, she's sixteen—I gave my mother a hard time at that age..."

"Eh, she probably had it coming," I replied, kneading her taut muscles.

She stiffened, then began to relax under my hands. "She told me the truth about my father when I was fifteen. What she *could* tell me, at least." Meggy glanced at me over her shoulder as I continued the massage. "Did I ever tell you that?"

"No."

"It explained why Dad doesn't want me around, at least," she sighed. "Haven't spoken to him in three years." She hissed as I hit a sore spot, then said, "Mom calls on Christmas and my birthday. Mike and Justin sent me birth announcements for three nephews I've never met. Nor do I plan to. It's...you know, better this way."

My stomach twisted as I heard the pain Meggy tried to hide. Charlie Bellamy was no saint, at least not when it came to his wife's daughter, but he'd been present in Meggy's life. I had moved to the fringe, at best, of Olive's orbit, and part of me berated myself for being a terrible parent. The other part pointed out that, given her true memories, Olive almost certainly wanted me dead, and that this was a shaky foundation for building any sort of father-daughter relationship.

"Say the word," I told Meggy, releasing her with a final squeeze, "and I'll take her elsewhere. If she's too much—"

"She's mine," she said with the same finality as always, but her eyes were still troubled. "We'll get through this if it kills me." Forcing a smile, she walked over to the counter and retrieved the car keys by their palm tree fob. "Enough about Olive's wardrobe. Still hungry?"

I followed her into the garage and waited until she cranked my old Accord, then asked, "So, would now be a good time to tell you about my little brother?"

Chen Yang, the owner, host, and half the wait staff at Szechuan Garden, seated us at a cozy table behind a cheap folding screen in the back of the restaurant, a spot he seemed to reserve for frequent diners and, I suppose, any passing Mafiosos in need of eggrolls. When he left us with a pair of laminated menus, Meggy let her mask of polite anticipation drop, leaned across the table, and furiously whispered, "I can't believe those asses waited until now to tell him! What were they *thinking*?"

"Wouldn't have been my choice," I replied, turning past a splotch of dried sweet and sour sauce. "But he was handling it well when I left him—with Joey," I quickly added, seeing her expression shift. "I left him with Joey and a baby dragon, and that should take his mind off the situation until I get back. Right?"

Meggy blinked. "Baby dragon?"

"She found Joey in the woods last night. He didn't want to leave her out there alone." The next page was stain-free, and if I concentrated, I could almost understand the dish descriptions. Chen kept a decent restaurant, but he had always seemed to get around Rigby by smiling and pointing. "What did you get last time, the one I kept stealing?"

"Cashew chicken, and quit changing the subject. Don't you think it's a tad risky to have a freaking dragon around the house?"

I looked up from the menu and saw that she was not to be ignored. "Just a hatchling right now. I'm sure Joey can handle her, and Aiden...well, he's a smart kid, he'll stay out of the way if she starts rampaging."

Sighing, Meggy lowered her gaze to the page of poorly-lit appetizer photographs. "Promise me you won't end up crispy, okay? I'd like to keep you around for a bit."

"Only a bit?"

"We'll see." She pursed her lips, scanned the options, and murmured, "I'm kind of in the mood to get dessert and go home. Olive's going to be out for a while, but just in case..."

The thought trailed off tantalizingly, and I was about to find Chen and order a plate of fortune cookies to go when Meggy's purse began playing wind chime scales. "Sorry, one sec," she said, pulling her phone free, then frowned at it and tapped the screen. "Hello?" she asked, keeping her voice down. "Oh, hi, Father...yeah, actually, he's right here, do you...okay, sure. Here you go." She passed the device across the table, righted it in my hand, and whispered, "Hold it up and talk like normal. The screen doesn't get in the way."

I didn't trust her phone and its discomfiting lack of buttons, but I could think of only one priest who would have Meggy's mobile number. "Paul?" I muttered toward the microphone. "Something wrong?"

"Sorry to interrupt," he replied, "but we have a slight

situation in Southport. Any chance you could stop by?"

"We? What we?"

He lowered his voice to a near whisper. "I've got a blasted camera crew, Colin. These fools called the paranormal investigators right after they called me."

I rubbed my forehead. "Why would they—"

"Ten-year-old girl seems possessed, which is why the diocese got involved and brought me in. When I pulled up, I had to fight past a pair of vans and an SUV to get in the door, and then they wanted me to sign a waiver. *Heathens.*"

"Let me guess, she's not possessed."

"Not in the traditional sense. Something's speaking through her and throwing half the house around, but I don't think it's demonic. Voice sounds a bit like the one from Harrow last spring. I made a recording if you want to hear it now."

"Don't bother, I'm on my way."

I passed the phone back to Meggy, who touched the screen until it went dark. "Got to go?" she asked.

"Unfortunately." I pushed back from the table, by turns seething and frustrated. "Paul's out of his depth, and whoever's messing around is doing so for ghost hunters."

She rolled her eyes in exasperation. "Be careful. Will I see you later tonight?"

I bent and kissed her one last time. "No. I'm afraid I'm going to have business in Florida when I'm finished here. Maybe tomorrow?"

Meggy mulled it over. "Could work. Olive wants to spend the night with a friend."

"Or you could come over and see the dragonet."

She smiled sadly and pushed me away from the table. "You know where to find me, Colin."

CHAPTER 6

For someone like me, there are few things more annoying than having to work around mortals who believe they have "the paranormal" studied, sorted, tagged, and catalogued. Witches with inferiority complexes I can handle. Run-of-the-mill nonbelievers are a cinch. But idiots with expensive cameras, gadgets used off-label to commune with the spirit world, and bags of sage and saint medallions make my work far more complicated than it need be.

Under ordinary circumstances, if I helped Paul on a job, he would corral the victims elsewhere while I convinced the faerie amusing himself at their expense to hit the road. But paranormal researchers refuse to be removed from the scene—they want to be in the middle of the exorcism, shouting down demons and shrieking every time the house settles—and thus, they try my patience. It's not easy to have a quiet conversation with an invisible entity in a language unknown to everyone else in the room—a conversation that occasionally devolves into a full-blown, fire-slinging, wall-smashing fight—when there's a boom mic hanging in your face.

Fortunately for Paul, I once spent a long weekend in Southport, a little seaside hamlet half an hour from Rigby and best described as long past its heyday. He and I had found a group of Oberon's thugs lying low in a farm outside the city limits, and I pursued them onto an abandoned cannery up the coast. A decrepit warehouse filled with bits of rusting equipment is roughly at the bottom of the list of places good for my health, but I'd made the best of it and managed to crawl out the back door while the complex burned. Paul deflected suspicion from us during the resulting arson investigation—which morphed into a homicide investigation once someone stumbled across the charred bones I'd left behind—and I holed up in a nondescript motel, treating my many wounds with copious quantities of liquor.

Southport was tiny, and the relatively central motel was as good a starting point as any. I opened a gate between Szechuan Garden's men's room and the alley behind the motel, then strolled out toward the main street and observed the deserted downtown square. Night had long since fallen, and Southport was the sort of place that rises and sleeps with the sun, but there was a light in the motel's office, and I rapped on the security glass to get the bored attendant's attention.

He lowered his magazine, the sort of periodical one finds sold in black plastic, and squinted at me through the sand-pitted window. "What do you want, a room?"

I supposed his confusion was due to my lack of companion, as Southport's finest accommodations were available for hourly rental. "Information," I replied, leaning against the counter.

"I don't deal, man."

"Not that sort of information."

His puzzlement deepened. "You want a girl?"

"No." I leaned close to the speaker and kept my voice low. "Looking for a camera crew. Not the kind from CNN, if you know what I mean. Couple of vans, probably a bunch of twenty- and thirty-somethings, and maybe someone in the bunch talking about residual energy. Got a lead for me?"

A glimmer of recognition crossed his face. "Maybe. Course, I see a lot of people around here…"

I could have read his mind, but it was simpler to produce a folded hundred-dollar bill from my back pocket. "Think hard," I said, holding it up to the glass.

The attendant hesitated only long enough to note the face on the currency. "Yeah, the freak show. They're staying here."

"Not here now?"

"Nah. Ghost huntin' or some shit like that."

"Indeed." I slid the bill through the slot in the window and pulled a second one out. "Any idea where they might have gone?"

"They might have mentioned the Monroe House." I tilted my head, and he explained, "Old Man Monroe used to own half the town. He haunts the house he built. Or that's what folks say, I don't know," he allowed. "Ain't never seen a ghost. Me and my girl went up there once before the new family bought it."

I had a strong suspicion that the attendant's girlfriend was attached to his wrist, but I let it slide. "Where would I find this place?"

He pointed toward the darkened brick courthouse. "Up the hill, hang a right on Third, go halfway down the street, and you'll see the driveway." He cleared his throat, and the second bribe joined its fellow.

I left him to his pornography and trekked off into the night, having helped myself to the attendant's mental map. True to his word, the house wasn't far—and true to Paul's, the driveway was choked with vans, black vehicles grossly out of place in a neighborhood of modest Hondas and Subarus. I stepped up to one and peered in the open back doors at a tangle of monitors and blinking computer components, all overseen by a skinny kid wearing thick-framed glasses and fat headphones over braided black pigtails. Before she could notice me, I slipped out of her line of sight and headed for the house.

As glad as I was to see Paul again, I suspected something was amiss when I found him sitting on the porch steps, drinking from a tiny flask. He saw me approach, lifted his metal box, and swigged. "Don't even start, Leffee," he warned. "I've had one hell of a day."

I sat beside him, and he shifted to make room. "What are you drinking?"

"Gin," he said miserably. "Found it in my trunk. I think you left it there a few years back."

"Just dump it," I told him as a bottle of port appeared at his feet.

He cut his eyes to the wine, nodded his thanks, and poured the rest of the gin in the bushes. "The imbeciles driving me to drink have decided that Madison—that's our little girl—is being haunted by the ghost of Henry Monroe."

"Former owner, heard the short version."

Paul eyed his miniature flask and the full-sized port bottle for a moment, and I dropped a funnel in his lap. "Got a cocktail shaker, too?" he asked as he commenced the operation. "I'm curious how much barware you're carrying these days."

"As always, whatever's needed," I replied, catching the old priest's smirk. "And should you require something a bit more potent, I can do a decent syringe and—"

"Don't tempt me tonight. I might take you up on it, and that's a confession I'd rather not make. Cheers." He handed me the funnel and drank deeply, careful to avoid dripping on his stole, then slipped the flask back into his pocket. "Did you want to hear the voice?"

"Sure," I said, and Paul slapped his recorder against my glove. I depressed the button and waited while the babbling subsided, and then a sweet, high voice I assumed to be Madison's growled insults against the mothers of everyone around her in Fae. "Yeah," I muttered when the sound ceased, "I think this is Harrow again."

"Another burger jingle?"

"Not nearly as polite. You know, Paul, my offer stands—"

"And my answer is unchanged," he replied. "Please stay out of my head."

I shrugged and passed back his recorder. "As you like.

Well, this isn't fixing the problem." I sighed, pushing myself off the step. "Coming?"

He looked sick. "Colin, they've got a damn *psychic* in there. She sees shadow figures in every room."

"I'll take point, then." I paused to check the integrity of my gloves, then picked up an abandoned trowel and tested its weight. "This may get messy, you know."

"It pains me to say this, but see if you can avoid killing the idiots, okay?"

I snorted and headed up the stairs. "Some priest you are, man."

"I'm only human," he called after me. "I've got limits."

At the door, I glanced back at him and raised an eyebrow. "You think mine are any higher?"

"No, and that's why I'm staying out here." Paul pulled his flask free again and unscrewed the cap. "Go on, have a good time. *Ego te absolvo.*"

Want to have a little fun with ghost hunters? Here's a tip: bear in mind that they're straining to pull meaningful sounds from silence.

Aside from a pair of tapers shoved into empty wine bottles in the foyer, the house was dark when I slammed the door open and stomped inside, earning a satisfying round of shrieks for my pains. The evening breeze caught the candle flames just so, sending them dancing before snuffing them out, and I set my hand ablaze to compensate. "You people like orbs, right?" I asked as they stared at the fire in my palm like terrified deer. "Time to pack up," I said quietly, meeting the eyes of the nine kids ringing the living room. "And turn off the recording devices before I do it for you."

The boy behind the camera, who looked as if he might be on a first-name basis with the proprietor of every pizza joint in a twenty-mile radius, gawked at me in shocked silence.

"Turn it off," I repeated, "or it's history."

His stubby fingers began to reach for the buttons, but before they could make contact, a boy in a black baseball cap barked, "Keep rolling! What the *hell* is that thing?"

The cameraman, too stunned to argue, swiveled the camera on its tripod until I stood in the center of the lens's field of view.

"Kid," I murmured, "I warned you. Close your eyes."

At least he had a modicum of self-preservation. By the time the camera exploded into shrapnel, he had flung himself behind an antique loveseat and was whimpering along with his crew's renewed shouts.

"Hey," their leader yelped, "that's expensive! The fuck—"

I didn't waste time asking nicely again. He shrieked as I sent a focused bolt of energy around the room, electrocuting every voice recorder and repurposed voltmeter in their arsenal as well as all of the family's lamps. Blue lightning flickered from pockets and bounced off the metal objects in its path, and the short hair on my arms stood on end as it returned to me, ricocheted off my trowel, and passed out the window.

By the time the light show ended, the would-be exorcists had become a cowering mob in the corner, shaking in the firelight. A girl near the front prayed and frantically rubbed a plastic rosary, while her leader had somehow slunk to the rear of the pack, putting his assistants between us for safety. As I finally spotted the little girl, who had been tied to a coffee table in the back of the room, a woman in a white broom skirt stepped forward and raised her hand. "Unclean spirit!" she bellowed, swishing her way toward me. "I banish you to the darkness from which you came. I banish—"

"Yeah, that's not going to work," I interrupted, turning up the flame to get a good look at her bottle-thick glasses. "I suppose you're the psychic, hmm?"

She flinched, thrown off balance. "Go into the light?"

she tried weakly.

"Nope," I replied. "Now, listen up, children. I've got a priest on the porch who actually knows what he's doing, and instead, I find you lot playing at *Ghostbusters*. So who's the spirit, then?" I asked, focusing on the alleged medium.

She held her composure remarkably well, considering that I was standing ten feet away from her with a large ball of spectral flame in my palm. "Henry Monroe," she said, fighting the quivering in her jaw. "He has unfinished business."

"He may well have buried a fortune in pirate gold in the garden, my dear, but he's got nothing to do with this mess." I turned from her to the bound child, who strained against her restraints, and switched into Fae. "Drop her, Benatin."

Little Madison sighed, and her eyes rolled back in her head as she slumped against the table. A disembodied voice to her right whined, "You have no right—"

"I have *every* right," I snapped, and threw the globe of fire into the air to free my hands. "And I thought we had this conversation already."

"My lord gave me—"

"Your lord is dead, or hadn't you heard?"

The voice hesitated. "My...my lord—"

"Robin? Yes. Our mother killed him. Now show yourself."

The shadows wavered, and the paranormal experts gasped as Benatin popped into view, all four feet and dimpled cheeks of him. I tapped the trowel against my glove and said, "Drop the glamour. You're not fooling anyone."

His tone turned petulant, but his eyes remained focused on the trowel. "Who are *you* to give orders? I don't have to drop it, not for you."

I stood in silence for a moment, long enough to make him twitch, then tucked the trowel into my belt and let myself explode in a white corona. Our observers screamed again, and Benatin staggered backward before tripping over the rug and falling on his side. By the time he righted himself, I had grabbed him by the shirt and pulled him toward me, then willed his glamour away until I found myself facing a petrified adult version of the little boy he chose to be. "Robin's not the only one lately dead," I said softly. "Now, what were you saying?"

His pronounced Adam's apple bobbed. "You...you can't...Lord Oberon will—"

"Oberon doesn't seem to give a damn. But I do." I yanked at his shirt, drawing him nearer. "What's it going to take to get through to you? Honestly, you didn't even leave the state. The damn *state*, Benatin! What sort of idiot lingers where he's been warned away?"

His panic mounted by the minute. "I wasn't hurting anything!" he wailed, squirming in my grip.

"You were using that child like a puppet!"

"I didn't hurt her!"

"*That's not the point!*" I shook him until his head snapped back and forth. "You did what I told you not to do, you got *those* morons mixed up in this mess," I continued, dragging him into view of the bug-eyed ghost hunters, "and you pulled me away from what was promising to be a *very* pleasant evening. What do you have to say for yourself?"

His defiance melted into begging. "My lord, please...Lord Coileán, I swear it, never again..."

I let him babble for a moment, then threw him onto the sofa beside the unconscious girl and pulled the trowel free. "This is the last time I let you live," I murmured, holding him down with a heavy wave of force. "Though I see that you've yet to learn the lesson I taught you. Let's try again."

I pushed the trowel's blade against his cheek, holding it steady as he screamed and thrashed with the pain, then pulled it out of his ruined flesh and stepped back. "Try to learn something this time, won't you?" I said, and waved the door open.

Benatin, still screaming in agony, ran for the door and vanished. A moment later, Paul stepped into the foyer, looked around, and peered at me. "Problem solved?"

"Problem solved," I replied, switching tongues again. "And I kind of like this thing," I added, turning the trowel's wooden handle over. "Good weight, bit of a buffer."

Paul cleared his throat pointedly. "Colin, uh…you're glowing."

"I'm aware of that."

He cut his eyes to the kids and their ruined equipment. "This isn't being recorded, then?"

I shook my head. "Anyone wearing a pacemaker would be on the floor by now. Remember those conversations we've had about why I'm not getting a computer?"

"Yeah, understood." He looked the team up and down and snorted. "All right, boys and girls, you've got no proof that any of this ever happened, and anyone you tell will think you're making it all up. And should you decide to go public, my shiny associate might be distressed, and that would be a *very* unfortunate turn of events. Is that quite clear?"

All of them, even the boy in the baseball cap, nodded.

"Good. Now, run along, all of you. I've got to see to Madison," he said, heading for the coffee table.

The praying girl spoke up. "Uh, Father Paul…if the feed died, her parents are going to be back here soon…"

"Good," he snapped, untying the sleeping child. "They should have been here from the get-go."

"But for control purposes—"

I willed a pair of candelabra onto a side table and shut off my brights. "This wasn't a damn experiment," I interrupted. "You've got a case of mind control on your hands, and you're worried about bad data? Moon and stars, what the hell is wrong with you?"

I never received an answer. Something firm and fast

slammed into the back of my head, and all I saw were stars flickering into blackness.

"Shit. Shit, shit, shit, shit, *shit.*"

The voice was female, moderately pitched with a slight drawl muddled by panic. I couldn't place it, but at that moment, as I was waking to a blinding headache, that detail was inconsequential. So there was an unknown woman nearby, probably young, definitely distressed. So what? I was almost certain that my skull had gone concave.

I must have moaned, because the next thing I heard was Paul's voice—darker, rougher, far deeper— somewhere in the haze. "He's coming around. Stand back."

"He's going to kill me," the woman protested. "If you don't let me go—"

"*Stand back*, but stay where I can see you."

The floor creaked, and then a hand landed on my forehead. "Come on, Colin. Wake up. You need to wake up," Paul murmured. "Rise and shine. Don't make me get a bucket."

At that, I forced one eye open, and he smiled tightly. "That's more like it. "Now the other one."

It took three tries, but I managed to get both eyes open and keep them that way. Paul, I saw, had knelt beside me with a camping lantern, but only one of his hands was free. The other was wrapped around a little pistol, which was pointed at the pigtailed girl from the van.

"*Shit*," she whispered.

I blinked a few times, trying to recall exactly why I was prone and in pain. "What—"

"Be still," Paul interrupted. "I've got the situation in hand, and you probably have a concussion, so take it easy while I—"

"No." I forced the screaming pain deep down and sat up, though the effort almost cost me my last meal. "What happened? Where did they go?"

His eyes disapproved, but his voice was resigned. "They ran while you were out. Victim's still sleeping it all off," he said, nodding toward the far table, then moved his gun hand closer to the girl. "*This* one sneaked in through the side door and smashed a candlestick into your head."

I glanced around and spotted a glint of brass in the lantern's glow, then carefully examined it while I prodded the wound. "No blood. She didn't break the skin."

"I'm more concerned about internal bleeding," he replied. "Swelling. Bruising. Cranial fractures."

"It's just a candlestick," I protested.

"You fell like a sack of potatoes. Now sit there and let me handle this." He rose slowly and turned his full attention on the girl, who remained frozen in the middle of the room. "All right, I need some answers," he said. "Unless you'd like to go down for aggravated assault, young lady."

Her glasses flashed as she tilted her face toward mine. "You think *he's* going to call the cops?"

"Wouldn't be the first time," I said, pushing myself off the floor over Paul's protestation. I turned the candlestick over in my hands—my appropriated trowel was nowhere to be found—and studied my apparent assailant more closely. "You were in the van. Technical oversight?"

She nodded. "Someone had to monitor the feeds."

Paul grunted beside me and muttered, "We've got to destroy that van." I looked at him quizzically, and he shrugged. "All you did was break the cameras. The real recording is in that vehicle."

"It's already been erased."

We whipped back to the girl, who crossed her arms and glared at the pistol. "I killed the whole thing once the lightning started. Little bug I wrote into the software, untraceable by anyone else on the team. They won't suspect me. Chalk it up to supernatural forces and move on."

"Why would you—"

"Want to put the gun down?"

I nodded, and Paul lowered the pistol. "Okay," I said, "I'm listening."

She exhaled in a soft rush, then dropped to one knee. "Lord Coileán, my name is Vivian Stowe," she muttered at the floor. "I apologize for the candlestick, but it was either that or the fireplace poker, and I figured you'd prefer my choice."

I gingerly rubbed the back of my head, which had begun healing. "Not sure I like either option, to be frank. And how do you—"

"My parents are of Lord Oberon's court."

"*Ah.* And you...are not?"

"My allegiance is to the Fringe," she replied, pulling a phone from her pocket as she stood. "And given the time since the feed went down, we should expect the victim's parents here any minute. I need you out of here so I can clean up your mess."

I laughed in disbelief. "*My* mess?"

"Yours. I had the situation under control before you barged in and lit up."

Her wristwatch caught the light when she returned her phone to its place, and I couldn't contain a smirk. "Under control, you say? You had a full-blooded faerie under control, kid?"

For a fraction of a second, she wavered. "The plan—"

"Whatever plan you had was moronic. Your parents—half fae, yes? Certainly not full, not if you're wearing *that.*" Her hand went to her wrist, covering the metal band. "Didn't get what they'd expected, did they? How's your skill?"

Her jaw rose in challenge. "Sufficient."

"Not if you're wearing steel. So what was this grand plan, ask him nicely?"

She paused at the sound of tires and a rumbling engine outside. "They're back. Are you going now, or are you going to explain to these folks how you lit your hand on fire?"

"Girl's got a point," Paul muttered. "I'll come up with something, call you when this is over. Are you, uh…going to be with Meggy?"

"This little outing killed the mood." I produced a phone like Joey's and handed it to the priest. "You can reach me here."

He flipped the cover up and frowned. "No buttons."

"No need." I spotted the shadows running up the driveway and gave Vivian a final glare. "This conversation isn't over."

"Talk to Rick. He'll explain everything," she replied, and made a little shooing motion.

And so, at a loss for a better idea, I opened a gate back to Rigby.

Since inserting myself back into Meggy's life, I'd thought my nights at Slim's were behind me. Walking past the knot of smokers on the street and through the front doors felt a bit like coming home, if home had grime-blacked windows and an omnipresent smell of beer and cheap floor cleaner. At least it was Wednesday, still twenty-four hours away from another round of karaoke.

I slid onto my old bar stool, nodded to the regulars flanking me, and caught Slim's attention when he looked away from the baseball game playing on the television mounted in the corner. He nodded curtly, grabbed a bottle of Johnnie Black from the shelf, and placed it in front of me with a glass that was almost clean. "Honor system," he muttered, and turned back to the game.

An inning and about four fingers later, I waited while Slim made the rounds, topping up drinks for his few patrons, then met his eyes when he passed. "Rick," I murmured, conscious of my neighbors, "we need to talk."

He ran one pudgy hand through his thinning hair, then

glanced up and down the line of drinkers, all of whom were focused on a commercial—for either a truck or erectile dysfunction pills, I couldn't tell. Satisfied that they were distracted, he nodded toward a door beside the empty stage. I followed him across the bar, drink in hand.

The door led to a flight of stairs, which terminated in a surprisingly well-appointed apartment. "Well, this is unexpected," I said, turning to examine the living room.

"Something wrong?" Slim puffed as he locked the door behind us.

"No, I'd just pictured you as more of the brown recliner and sagging couch type," I replied, taking in the sleek lines of Slim's white leather sofas and matching ottoman. "Scandinavian?"

"Try not to spill anything," he said, sinking onto the larger of the pair. "What happened? Did she throw you out?"

"Aren't you a beacon of hope," I muttered, taking a seat on the empty couch. "And no, this has nothing to do with Meggy. I was sent to you for information."

"*Me*? By whom?"

I studied his posture—back tense against the cushion and trying to disguise it, hands tightly locked across his ample stomach. "She called herself Vivian," I said, waiting for his reaction. "Vivian Stowe, I believe. Sound familiar?"

Slim sat motionless, expressionless, for a full five seconds, and then he puffed his cheeks and exhaled. "What's she gotten into now?"

"Ghost hunting, apparently."

"Oh, for crying out loud." He rubbed his face and softly groaned. "Kid means well, she really does, but she's…rash, you know. Young." He hesitated, then asked, "How did y'all cross paths?"

"Coincidentally," I replied, leaning back into my couch, "but fortuitously enough for her. Thought she could take on a faerie by herself."

My bartender continued to massage his forehead.

"How bad a faerie are we talking, here?"

"Does it matter? She's a quarter-blood at best. No power to speak of, right?"

"None at all, actually." Seeing my confusion, Slim stopped trying to rub his headache away and regarded me quizzically. "You don't have much experience with lesser bloods, do you?"

"Not a great deal, no," I admitted. "I've known one or two, but—"

"But you're terrifying, you've been terrifying a long time, and the smart ones know to avoid you. And then there's me."

I raised my glass to him and drank.

Slim smirked at the salute. "Did Vivi tell you about the Fringe?"

"She mentioned it," I said, producing a fresh bottle of scotch and giving myself a refill. Slim's eyebrow rose, and I offered him the bottle across the ottoman.

He took it from me silently, inspected the label, and gave it a tentative sniff. "Smells like the real article."

"It's close. Never quite perfect, but I've got the taste down well enough to replicate it almost faithfully."

He held out his hand, and I created a crystal tumbler in his palm. "Classy," he muttered, taking a test pour.

"Keep it. I'm sure I still owe you for a drink or two."

Slim sipped, then nodded. "Close enough to fool me. Shit, man, if you've got this on tap, why've you been darkening my door, huh?"

"Because I like you," I replied with a shrug, "and because eventually, the walls close in. Now, you were saying about this Fringe?"

He drank slowly, almost carefully, and I joined him in silently imbibing, listening to the faint voices of the game downstairs. After a moment, he set his glass aside and crossed his legs, adding unwise strain to his trousers' seams. "You see things as a binary, yeah? Court and not court?"

"Sometimes. I mean, there are nuances—"

"Just say yes for purposes of this exercise, okay?" he interrupted. "Well, the Arcanum's even worse about it— you're either Arcanum or a potential danger. Trust me," he muttered. "So given that all of the organizations of magic-wielding peoples have an in-or-out mentality, what do you do with the ones who don't fit into either category?"

I frowned, trying to discern where this was going. "Meaning?"

"Meaning you've got Column A and Column B, but there's a bunch of us who straddle the line between them." Slim lifted his empty glass, considered it, then poured a refill. "Mongrels. Witches. Duds. Quarter-fae, eighth-fae, one guy with a little drop of fae blood on his dad's side, maybe ten generations deep. I've known quarter-fae who can't even sense magic, and that old bastard runs circles around them. Weird world," he mused, raising his glass to his lips. "We're the Fringe," he said when the whisky was gone once more. "A support network for the rejects, if you like."

I took the bottle back and poured a double. "*All* of them?"

"We don't discriminate," he replied. "There's no point. Arcanum won't take us, courts certainly won't, but we have each other."

"Fair enough, but why not just blend into Column B, then?"

Slim's mouth twitched. "We do, more or less. You wouldn't have known about me had Toula not blown my cover, right?"

He had a point. "So this Fringe is…what, group therapy?"

"Sometimes. But it's bigger than that." Taking up the scotch once more, Slim explained, "Let's say the mundanes find out about wizards, for example. Everyone freaks out. Time for torches and pitchforks, yeah? Only the real wizards are sealed off and safe, maybe in Montana, maybe in another of their hidey-holes. That leaves us—the ones who might seem a little odd but don't warrant protection. If you've got a town on a witch hunt, they're not going to find a real wizard. They're going to grab a witch because he can't stop them. Or *she*, more likely," he amended. "The mundanes expect witches to be female, after all."

I put my drink on the carpet and folded my arms. "Come on, when was the last time you saw a torch-wielding mob?"

"It's happened before," he said defensively, "and there's nothing preventing it from happening again. They might come with tranquilizer guns and vivisection next time, for all I know, but the principle's the same: they fear what they don't understand, and they don't realize that we're bit players. Or care, I guess. A dead witch is a dead witch, right?" Slim collected his thoughts as the drinkers downstairs cheered. "Sure, I guess we could hide it all and blend in, but...you know, it's part of you. We've all seen what we could have been. A good chunk of us grew up with the Arcanum in our lives, and then you've got kids like Vivi—half-fae parents whose kid got all the mortal bits. I've met them, you know," he added after a drink. "Nice folks. They look like her siblings now."

"What were they doing—"

"Came in to find out what we were about after I got her hooked into the network. I told you, we don't discriminate." Slim shrugged. "They're married, oddly enough. Live up north of Anchorage. They've had a few kids over the years, all relatively fae—Vivi's the first to come out wrong. They're devastated, but what do you do? Kid's going to die in seventy years, give or take. I think they're still trying to come to terms with it."

My thoughts ran to Olive, who was solidly fae, and I flinched inside at the surge of relief I felt. Never mind the fact that I barely knew my daughter—we had time to work on that. But the Stowes, having a child, loving her, raising her, only to know her end was inevitable...

"I'm surprised they let her out of their sight," I replied.

"There was no 'letting' about it," said Slim. "She moved down here two years ago. It was easier, I think." He stared into his once-again empty glass, muttered, "Screw it," and reached for the bottle. "Vivi's got a little streak of paranoia, but she's not entirely off-base. She and a few others have been inserting themselves into these paranormal groups, keeping them focused on ghosts and Bigfoot and the Loch Ness Monster and whatnot to draw attention away from the rest of us. I've seen a couple of our guys on TV, actually," he said, passing me the scotch. "Fake psychics, researchers, tech people—Fringe folks do it all."

"And get cocky, and get killed," I said, refilling. "Her team was up against a guy who loves nothing more than tormenting mortals. He must have found her extermination squad amusing."

Slim shook his head. "I've warned her—"

"Obviously, it didn't stick." I rose and threw back my drink. "Tell your people not to be stupid, all right? If there's a genuine problem, I'm willing to help, but I work best without half a dozen cameras in my face."

"Shit," he muttered, and pushed himself to his feet. "I'll pass it along. Want this?" he asked, lifting the scotch.

"Nah, keep it."

As I abandoned my glass and turned for the door, Slim said quietly, "You should know there are rumors of a mongrel in the silo."

I paused. "Oh?"

"Nothing verifiable, but word is he might be one of Titania's."

I looked back at Slim's carefully neutral face and blanked my expression to match. "Do him a favor and keep your silence, would you?"

"They're true, then?"

"He's safe. That's all that needs to be said for now."

With a nod, he muttered, "Understood. Poor little

bastard." My eyes twitched, and Slim's mouth tightened. "You grow up Arcanum," he murmured, "and you're taught that anything coming out of Faerie is the Great Satan, more or less. And then you get a little older, and someone finally tells you that you're tainted…" He let the thought hang, then said, "I mean no disrespect, Colin. I've got no beef with you, and I know what you're about. But I've had a few years to let everything sink in, and I don't constantly have a mob of wizards looking down their noses at me. Not anymore." Slim hesitated and folded his arms. "It's…well, it's a lot to digest, you know? It's bad enough that you can't do magic, but when the real wizards look at you like you're evil incarnate…and then you add on something like, I don't know, a rapist father who wants you dead…" He cleared his throat self-consciously. "There's a support group for a very good reason. If this hypothetical kid needs to talk…"

"I'll keep that in mind," I said, shaken to finally see beneath Slim's unflappable façade. "Listen, Rick—"

"I'm sorry, I just wanted to put that out there," he said in a sudden rush. "No big deal. In case…you know."

"I only met him a few hours ago. He's at my place now, safe." I stepped away from the door and shoved my hands in my pockets. "The rumors are right, he's my half brother. His sister—his father's daughter—is on track to be grand magus."

Slim's pudgy face contorted in a grimace. "He's going to need more than therapy."

"Yeah." I studied my loafers for a moment, then met his eyes. "So tell me what to do."

The sun was beginning to rise over the Atlantic by the time I took my leave. Slim punctuated our talk with occasional trips down to the bar to pour and tally, but we spoke long after the regulars had stumbled off into the night. He didn't mention Vivian again, but her specter remained in my thoughts as we talked of Aiden.

Finally, when the last of the scotch was long gone, Slim told me, "The important thing to remember is that this isn't an overnight process. You're going to have to go easy on him—the Arcanum's in his blood and in his head. That's not something he's just going to forget." He paused, thinking. "You left him with the priest, you said?"

"Ex-seminarian, but yes. Why?"

Slim smiled faintly. "You left him with a guy ten years his senior who's completely non-fae. I can't think of a less threatening guide, can you?"

"Aside from the minor detail that Joey goes armed, you mean?"

"You're being too literal." He perched on the edge of the ottoman, grimacing as it creaked. "Joey's still young. Talks the talk, knows the music, probably has a favorite Avenger. Old enough to be responsible, but young enough to be cool to a teenager—aside from the priest thing," he muttered. "I can't do anything with that."

For some reason, I felt slightly miffed. "You're saying I'm not *cool*, then?"

Slim's eyebrow rose. "Weird old alcoholic loner with a thing for a much younger woman, who employs a good-looking young man as…well, what is it that Joey does for you, again?"

"Touché," I mumbled.

He shrugged in reply. "If I were you, I'd give Aiden his space. Let him get his bearings, and then let him come to you. Don't try to rush this—he's got a lot on his plate." Slim scratched at his stomach and yawned. "Breakfast? The Waffle House still stands."

"Thanks, but no." I opened a gate beside me, giving Slim a peek at dawn-pink sand on the far side. "I've got an appointment to keep."

He craned his neck and scowled at the view. "You sure about that? Looks like the morning after an orgy to me."

I looked more closely through the window to the Keys,

took in the dozen half-naked bodies strewn about the beach, and sighed. "That may not be far off. Wish me luck," I said, and headed for Florida.

CHAPTER 7

That quiet Thursday morning, Red's could have been any beachside dive long after last call. Darkened strings of icicle lights drooped from the rusty roof, their nighttime allure cheapened by the white cords glinting in the dawn. A handful of clear plastic cups littered the long bar, some bearing traces of suds, others laced with colorful stains and smeared lipstick prints. Half a bowl of shelled peanuts remained as testament to the night's revels and the bartender's lazy cleanup. Really, if not for the people passed out between the shack and the shore, Red's could be instantly forgotten.

As could its proprietor, whom I found sitting on a wooden folding chair at the tide line, bare feet in the surf and green eyes trained on the southern horizon. A salt-stained Marlins cap hid most of his hair, but a few ginger strands waved around his face as the wind whipped up from the sea. With his long black shorts and bare, well-bronzed chest, he could have been any local boy, another twenty-something kid wasting time in a lonely corner of the Keys.

Not until he turned to face me did the truth begin to peek through. Oberon looked like a beach bum those days, but his eyes belied his apparent youth—unlined, unclouded, but if you knew how to see, they were so striking in their age.

Fleetingly, I wondered if that was what Meggy saw when she looked at me.

"You're overdressed," he called, raising his voice to be

heard over the breaking waves. "As usual."

"Not a social call," I replied, slogging through the trampled sand. "As usual."

He gave me a once-over and snorted. "Drop the glamour. At *least* get rid of the loafers."

"And walk on broken glass? No, thanks." I made my way to his side, waved an identical chair into existence, and wedged it above the waves as my glamour fell. "Or whatever else you throw around out here. Needles—"

"No, nothing more than pot. I don't allow it. There's no point in drawing attention."

"Care to explain *that*, then?" I asked, cocking my thumb at the nearest clump of sleeping patrons.

Oberon looked over his shoulder at the scene and smiled. "Tell me, boy, what draws bad press to a bar like nothing else?"

"Fights? Fires? Dead hookers in the bathroom?"

"Drunk drivers." He leaned back and dug his heels into the wet sand. "You don't want to be the guy who last served the fool who swerved off the road and into a van full of photogenic children, yes? So I take precautions." The hint of pride in his voice was unmistakable, satisfaction with a problem solved. "Anyone still here at closing time takes a little nap. They'll wake around eight," he continued, turning again to survey his work. "Sandy, maybe bitten, hung-over as hell, but relatively sober."

I took another look at the sprawl and realized that the sleepers had fallen into same-sex pairs. The nearest, a couple of deeply tanned guys in cutoffs, flip-flops, and oversized shirts proclaiming their fondness for the Confederacy, practically spooned. "Relatively sober and…confused?"

Oberon's predatory grin was immediate and inculpatory. "I never said I didn't have any fun with them."

"They're helpless and—"

"Don't start, Coileán," he sighed, once more turning to

the sea. "Indignant rants are obnoxious as hell, has anyone ever told you that?"

"And entirely warranted," I snapped. "They're going to wake and think—"

"Think what? It's good for them." He tucked his hands behind his head. "When they get drunk enough, they drop their defenses. I've got a dozen regulars here who flirt shamelessly with *anyone* if the hour is right. Not those two," he admitted, pointing to the nearest couple. "But their girlfriends were busy, and I thought, why not? They have matching tattoos, at least."

I noted the barbed wire inked around the big spoon's thick bicep. "That's cruel."

"But so very amusing, you must admit. I didn't choose this viewing spot on a whim." With a last little chuckle for the drama to come, he looked at me and folded his arms across his chest. "So. Who's annoyed you today?"

"Benatin."

"And this is my problem because…"

He left the question dangling, and I fought to keep my temper down. "He used a child as a puppet and convinced her parents that she'd been possessed. I got the call in the middle of dinner when my priest realized what was going on, and then I had to get rid of a bunch of ghost hunters. And you're still smiling."

"Oh, please," he said, grinning smugly, "don't let me stop the story. Let me guess: Benatin's in pain but not dead, your little priest is doing the cleanup, and you"—he paused and sniffed deeply—"you spent a few hours drinking it off. Close?"

"He terrorized those people," I replied, not rising to the bait, "and on top of that, he ruined my evening. What are you going to do about it?"

Oberon laughed to himself. "Benatin kept you from screwing my daughter, and I'm supposed to be upset?"

I stiffened. "Since when have you cared about Meggy?"

"Since you started bedding her," he replied,

nonplussed. "I thought you'd be pleased. You wanted me to show her a little attention, didn't you?"

The only factors standing between Oberon and a new face at that moment were my strained self-restraint and my stronger sense of self-preservation. Yes, Oberon had moved out of Faerie, but he hadn't relinquished his claim, nor the power that came with it—and with that equalizer in force, I wasn't his match in a fair fight. Eight hundred years of practice was sufficient in most situations, but not against a faerie who, I suspected, had long ago given up keeping count of his years as tedious.

"You know," I muttered, "you don't actually have to be an asshole."

"Careful, boy." His tone was light, but I heard the edge below the surface. "You presume."

"Touch Meggy, and I'll show you what presumption looks like."

He smirked and looked away. "I'm going to let that one slide because you've obviously been drinking. Consider it a favor."

I started to protest that I had my faculties well in hand, then realized what a stupid mistake that would be. Instead, I squinted past Oberon across the beach at the rising sun. "My offer stands."

"Does it, now?" he asked the sea.

"Let them come home. Less work for you, less work for me—"

"And my court disintegrates. No."

The light was strengthening toward yellow, and I produced a pair of sunglasses against the glare. "I'm not asking that they swear fealty, Oberon. Just follow some basic dictates to keep order. I assure you, I'm not trying to take them."

He looked at me again, his face backlit by the sun. "A hypothetical, then. Suppose I give an order. Suppose you contradict it. What do they do?"

I chose my words carefully. "Within Faerie, as long as

they live in the realm—"

"The correct answer," he quietly interrupted, "is they do as I say. Anything less, and they're no longer my court to command. Do you see the conundrum, Coileán?" He pulled his cap off, and the wind and sun turned his hair into a coppery corona. "This realm is mine. You may have Faerie for now because I have no need for it. But if you think you're taking my court away from me, we're going to have a problem."

"*Your* realm?" I replied. "I'm sure the Arcanum would take umbrage at that. Or did you mean this island? I'll grant you the rock, now."

Oberon smiled. "My realm," he murmured. "You have one minute to leave."

I knew better than to fight a senseless battle, and so I stood and turned my beach chair into atoms. "The offer stands," I said, wincing as a wave soaked my shoes and cuffs. "They just want to go home."

"I'm well aware." Oberon's eyes flicked to the water as a trio of dolphins passed through the shallows. "Oh, and Coileán?"

"Yes?"

His smile never faltered. "How *is* that daughter of yours these days?"

I opened a gate without another word. There was nothing to be gained by meeting that threat.

I should have gone home, but instead, I found myself standing outside my old shop, looking through the plate window at the long racks of discarded books. Meggy had changed nothing—not even the faded wooden "Ex Libris" sign I'd hung over the door years ago—and I fought the urge to let myself in and surround myself with the comforting perfume of old paper. There was too much magic in Faerie to appreciate such scents properly. My awareness of the overwhelming smell of magic faded a short while after each return, but still, the scent of not-quite-citronella lingered like strong cologne, masking the subtler odors to which I'd become accustomed in the mortal realm.

Not Oberon's realm. *Never* Oberon's realm.

I didn't realize I had dug my fingernails into my palms until a hand on my shoulder cut short my inner raging and made me aware once more of little things like pain. Startled from my reverie, I jumped and whipped around to find my former neighbor standing behind me on the sidewalk, newspaper in hand. I didn't recognize her purple sweatsuit, but her hair didn't budge in the breeze, and I was momentarily heartened to see that some things in my life remained constant.

"Out for a jog, Mrs. Cooper?" I asked.

Her rouged lips tightened into a wrinkled line. "A lady does not *run*, Mr. Leffee. Are you insinuating something?"

I had a mental flash of Mrs. Cooper puffing down the street in overstuffed yoga pants and a sports bra, then pushed that thought back into the hell from which it had arisen. "Never, madam. You're looking quite dressed for the hour."

"It's seven-thirty, dear. The day's half over, and"—her lips briefly tightened to white—"I have company. Taking a break from said company, in fact." She gave me an appraising glance, then murmured, "You're looking rather youthful today."

I closed my eyes, kicking myself for the lapse, and threw the glamour back on. "Better?"

"Much." She studied my features a moment longer, then nodded. "You'll excuse me, I know, but you look terrible. I don't want to pry…"

She let the question hang, and I shrugged. "Long night. Lot on my mind, nothing to worry about. I should be going—"

"Cup of tea, dear?"

There was something entirely too hopeful in her voice

for that offer to have been purely altruistic. "What about your company?"

Mrs. Cooper pushed her bifocals down her nose. "*Please* come have tea."

"That bad, is it?"

She sighed. "I don't like to speak ill of family, but—"

"I do it all the time, and it's remarkably cathartic. Go ahead."

Before she could begin, however, the door to Tea for Two opened, and a skinny man with a mop of mousy brown hair wandered onto the sidewalk. "Auntie Eunice!" he called across the street, cupping his hands around his mouth as a megaphone. "Are you all right? Do I need to call a doctor?"

Her eyes met mine and held my questioning gaze.

"Tea sounds lovely, Mrs. Cooper," I said, and escorted her back to her shop.

Her company, Mrs. Cooper explained with as much civility as she could muster before breakfast, was her grandnephew, Stuart Purcell. "My only brother's only daughter's only son," she said by way of introduction, "who's recently come from California to look after me. Isn't that nice?"

I extended my hand and waited for Stuart to make contact, but he held back and locked his fingers together, and I awkwardly aborted the gesture. "Colin Leffee. Welcome to Rigby."

"Mr. Leffee used to live here," Mrs. Cooper told Stuart. "And he's seeing Ms. Horn across the street—have you two met?"

Stuart's dark eyes—wide-set and slightly bulging—lit up. "Meghan? Sure! Lovely lady. I, uh…" He paused, giving me a second look. "I didn't know she was taken."

"We keep a low profile," I told him. "For Olive's sake, you know. She's at that age, and for everyone to know that her mom's dating…"

"Understood," he said, but looked disappointed.

I took the seat Mrs. Cooper offered at her dinette and helped myself to the teapot. "So, Stuart, what do you do?"

Across the table, Mrs. Cooper's eyes squeezed closed as if tensing for a blow, but Stuart, oblivious to her distress, sat between us and wrapped his long fingers around his teacup. "Perhaps you've seen my store, The Endless Knot?"

"Can't say that I have," I replied, trying not to cut my eyes to my hostess. "But I haven't done much shopping in Rigby of late."

He leaned toward me, eyes sparkling with the sort of excitement seen only on the faces of street-corner evangelists. "Now, I don't want to alarm you, Connor—"

"It's Colin. Or Coileán, I answer to either."

Stuart paused, thrown off his rhythm, but quickly found the beat again. "Sorry, Colin. Anyway, I don't want to alarm you, but I"—he smiled and steepled his fingers— "am a *wizard*."

"You don't say," I murmured, and sipped my tea.

He seemed to deflate a degree, but pressed on. "I've studied The Craft"—I swear, he pronounced the capital letters—"for many years. It's a passion, a…a calling, you see? My life's work." Stuart began to tear bites off a scone and roll them in the mound of raspberry jam in the center of his plate. "Now, that said, you have nothing to fear from me. I'm a white wizard."

"Well," I said, helping myself to the scone plate, "you've come to the right place, then. The American south has had more than its share of white wizards through the years. Though I don't suppose most were *practitioners* as such…"

"Mostly in New Orleans and South Carolina," he replied, popping a jellied scone ball in his mouth. "And those communities were more heavily involved with Voodoo…"

As he launched into a practiced lecture, I glanced at Mrs. Cooper, who alone of my companions had caught the reference. She silently covered her eyes, and I tried to pick up the thread of Stuart's monologue. "So you're a bit of a trendsetter, then?" I interrupted.

Stuart nodded. "Indeed. But the magickal community is growing, you know."

He pronounced it with a *k*, I was sure of it.

I poured the last of the tea, then brushed past Mrs. Cooper to the kitchen and was surprised to see my chintz kettle on the range. "That's all well and good," I called back to the dining room, turning on the tap with a quilted potholder, "but what do you *do*, exactly?"

"To pay the bills, you mean? Manage my store," he replied, raising his voice above the running water. "I do private readings—palm, aura, Tarot. Thinking of starting some classes later this fall, beginner stuff, nothing too esoteric. And spellwork, of course."

"Of course." I set the kettle back on the warm eye and leaned against the dining room wall. "Anything skyclad?"

Stuart resumed playing with his scone. "You jest, but only because you don't know what a wizard can do."

"Oh, I don't doubt it. But do us all a favor, hmm?" I said, folding my arms. "If you're doing anything in the buff, take it outside of town. Folks around here are a little touchy about, uh…magic *wands*, if you catch my drift."

Poor Mrs. Cooper looked like she wanted to crawl into the teapot and die.

The fool sighed and shook his head. "It's amazing how much prejudice there still is against people like me. I only want to help," he protested, spreading his palms. "Love spells, lucky charms—I'm happy to use my gift for the common good."

"For a modest fee," I countered.

Stuart shrugged. "Keeps the lights on and the lease intact. Wisdom is free."

I forced myself to keep a straight face at that—Stuart

couldn't have been more than thirty-five, and I could only imagine the sort of wisdom he'd provide. "Good of you," I managed, and headed back into the kitchen to locate the tea. "So, uh…how does magic work, anyway?" I called from around the corner.

As Stuart started up again, Mrs. Cooper joined me by the cabinet and muttered, "Two shelves from the bottom, and did you have to set him off, dear?"

"Just let him get it out of his system," I replied in kind, reaching for the wooden tea chest. "Want me to knock him out for you? It's no trouble."

She snorted quietly. "Correct me if I'm wrong, but don't all the stories say *not* to accept favors from faeries?"

"This is an exception, but aren't you the clever girl."

"I like to think I've amassed slightly more wisdom than my nephew," she retorted, "and yes, I know exactly what *skyclad* means. 'Magic wands,' my sainted aunt," she muttered, lifting the lid from the teapot. "But you see what I'm up against. What do I do with him?"

"Do? Who said you had to do anything about *that*?" I handed her the chest and leaned against the cabinet, keeping my voice lower than Stuart's half-shouted monologue. "He's harmless, Eunice. Confused, maybe delusional, but probably harmless. How many cats does he have, anyway?"

"Five." She measured out the tea by sight, squinting into the damp pot to gauge the strength. "He tried to give me one. I wouldn't have it."

"No?"

"If I'd wanted to clean up someone else's excrement, I'd have bought my own damn cat."

Mrs. Cooper's spoon was showing no sign of slowing, and so I patted her shoulder and took the tea chest away before she could brew up something vile in her distress. "I'll grant you he's odd, but he's nothing to worry about."

"He's embarrassing," she mumbled, yanking the kettle off the range.

"There's a lunatic in every family, you know." I paused in time to catch Stuart embarking on a discussion of thaumic principles, then caught Mrs. Cooper shaking her head. "What is it?"

"He's *embarrassing*," she repeated, and gave me a long look over her bifocals. "It's bad enough that he's trying to sell rabbit's feet and…"—she paused, flustered and momentarily stumped—"and Lord knows what else down there. You know why he won't shake hands?" she continued, forcing the teapot's lid back into its hole with a solid *clink*. "Says he's afraid of aural contamination. Like you might be carrying some contagious juju, right, and he might get it on contact?"

"He told you that, did he?"

"He told *Reverend Martin*," she quietly wailed. "We met for Sunday lunch after service last week, and Reverend Martin was there with his family, and, silly me, I introduced them…" She closed her eyes and exhaled softly. "And so my great-nephew's sitting there, telling my pastor he's a wizard and that Mrs. Martin's aura shows evidence of psychic scars. I'm never going to live that down."

In the other room, Stuart launched into an impassioned diatribe against Jack Chick.

"He can't really see auras, can he?" Mrs. Cooper murmured.

I could only shrug. "It's possible. I've run into a few sensitives over the years—they can barely see magic, and they certainly can't do anything with it." Her brow knit, and I explained, "You're always standing in the middle of a magical field, with the exception of those few days last March. Living things give off certain energies, yes? Well, when those energies pass through a magical field, they interact. If you're on the cusp of visual sensitivity to magic, you might see those interactions as color fluctuations. Following me?"

"I suppose." She passed me the warm teapot and

cocked her head toward the kitchen. "Shall we get this over with?"

"Really, I can get him out of your hair—"

Mrs. Cooper pushed her glasses to the tip of her nose and gave me a silencing stare. "Colin, dear, I am quite fond of you, but I'm not about to sic a faerie on my own blood. Is that understood?"

"Auntie Eunice," Stuart called from the next room, "you really should let me guide you through a past-life regression. It's so...*cleansing.*"

I met her eyes and smirked. "You're sure about that, are you?"

"Should I forget, I expect you to remind me," she muttered, and nudged me toward the table.

I slid back into my seat and passed Stuart the teapot. "Sorry about that. Your work sounds fascinating, really. Refill?"

He helped himself and grabbed another scone. "I don't expect a layman to understand the technicalities, of course, but that should give you a better picture of my profession."

"Indeed." I filled Mrs. Cooper's cup, then my own. "You'll forgive a silly question, then, but how the hell are you planning to pay the bills in *Rigby*?"

Stuart flinched, though I couldn't tell whether the enquiry or the profanity unsettled him more. "I don't underst—"

"Come on, this isn't Glastonbury. You're trying to peddle witchcraft in a town of nice, churchgoing folks. How much success do you honestly anticipate?"

He paused, sweetened his tea, broke his scone into crumbs, and finally let out a little sigh. "If you must know," he said stiffly, "I'm living off the family trust until I can get the online shop up and running. I'm here for Auntie Eunice."

"Isn't that sweet," she mumbled into her teacup.

Stuart gave Mrs. Cooper a patronizing smile, then

turned his attention to his crumbs and jam. "I'm also doing some investigative work in my off-hours," he continued. "Research for a book."

"Oh? On what?" I asked, and took a sip of tea.

"Fairies."

I tried to laugh, but ended up choking and on the receiving end of a hearty thump between the shoulder blades from Mrs. Cooper. "Come again?" I wheezed once the worst of the fit had passed.

"Fairies," he repeated, seemingly unfazed by my brush with scalding death. "And I'm quite serious about this, so there's no need to mock me."

"Not mocking," I replied, cutting my eyes to Mrs. Cooper in time to catch her grimace, "just...curious."

Looking up from his pastry deconstruction, Stuart drummed his jammy fingers together and grinned across the table. "You've heard of the Cottingley Fairies, I hope?"

The twinge of foreboding I'd felt on the announcement of Stuart's research interest dissolved immediately, but I tried to play along. "Yeah, maybe...Victorian photos, right? Little girls, dancing fairies?"

"Exactly," he said with a satisfied nod. "Five photographs in total, taken in the first two decades of the twentieth century by a pair of cousins."

"Think I saw something on TV about those," I said, and sipped with greater care. "All a hoax, yeah? The fairies were cutouts from a book or something—"

"An unfortunate cover-up," Stuart interrupted, looking pained.

"No, didn't the girls themselves admit—"

"They were just village girls!" he exclaimed, banging the table. "Imagine the *pressure* on them! Believers on the one hand, skeptics on the other. Wouldn't you have wanted it all to go away after a certain point?"

His agitated slap had left two shiny red fingerprints on the tablecloth. "Okay, maybe," I allowed. "But...you don't honestly believe..."

"I honestly do," he said gravely.

"Tiny winged humanoids? *Really*?"

Stuart leaned across the table and lowered his voice. "I've *seen* them, Clark. At a distance, of course," he added apologetically, "but they have the most beautiful aural glow, such…such *vibrant* colors…" He paused, blinked a few times as if clearing an image, then said, "You know, Ms. Horn's seen them, too."

"Oh?" I managed, not trusting myself to hold it together through a longer response.

His head bobbed. "She said she'd seen them out on the beach at night. They fly up to fifty yards off shore, apparently. Must like the breeze out there."

I thought of reminding Stuart of how quickly a glowing food source would be snapped up, then decided that some delusions weren't worth addressing. "Well, happy hunting."

"You don't believe me," he replied, resting his chin in his hand. "I mean, I'm not surprised. Mundanes seldom believe in the supernatural, even when it's right before their eyes." He sighed deeply and patted his cheek with his supporting hand, oblivious to the jam smeared near his ear. "Those of us in the community talk, you know, share our findings. More stories circulate about this town than you'd think."

That piqued my interest, but I feigned polite disbelief. "Such as?"

"Fairy activity, mostly. Up and down the coast, but there's a hub of it near this place. If you ask me, I think there's a ley line running through the Outer Banks and up toward Virginia Beach, but that's all speculation, you understand. Work to be done."

"Then I'll leave you to it," I replied, and made a show of looking at the clock on the wall. "Mrs. Cooper, I'm so sorry, but I've got appointments to keep…"

"I'll show you out, dear," she said, pushing back from the table. "Back shortly, Stuart," she added, seeing him half-rise, and he plopped into his chair once more, where he resumed his assault on the scone plate after a muttered goodbye.

I followed Mrs. Cooper through her shop and out into the morning, waited until she'd closed the front door, then shook my head and laughed. "I'm so sorry, but that's—"

"Embarrassing," she interrupted. "Unbelievable. But my problem, I suppose."

I wiped a stray tear from my eye. "Try to keep him out of the shallows at dusk, yes?"

"Oh, I don't know, maybe a shark would knock some sense into him. Of course, knowing Stuart, he'd probably blame a kelpie." She folded her arms and squinted at the sun. "You're not going to disabuse him of these notions, I take it?"

"Not unless I have to."

"Sound choice, Mr. Leffee. Sound choice." With that, Mrs. Cooper patted my arm and pushed the front door open. "Don't be a stranger, now," she called over her shoulder, and then I was alone once more.

Twilight had descended over the realm by the time I let myself back into my office, and I sprawled on one of my twin couches, trying to get my bearings once more. I needed to make the aborted date up to Meggy, and then there was the matter of Olive's growing defiance…Vivian's foolhardy exploits…Oberon…Aiden, what the hell was I to do with Aiden…

Come to mention it, where *was* Aiden?

I'd left him with Joey, Valerius, and a giant lizard, but that had been hours ago. There was no telling…

I rose to find my brother, but before I took two steps, someone knocked on my office door. "Enter!" I called across the room, rubbing my head as weariness finally began to set in, and looked up as Valerius poked his head through the gap. "Captain," I sighed. "Please tell me

Aiden's still alive and well."

"Asleep in the loft," he replied, letting himself fully into the room. "Joey put him to work. Last I saw, the boy was grilling mutton shanks."

"What loft?"

"In the barn."

"I didn't build a loft—"

"I did, my lord. I..." He paused, uncertain. "Lord Aiden was weary, and the dragon was not. I put him out of the way to avoid trampling." He hesitated again, then said, "If I've erred, I'll take it down..."

"No, that...that actually sounds great. Thank you." I leaned against the back of a couch, mentally checking one item off my list. "Grilled mutton, you said?"

"The first attempts seemed a bit charred."

"Huh." I folded my arms, stared at the rug for a moment, then met the captain's eyes. "Think he's grilling extra?"

"There's really no lack of sheep, my lord." He closed the door quietly and crossed the room. "Grivam asks an audience as well," he said, keeping his voice low. "He's been made comfortable until you can hear him, but if you have more certain plans, I'll see that he's informed."

I frowned. "Grivam of the merrow?"

"The same."

"Moon and stars," I muttered, wishing I'd thought to spike my tea. "How long has he been waiting?"

Valerius squinted at the ceiling. "Since midday, perhaps. Not particularly long."

"And you didn't think I needed to know?"

He stepped back, flummoxed. "My lord...the queen gave me permission to leave the realm only in time of severe emergency. I didn't—"

"New rule," I replied, cutting him off. "If you think I might want to know about it, find me." I ran that back, thinking it over, then added, "Except on date nights, in which case, use your best judgment." With that, I changed my button-down and jeans for a slightly less ornamented version of the robe I'd discarded that morning and headed for the hallway, my captain on my heels. "When did she last let you out, anyway?" I asked over my shoulder.

"She didn't," Valerius replied, easily keeping pace with my quick strides. "I've not been back since I first crossed the border. Except for hiding your brother, I mean, but that was a moment's work."

I stopped in my tracks and stared at him. "You haven't seen the mortal realm in all this time?"

"I suppose not." He shrugged and chuckled at my disbelief. "It can't have changed that greatly, can it?"

I tried to imagine a worldview in which history stopped well before the Middle Ages, but the exercise only made my headache worse. "Captain, uh...I'll show you later. Where've you hidden Grivam, anyway, the pool? Come to think of it, do I *have* a pool?"

The merrow are a curious race, natively aquatic but eager to make shore excursions when their nosiness gets the best of them. Said excursions naturally require a change of form—legs are far more practical than a tail for dry locomotion, after all—and once ashore, merrow are indistinguishable from humans but for their propensity to stagger about like sailors on shore leave. Bipedal balance is a tricky thing for those without constant practice, and I've seen two-year-olds totter around with far more grace and poise than a two-hundred-year-old merrow freshly risen from the sea like Venus after a hard night of clubbing.

The merrow are, in my admittedly limited experience, much like magpies with a propensity for hoarding. Flash something shiny or even vaguely interesting in their direction, and they're hooked—they'll beg, cajole, and dicker their way to getting what they want. The kids are understandably ignorant of the value of human-made detritus—after a night with one adventurous lady, for instance, I was given no rest until I procured for her that most expensive of parting gifts, a pink paper-and-toothpick drink umbrella from the bar up the beach—but a merrow with a few years on him knows what the surface-dwellers prize, and he'll inevitably drive a hard bargain if asked to part with something of use.

Grivam was master of the lopsided trade when he was of a mood. Then again, he'd had ample practice—as far as I could tell, he considered me a child.

I tried not to show Valerius, but the news that Grivam had come left me unsettled. The merrow moved out of Faerie millennia ago—they had never been thrown out, but they seemed to prefer their own company, far from the lot of us, with the exception of the occasional hunting trip through our waters. I couldn't blame them, but that made finding one on my doorstep all the more worrying. Finding *Grivam* in the realm of his own accord made me want to double-check our defenses.

Grivam didn't just leave the sea. If you wanted a word with the merrow's king, you went to him and waited—he didn't give a damn whose court you claimed, and he didn't care if you got sunburned while waiting for him to surface. One typically bartered with him from a boat, a precarious position at the best of times, which seemed to suit him nicely. On the few occasions on which I'd seen him, Grivam had been a smiler. This was an unfortunate circumstance, as Grivam's smile did little to set anyone at ease. In fact, all his smile did was remind his companions that he had teeth to rival a shark's, and that those dealing with him were quite out of their element.

I had never seen Grivam shapeshift, and so my mental image of him was vaguely cetacean and toothy. Keeping my face neutral and unconcerned, I settled back on the throne and waited while Valerius fetched him, then took to pacing when the minutes stretched to half an hour, wondering what was delaying the audience. Surely Grivam hadn't wandered off, I mused, sorting through the possibilities. Surely Georgie hadn't developed a sudden taste for seafood.

As I stalked back and forth, I tried to prepare myself for what was to come, but even still, it threw me for a loop when Valerius opened the ceremonial doors and led in a pale, white-haired old man. The creature clinging to the captain's arm was sinewy, but his papery skin drooped in translucent folds, and he peered at me through deep-set eyes as he shuffled up the blue runner.

I watched their slow progress, stunned. The merrow aged, yes, but slowly—I was with a five-hundred-year-old lady once who barely looked a day over twenty. Seeing the true mark of Grivam's years startled me far more than did his eschewal, in typical merrow fashion, of the frivolity of clothing.

He took another slow step and grimaced, and I shook off the paralysis. "Grivam," I said, half-jogging down the blue runner to intercept him, "be welcome. I apologize for keeping you waiting, but I was away and didn't hear of your coming."

The old merrow shifted his arm from the captain's to mine and held on tightly as I led him toward a row of chairs. "I came unannounced, young Coileán," he replied, squeezing my arm as he stepped off the thick rug. "I expected a longer wait, in truth. Things are calm here?"

"Not exactly." I helped him to a seat and took the chair beside him. "But I hate to inconvenience you. What, uh—"

"My condolences to you as well," he quietly interrupted, patting my hand. "The loss of a parent is never an easy thing."

"I…" I began, but paused, trying to discern the truth behind Grivam's words. "Thank you. She is missed."

"Of course." He locked and unlocked his long fingers—I could only suppose he found the lack of webbing a novel sensation—and pursed his thin lips. "And in this difficult time, I'm afraid I only add to your troubles.

I come to ask a boon."

The expression in his dark eyes was difficult to read, though I thought I saw a trace of fear in the mix.

"What sort of boon?" I asked warily.

Grivam's finger locking increased in tempo. "There is something in the shallows. It found us, it stalks us, and it's taken sixteen. I ask that you give us refuge until it returns to the deeps." His eyes bored into mine, and I tried not to focus on the skeletal contours of his unfamiliar second face. "Name your price."

"Excuse me?"

"The price for your protection. Name it." He grabbed my wrists with surprising strength. "Anything you ask, up to my life, if you will help us."

Behind him, Valerius cocked an eyebrow, and I fought to keep my expression in check. Grivam *never* showed his hand, and only a fool would have been at ease seeing him so desperate.

I took a slow breath, then nodded. "You have it."

His brows knit. "The price—"

"A favor on a later date," I interrupted. "A favor agreeable to you. Acceptable?"

The suspicion in his look slowly turned to understanding. "I could reject your request for this favor as disagreeable, under these terms. *Any* request."

"And I trust you are a man of honor in your dealings," I replied.

"Indeed." He released me and nodded in turn. "A deal, then. You will have your favor, should I find it agreeable to grant it, at a time to come."

Grivam pushed himself to his feet, wincing at the stress, and I produced a gold-topped cane. "The path back to the water is uneven," I said, pressing it into his hand. "This should steady your steps."

He twisted the stick, watching the knob glint. "A gift, young Coileán?"

"A token of my good faith." I rose and waited while

Valerius opened the door, then escorted Grivam back to the rug. "Bring your people as soon as you like. The gate will remain unlocked."

He glanced at me over his thin shoulder with a half-smile. "You barter poorly, you know."

"I let my guard slip on occasion." Watching him slowly make his way toward the exit, I asked, "How did you come?"

"On these useless things," Grivam replied, leaning on his new cane.

"You *walked?*"

He nodded, not looking back. "From here, it is two days' journey to the sea. And another day's journey to the gate."

I caught his free arm to stop him, then opened a gate to the shore in the middle of the throne room. "Unless you have business between here and there…"

His teeth flashed, and Grivam shuffled from the rug onto the pale brown sand, which had shifted toward black with nightfall. Valerius stepped around the gate and watched beside me as the merrow reached the lapping waves, then continued his slow walk into the dark shallows. When the water reached his hips, his body shuddered, and a hairless form, sleek and gray, disappeared with barely a splash.

I closed the gate and looked at Valerius. "Make it sound like I worked a fair deal, won't you?"

"My lord." He hesitated, then awkwardly patted my back.

"Thanks," I mumbled, and wandered off to find my brother.

CHAPTER 8

I should have been proactive when Grivam announced there was a merrow-eating monster in the Keys. Had I caught it and traced its source then, I might have saved myself the trouble to come. But I was as yet inexperienced, and my thoughts that season vacillated between Meggy and Aiden, making forays toward the task of running the realm only when strictly necessary. Valerius quietly reminded me on occasion that the list of audience requests wasn't going to disappear if I ignored it, but I simply hadn't the time or inclination to deal with petty grievances. I had a relationship to salvage and a teenage brother to keep alive, and as far as I was concerned, the rest could sort itself out.

Of my two tasks, the former was, surprisingly, simpler. I knew where Meggy lived, I had a decent sense of how not to provoke her, and I listened when she needed to unload about our daughter. *That* was a delicate area— Meggy was a single mother by choice, but that didn't make her situation any easier, and she seemed to enjoy escaping while Olive was off at cheerleading practice or with her new friends, doing whatever it was that adolescent girls do when they're alone together, which remains something of a mystery to me. Meggy explained that she'd never been a typical girl, and she could give only educated guesses as to Olive's evening schedule. "But really, I'm not that concerned," she told me one night over chow mein. "It's *Rigby*. They'll go to the pier, smoke something, maybe drink something vile, and feel grown-up."

"Nothing else?" I'd pressed.

Meggy smirked and pointed her chopsticks at my chest. "We've had talks."

I wasn't entirely convinced, but I reminded myself that Meggy knew this territory far better than I did. With the matter of Olive's evening doings relegated to the back burner, Meggy and I were free to...well, date.

The process was novel for us both. Meggy had dated Jack Horn in high school, but their relationship had largely been built around school and the things that might come after—Jack would go east for college and pray for a spot in the NFL, Meggy would wait for him in Arizona, and in the far distant future, they'd start a family. They had been children, still figuring themselves out over hamburgers and cheap beer. By the time Meggy realized she didn't want Jack, she was pregnant, I was gone, and Jack was dying. She had never dated anyone but Jack, and suddenly, she found herself married and a mother—and too soon, a widow with a missing child. She hadn't felt like exploring a new relationship while she put her life back together.

That said, if Meggy was a bit out to sea on the particulars of adult courtship, I was clinging to a life raft in the middle of the ocean, trying to keep my head on the right side of the water. I'd never *dated*—the few relationships I'd had before Meggy, if you could fairly call them relationships, were brief and largely sexual. What made our evenings stranger was the fact that we had a history. My prior understanding was that dating is supposed to be about getting to know someone and whether you would like to eventually climb in bed together, but that wasn't the case with Meggy—I knew her, I liked her, and whether I chose to admit it to myself, I'd very much enjoyed the events that led to Olive. Then again, I soon realized that the Meggy I'd known was a young woman barely out of her teens. *This* Meggy, who drank vodka martinis at dinner and listened to the Ramones when she was tidying her store, was in many aspects a stranger to me, a creature hinted at by her younger incarnation but hardened by too much grief, too young. She was still unsure around me—in one moment, laughing at a joke we'd made twenty years before, in the next, squinting slightly at me with her head cocked, perhaps looking for traces of the man she'd known in my face. But as the weeks of our re-acquaintance grew into months, I noticed more laughter and less reticence, and I saw the Meggy I knew in this other Meggy's eyes.

I loved her. I *had* loved her, and I loved the person she had become. But it was far too early to press her to move in with me, not when Meggy had yet to come to terms with who and what she and I were. If she needed to pretend that we were two ordinary friends meeting for Chinese and sex with a view to something more, I could play along. I knew she was working through the cognitive dissonance inherent in our relationship. Meggy had been dealing with Arcanum contacts long enough to cultivate a mistrust of faeries—and now, not only was she fae, but *I* kept showing up, wanting to buy her dinner. If it made her happier to focus on books and movies and songs I'd never heard, I wasn't going to make a fuss.

Still, even if Meggy and I had our uncertain moments, at least I could rest comfortably knowing that no one was trying to kill my girlfriend. The same couldn't be said for my brother.

Simply put, I had no clue what to do with Aiden. I'd felt terrible about abandoning him with Joey for most of his first day in the realm, but when I stopped by after seeing Grivam off to look for leftover mutton, I found Aiden sound asleep in the new loft and Joey stretched out by the fire, feeding blackened bits of meat to Georgie by hand. "He's fine," Joey assured me, passing the platter of rare, yet well-charred, chops. "Tuckered out. He's been a big help, really."

After dinner, I floated Aiden, still unconscious, to his room, leaving Joey to spend another night alone with his dragon, who sent up psychic distress calls if he was out of her sight for five minutes. Eventually, I collapsed into bed myself, making a note to catch up with Aiden—hell, to try to get to *know* Aiden—over breakfast. When morning came, however, he was nowhere to be found in the palace, and after a few minutes' frantic search, I tracked him back to the barn, where he was shoveling muck at Joey's side. We said our awkward hellos, and I told him I'd be in my office if he needed anything.

He never came by.

That evening, I sent an aide down to the barn to bring Joey to my office. He jogged in ten minutes later, closed the door behind him, and picked a piece of straw out of his hair as he headed for my desk. "You wanted to see me?" he asked, smoothing a stray lock back into place.

I held out my hand and beckoned for the straw, then incinerated it and sank onto one of the couches. "I've got to take Aiden home tonight," I said, watching Joey claim the couch opposite mine. "Promised his mother."

"Okay. I'll see that he gets a shower. Don't want him going back smelling like manure, eh?"

"Sure. Thanks."

Joey waited for a moment for a follow-up that didn't come, then frowned, leaned over his knees, and rested his chin in his palm. "What's up, boss?"

I sighed and massaged my scalp. "What am I doing wrong?"

"What do you mean?"

"With Aiden. He's avoiding me."

Joey steepled his fingers and glanced at the ceiling. "He's working through a mess right now, Colin. You've got to give him time."

"Meaning?"

"Correct me if I'm wrong, but didn't Aiden grow up Arcanum?" he replied, giving me a knowing look. "Come on, man, don't make me spell it out for you."

I squeezed my eyes closed. "I'm still the Antichrist?"

"Hail, Damien," Joey said with a snort, then leaned

back against the cushions and shrugged. "Okay, it's not quite that bad. He's working through it. Keeps telling me you've been awesome—his word, not mine," he added, "but he's twitchy as hell right now. I'm pretty sure that little revelation from Val didn't help the situation." He paused, then folded his arms and waited for me to look back at him. "Don't take it personally, eh? You're a lot to take in, even in ideal circumstances, and this ain't ideal by a long shot."

"I just thought we'd made progress," I muttered.

"Well, he's not rocking in the corner, so I'd say it's a start." Joey flashed a conspiratorial half-smile. "Listen, there's this stable hand on the Faire circuit, Rodney Delgado. You want to talk about horse whisperers, that guy's a friggin' magician—and yes, I meant to say that," he rushed, catching my smirk. "Anyway, I saw a lot of him during the summers growing up. He's the kind of guy who'll sit there and listen, not say anything, just let you vent."

"Yeah?"

"Yeah. And when you've explained how the universe hates you and your parents are *completely* uncool, and unfair, and lots of other things that start with *un-*, he puts a handle in your hand and sets you to work. And by the end of whatever he's told you to do, you're tired and sore in places you didn't know you had, but you feel better about life."

I nodded. "And this is why you've had Aiden shoveling shit for two days?"

"More or less. If he's exhausted, he's less likely to worry about all the messy ways to die here."

"I suppose I owe you one, Joey."

He grunted. "Nah. Aiden needed a sounding board, and I haven't had much company of late—we're good. I like him."

"You do?"

Joey rolled his eyes. "Well, I mean—*youths*, you know.

But he's got potential."

I chuckled. "You're not one to talk about youths, kid."

"Me?" he replied in wide-eyed mock offense. "I'll have you know I'm a well-seasoned, well-adjusted man of the world."

"You're barely twenty-five."

"I'm a *mature* twenty-five," he countered.

"We'll continue this conversation once you've reached your centennial," I said, and pushed myself off the couch. "Okay, I did promise I'd swing Aiden by his parents' apartment. Once he's presentable, would you send him this way?"

"I'll do you one better and escort him because I'm a mature guy like that," said Joey, then touched an imaginary hat brim and let himself out.

An hour later, as I watched the stars rise out my office's bay windows, Joey rapped on the door and led Aiden in, clean once more if still somewhat damp. "Have fun, I guess," he said, and showed himself out as quickly as he'd come.

Aiden straightened the collar of his golf shirt and cleared his throat. "So, uh…we're going back to Montana?"

"I promised your mother," I replied, maintaining what I hoped was a non-threatening distance. "And…you know, we can stay as long as you like. Or you can stay permanently, if that's what you'd prefer. I mean," I rushed, "no pressure, you're welcome here, but if you'd rather, um…stay…"

"I don't think this'll take too long," he replied a few seconds later, breaking the uncomfortable silence that had fallen between us. "Can we get it over with?"

"Yeah, sure." I stepped around the desk and gestured at the wall, and a gate opened into Greg's office. "Look, Aiden, before we go…"

His eyes met mine, and I struggled to read what was written there. The kid's face was a mask but for a few minor tells, a slow tic at his left eye, a tension wrinkle between his eyebrows, a certain tightness around his mouth. In other words, nervous and trying not to show it.

"I'm not going to hurt you," I said quietly. "Not intentionally, I mean—accidents happen—but I won't make plans to do you ill. And I know it's asking a lot of you, but please try to believe me."

He studied me for a moment, then folded his arms and nodded.

"I'm sorry I've been so busy of late," I continued as Aiden hugged himself. "You've yet to even have a proper tour, and that's my fault. I just, uh…well, you and Joey seemed to be getting on, and…I didn't want to intrude."

Aiden mulled that over, then looked back at me. "You're not mad?"

"*Mad*? At you? Whatever for?"

He shrugged. "After what Val said…about me—"

"Moon and stars," I sighed, cutting his explanation short. "Aiden, if I were angry with anyone over that, the very last person on my list would be you."

It could have been my imagination, but I thought I saw his shoulders relax a degree. "I didn't want to make things worse," he said in a rushed mumble, "and Joey let me hang out, and Georgie wants a lot of attention…"

I waited until he ran out of steam, then said, "If you're having fun with Joey, that's great. I don't want to interrupt. But, uh…you know, if you…you get bored or something…"

Aiden glanced at the open gate. "We should probably—"

"Yeah, go ahead." I waited until he was through, then stepped across after him and closed the gate behind me. The realm sent up its usual mental protest at my departure, but I'd become more adept at ignoring it and pushed it to the back of my mind. I sniffed deeply, conscious of the odd smell of the air—recycled and dry, yes, but also devoid of much of the scent of magic to which I'd grown numb of late. Funny, I mused, how quickly one acclimates and forgets.

Greg's office was empty, and Aiden looked around at the bookcases and wet bar nervously. "Are we supposed to be in here?" he whispered.

"Probably not," I replied, heading for the beverages, "but there's not much Greg can do about it, and I doubt he wants me taking a self-guided tour of the silo. I trust you know the way home?"

He headed for the door, but looked back before leaving. "You're not coming?"

I snorted and reached for a tumbler. "I'd rather not get into a fight with your parents, if it's all the same to you."

"Good call," he said, sounding relieved, and slipped off down the darkened hallway.

Shortly after I'd settled onto the couch with a glass of small-batch bourbon and a three-year-old *National Geographic*, the door opened again. I glanced up over my magazine, and the gray-haired newcomer harrumphed as she crossed her arms over her ample bosom. "Why am I not surprised?" she muttered.

"Hello, Missy," I replied, turning back to the article I'd left. "Don't let me keep you."

"Small chance of that." She walked around the room to Greg's desk and pulled something flat and slim off the blotter. "You here to see him?"

"No. Just waiting."

Missy sniffed and leaned against the wall. "So I'm supposed to leave you alone with Greg's things, am I? His computer? All the Arcanum records?"

I looked up again, holding my finger on my place. "Do I look like I'm here to dig through your files?"

She cut her eyes to his desk and the darkened computer monitor.

"I don't touch the damn things," I added, following her

glance. "Greg knows that. Really, don't let me keep you."

I could feel her eyes on me as I bent back to my reading. After a moment of listening to the wall clock tick, she asked, "How's the view up there?"

"Up where?"

"On your high horse. Must be nice."

Sighing, I closed the magazine and put it aside. "Be plain, would you? It's been a long week."

"You know what I'm talking about." She put her flat thing aside—something computer-related, I supposed, seeing no practical use for it—and stared at me over the back of the opposite sofa. "Tell me, what's it like being right all the time? Knowing everything there is to know about Arcanum politics? Oh, wait—you don't, do you?"

Her sarcasm was trying my patience, but I knew nothing good would come of unnecessarily antagonizing Missy Harrison. "I'm going to assume you're hinting at something related to Aiden. In that case, yes, I think Greg fucked up in a colossal way, and all of your wit and charm isn't going to change my mind. Anything else?"

She shook her head, and her short hair barely bounced with her displeasure. "You've got some nerve, faerie boy," she muttered.

"As do you."

"*I'm* not the one sneaking into other people's offices uninvited."

"I'm waiting for my brother," I replied, picking up my drink. "Where else would you like me to go?"

Her thin eyebrows rose. "You really want to know?"

"Good night, Missy."

"Oh no," she retorted, "as long as you're here, you're going to hear me out."

I sighed and folded my arms in mimicry of hers. "If this is the Batman speech, Greg already gave it."

"Just shut your mouth and listen," she said, glaring down at me. "That man has done a *damn* fine job keeping this organization from imploding, all right? And sometimes, for the greater good, he's made decisions he didn't want to make. Believe me, I've been hearing about it almost every night since 1970."

I stared back at her, drumming my fingers on my knee.

"Howard didn't want that boy," Missy continued. "Half the Council wanted to pack him off to foster care, and a few magi—I'm not going to name names, but it was more than three—suggested putting him back up top and letting the cold take care of the problem. That child is alive right now—"

"You could have brought him to me from the start."

"Right, because you have such an excellent track record with children," she snapped. "Let's see, late nineties—were you still snorting then, or were you just an old drunk?"

She had a point, and I felt my neck begin to flush. "Be careful."

"Or what? You're going to strike me dead in my husband's office?" She grunted and rolled her eyes. "I'm sorry, did I upset you?"

"I'd tell you to go screw yourself, but that wouldn't be polite."

"Such a gentleman," she said with a smirk. "And I'm not finished yet. You know the Matherson boy? Want to know why he's still around?"

I put my drink on the table and leaned back against the sofa. "Because Mrs. Matherson knows which is the business end of a sword?"

"And because Greg didn't let the Council kill him before June ever had a chance to swing that sword," she said quietly. "I'm not even going to get started on little Ms. Pavli."

"All right," I said, "he didn't kill three children. Does that generally warrant a medal among you people, or am I missing something?"

"I'm saying he did the best he could." Missy planted her hands on the back of the couch and gave me an unblinking stare. "Let me put it in terms you'll understand.

If Greg upsets the Council enough, they'll kick him out. Then we won't have a clear succession. There could be multiple contenders. Couple three grand magi running around, each claiming he's the real one. Hell, you might get a grand magus out of each installation. Know what happened the last time we had a problem like that?"

"Great War," I replied, holding her gaze.

"Uh-huh. You want to go through another one of those?"

"Wouldn't be my problem, would it?"

She seemed taken aback at that. "The Arcanum eats itself alive, and that's not your problem?"

"Nope." I glanced at the ceiling tiles. "What's the Arcanum's refrain...ah, right, 'We don't get involved in court politics.' Works both ways, my dear."

Missy slowly shook her head. "I have no idea how he's put up with you this long."

"Because," I said, going to my feet for a moment's height leverage, "Greg knows I'm not the enemy. I'm the closest thing to an ally you have." Her defiant stare didn't waiver as I finished my drink. "So you can make excuses for him all you want, Missy, but he knows damn well why I'm peeved. That's not some poor little foundling he kept alive out of the goodness of his heart—that's *my brother*. And I saw too well what Greg's kindness looks like."

She sniffed. "Since when has family mattered to any of you?"

"Since someone named him Aiden."

Before Missy could snap back at me, the door opened again, and Aiden slipped into the room. "Magus," he mumbled, glancing at her. "Um...am I interrupting?"

"That was quick," I interjected. "Is everything—"

"Can we go?"

"Sure." I reopened the gate, traded a final look with Missy, then followed Aiden back into my office. When the gate was closed again, I asked, "What happened?"

He said nothing for a few seconds, then muttered,

"Locked me out."

"Maybe they weren't home."

"No, they were there," he said, sounding oddly calm. "Mom was crying. Dad did the shouting." He met my eyes and added, "I'd rather not repeat it."

I floundered for the right words for a moment, then managed, "Aiden...I'm so sorry."

He shrugged. "Screw them."

"What?"

"*Screw them*," he repeated. "They don't want me? Screw them."

We stood there in silence, listening to the muffled bleating of Georgie's sheep as they multiplied.

"This is probably a dumb question," Aiden mumbled after a time, "but do you play Mario Kart?"

"I...can't say that I have, no."

"I brought my Wii," he said, sounding hopeful. "If Hel could figure it out, anyone can. I mean," he added quickly, "I know you're busy and all, but...if you wanted. You know. No pressure."

I hesitated, wondering if I should divulge my track record with sensitive electronics, then nodded. "Nothing on the schedule tonight. How difficult is this?"

"You ever played with a Wii?" he asked, then saw my expression and waved the question aside. "Okay, we'll start with the basics. Come on."

Halfway down the hall, Aiden paused and rubbed the back of his neck. "Oh, hey, I meant to ask—wall sockets."

"What about them?"

"None in my room. I kind of need electricity." His brow scrunched into thick wrinkles. "Is that going to be a problem?"

"We'll work something out," I said, following him down the corridor. "And you're going to go easy on me with this game, yes?"

"Of course not."

I punched him in the shoulder, and Aiden laughed.

Given my druthers that season, I would have rounded up my siblings—save Aiden—and shipped them off to a nice, secluded island, somewhere without the possibility of return passage. A little separation would have been good for all of us, as they'd made it clear from the start that they resented my presence. The five of them had always been the few children in Mother's favor, and suddenly there was no more Mother to protect them—just me, the greatest asshole of the family, if not the race. It had to be a bit of a shock to the system.

I knew they blamed me for Mother's death, and in all honesty, that blame wasn't entirely undeserved. I hadn't exactly tried to *stop* Toula, after all. But then none of them had been there when Mother set Robin on fire and left it up to me to mercy-kill him. They hadn't smelled him roasting alive or heard him scream like an animal. None of them had yet been born when Mother murdered little Áed in front of me—not for anything the boy had done, but rather to plunge the knife in my gut and twist, amusing herself at my expense. Of course, they probably wouldn't have cared. These were the same siblings who stood by while Mother dispatched her less favored children, who went on with their lives as if nothing were amiss when Mother sent Aiden to his supposed execution and raised Meggy's stolen daughter as her own.

They still asked about Moyna on occasion, and Ji had once whined that I was being unfair, that I should bring her back where she belonged. I had driven my sister from the building with fireballs that morning, too furious to express myself any other way. I couldn't forgive them for letting Mother ruin Olive and torment Meggy, and in that moment, as Ji dashed across the gardens with the hem of her dress smoking, I regretted only that my aim had been inaccurate.

But I couldn't kill them.

Well, that's not entirely correct—I could have done the job without much effort, possibly even in a five-on-one scenario. Aside from the power the realm gave me, I had almost two centuries on Doran, the eldest of the lot, and I'd had plenty of time to learn to fight dirty. Nanine wasn't even three hundred, and she'd probably spent the bulk of those years in Faerie, sitting at Mother's feet and trying out hairdos. Physically, I could have rid myself of them.

Then again, you don't just kill your siblings because they annoy you. The realm protested in my head every time I so much as entertained a daydream in that direction, and I was sure there would be blowback from the court if I eliminated the rest of Mother's line. My siblings I could have handled, but a full-scale revolt would have been unbeatable, especially considering that Valerius wasn't the eldest of my subjects by a long shot. Nor was exile a feasible option. As little as I liked having them in Faerie, at least I could keep an eye on them there, and the thought of adding to the problem Oberon had created by moving his court out of the realm sat ill with me. And so I continued with the status quo, suffering as few of my siblings' visits as possible and dreaming of taking them to unspoiled tropical paradises with nothing but open ocean for miles around.

Unspoiled tropical paradises with rabid jaguar populations, when I was of a mood.

Still, I knew that if Aiden was staying, I would have to make the introductions sooner rather than later, if for no other reason than his safety. The sooner the others knew to avoid him, the better I would feel about not keeping him supervised around the clock. To that end, two days after his brief return to the silo, I sent dinner invitations to the rest of the family and mentioned to Joey that if he felt like praying, I could use a favor.

Having spent most of my adult life alone to that point, I didn't *do* dinner parties, and so I left the details to my staff and spent Sunday with Meggy on the beach, sitting on a blanket in the late September afternoon, reading a paperback with a mildly intriguing cover, and trying to forget the duties I was shirking. When I eventually dragged myself home, I found the smallest of my dining rooms set with a round table and gold china—all standard, as far as I could tell, but for the illumination. Someone had thrown about a thousand tiny floating lights up near the high ceiling, giving the overall ambiance more than a passing resemblance to that of Rigby's tiki bar's beachfront deck. Watching me appraise the work, one of my aides explained, "Considering the guest list, we thought a round table would be best—fewer ways to offend through seating."

"Understood," I said, noting that Syral and Doran's place settings had been situated out of each other's line of sight. "And the, uh…decoration?" I asked, pointing to the light show.

She grinned apologetically. "Lord Aiden's idea. If it displeases—"

"It's fine," I interjected, and saw Aiden's head poke around the doorway. "Going into interior design, are you?" I called.

"Nah," he replied, shoving his hands into his pockets as he slipped into the room. "There's this Mexican place, closest thing to the silo—they go a little crazy with the Christmas lights, but I've always kind of liked it. Festive, you know?" He glanced at the riot of twinkling colors above us, then shrugged. "Okay, maybe it's not exactly *formal*…"

"So how good is the Mexican in Montana?"

Aiden made a face. "Well, I'm probably not the best judge of authenticity, all things considered, but let's just say the owner's name is Stan."

"Yeah," I muttered, suddenly missing Phoenix. "We'll do something about that later."

I left him with the aide, a soft-spoken half-blood who seemed to have an intuitive understanding of the situation, and returned to my chambers to get the sand out of my hair. Valerius caught me poking my cheeks in front of the mirror, trying to see how bad my fresh sunburn was going to be, and cleared his throat to announce his presence. "Pleasant outing, my lord?"

"Most things are pleasant beside the sea," I replied, patting my windblown hair into order. "No emergencies?"

"None, though I may have taken the liberty of doubling the guard tonight." I turned and cocked my eyebrow, and he nodded. "The last time Lord Doran and Lady Syral had a disagreement, the damage was rather...*extensive*."

I flipped back to the mirror and started to try on different shirts, running through my mental catalogue of garments worn in the last fifty years. The Hawaiian number, at least, was definitely out. "Going to satisfy my morbid curiosity?"

Valerius had been at his job long enough to be unfazed as my clothes kept popping into and out of existence. "They destroyed the north wing of the palace. Your mother threatened to skin them alive if they didn't clean up the mess."

"She meant it, I'd wager." The white button-down was easy, but I wasn't convinced.

"She had a knife on hand. You know, togas make things much simpler. Always appropriate for formal occasions."

I paused and gave him a look in the mirror. "And when was the last time you wore a toga? Within the past millennium?"

"It's never been the fashion here, my lord."

The captain hadn't gone far from his roots—I'd yet to see him sport anything but a belted tunic and pants—but I couldn't imagine even Valerius pulling off a toga in Faerie without ridicule. "And it hasn't been the fashion outside the realm for quite some time," I said, settling on a subdued green blazer. "Aside from toga parties..."

"Toga parties?" he echoed, perplexed.

I tried to find an explanation that wouldn't offend him

and realized the effort was wasted. "An excuse for students to wrap themselves in bedsheets and drink until they vomit."

As Valerius tried to process this, I turned when someone rapped at the door, then relaxed and beckoned when Joey cracked it open. "Princess Buttercup is on a rampage?"

"No, Georgie's napping off her tea," he said, closing the door behind him. "Aiden wasn't sure of the dress code tonight. I said I'd check on it for him."

"Pajamas, for all I care," I replied. "Look, Joey, you don't have to babysit—"

"I'm not," he said with a little shrug. "Been kicking his ass at Mario Kart all afternoon—porta-generator, good call. Georgie wants to play, but it's tough without thumbs, you know?"

"Glad someone can challenge him," I muttered, giving the mirror a final inspection.

"Yeah, he said you were still figuring it out."

"Damn bananas."

"Welcome to the club. Hey, Val," he added, leaving me to brood. "Are we still on for tomorrow?"

Valerius nodded, then stopped and frowned at Joey. "Have you heard of this 'toga party' phenomenon?"

"Sure," he began, then paused, a look of realization crossing his face. "*Oh*, this is news to you."

"You've been to one?"

Joey had the grace to look sheepish. "Maybe?"

"*Maybe?*"

"Okay, yes. College is a time for doing things you'd never do as a real adult."

The captain closed his eyes and sighed softly. "Please tell me you at least had the sense to wear a tunic underneath," he said, then looked at Joey again in time to catch his confusion. "Tunic. Sleeves. No?"

Joey shook his head.

"You walked around in a bedsheet. And...drank?"

"A fair bit," he reluctantly admitted.

He crossed his arms and scowled. "You can't possibly make a toga out of a sheet! The proportions are wrong, you can't drape it properly—"

"Knots, safety pins, gallon jugs of wine. Presto."

"Was it at least a white sheet?" I asked as I experimented with cufflinks.

Joey's face had begun to burn. "If you must know," he said with affected dignity, "it was floral. But it was clean, and that's saying something. One of the girls had a tie-dyed flannel toga, so I wasn't the worst."

Valerius snorted. "Your women walked around in togas as well, did they?"

"It was a theme party!" he protested.

"Only prostitutes wear togas!"

"Says who?"

He spread his arms and looked at Joey with deep incredulity. "Apparently, the one man in this room who has ever worn one properly!"

"Good point," Joey mumbled, and saw me trying not to laugh. "Don't even start, Colin."

"At least you figured maille out on your own," I replied.

He rolled his eyes, muttered threats about Ren Faires, and slinked off to find Aiden.

The first of my guests arrived a few hours after sundown—and five minutes late, but then I hadn't anticipated anything less from them. Syral and Huc often traveled as a pair, dark-haired and remarkably alike in their features but for their eyes, her father's blue and his father's black. Syral seemed to take her fashion cues those days from Jane Austen and Huc from Ziggy Stardust, but their motions were strangely synchronized, their affectations similarly disinterested, their glances at each other frequent and indicative of silent conversation. From what I had gathered, Huc had been Syral's pet when he was small and she was between lovers, and he had absorbed many of his sister's mannerisms by observation. Then again, their difference in age was perhaps only seventy-five years, so they had had ample time to adapt to each other.

I let the staff seat them beside each other and bided my time in another room, watching them. I had no need of hidden cameras—not when the realm itself was only too happy to show me what was transpiring outside of my sight. The sensation was beyond strange, like seeing a second reality layered onto the one before me (and leaving me confused as to which I was actually viewing if I paid too much attention to the vision), but it had its uses. That night, I was trying to see how the alliances had shifted before I threw Aiden into the middle of a war.

Syral gave a lazy wave when Nanine was shown in, but Huc stood and kissed our youngest sister's hand. She was always pretty, but that evening, Nanine had swept her blonde waves—Mother's hair with better style—into a pearl-studded chignon. She sported an absurd confection of pink lace and black opera gloves, looking rather like she'd been playing dress-up in an attic, but somehow still seemed radiant, a brown-eyed angel with a child's ringing laugh and at least three confirmed murders, changelings she had wearied of and sent my way for disposal.

Mistress was so beautiful, the last told me as she died at my feet, suddenly finding herself wizened and too ancient to stand. Beautiful and cold, like autumn's first killing frost.

Next was Ji, petite in every sense but for her mass of black curls, which bounced around her as if to make up for Nanine's subdued tresses. It was Syral's turn to rise and greet, a perfunctory exchange of kissed cheeks, followed by a quick look at Huc, whose slow blink seemed to speak volumes in reply. Nanine giggled as Ji produced a fishbowl-sized margarita, then considered the others, glanced down at her red sheath of a dress, and changed into something Marie Antoinette might have commissioned.

Finally, nearly an hour late, Doran showed himself into the room, sporting a blue robe embroidered with gold and glittering with what I assumed to be diamonds. Ji rose to embrace him, but the others sat and stared, silently drinking in the quasi-festive glow.

"Any bloodshed yet?" Valerius asked beside me.

I let the vision fade and blinked until he came back into focus. "No, but the night is young. How do the wagers stand?"

"If I told you," he said with a faint smirk, "that might change the odds."

"Fair enough." I rose, straightened my shirt, and took a deep breath. "Think this is a bad idea?"

"Honestly, my lord?"

"Don't answer that," I muttered, and set off to greet my guests.

Doran was the first to notice my entrance, which he acknowledged with a sigh. "I was beginning to wonder if you were ever going to grace us," he said, leaning back in his chair and studiously avoiding Syral's dagger eyes. "Or starve us. Suppose they're equally likely, aren't they?"

"My sincere apologies," I lied through a smile, "but I was unavoidably detained. I see the drinking has commenced," I added, glancing at the ring of unmatched stems and highballs around the table as I took my chair.

"Just passing the time," Syral chimed in, and raised her glass in brief salute. "And...we're expecting a seventh?" she asked, indicating the empty place beside mine. "Not Moyna, surely?"

"No, I'm afraid she has an early morning," I replied, straining to keep my smile in place. "There's someone I want you to meet."

"Who, the mongrel?"

I glared across the table at Nanine, who smiled back at me and shrugged. "Word travels," she said. "I could think of no other reason for this gathering."

Huc's eyes narrowed, and he looked back and forth between Nanine and me. "What mongrel?"

She examined her pink fingernails with practiced carelessness. "Mother's little mongrel. You remember, Moyna was an infant, and then Mother had the boy…"

His dark eyes widened in recollection. "Yes, *that* mongrel. I thought she got rid of it."

"So did I," said Syral, leaning around Huc to stare me in the face. "Were we mistaken, dear brother?"

I studied the table, trying to decipher Ji's well-rouged smirk and Nanine's little grin. Doran's expression was unmistakable, however, and I hurried on before he could come up with any ideas involving homicide. "Aiden's fifteen," I said, trying to meet every gaze simultaneously, "and he's come home. I thought you should meet him."

There was silence for a moment, and then Doran snorted. "You called us here to see a *mongrel*, Coileán? Is that how little you think of us?"

"Witch-blood," I said quietly. "And our brother."

"You'd bring *that* here," Ji interrupted, "but you won't bring our Moyna home?"

Doran had begun to color, and he went to his feet before Ji finished speaking. "I will not break bread with *her*," he said, pointing at Syral, "on account of a damn mongrel!"

Huc started to rise, but Syral pushed him back into his chair. "Sit, dear," she said, giving Doran a particularly venomous look. "He's not worth the effort. Let him rage in peace."

"Come over here and say that," Doran spat.

From his position in the shadows at the back of the room, Valerius pointedly cleared his throat, and my siblings turned as one. "Lords and ladies," he said calmly, "I've been instructed to inform you that there will be no violence this evening."

"Oh, you're going to stop us?" Doran shot back. "*Really*? You would come between—"

"No, but *he* will," Valerius interrupted, cutting his eyes to me. "I'm only the messenger. And should the situation deteriorate, I've been authorized to bring in Lord Coileán's…associate," he continued. "Who wields a weapon that fires iron projectiles. Effectively, I might add," he muttered, absently rubbing a small burn scar on his forearm.

Syral looked back at me, pursing her pale lips as she considered the situation. "You're threatening us, then? Whatever you've been told about our last quarrel, really, it must have been exaggerated."

"I don't care what you two do to each other outside my presence," I replied, bringing forth a glass of scotch to give my hands something to do other than ball into fists. "Nor do I give a damn whether anyone eats here tonight. I brought you here to explain that no one is to touch Aiden."

Ji and Nanine exchanged a quick glance, and I downed my drink to calm my temper. "Let me clarify, since there seems to be some confusion," I continued when the glass was empty. "No one kills Aiden. No one maims Aiden. No one sets up any sort of trap in which Aiden will come to harm. No one tries to sell Aiden to anything out of the Gray Lands. No one imprisons Aiden. No one throws Aiden out of the realm. No one enlists the help of a third party to do any of the aforementioned to Aiden. Have I forgotten anything?"

"General enchantment," Valerius offered.

"Right. No enchanting Aiden against his will or to do him ill, understood?"

The others glared at me sullenly, and I nodded. "Glad we had this chat. Stay if you like. I've lost my appetite." With that, I rose and marched out of the room, leaving the silent table to take care of itself.

I found Aiden waiting a few yards down the corridor, hands in his pockets and shoulders slumped. "Didn't go so well?" he mumbled.

"No one's dead, so I think it's a success," I replied, changing into jeans and a T-shirt. "Want to go bother Joey?"

"Lamb chops again?"

"We'll raid the kitchen on the way out.'"

"Sounds good," he said, pulling himself off the wall. "Hey, I left my Wii out there if—"

"Coileán!"

I whirled around to find Syral approaching, followed closely by her younger shadow. "Problem?" I asked.

"Nothing new. I just wanted to see the little mongrel for myself," she said, and peered up at Aiden. "Hmm. I suppose he has Mother's look about him, doesn't he?"

She continued to stare, circling Aiden for a closer view. "Uh…hi?" he mumbled, swiveling his head to keep an eye on her. "Have we—"

"All right, no one plays with your little pets," she interrupted, then patted Aiden's cheek and flounced back the way she had come, arm-in-arm with Huc.

Aiden stared after them. "What…"

"Sister. Brother. Not the most antagonistic of the lot, either."

"*Right*," he whispered, then shook his head and pointed toward the kitchen.

CHAPTER 9

A few months after I moved to Arizona, when Meggy was still living at my place, a traveling ballet troupe passed through Phoenix. I've never been the greatest patron of the arts, and what I knew of ballet made my feet hurt in sympathy, but Meggy thought the show seemed promising. After two weeks of needling—and since we were together night and day, Meggy had plenty of time to work on me—I finally caved and procured a pair of decent tickets.

The evening's entertainment was *Swan Lake*, and Meggy sat on the edge of her chair, entranced by the lithe young things in feathers and spandex that twirled and leapt across the stage. I found myself engrossed as well, as overall, the dancing was beautiful. But shortly after the lovers ascended into the heavens and the curtain fell on the final bows, an erratic percussion sounded backstage, and the curtain lifted to reveal a few of the lesser members of the company still standing about, surrounded by little girls in tutus and one very uncomfortable little boy in white tights.

The music started up again, and the children began to cavort around the legitimate ballerinas, some with a modicum of grace and skill, but most flailing about like epileptic puppies. The boy managed to sneak offstage in the chaos—with half the dancers moving the wrong way, he had a ready-made distraction—and one girl, overtaken by the moment, leapt from the stage and ran to her mother's seat in tears. Meggy covered her mouth and looked at me, physically trying to hold the laughter in. As I was on the verge myself, I did nothing to help the situation, and she ended the evening with her face pressed against my shirt, shaking in a fit of barely muffled giggles.

I thought back to those eager, awkward little dancers as I sat on the sheep fence in the afternoon sun and watched Valerius knock Joey off his feet for the ninth time in twenty minutes.

A man who knows his sword and can wield it as an extension of his will can make an art out of dealing death. The captain was a virtuoso, light on his feet and lightning-fast with his strikes, and by the second day of lessons, he could anticipate Joey's moves from the subtle cues of his opponent's eyes and feet. Joey was no slouch, all things considered—I had to award him a few points for knowing how to hold a sword at all, given his age—but for every blow he attempted, Valerius delivered two.

It was painful to watch, though I'm sure Joey had it worse than I did.

They fought with wooden practice swords, partly due to the captain's wariness of Joey's usual steel, but mostly so that Valerius wouldn't accidentally kill him. The blades weren't sharp by any means, but fast-moving wood against skin provides its own brand of sting, and Joey limped as he rose from the dirt. Valerius stood a few feet away, relaxed and waiting as Joey struggled to find his feet. "Your leg is now useless," he said, "and I've probably hamstrung you. Watch your flank—you turn too much when you lunge, and you're making yourself a target."

Joey gritted his teeth and wiped his sweaty hair from his eyes. He was breathing heavily, though I couldn't tell whether it was from the exertion or the pain. "You said I wasn't turning enough."

"You weren't," he replied. "But you overdid it. Again, now."

Joey dragged himself back into a fighting stance, waited for Valerius's nod, then started to weave around him. The captain watched calmly, parried Joey's first blow, then hooked his ankle around the boy's leg and threw him to the ground. "And now you're dead," he said, holding the blunt sword against Joey's chest. "Again."

"All right, kid?" I called from the safety of my perch.

"Fine," he said wearily. "I'm fine." He waited until Valerius stepped back, then used his sword as a crutch and pulled himself upright. "Water break?"

Valerius consulted the sun, then shook his head. "You can go longer. Again."

While Joey continued to earn a fine set of bruises, I looked across their makeshift ring into the barn, where Aiden sat with Georgie, stroking her head to keep her calm. The dragonet had lengthened at least three feet in the two weeks since Joey had found her, and her girth was almost keeping pace with the rest of her growth. More troublingly, her first teeth were fully in, and she bared them every time Joey hit the ground.

Aiden murmured to her when he tripped and bounced, but Georgie's response was all too clear: *Bad. Don't like.*

She was no longer broadcasting her every mood to all minds in a fifty-foot radius, but Georgie was vocal—relatively speaking—about her dislike of combat practice. Joey was *hers*, apparently, and she took it extremely personally when he was hurt. After their first lesson, when Valerius had almost lost his sword arm to a pissed-off dragon, he had suggested taking their activity elsewhere, but Georgie had liked that idea even less. And so they continued to fight by the barn under her wary eye, with Aiden sitting beside her to stave off bystander-inflicted casualties. The idea of leaving my brother that close to a dragon didn't sit easily with me, but Aiden had quickly learned where to scratch Georgie for maximum effect. After watching a few sessions, she tolerated Joey's lessons with minimal grumbling, but only with her head in range of Aiden's hand.

I slipped off the fence and skirted the combatants, then joined Aiden on his hay bale. "How much longer does this usually last?" I asked.

He considered the tableau for a moment, then winced as Joey went down again. "Give them half an hour. Val's going to keep beating Joey until Joey gets a hit in."

"Really?" I watched Joey stagger back to his feet, clutching his side. "You think he can do it in half an hour?"

"No. But I think Val will give him a mercy shot by then," he replied, scratching the base of Georgie's horns as she broadcast her continued displeasure with the lesson in progress. "He hasn't broken anything yet, at least."

I produced a hip flask of bourbon and swigged. "Does that usually happen?"

"Do you see bits of Val in Georgie's teeth?"

"Point taken."

Aiden murmured reassurance to the dragon, then glanced down at my flask. "Sharing?"

"This?" I asked, lifting the flask for inspection. "You wouldn't like it."

"I *might*..."

I gave him a look. "If Meggy thought I was letting you drink hard liquor, she'd throw a fit."

"How about a beer?" he asked hopefully.

"You said you don't like beer."

"I'm learning to like it!" He read my face and huffed. "How am I supposed to acquire a taste for it if I never try it, huh?"

"And how am I supposed to explain it to Meggy if you show up tonight smelling like a frat house?" I retorted.

Georgie lifted her head and snorted. *Nervous.*

"Stop ratting me out, Godzilla," he muttered.

Keep scratching.

Aiden bent back to his task, but he sighed when I kept my silence and waited for an explanation. "I haven't been to anything like this in years," he mumbled, "and the last time I did, I ended up getting my face rearranged under the bleachers. Not a lot of happy memories, you know?"

"First," I said, capping my flask, "the bleachers are a concrete block. No one's getting beaten underneath them."

"There are other places—"

"And no one who would want to beat you is going to be there. Meggy's not usually the violent type."

Joey yelped as he fell onto his bruised knees, and Georgie stiffened beside us, ready for attack.

"I promise you," I said, reaching behind Aiden to pat the dragon before she could get any rash notions of heroics, "I'm not going to let anything happen to you. Unless you eat the hot dogs—I'm not responsible for those."

His mouth twitched. "You're sure about this?"

I looked around us—the unsettled dragon, the swordfighters in the yard, the flask in my hand—and nodded. "A little normalcy will do you good, don't you think?" I looked up when Joey yelled again, then called into the yard, "Valerius! I want him left alive, please!"

The most that could be said for the Rigby Buccaneers was that they tried.

The boys seemed to know which way to run and whom to sack, which was promising, at least from a technical standpoint. Hampering their attempts to run and sack was the slight problem that no one on the team was more than five-ten or two hundred pounds. A few of them that season looked like fantastic contenders for college benchwarmers. Their parents said the team had a lot of heart, which made their inevitable trouncing all the worse—not disappointing, just painful.

But Olive had secured a position on the cheerleading squad, and so Meggy's Friday nights that fall were booked solid. Considering the low entertainment value of Rigby's football games, I couldn't help but wonder if Olive had subconsciously picked up pompoms to spite me.

The sky threatened an overnight rain, but the weather was holding well enough for the evening's game to go on as planned. I found Meggy sitting in the middle of the old bleachers, wrapped in a blue anorak against the wind and clutching a thermos of coffee. "Hey!" she said, patting the vacant concrete beside her. "My money's on a washout by halftime. And you must be Aiden!" she added, spotting my brother as he trailed me up the bleachers. "Come on over, plenty of room!"

Aiden looked around at the half-empty stands and grinned. "Rain scared everyone off?"

"No, this is a good crowd. We just suck," she replied, and grabbed him in a quick hug. "Welcome aboard the crazy train," she murmured. "How's he treating you?"

"Terribly."

"Figures." She stepped back and gave him an appraising look as she sipped her drink. "Okay, there's a *little* resemblance with you two," she said after a moment, "but you've got to squint to see it. You, uh...you look like your mother."

"So I hear," he mumbled, rubbing his neck, then pointed to the bench of cheerleaders. "Which one is Olive, Ms. Horn?"

"It's Meg, hon, and *that* one," she said, indicating the other end of the row. "I'd say the skinny blonde, but that's about half the group. And if I try to get her to wave, she'll disown me. Um...two in from the left, the one with the cockeyed ponytail—that's Olive." She hesitated, then added, "Takes after her grandmother. You'll see it when she turns around. But hey, enough of that," Meggy continued with affected brightness, trying to dispel the unintended tension. "Welcome to Virginia! Any interest in the ocean? That's really about all Rigby's got going for it, but the beach isn't half bad."

Aiden perked at that. "Yeah?"

"About a mile that way," she replied, pointing over the visiting team's bleachers. "Not the warmest right now, but that's what you get in October, you know? And if this storm blows up, we might have decent waves tomorrow. You don't surf, do you?"

He made a face. "I've, uh...never actually seen the ocean. Montana's kind of landlocked."

Meggy reached across me and squeezed Aiden's knee. "Been there, know the feeling. Tell you what, we'll go down in the morning—it's more impressive when you can see where you're going. And hey," she said with a snap, "you like boats? I know a guy in town who does charters—we could get you out, let you get a little salt in your lungs, eh? You can swim, right?"

While Meggy and Aiden discussed lifejackets and the statistical probability of rogue waves, I slipped out from between them and headed down the bleachers for a walk, trying not to remember Meggy's first time at the land's end and the things we'd done in the sand. Meggy and I had made up for lost time in the months since our reconnection, but part of me still hated myself for what had transpired in California, and all of her reassurances that the desire had been mutual did nothing to make me feel less filthy.

Maybe, I mused in the small hours, Meggy was clinging to the ghost of her dream of a family, looking for something to help her through the changes in her life. Maybe I was only a diversion until something real came along. Maybe I would never measure up to whatever version of me had resided inside her head all of those years. Or maybe, somehow, this thing between us *was* real, and my Meggy was trying to move past what I'd done to her.

I wanted a drink, but Rigby High didn't sell beer at their games, and I wasn't going to embarrass Olive further by being not only her mother's creepy boyfriend, but also the alcoholic who couldn't stay away from a flask for one measly game.

And so I struck out in search of nachos.

There are times in life when one's masochistic stomach demands tribute of the basest form. For me, that meant stale corn chips smothered in a lukewarm orange goop generously described as "process cheese product."

Rigby's band booster nachos were overpriced at three dollars, but the jalapeños were free, and standing in line beside the concessions building gave me an excuse to get out of the wet wind. I handed over the money, cursed my life choices, and was making the most of the toppings bar when I heard a woman behind me say, "You do know that's not really cheese, right?"

I put the chili flakes down and turned to find a familiar pair of dark-rimmed glasses watching me. "Ms. Stowe?" I replied quietly, dropping the nachos to free my hands.

She slurped her slushie and grinned. "Not going to hit a girl, are you?"

"Not if you tell me what the hell you're doing here."

Vivian prodded her sweatshirt, blue with a white screen-printed pirate sneering monocularly on her chest. "Dating the coach. I'm serious!" she insisted, seeing my expression creep toward incredulity. "Hal's an occasional amateur paranormal investigator during the off season."

I rolled my eyes and resumed my nacho customization. "And did the spirits tell him whether he'd have a winning record this year?"

"No, but they probably didn't want to crush his dream." She joined me at the folding table of condiments and contemplated the vat of relish. "And you're here because…"

"My daughter cheers."

"Ah. This would be the kid with the memory wipe?" I looked up sharply, and Vivian shrugged. "Rick filled me in. My spider sense goes off around her, and I wanted the details before I went recruiting."

"You have a spider sense?"

"I'm not *completely* vanilla," she muttered.

"And your beau?"

"One hundred percent Madagascar, so do me a solid and don't blow my cover, eh?"

Moving on to the sad jar of mild salsa, I replied, "I have other things to worry about than ruining your love life, kid."

"So I hear. And ew, that shit's more water than tomato." She leaned closer and muttered, "I understand there's some trouble in the Gulf."

"We're not having this discussion."

"Yes, we are. I've got people down there."

I paused, put down my food again, and stared her full in the face, but Vivian didn't blink. "If there's something going down, we need to know about it," she said. "Folks need to get to safety. You've got nothing to gain by holding out on me."

"You don't know when to quit, do you?"

"Character flaw." She sipped her drink and flashed a blue-tinged smile.

I sighed, wished for patience, and picked up my rapidly congealing nachos. "Somewhere private?"

She pulled a key ring from her pocket and cocked her head toward the gymnasium, and I followed her through the building, across a basketball court, and into a tiny, green-carpeted office full of filing cabinets and steel-framed chairs. "Just try not to brush up against anything," said Vivian, seeing my shoulders tighten, and closed the door. "Hal won't be back by here until after the game. So go on, spill it."

I leaned against the door and ate a chip. "The merrow are spooked. That's all I've got."

"I heard there'd been a mass exodus," she replied, perching on the edge of the coach's dented desk. "None spotted in a week."

"They're in the realm."

"Want to tell me why?"

I licked a bit of cheese off my knuckle. "Something about a merrow-eating monster. I was offered no further specifics."

She folded her arms, obviously exasperated. "Are you following up on this?"

"No." I ate another chip, making her wait. "That's Oberon's turf. I'm not going anywhere near there without an invitation."

"You know *he's* not going to do anything about it."

"If you're so concerned, you could try asking him yourself."

Vivian pushed her glasses down her nose and glared at me. "This is all some sort of joke to you? Giant sea monster, total merrow evacuation, and…and you sit there eating Doritos?"

"Doritos would be an improvement." I put the nachos on a bookshelf and spread my hands. "Look, you understand how the courts work, yes? We stay out of each other's way. I can't just tell Oberon that I'll be poking around his backyard for a while, looking for Nessie."

"Why not? If he's not going to—"

"Because he'd lose face if he didn't stop me." I stared down at her until she let her next protest die unspoken. "I was a vigilante for a long time," I said slowly. "He let me get away with it because coming after me would have made Titania lose face. They had their own sort of truce worked out, and I wasn't worth upsetting the arrangement over. But I'm not a random nuisance now—I've got a court behind me. If I act, he *has* to acknowledge it. And if he acknowledges it, it won't be with a thank-you fruit basket. Do you understand?"

She nodded.

"Good," I said, resuming work on my nachos. "And if you *ever* presume to demand answers from me again, little girl, I'll repay you with interest for that concussion."

Her mouth tightened, but her eyes remained defiant. "I'm not afraid of you," she muttered.

"Then you're either a liar or a moron, and I don't think Rick would associate with you if you were a complete imbecile." I poked at the disappointingly hardened cheese and settled for a pepper slice. "But since this game is going to be painful to watch, was there anything else you wanted to discuss?"

Vivian hesitated, then said, "Yeah. One more thing."

"Go ahead."

"I've been seeing a kid hanging around near the school. Hal says he's not a Rigby student, as far as he knows. Sets off my spider sense."

"Again with the spiders."

She stared at the water-stained ceiling. "I'm sensitive to magical fields, yeah? It's verbal shorthand."

"Go on," I said, gesturing with a broken chip.

"Well, my alarm goes off around him. Haven't gotten close enough to say why, but he makes me uncomfortable. Could be glamour, could be a bind, could be something else entirely. He's not Fringe, but I don't know *what* he is."

"Got a name for me?"

"Nope," she said, shaking her head until her pigtails bounced. "Dark hair, about your height, kind of skinny. Looks a little emo. Maybe a junior or senior. That's all I've got."

"I'll keep an eye out for him," I told her, then glanced at the steel door handle. "Are you going to get that, or are you going to make me glove up?"

She slid off the desk and brushed past me. "Limitless power," she muttered, "and you're foiled by a damn door."

"I'm not *foiled*," I protested, following her back across the empty gym. "It's merely a situation requiring certain precautions. The alternative is expending an obscene amount of magic to make iron cooperate."

"It's a doorknob."

"If you want to see what limitless power looks like," I said, "then keep trying to piss me off."

Vivian smirked as we got to the exit door, then swung the bar down and gestured toward the field with a sweeping bow. "Crisis averted yet again. After you, Your

Majesty."

"Thank you, smartass, but 'Lord Coileán' will suffice," I said, then headed back to the bleachers to the sound of the visitors' cheers.

To the deep regret of all but the most die-hard Rigby fans, the rain held off throughout the game, letting the contest run to its foreseen lopsided conclusion. Aiden, at least, was in good spirits as the team limped off the field—fresh air was still a novelty for him—and he cleaned up the trash as Meggy coaxed Olive to make her sullen approach. "I'm going to be late!" Olive yelled up the stands when she was still five rows below us. "What do you need?"

Meggy continued to beckon, and Olive, heaving a sigh, made the climb. "*What?*" she whined. "I'm going to miss my carpool!"

To her credit, Meggy smiled and ignored the performance. "Olive, honey," she said, prodding my brother until he put the wrappers down and straightened his sweater, "this is Aiden. I wanted to introduce you two."

"My nephew," I quickly volunteered as Aiden stuck out his hand. "He's staying with me for a while. Since he'll be around, your mother and I thought you should meet."

Olive remained unmoved by this information and ignored Aiden's hand until he dropped it. "What, you're transferring?" she asked him.

Aiden picked up the trash again and shrugged. "No, uh...I graduated early, so I'm actually out of high school—"

"And it would be great if he could make some friends around here," Meggy interrupted, "so why don't you take him along to the after-party tonight?"

Olive looked at Meggy as if her mother had suggested a pleasant evening of ritually slaughtering kittens. "*Mom!*" she wailed. "Why do you *hate* me?"

"Come on, honey, it'd be a nice thing to do..."

But Olive was already fuming. "If I show up with some...some..."

"Nerd?" Aiden offered.

She glared at him. "Some loser, then I'm going to be ruined. And the seniors are going to be there! Everyone's going to laugh at me, and I won't have any friends, and why don't you go ahead and kill me now, huh?"

Meggy crossed her arms. "Fifty bucks."

"You're so *mean*."

"Seventy."

Olive paused, and I could see the wheels turning behind her eyes.

"One hundred, and that's my firm offer," said Meggy, reaching into her purse. "I'm not asking you to babysit Aiden. Take him to the party, maybe make a few introductions, be a team player. Okay?" She pulled five twenties from her wallet and held them out to Olive. "Come on, you know it's not easy being new. What's it going to hurt to be nice, hmm?"

"I bathed before I came," said Aiden. "You'll never know I'm there."

She took the bribe, but her eyes narrowed as she looked at Meggy and me. "You want him gone so you can screw around. I know what you're up to."

Aiden slipped past Meggy and headed for the stairs. "And that would be a '*duh*.' Shall we?"

"God, you're annoying," she muttered at no one in particular, then stomped off after him.

Olive might have been young and temperamental, but she wasn't stupid.

Meggy and I made the most of the empty apartment, and I woke beside her shortly after dawn, squinting in momentary confusion at the pink light in the bedroom. She mumbled when I sat up, then buried her head beneath the blankets. "Breakfast?" I asked, poking her shoulder through the comforter.

"Hashbrowns."

"Do you have any here?"

"Freezer," she said, pulling the blankets more tightly around her against the chill, and I rose and produced a bathrobe. After giving the dresser mirror a quick check to be sure the glamour was still in place, I padded down the hallway and peeked through the cracked door into Olive's bedroom. The lump beneath the pink quilt seemed the right size and shape, and so I headed on toward the kitchen, expecting I'd find Aiden crashed on the couch.

As it so happened, I was mistaken, and breakfast was quickly abandoned.

Throwing propriety aside, I barged into Olive's bedroom and shook her shoulder until she rolled over and favored me with a bleary, yet baleful, glare. "Where's Aiden?" I asked.

"Dunno," she grunted, flipping back onto her stomach.

"Olive, *wake up*. Where's my br—nephew?"

Fortunately, she was too groggy to have caught my slip. "Dunno."

"Well, where did you last see him?"

"Party."

"*Olive*," I said, trying for Meggy's no-nonsense tone, but my daughter remained unfazed. As I contemplated the ramifications of ripping her blankets off, Meggy shuffled into the room and peered at the tableau.

"No hashbrowns?" she asked through a yawn.

"Aiden's missing. Olive left him somewhere."

"*Shit*," she hissed, suddenly awake. "Olive, get up!"

The girl groaned something at us—I assumed she was trying to make us leave her alone, though the pillow made every third word incomprehensible—but Meggy shook her until she raised her head. "Where did you leave Aiden?" she asked, bending to within inches of Olive's face.

Olive squinted against the light. "Told you, party," she protested, then flopped back into position.

"And where was the party?" Meggy demanded.

"Leo's," was the muffled response.

Meggy straightened and gave me a look that spoke of long suffering, then pointed down at the bed. "Can you do something about that?" she murmured.

I nodded, then closed my eyes and concentrated, seeking the pertinent information in the jumble of Olive's semi-conscious mind. A few seconds later, I caught flashes of the night before, then retreated before I could tempt fate and the bind. "The blue colonial on Piedmont," I whispered, heading for the door. "Big place with the crape myrtles up the drive. I know the way, let's go."

I slipped back into the master bedroom and was pulling on the previous day's clothes by the time Meggy located her sweatpants. "How do you know—"

"Wait until the Christmas lights come out, and you'll know it, too." I found my shoes and pushed my hair into a vague facsimile of order. "The reindeer on the roof are life-sized."

Her head popped out the top of a T-shirt. "One of those families, huh?"

"Pretty sure their power bill doubles in December. Here," I added, tossing Meggy her anorak. "Better let me drive."

She mulled this over briefly, then nodded. "Yeah, coffee wore off. Don't wreck my car."

Ten minutes and several longing looks at coffee vendors later, we parked at the end of a crooked snake of cars stretching well past the party house on either side. A light scattering of red plastic cups in the wet grass hinted that we'd found our destination, and I looked around for signs of life as I took in the scene. The windows appeared to be intact, but a few pieces of clothing had somehow landed in the shrubbery—as had an empty keg, I noticed as I walked toward the front door, wincing at the broken bush beneath it. Whoever Leo was, he was going to have some explaining to do when his parents returned.

The doorbell proved ineffective, and so I hammered on the door for two minutes before it opened to reveal a puffy-eyed young man who'd probably been feeling excellent a few hours before. "We'll keep it down," he mumbled, starting to close the door again, but I shoved my foot in the gap and pushed it open.

"Looking for Aiden. Seen him lately?"

The boy stared into space, trying to process those complex, unfamiliar words, and then nodded as his brain caught up with his body. "Upstairs. Hey, he's not in trouble, is he?" he asked as I brushed past him into the foyer.

"Not yet."

"Okay," said my guide, trailing two steps behind me as we climbed. "You're not going to call my mom, are you?" he asked in a rush, finally realizing the implications of admitting an adult into a house full of hung-over teenagers.

"Is anyone dead?"

He had to think for a minute. "No…"

"Then it's not my business. Where is he?"

The boy—I supposed I was in the presence of Leo—stopped in the middle of the upstairs landing, which revealed a hallway with five closed doors. "*Octobong!*" he shouted, his morning rasp echoing off the high staircase. "*Hey, Octobong! Your dad's here!*"

"'Octobong'?" I muttered, but before Leo could explain, the door to my left opened, and Aiden stumbled out into the hall, his hair a mess of blond fuzz and his sweater tied around his chest like a pageant sash. "Have fun?" I asked.

He grinned and stretched. "Hey. Uh-huh."

"Some reason why you stayed out all night?"

Aiden blinked slowly, studying my expression, then saw I wasn't furious. "Olive left. I didn't have Meggy's number, so I thought, what the heck, plenty of floor here." He and Leo exchanged a sloppy high-five, and I steered him toward the staircase.

When the front door had closed behind us, I muttered, "Sorry, kid. I'll give you a phone next time."

"It's okay," he said, yawning. "Guys're awesome. Said I can come back next week."

"If you like." I waited until he climbed into the back seat, then asked, "What the hell is an octobong?"

Aiden smiled in the rearview mirror. "A plastic mixing bowl, some tubing, and a ton of duct tape."

Meggy turned around in her seat. "Simultaneous funneling?"

"Bingo." He yawned again and scratched his stomach. "It was a hit."

"Yeah?"

"Yeah. If you're going to be a nerd, you might as well do something socially useful with it." He leaned back and closed his eyes. "One of the juniors, Micah, his parents are going out of town next weekend, and they've got a beachfront place. Should be good. Thought I'd whip up a robotic cooler before then. Put some sand tires on it, basic steering. Think I've got most of the important parts already—hey, anyone have a spare cooler?"

"Not a problem," I replied, giving in to Meggy's pointed glances at the McDonald's up the road. "So you actually know something about robotics, do you?"

"I've had a lot of free time on my hands." He opened his eyes again as we turned into the drive-through lane. "Ooh, *hashbrowns*."

Apparently, Olive considered her happiness and Aiden's a zero-sum game. She moped about in her room while we began eating, ventured out only once the cloud of scented grease grew too intoxicating, and sullenly chewed in silence while Aiden described the night's revels. Meggy asked if she'd had fun, to which Olive muttered that she would have had a great time, had *someone* not been trying to steal her friends. Aiden's announcement that she was invited to the following Friday's scheduled bout of underage intoxication was greeted with a snort, a reprimand that she didn't hang around with losers, and a flounced exit to her room, complete with slammed door.

"And that's our cue," I said, cleaning up the leavings. "Meggy, just say the word."

But she shook her head and set her mouth into a grim line. "We'll get through this," she said. "It may kill us both, but we're going to get through this."

CHAPTER 10

Anyone who spent time around my mother quickly realized she was an unapologetic magpie. Anything—or anyone—that caught her eye was fair game, and much of her collection (the inanimate bits, at least) ended up in a grand storage room her staff had dubbed "the library." True, she had stolen her fair share of books, including a few the Arcanum would gladly have bought from me with first-born children, but her hoard was so much more than literary. As I began sorting through the mess, I found paintings, sculptures, jewels, maps, bits of colored glass, several centuries' worth of fancy dress—female and male—and even some pieces of armor and battered swords, which she had left scattered around like booby traps for unwary rummagers.

With the realm momentarily calm, Joey splitting his time between feeding Georgie and learning new types of pain, and Aiden holed up with a soldering iron, I had a chance to make progress on the library in peace. After hanging a canvas that looked suspiciously like a Van Gogh, I turned my efforts toward cleaning and cataloguing the massive book and manuscript collection. It couldn't be avoided. By then, I'd dabbled in books, either production or retail, for the better part of seven hundred years, and some habits die hard. Besides, there's something inherently soothing about a well-organized library.

And Mother's ran the gamut, from treatises on parchment (one partly in my hand, to my surprise) to a box of mass-market romance novels, all sporting a certain blond Italian on their covers. I was digging through a pile of paperbacks, pulling a few to offer Meggy for the discount rack, when a slim black box near the bottom caught my eye. Lifting the lid, I found a roll of vellum inside—the good stuff, white and hairless—and brought it to a cleared table for closer inspection.

It wasn't a monastic manuscript, as I'd first assumed. The hand was neat, but I puzzled over the script for a moment before I realized I was staring at written Fae, a rarity in a place run largely on institutional memory. The vellum struck me as odd, too, until I pinpointed what was bothering me about it: vellum, even the finest, often bears pores or veining on one side, marks of the animal from which it came. *This* vellum had no traces of follicles, but rather showed a strange pattern of lines...

And then it hit me—scales. The vellum had come from something scaled, and for a scroll that size, there was only one contender.

I was looking at dragonhide.

I caught myself glancing at the door guiltily, hoping Joey hadn't wandered in, but the door was still bolted, and I was alone with what appeared to be the underbelly of a dragon. Anchoring the end of the scroll, I started to unwind it down the table, then stretched the room and the tabletop until it gave out a hundred-odd feet later. I was momentarily impressed with the size of the beast, but then I recognized that I was probably seeing a juvenile spread before me.

The thought of housing a dragon twice that size gave me pause yet again. Feeding Georgie would present no problem, but if she were to get irked...

Pushing that possibility aside, I bent over the scroll to see what I'd discovered, other than an ulcer.

The work appeared to be in one hand, though the ink colors varied—not a single-day project by any means, especially considering the quantity of text crammed onto the hide. I found no trace of a signature, but I doubted I'd have recognized the author, given the subject matter. The scroll described years of dragon study, and I'd never known of anyone actively *raising* them in Faerie. Killing them or shooing them away, yes, but breeding a captive population? The idea was ludicrous.

My anonymous expert had seemingly lacked common sense or caution, however, as his notes and accompanying illustrations spoke of decades of research. He'd had at least sixty dragons on his hands over the course of his study, and he listed detailed specs on each, from size and weight to sire and clutch size. A convoluted table offered theories as to draconic coloration patterns, an attempt at Mendelian work with a species that only bred once or twice a century. He stressed that a black dragon could throw any color young, much to his apparent consternation, and described a piebald effect present in some of his subjects, leading to odd white beasts with purple or green splotches. A second-generation piebald was mostly white with black spots, and I tried to picture the sight of an overgrown, fire-breathing Dalmatian blocking out the sky.

Beyond the proto-genetics and breeding records, he had left a brief note in red ink that stirred my curiosity:

> *Draconic affection is fickle. The clutches I raised showed some degree of loyalty to me, but in general, the dragonets were more loyal to their mother than anyone. The lone exception is the fifteenth, a late hatch. I alone was present at the hatching, and the dragonet always showed me great affection. He could not bear to be separated from me as a juvenile, and consequently, he was amenable to training and instruction. Fifteen was willing to carry me. The same could not be said for his clutchmates.*

> *It seems that dragons look to the first conceivably parental figure as their mother, and their loyalty cannot be swayed, even when presented with their true dam. A breeder with well-timed hatching could, in theory, create a clutch of dragons*

loyal only to him. The drawback to this phenomenon is that a bonded dragon is loath to part from his "mother" while young, making it difficult to obtain privacy during the juvenile phase.

Georgie had clearly bonded with Joey, then, and if what I was seeing was accurate, she wasn't going anywhere as long as she had a vote in the matter. But conceivably, as long as she listened to Joey and I was on good terms with him, I wouldn't have a rampaging lizard to worry about. Feeling better about his new pet, I stepped a few feet down the scroll and continued to read:

Fire nearly impossible to produce in Faerie. Triggered by native ether of Gray Lands (investigate properties). Adequate etheric content in mortal realm to sustain production.

The notation was brief, but a clearer picture of the dragon breeder's research methods was coming into focus. I could only imagine good old Fifteen, sailing across the sky over some little village, setting fire to everything in its path. Small wonder dragons had fared so poorly in the literature.

I wanted to read on, but I suspected that Joey had a more pressing need for the information in the scroll, and so I carefully rolled it back into its box and recompressed the library to its usual dimensions. Tucking the box under my arm, I slipped outside and down to the barn, where I found Georgie eye-deep in a sheep, watching warily as Joey and Valerius took a water break. "Found something that might interest you," I told Joey, putting the box on a bale out of the way. "Someone did quite a bit of research on dragons. You should have a read when you're, uh…not busy."

"I could be not busy now," he replied too quickly.

Valerius shook his head. "The afternoon is young yet— we have work to do." He peered at the box, then nodded.

"Tyrel's notes?"

"They're unsigned," I said, leaning against the fence beside him. "Raised a bunch of dragons, maybe a touch obsessive?"

"Yes, that was Tyrel."

Up close, I could see a sheen on the captain's brow. It was nothing compared to the sweat and grime caked onto Joey, but it was a start. "He gave up the hobby?"

"You could say that." He caught my eye as Joey slipped off to hydrate, then looked at the dragonet ripping a carcass apart ten yards away. "Concluded his research. Started killing off his test subjects."

I whistled softly. "All of them?"

Valerius gulped his water and wiped his face on his tunic. "All but one. He'd hand-reared this little blue dragon...I guess he was saving that one for last, and the dragon got wise to him and struck first."

"You mean—"

"Ate him," he confirmed. "Well, his top half— someone found the dragon curled up around his legs." He shrugged and drank again. "No choice but to kill it. The queen was most displeased with Tyrel's death." He frowned in thought as his empty cup refilled. "Lizard was acting in self-defense, if you ask me, but she didn't."

I watched Joey climb over the fence into the sheep pen and give Georgie a deep rub over the eyes. "Maybe we shouldn't mention that story to him yet."

Valerius snorted into his drink. "Understatement, my lord?"

It was strange, I mused, watching Joey and the dragonet interact from the safety of the other side of the fence. Joey had experience with horses, that I knew, but I hadn't expected it to translate so easily. Then again, what did I know? I'd kept my dealings with horses to a minimum, making them work for me only with a liberal dose of enchantment. Horses inevitably shied and went white-eyed around me, and they fought the magic that kept them from fleeing. Whenever I had to borrow one, I'd let someone else stable it and calm it down, as there was no sense in prolonging the animal's distress with my continued proximity.

But Joey and Georgie were perfectly relaxed with each other, and the little dragon continued to eat and grunt with pleasure as he gave her a sort of deep-tissue massage. He even straddled her back to rub her shoulders, and Georgie never so much as looked up from her carcass. As he moved down toward her wings, Joey hesitated, then lowered his full weight onto Georgie's back. She glanced up at that and turned her head to see what he was doing, but seemed only curious. He stood again and scratched her blood-spattered nose, and she resumed her attack on lunch.

"Valerius," I said quietly, "how soon until she flies?"

The captain leaned on the fence and rubbed his chin. "Difficult to say, my lord. It's been years since Tyrel…" He considered the subject before him in silence, then asked, "How old is she, would you estimate?"

"No more than twenty days, I'd say. Surely we have some time yet before she's airborne."

"Some," he allowed, "but they mature rapidly, as I recall. What did Tyrel say?"

"I didn't read that far. Let's see, shall we?"

While Joey was occupied, we took the box into the barn and unrolled the scroll again on a stone bench I created for the moment. Valerius and I took opposite ends, scanning for useful information. I'd not progressed more than five feet when he called, "My lord? There's a chart down here."

I jogged to the other end of the hide and followed Valerius's finger down to a neat calendar in green ink. A few seconds later, I looked up again and realized why his face was drawn. "A week? We've got a bare *week*?"

"If this is accurate—"

"Why wouldn't it be? The fool raised his own…uh…"

I paused, flummoxed. "A collective of dragons is called what, exactly?"

"A pestilence? An inferno?" he suggested, leaning against a stack of bales. "A flock?"

"A mess, perhaps. He had a mess of dragons. Anyway, he'd be the expert, yes?" I tapped the scroll, mentally berating myself for getting oil on the vellum. "Flying by their thirtieth day. Even if she's just testing her wings by then…"

Valerius nodded. "The boy's going to need equipment."

"You think *he* can hold her down?" I scoffed. "Look, there's a growth chart…she's going to double in size in a few weeks! I doubt he has the strength now, let alone—"

"That's not what I meant," he replied, staring out the barn door as Georgie nudged the remnants of the sheep toward Joey. "He's going to need a saddle."

I joined him in a moment of silent observation. "You think he's going to try it?"

"Why wouldn't he? Wouldn't you, were you in his position?"

"I don't know, a fall from *that*…"

Valerius shrugged and refilled his cup again. "He said he's a horseman. It can't be too difficult transitioning to dragonback, can it?"

I snorted at that. "You've had ample experience with horses, have you, Captain?"

"Of course not," he muttered into his cup. "They won't tolerate me." He drank and glanced at me out of the corner of his eye. "I served as a legionary and not a cavalryman for a reason, my lord. Difficult to progress in the equites if you can't get near the damn mounts."

"I didn't know you'd served."

"Briefly. My father had the wealth and the clout to put me among the equites, but we both knew that wouldn't work, and I landed with the principes. Something of an embarrassment to the family, I suppose, but at least there were no horses."

I hesitated, unaccustomed to hearing Valerius offer anything about his past. "What happened?"

He drank slowly, then destroyed the cup and folded his arms. "Ever worn armor, my lord?"

"Managed to avoid it."

"Congratulations. It's a special sort of torment. A necessary evil, but you pray your tunic doesn't rip." He sighed softly as his mouth tightened. "I went to Celtiberia when I was twenty-three. We skirmished with the natives outside a village—I never knew its name. One of my friends fell. I couldn't get to him in time, not on foot, but—"

"Shielded?" I guessed.

Valerius continued to gaze into the distance. "Saved his life. I didn't know what I was doing, but I knew I was doing it—I knew nothing of magic, and yet I *knew* what I was doing. Does that make sense?" He closed his eyes and rubbed his temples. "Confusing for me, terrifying for the rest of the men. They drove me off at swordpoint that night." When he looked in my direction again, I could tell he wasn't seeing me. "Wandered for a time, lived off the land, and then one of the queen's guards found me—she was traveling in Hispania, and I stumbled into camp. Offered my sword for my life, and that was that."

"And you never went home again."

He shook his head. "She always wanted me at her side when she was here, and she never gave me leave to travel. But it was for the best," he added, brightening. "She granted me a boon for my service—a complex enchantment. Rome will be protected as long as I serve the court." He smiled to himself and briefly chuckled. "My brothers' distant grandsons may be senators now. I've often wondered."

I stared at Valerius, momentarily speechless, then managed to lift my jaw off the proverbial floor while I scrambled for a response. "Captain...I'm not sure how to tell you this, but there hasn't been a senate in years."

His brows furrowed. "My lord?"

Before I could begin to explain, Joey limped into the barn and past the dragon scroll. "All right, I'm hydrated," he said, taking a seat on a low bale, "so let the beating resume." He paused, looked at our expressions, then asked, "Something wrong?"

"What do you know of the Senate?" Valerius asked him.

"Which one?" he replied, frowning in confusion.

I caught his eye, trying to silently warn him as I mumbled, "Roman Republic."

"The king said it has disbanded," Valerius continued, focusing on Joey. "Do you know about this?"

"Uh…crap," he muttered, oblivious to the situation, "I've never been good with dates. Help me out, Colin, Rome fell in the fifth century, right?"

The captain looked stricken, and Joey turned to me for a hint as to his sudden distress. "The capital still exists," I said quickly to Valerius before Joey could make matters worse.

"Yeah, I visited Rome during seminary," Joey added. "Vatican museums, you know? Hey, I saw the Colosseum. It's, uh…it's still there. Really nice city—"

"The *what?*" Valerius interrupted, his voice colored with panic.

"Built in the first century A.D.," I muttered to Joey. "After his time."

"Seriously?" Joey cocked his head and stared at Valerius. "How old *are* you, anyway?"

But Valerius had begun to pace and clutched at his head. "She swore to me, on her life she swore," he mumbled. "I served her, she protected Rome. That was all I asked, and she…" He whipped around and pointed at me, demanding, "Does Rome stand, yes or no?"

I sensed rather than saw Joey's hand creep toward the practice blade at his hip—Valerius's wild eyes were enough to give any sane man pause—and I shoved the kid behind me. "No," I said as calmly as I could. "Not for many years."

His breathing quickened. "How long?"

At a loss for a better solution, I opted for the truth. "If I remember my history, Rome as you knew it ended a little over two thousand years ago. You couldn't have been here that long when the Empire began."

He sank onto a bale and shook his head, then croaked, "What happened?"

"Augustus Caesar, as I recall. The Senate transferred power to a dictator, and then a string of emperors." I paused, watching his face work. "And then the Empire split in two. The Germanic tribes took care of the west, and the Ottomans finished off the east. But the capital stands—there's a successor state built around it. It's...well, it's not what it once was," I admitted, "but that's the story of Europe. I mean, look, I lived in my father's land for years. We had Normans, and then we had the Tudors—there wasn't a free Ireland until 1949." Valerius looked at me blankly, and I amended, "Sixty-four years ago. What I'm trying to say is that the damn continent seldom remains stable."

He continued to watch me despondently, and I was struggling with a response when Joey slipped past me and into Valerius's line of sight. "Let me get this straight," he said. "Titania promised to protect Rome if you worked for her?" Valerius nodded silently, and Joey rubbed his stubble. "Shit, man. All this time, and no one mentioned that it fell? Or the—" He paused, nodded curtly, then turned and gripped my shoulder. "Come on, walk with me," he muttered. "I need to show you something in the sheep pen."

I, too, had seen the wet glint in the captain's eyes, and I didn't need further encouragement to leave him to his thoughts.

The stars came out that evening, and still Valerius had yet to check in with me, a deviation that portended nothing good. I waited until the crescent moon was high, then strolled back to the barn, where I found Joey asleep in the loft, Georgie curled up below him, and Valerius sitting on the fence, watching the herd grow. "Tell me to go away if you're not in the mood," I began, leaning on the rail beside him. "You're not going to hurt my feelings."

He sighed to himself. "Do you need me, my lord?"

"No. But I'm worried about you."

"I'm not going to borrow Joey's sword, if that's what you were insinuating," he replied, then slid down the fence to make room. "Not tonight, at least."

I climbed up next to him and passed a flask. "Hate to tell you, but I incinerated what was left of Mother. There's nothing to stab."

"I wasn't planning to use it on her." He considered the flask, then drank deeply and coughed. "Ever think of being finished with this business?"

His expression was inscrutable in the low light, but his tone betrayed his unspoken thoughts. "Honestly? Yes. Who hasn't after a few centuries?" I said, taking my turn with the bourbon. "But somehow, I keep finding reasons to press on."

Valerius waited until the flask returned to him, then quietly said, "I've thought of it many times. How best to do it. Angering the queen would have been too risky, so I thought iron was the safest method. And after some of the things she asked me to do..." He considered the open flask, then drank until he gasped for air. "Do you know what stayed my hand?" he choked out. "She'd promised protection as long as I served her court. Can't serve her dead, can I? Can't serve her at all now." He nudged a wayward sheep back toward the herd with his boot. "And it was all a lie—a joke to her? Has my life been nothing but a long *joke*?"

We sat mutely until the silence was broken by a

surprised bleating in the distance.

"Boy's right about the sheep," he mumbled.

"I know," I said, and rubbed my arms against the growing chill. "Valerius...you owe me nothing. If you want to remain in my service, I'll gladly have you. But if there's something you'd rather do—"

"Such as? What would I do? I've done nothing else here, and if the world I knew is truly dust..." He hesitated, then added, "I'd hoped to meet some of my brothers' kin someday. A foolish thought, wasn't it?"

"It's...unlikely," I allowed. "Not *impossible*, but with so many generations...when, exactly, were you born?"

He shifted his weight on the rail. "The summer before we defeated the Poeni for the second time."

I thought hard, trying to remember what I'd learned of the ancient Mediterranean. "Hannibal?"

"Yes. The consulship of Servilius and Claudius Nero. Do you know their names, my lord?"

"I don't, but I can estimate from that. Twenty-two centuries? That's sixty or seventy generations, but there's a chance..." I pulled my homemade phone from my pocket, dialed, and waited while it rang on the other end as Valerius watched me curiously. The ringing gave way to a low grunt quickly enough, and I wondered what time it was in Montana. "Toula? Hi. I need a witch."

"Screw you," she grumbled, and the phone went dead in my hand.

Valerius frowned, but I put the phone away and pointed to the gate opening behind us. "She loves me, she just doesn't know it. Ah, Glinda," I called as Toula stomped through, sporting a ragged gray T-shirt and plaid boxers. "A vision, as always."

One finger rose in an unmistakable salute as she smoothed her drooping spikes with her other hand. "You got a death wish, Gramps?"

"Not tonight. How's your blood magic?"

Toula closed the gate and folded her arms. "Decent.

What were you after, and will this piss Greg off?"

"I'm looking for a kinship trace, and no," I replied, cocking my head at Valerius. "Living relatives—can you work with him?"

She mumbled under her breath until a glowing orb rose before her, lighting a path through the grass. "With whom? *You?*" she asked Valerius. "Misplaced your kids or something?"

"I have none," he said, eyeing her with caution. "My brothers' descendants—"

"Ooh, that's a problem," she replied, and sucked her teeth. "Blood works vertically—anyone in your direct line. Parents, children, grandparents, grandkids, you get the drill. But tell you what," she added, seeing his face fall, "it would work from your parents. A blood trace from either of them would lead to your nephews and nieces."

"Impossible," he mumbled. "My father's long dead, and my brothers were his alone."

She squinted back at him. "So…you're half fae?"

"Presumably. Affinity for magic, allergy to iron."

"Yeah, sounds about right. Well, shit," she muttered, and frowned at the night as she thought. "Who's your mother, then?"

"She never claimed me. All I know is I'm not the queen's," he said with a weak smile.

"Ah." She scratched her ribs and yawned. "If you think she's still around, I could use blood magic to track her. But if you're looking for mortal relatives…well, there's an option, but it's a long shot." She propped one foot on the fence and leaned past me to talk to the captain. "Aural comparison. I've never worked with mundane lines, but that doesn't mean I *can't*. It just means the pool is massive. But here's what I can do: I'll store your signature—your paternal half, at least—and if I get a chance to look at anyone promising, I'll see if I can get a match. Your ancestry is…"

"Roman, back to the founding."

Toula cut her eyes to me, and I nodded. "Born in the Republic."

"Oy," she said, rubbing a quartz band on her left index finger. "Lot of generations in there. Half of Italy might conceivably be part of that line, you know?" She shrugged. "Hell, maybe it'll help my odds. I'm Toula, by the way," she added, jutting her hand toward Valerius. "Don't think Colin's ever made the formal introductions. Grand magus's go-between."

He clasped her hand and smiled with more enthusiasm. "Valerius. You're the wizard the realm dislikes, yes?" he asked, glancing at me for verification.

"The realm dislikes all wizards," I replied before Toula could protest. "And she's actually a witch-blood."

Valerius examined her face more closely in the orb's light, and his eyes widened in recognition. "Of course. I arrived late, but you were there…"

"I offed Titania," she finished for him, releasing her grip. "And Gramps offed *my* mother, but that still doesn't give him permission to get me out of bed at ungodly hours," she added, glaring for good measure.

He frowned bemusedly. "Your mother—"

"Mab. Ready?" she asked, avoiding the conversation. Valerius nodded, and Toula started muttering her incantation, a long string of bastardized Latin I assumed to be of her own creation.

As the ghost of a sphere began to materialize, Valerius murmured, "Your accent is terrible."

Toula opened one eye and paused the spell. "Man, *you* try learning a dead language, and then we can talk about nuances. Now let me work."

He withheld further criticism, and a moment later, a red and blue sphere appeared before him. Toula cracked her neck and peered at the lattice, then split it into its component halves. "Okay, that's your father," she explained, pointing to the blue side. "Your half brothers carried that as well, and anyone down their line would have a hint of it. See how tight the weave is?" she said, then pointed to the red side. "Fae. Fewer generations, less complex. Your mother…"

Toula studied the red lattice for a moment in silence, then tapped out a complicated pattern on her ring. The quartz illuminated from within, and a set of spheres appeared above her hand, mostly green and blue. "I store what I've seen for later comparison," she said, beating me to my question, "and that lattice looks familiar." She repeatedly flicked her wrist to the side, cycling through the projected orbs until a red lattice appeared. "Bingo," she muttered, then held her hand near Valerius's lattice to compare.

"Identical," he whispered as the images aligned. "What does that mean?"

She looked up from her work and bit her lip. "Well, um…all full siblings carry the same aural signatures. A common partial lattice in two people's signatures means they have either a shared ancestor or ancestors who had the same parents, yes?"

He nodded. "So…that thing in your hand, that's either my mother or one of her siblings?"

"Exactly. And it would have to be a full sibling." Toula turned to me with a strange expression on her face. "Was Mab an only child?"

Valerius jumped in before I could answer. "None of the Three had full siblings," he replied. "And by the time I came to the realm, they had eliminated their half siblings." He paused briefly, puzzling over the question, before the realization hit. "That's from *Mab*?" he exclaimed. "My mother was of Mab's line?"

"No. She *was* Mab," said Toula, and projected a red and green sphere from her ring. "This is my signature—it's where I got her lattice to start with. I, uh…I guess that means we're…you know." She closed her hand into a fist, and both the projection and Valerius's sphere vanished. "Look, you don't have to worry," she said quietly, "I'm not going to say anything. If I come across any of your other people, I'll be in touch." She cleared her throat, nodded curtly, and ripped open a new gate with a wave of her hand. "Good night," she mumbled, and started toward home.

"Toula, wait!" Valerius called after her, jumping off the fence. "Don't go, I—"

She stopped in her tracks, took a deep breath, and turned around. "Really, I promise," she said, holding her empty palms up to stop his progress, "no one's going to know. I can keep my mouth shut."

He paused a few feet from her, watching her redden in the glow of her lantern orb. "You...you're my sister?" he murmured.

"I'm sorry."

"For what?"

Toula hugged herself and scowled at the grass. "My name is Toula Pavli," she muttered. When that garnered no response, she added, "My father was Apollonios Pavli." Valerius remained silent, and she sighed. "You don't know who he was, do you?"

"Should I?"

"Arcanum executed him for mass murder," she said, her face hardening even as it burned. "So, that plus Mab...yeah, sorry, I'll keep quiet. No one's going to know."

He caught her arm before she could slip through the gate, and she turned again, confused. "Please stay. Please, I..." he started, then faltered and tried again. "Please."

She looked down at his hand, perplexed by its presence on her triceps. "You have my word, I won't—"

"You're my *sister*."

I couldn't see his expression from my perch, but Toula's brows knit as she looked back at him. "I won't tell—"

"I've never had a sister," he interrupted in a rush. "Well, perhaps I *have*," he amended, "but none I've known as mine..." He grabbed her hands and peered at her flushed face. "You're really my sister? Truly?"

Toula's mouth opened and closed silently, and then she found her voice once more. "I...yeah, I guess I'm your half sister..."

The end of that thought was squeezed from her as Valerius pulled her into a rib-crushing embrace. When he let her breathe once more, she took a step back and shook her head. "I don't understand, you, uh...you're not upset?"

"Why would I be upset?" he exclaimed, still clinging to her arms. "Have you any idea how long I've been alone? I haven't known any family in...how long was it, my lord?" he asked, glancing over his shoulder.

"Twenty-two hundred years, give or take," I replied, slipping off the fence.

Valerius nodded emphatically at Toula. "And this is the best thing to happen in many of them, so please stay. Will you stay? Say you will, please..."

I approached in time to see Toula's eyes well. "I don't...I mean...you actually *want* to be kin to me?" she asked incredulously, her voice wavering.

"Why wouldn't I?"

"*No one* wants me," was all she managed before the tears began to spill. Valerius pulled her back into his arms as Toula, who had watched her own mother die without flinching, sobbed like a child.

One of the gifts that come with age is knowing when one's presence is no longer desired. I closed the gate Toula had opened and sneaked away, leaving them to get acquainted in private. Although I intended to retire, however, I soon found myself lingering outside the open door of Aiden's room.

He looked up from his cooler—now equipped with tires and a little antenna—and grinned at my knock. "Hey! Check it out, I got the wheels synchronized," he said, climbing off the floor to grab a joystick from his desk. "The basics are down, but I want to program a few tricks in—make it pop a wheelie or something. Maybe tomorrow, huh?"

Aiden tiptoed barefoot through a minefield of spare parts to join me, then coaxed the cooler to life and promptly drove it into the wall. "Steering's a little touchy," he muttered, throwing it into reverse and nudging it into a five-point turn, "but that's adjustable."

The cooler drove straight into my shins, and Aiden mumbled an apology as he parked it. "Impressive," I said, rubbing the impact site. "Have you tried it loaded?"

He flipped the lid up with the touch of a button. "Not yet. Want to do the honors?"

I filled the bin with ice and brown bottles, and Aiden plucked one out for an inspection. "Root beer?" he enquired, flipping the unlabeled bottle around in his hand.

"Small beer," I explained. "Slakes your thirst, but won't get you drunk quite as quickly. It's about three proof."

Aiden nodded, seemingly satisfied, and popped the cap against the edge of the cooler's new wheel frame. "Not bad," he said after a quick swig. "Not great, but not bad. You want one?" he added, lifting another bottle from the ice.

The hour was late, the room was a steel-strewn disaster, but my little brother's eyes were hopeful. "Sure," I said, and made myself a couch in a distant corner free of scrap metal while he practiced drinking and driving his new toy.

Perhaps, I mused—and not for the first time that season—I wasn't the world's best role model.

CHAPTER 11

I woke the next morning with a vague sense that something was amiss. The bed was as I had last seen it, and the sunlight was the proper shade of orange-pink— not too early, not too late—but the atmosphere of my chambers felt *off*, and I struggled to put a label on the problem while I rose and ran through my mental to-do list. And then it hit me: it was too quiet. Oh, the realm was still there at the back of my thoughts, omnipresent and finicky as always, but something in the quality of the sound around me had changed. I sat on the edge of the bed, hearing nothing but my own breathing, and listened, trying to pinpoint what was different.

I was alone.

Seldom did my suite go unguarded, and so I sneaked over to the door, called up a fireball, and cracked the door open, halfway expecting to find a mob quietly skulking in the corridor—but there was no one present, and I let the fire die. Puzzled, I barricaded myself in the room and tried to piece together what could have happened. Valerius made the rota for my guards, but he always checked with me first thing in the morning in case something had happened overnight…

Valerius. I'd left him with Toula, and then there had been Aiden's pet project, and finding my way to bed a few hours before…

The problem, I concluded with relative rapidity, considering the hour, was that I'd misplaced my captain.

Two minutes later, I let myself into my office and

found a folded piece of paper on the floor waiting for me. A note under the door, I realized, and opened it to see a nearly illegible blue scrawl:

Hey Gramps,

I'm taking V on vacation for a bit. Don't be difficult—I told him you wouldn't mind, and he needs this. Try to be cool and deal with it, okay?

XOXO,
T

I leaned against one of the couches and endeavored to let that sink in, but was finding the exercise trying without coffee. The Arcanum's punkish problem child and my shaken, depressed captain, a man who'd probably never even heard of electricity, running around together somewhere in the mortal realm—the thought was enough to knot my stomach, but I attempted to relax. Toula wasn't stupid. Surely she wouldn't let Valerius play in traffic. Surely she'd warn him about the iron hidden everywhere. Surely she wouldn't take him anywhere with a strong Arcanum presence.

Moon and stars, surely he hadn't gone *armed.*

I was fairly confident that I could have tracked them down—Greg would have known how to find Toula, at least—but I forced myself to let the matter go. Valerius was no child, and Toula...well, technically, she wasn't one, either. I could manage without them for a time, and I knew Joey wouldn't mind a chance to lick his wounds.

And so I went about my business for the next two days, arbitrating a few disputes, making sure Aiden stopped working for food breaks, but generally slipping off to see Meggy. With Olive in school and the bookstore traffic slow, I assumed she would have time to meet me. Wednesday passed pleasantly enough—Olive had practice that evening, and so we had a chance to grab a midweek dinner in front of the television before our daughter dragged herself in, caught me on the couch with a pizza, and wailed that Meggy's rules about boyfriends were completely arbitrary and unfair, and that we were trying to make her life miserable. I explained that the first thing on my mind every morning was finding new ways to torture her, which merited rolled eyes, a slammed door, and Meggy's pursed-lip disapproval.

I'd planned to coax Meggy out for a picnic the next day, but when I showed up at the store around ten, I discovered that she had company. Meggy glanced away from her customer at the sound of the bell and shot me a quick look of desperation, then turned her attention and polite smile back to the thin man lecturing her from the far side of the counter. "Really? And how's that going for you?" she asked him as I closed the door, but piercing his monologue did nothing to impede its progress.

The shadows obscured his features, but I recognized Stuart the White's slightly nasal tone and skinny frame. "Early lunch break, Stu?" I asked, hoping to distract him.

Stuart jerked in surprise, peered down the aisle at me, and frowned. "Christophe."

"Close enough," I replied, striding toward the counter. "Hi, Meggy. Any chance of stealing you for lunch?"

She cocked her head at the ceiling. "Well, I'd have to consider my day planner, but yeah, on preliminary assessment, I think I can squeeze you in. Thoughts?"

"Beach picnic? The pavilion's empty—"

Before I could finish my sentence, Stuart's eyes widened. "An excellent idea! You know, I saw evidence of fairy activity there about a week ago…"

As he launched into his story, I locked eyes with Meggy and silently sighed. The only faerie activity that pavilion had ever seen was on a moonless night the previous August when Meggy and I thought we had the beach to ourselves—and *that* was almost interrupted by a quartet of marauding teenagers—but there's no dissuading a true believer, and the chance to further his research brought color to Stuart's cheeks. Before I quite realized what had happened, our lunch for two had become a three-top, and Stuart walked between us all the way to the corner market and back down to the shore, chatting nonstop about lights in the sky and his "little wingèd friends."

"You know," I managed to interject when he broke for air, "I was recently talking to a paranormal investigator who lives in the area—"

"Please," Stuart scoffed, dropping his heavy shopping bag onto a splintering picnic table, "those amateurs wouldn't know a ghost if one came up and socked them in the jaw. Now, to summon and trap a spirit, one must take proper precautions…"

Across the table, Meggy's eyebrow rose in silent accusation: *You had to start him up again.*

Sorry, I mouthed, and set about unpacking the provisions while listening to Stuart just attentively enough to make noncommittal sounds in the proper places. I'd located the wine and was crafting a plausible pocket corkscrew under the table when I heard him say, "I'm afraid these charlatans are like bees to honey with conventions, Meghan, so we may run across a few on Saturday. Never fear, I know how to spot them a mile away."

You're thinking of flies to honey, I almost said, then replayed what I had heard and snapped up from my work. "Saturday? What's happening Saturday?"

Stuart's eyes practically twinkled. "Paranormal convention in Richmond," he replied. "Meghan and I are driving over to see the wares. We're expecting several of the top small-press publishers in the field, excellent material. I'd invite you along," he added with a mockery of an apologetic smile, "but I'm afraid you'd find it incredibly dull. And anyway, my car only seats two."

"Meggy has a sedan," I said, fighting the urge to slap

the grin off his face.

"Yes, but I'd hate to ask her to drive," he replied, calmly unwrapping his pastrami on rye. "Besides, this really is an industry event—we'll be looking at books all day, and you…" He paused to give me a condescending once-over. "Well, Chip, all you'd bring to the party would be bad vibes. A convention like this is no place for a *skeptic*," he concluded, pronouncing the final word as if he desperately needed to spit out something foul and was trying to be polite.

I kept telling myself to be the bigger man and let it go, but then Stuart reached over and patted my Meggy's hand.

There were six picnic tables in that pavilion. The unoccupied five burst into splinters, one by one, as Meggy screamed and ducked under our table for safety. Stuart jumped onto the cluttered tabletop, spread his hands, and began yelling an incantation at the troublesome spirit, but then a log just happened to fly up from the closest table explosion, slam into his stomach, and throw him off his feet.

I admit now that it was petty, childish, and completely unnecessary, but I felt so much better once I'd knocked the wind out of him.

As I sat there, placidly soaking in the destruction, Meggy grabbed my ankle and dragged me under the table. "The hell?" she hissed as Stuart wheezed above us. "What is your *problem*?"

"Run…" Stuart gasped. "Run, Meghan…I…fight…"

"You could have killed him," she whispered. Her furious glare suggested she'd rather be shouting.

"Just say the word," I whispered back.

She slid away from me, her expression a blend of shock and disgust, then slapped me across the face. "Hold on, Stuart, I'm going to help you," she said, climbing out from under the table. "You hang on, buddy, I think it's gone. Come on, up and at 'em."

Stunned, I sat in the sand and dirt under the table,

rubbing my smarting cheek, as Meggy coaxed Stuart to his feet and half-carried him out of the pavilion. And when they had shrunk to shadows in the parking lot, I finally looked around again, watched the fine wood particles fall through a shaft of sunlight from the leaking roof, and felt very small indeed.

Repairing the picnic tables was a moment's work, but I had no idea what to do about Meggy. I'd never seen her so angry, and experience counseled that the last person she wanted to see at that moment was me, regardless of whether I came with an apology. But that left me with a conundrum—Valerius was gone, Greg and I hadn't spoken since Aiden left the silo, and I knew with all certainty that I had no desire to relate what I'd done to Joey or my brother. Slim wouldn't open his doors until six, and something told me that Mrs. Cooper, though exasperated with her grandnephew's antics, would be less than sympathetic.

And so, fresh out of options, I found myself walking into the lobby of Sacred Heart's parish office. It might have been my imagination, but I thought I felt a twinge of the Catholic guilt that seemed to permeate the building. "Is Father Paul in?" I asked the receptionist, a dour-looking crone in an incongruously cheery pink sweater with frolicking cats around the collar.

She glanced up from her computer and pursed her pale lips. "Do you have an appointment, young man?"

"No. Tell him it's Colin."

She seemed to disapprove of my continued presence in the lobby, but she picked up the phone and tapped out an extension. "Colin…"

"Leffee," I finished, retreating to the sofa and its faded needlepoint pillows of the Virgin and Child. "If he's not busy."

The person at the other end answered, and she shushed

me with her free hand. "Father, there's someone here to see you, a Mr. Leffee? Are you…yes, all right, I'll tell him." She hung up and frowned back at me. "He'll see you. Down the hall, third door on the left."

I mumbled the requisite thanks and slipped past her, then rapped on Paul's door and let myself in. "Got a moment?"

"Should have a few left," he replied, wincing as he rose from his desk. "What, your phone's tapped now? Come in, sit down," he said, and pointed to a pair of well-worn armchairs. "What's the trouble? I haven't been called in—"

"Nothing like that," I said, closing the door. "And that's a lovely receptionist you have."

"Yes, Doris is a peach," he muttered, settling into one of the chairs, "but she's the only person around here who understands the payroll software, so we're stuck together. Is Joseph all right? I haven't seen him in a few weeks— what's he doing these days, anyhow?"

I took the other chair and rested my forehead on my fingertips. "Raising a dragon, but that's not why I'm here."

"He's doing *what?*"

"He can tell you himself at his next confession. I…" I exhaled slowly and closed my eyes. "I fucked up with Meggy."

His chair creaked as he settled himself in. "You want to tell me about it?"

And so I did—Stuart, lunch, the pavilion, the tables, the slap that still stung, everything. When I finished, I looked up again and found him watching me, legs crossed, fingers steepled under his chin. "So what do I do?" I asked.

The priest blinked, then glanced at the brown water stain on the ceiling. "Well, setting aside for the moment the fact that you've come to *me*, of all people, for relationship advice," he replied, "you give it time, and you give her space, because yeah, old timer, you fucked that one up pretty thoroughly."

"No absolution and Hail Marys?"

"You know, something tells me the Blessed Mother's not going to help you out on this one," he said with a smirk. "In all seriousness, I'd give it at least a few days before you come crawling back—and I do mean the crawling bit," he added, giving me a hard look over his reading glasses. "One doesn't just get over seeing one's, uh...*partner* in a jealous rage, particularly when said partner is *you*. For heaven's sake, Colin, what were you thinking?"

I leaned back against the chair and sighed. "I have a temper—"

"Tell me something I didn't know."

"I have a temper," I repeated, giving him a pointed glare, "and he was provoking me. I mean, when you think about it, he was practically asking for it."

"*Colin.*"

"And he's trying to steal Meggy!" I continued, ignoring Paul's disapproval. "I'm sitting right there, and he's going on about taking her on a trip, and he looks at me like I'm some sort of *imbecile*—"

"So you knock the ever-loving crap out of him? Scare him half to death?" he retorted. "You think the way to Meggy's heart is by making her fear you?"

"Of course not!" I protested. "He—"

"Forget about him. This is about you." Paul leaned forward and stared at me silently until I met his eyes. "I've seen what you're capable of," he said softly. "There have been times out there that you've put the fear of God in me, and I had a pretty healthy fear of Him to begin with."

I sputtered for a few seconds before I could formulate a response. "Paul, you know me! Have I *ever* hurt you?"

"Not seriously. Not on purpose, anyway," he allowed. "But when you lose it...Colin," he sighed, "I've seen you in judge-jury-executioner mode. Don't get me wrong," he hastily added, "you're damn good at what you do, and anyone in the know appreciates it. But it's one thing to know how you operate, and it's quite another to be standing two feet away from the firefight." Paul spread his gnarled hands. "I like you, Colin. I've trusted you more times than I can count. But I'm going to be honest—you scare me sometimes."

"But I—"

"I know you wouldn't hurt me on purpose," he continued over my protestations. "But step back and try to put yourself in my shoes, eh? I like to think I'm a halfway decent priest, but I was a lousy fighter in my prime, and that was ages ago. And I'm out there pitted against something I can't see half the damn time, fighting with you—and let's face it, unless you wind up down a silver mine, you're pretty much invincible."

"Hardly."

"Compared to me, you are. And then there's the fireballs, the lightning, the acid that once—remember, you melted holes in that hotel's carpet?—the...you know, the *magic*. I can't wield magic," he murmured. "I can't even sense it. It could be all around me, and I'd never know it."

I sniffed, detecting a faint, familiar whiff of citronella. "It *is* all around you."

"Exactly. Can't see it, can't touch it, can't use it—can't protect myself from it. I know you've looked out for me," he said before I could counter that, "but when we're out there together, I'm at your mercy. And having seen what happens to those who make you angry..."

He let that thought die unfinished and waited.

After a long moment, I cleared my throat. "I've never lashed out at you. I never would."

"I realize that. You're still one scary son of a bitch." He paused, but I had no defense to offer. "If you really love Meggy—and something tells me you do—you'll rein it in," he continued. "Prove to her you're not a complete psychopath." He saw me stiffen and held up one finger. "I'm not saying you *are*—I'm saying you acted like one. Am I wrong?"

"No," I admitted, dropping my eyes to the rug to avoid

his stare. "I try not to."

"I know that. And I know it's in you," he said gently. "You are what you are, I'm not damning you. But I know that my friend can be better than that. Yes?"

His words hung there for a long moment, and I finally nodded. "Thank you."

"Of course. But do us all a favor and stay away from Meggy for a while, hmm? I'm sure she's doing her own thinking right now." He leaned back again and snorted. "Seriously, you threw a *bench* into him?"

"Not a whole bench…"

"The fact that we're using qualifiers is enough. Are you really that insecure? You think you're going to lose her to some third-rate pagan?"

"I lost her once," I snapped. "Jack Horn, remember?"

"Oh, I remember," said Paul as he folded his arms. "I remember how Meggy came to me for weeks after you ran off, begging me to help her find you. And I *certainly* remember how I lied to that girl's face to cover your ass."

Paul had a point, and we both knew it. "I've never felt about anyone how I feel about her," I muttered. "And for that little shit to try to take her from me—"

"What you're not understanding is that she's not his to take. She's not yours to take, either. She's not a damn trophy, Colin."

"You know what I mean."

"I'm not entirely certain that I do, actually," he replied. "Do we need to have a talk about women's liberation? They haven't been chattel in quite a while."

"I *did* live through the twentieth century," I retorted. "And I've never thought of Meggy as…*chattel*. But he's blatantly trying to steal—"

"Again with the property," Paul interrupted. "Here, try to see it like this instead: she's not a possession you two idiots fight to own. She *gives* an interest in herself to whomsoever she chooses, just as you give an interest in yourself to her. And if something changes, she takes that interest back." He let that sink in, then said, "You don't fight for her by annihilating anyone who crosses her path and gives her a second look. You fight with yourself to be the man she loves. But what do I know?" he asked, linking his hands behind his head. "I'm only the exorcist in the room. That's my two cents' worth, whatever it means to you."

"Appreciated," I replied, leaning on the armrest. "And what's your going rate for therapy these days?"

"Seeing as I'm still unlicensed," he said with a grin, "it's gratis. Just tell Joseph to stop by. I need to hear about this new enterprise of his." He pushed himself from his chair with a little grunt. "Dragon, you say?"

"She's kind of cute for an oversized lizard."

He shook his head brusquely. "No such thing as a cute lizard. What are we talking, something like a komodo dragon?"

"Something like a *dragon* dragon."

Paul looked down at me, then slowly rubbed his hand over his face. "Colin, I'm trusting you with that nice kid," he muttered. "Please don't let him get eaten. I'm already on the seminary's blacklist since he dropped out—they're never going to give me an assistant again if I get one killed. Just…tell him to come to confession. I'm sure he needs it by now."

Some might suggest that taking relationship advice from a man who considered himself married to the Church was a risky proposition, but Paul had a sense for people, and he'd never shied away from telling me when I was making an ass of myself. And so I resolved to keep my distance from Meggy for a time—at least through the weekend. Surely, I reasoned, I could last that long.

Of course, that meant avoiding Rigby's game that Friday.

I tried breaking the news to Aiden with little

explanation, but he saw the truth almost immediately. "You and Meggy had a fight, didn't you?" he said, continuing to tighten a wrist screw on the sort of exoskeleton he'd constructed around his left hand.

"Something like that," I muttered. "And what the hell is—"

"Bioelectric control unit." He dropped the screwdriver onto the midden masquerading as a desk, then swiveled in his chair, extended his hand toward the cooler, and beckoned with two fingers. A light atop the cooler's lid switched from amber to green, the motor purred, and the cooler lurched forward across the field of detritus hiding Aiden's floor. He waited until it had almost closed the distance, then turned his palm out, throwing on the brakes. A flick of finger and thumb opened the lid, and he looked back at me with a cocked eyebrow.

"*How* much time did you spend alone in your room last year?" I asked, trying to puzzle out how he'd accomplished the trick without betraying my own ignorance.

"Enough." He gestured until the cooler's light flipped back to amber, then slid his hand out of the control scaffolding and set it aside. "I'd offer you a go with it, but it's mostly steel," he said apologetically. "Well, that, and it's sized for my hand. No point in building a robot army if anyone could steal the controls, right? So, since you're not going to the game, how about dropping me off after halftime so I can make it to the beach before the keg gets tapped?" My expression must have shifted, as he quickly added, "Hey, *I'm* not the one with girl problems. And I've never been to a beach party—there's a distinct lack of beaches in Montana."

"There's a beach here, you know," I pointed out. "And a visiting horde of merrow, which is one up on Rigby."

His brow knit. "Of what?"

"Merrow. Mermaids, but don't call them that, it's offensive."

"*Seriously?*" he yelped. "Like in—"

"Ask Joey for the details," I replied. "He has stories. And kickoff's at six tomorrow night, so if you're still set on this bacchanalia, I'll drop you at Meggy's around seven."

I left Aiden to his own devices and retired to my office to flip through correspondence—several of my more frequent petitioners, having wised up to the fact that I was avoiding them, had put their disputes in writing instead. Three letters in, however, my phone began to beep, and I flipped it open with hope in my heart. "Hello, Meggy?"

"I thought we'd agreed never to speak of the merrow incident again," Joey muttered on the other end. "Dude, not cool."

I heard not a peep from Aiden all Friday night, which left me torn between assuming the festivities were going well and fearing my brother was enjoying the warm hospitality of the Rigby PD. When my office clock told me dawn had come to Virginia, I popped over and wandered down to the public beach, but found the shore deserted. The tide was washing in a telltale red plastic cup, however, and so I backtracked against the current, crossing the private acreage of Rigby's wealthier families until I stumbled upon the scene of the night's revels. The few girls remaining had either passed out on the party house's sprawling porch or in the pair of hammocks, but the boys had bedded down in the sand, which had chilled unpleasantly during the clear night. I found Aiden shivering in his sleep a foot above the rising tide line, curled around his now empty cooler, and nudged him awake. "Ready to go?" I asked as he sat up and shook the sand from his hair.

"Nng," he agreed, powering the cooler on for the trip home, and trudged after me up to the main road and onto a pine-covered vacant lot, an unimproved victim of the last hurricane. When I was sure we were alone, I opened a gate into his bedroom, and Aiden, nearly sleepwalking, stumbled through with his toy. The sight of his bed triggered something instinctive within him, and he shuffled through his workshop, tapped the cooler off, and flopped onto his stomach, still wearing his control unit. I hesitated, considering whether I should try to work it off his hand, then gave up, covered him, and headed to breakfast.

Before I could cross the scrap heap, however, I heard Aiden mumble, "Olive's got a boyfriend."

"She does?" I asked, turning about, but Aiden's breathing had slowed. A few seconds later, he began to snore.

"Narcing in your sleep. Well done," I whispered, and saw myself out.

As befit a young man of his age and degree of inebriation, Aiden slept until the late afternoon, then wandered into my office with a large tumbler of water, a pair of sunglasses, and mismatched socks. "Have fun last night?" I enquired as he curled up on the couch and pulled his sweatshirt's hood down over his face.

"Yeah," he grunted in a rasping bass. "'Bot was a hit. Did a kegstand."

"You or the robot?"

His glasses hid his eyes, but Aiden's expression suggested he was in the mood for none of that nonsense. "Hung over?" I asked, coming around my desk.

"Maybe. Head hurts, feels like something furry crawled in my mouth and died."

"Sounds right." I touched the side of his head and concentrated, and Aiden looked up in surprise. "Those headaches are easy enough to fix," I explained. "I can't help you with the dehydration, though. Live and learn, kid."

He pulled his glasses off, blinking at the low light, then nodded. "Thanks."

"My pleasure." I took the couch opposite him and waited while he downed a pint of water. "Now, tell me about Olive's boyfriend."

Aiden looked momentarily panicked, then guilty. "How did you—"

"Has anyone ever told you that you talk in your sleep?"

"Damn it," he muttered, and drank again—stalling, I assumed. When he came up for air, he said, "Look, I don't know if they're really going out. I only saw her there for, like, half an hour, and then they left together."

"That's supposed to reassure me, is it?"

"No," he countered, "that's to say I don't know for sure what's going on. But they kind of had a boyfriend-girlfriend vibe, you know? Touchy, always together. She got giggly before they split."

"And does Prince Charming have a name?"

Aiden made a face at the ceiling mosaic. "He wasn't a football player—they all came in their jerseys. Everyone called him 'G.'"

"As in the letter?"

"Yeah. Nickname, I guess," he said with a shrug. "Hey, you're not going to tell Olive I told you, are you? She's getting close to tolerating me. I mean," he backpedaled, "she doesn't roll her eyes every time she sees me anymore, so I think we're making progress."

"You're doing better than I am," I muttered, refilling his glass. "And keep drinking, you have a long way to go."

"Noted," he said, but paused with the tumbler halfway to his lips. "Hey, you remember how you said Joey knew about the merrow? He said I should talk to you. What gives?"

I was wrestling with the proper response when a large shadow flashed against the wall, momentarily blotting out the sun. "Hold that thought," I said, racing to the window, and threw it up in time to hear Joey yell from the garden, "Trees ahead! Bank! *BANK!*"

A thud followed, and I climbed out the window onto the balcony for a better look at my stately oak stand, which was now adorned with a black dragonet flailing in the treetops. "Need a hand?" I called down to Joey.

"Need a ladder!" he bellowed, and sprinted off to coax Georgie back to earth.

By the time Aiden and I ran downstairs and out the back, Joey was dancing around beneath a rain of leaves and broken branches, yelling reassurance to Georgie, who was terrified and floundering for her footing. She had crashed into the confluence of two canopies and was being held aloft by their joint support, but only barely. "Just stay still!" Joey begged. "It's all right, hon, we're going to get you down! *Stop moving!*"

Before I could assist, Georgie rose into the air, squawking in panic to find herself floating, then drifted down through a clearing and landed, scratched and scared but unbroken. Joey ran to her side to stroke her face and murmur reassurance, and I turned to see Valerius behind me, shaking his head and grinning. "Ahead of schedule, that one," he remarked. "And about as graceful as her predecessors. I'd hide anything breakable until she learns to steer."

"Nice to see you back," I replied as Aiden jogged over to join the dragon consolation effort. "You had a pleasant trip, I trust?"

The captain seemed suddenly uneasy. "My lord, I apologize, Toula insisted you wouldn't mind—"

"She's right, and I don't," I interrupted, cutting his explanation short. "I'm glad you got out. Just…if you intend to remain in my guard, please give me some sort of a rough timetable before you disappear. In case of emergency, yes?"

His face clouded. "Yes, my lord, of course, I…" He paused, trying to interpret my expression. "I suppose this is probation, then?"

"No, but I…uh…" I glanced over my shoulder, but Aiden and Joey were still occupied, and I drew closer to Valerius. "I didn't know if you would want to keep the position, all things considered."

"Is this about Mab?" he asked, frowning. "I was there, I did nothing to help her. If any blame should fall, it must fall partly on me for not stopping you."

"Besides that." I took a deep breath, searching for the right words. "Valerius…you were a high lord long before I was born. Why would you want to serve me now?"

He folded his arms and watched as Joey coaxed the dragon back to her feet, then said quietly, "I've been a soldier most of my life. It's who I am. If I was ever a high lord, I knew nothing about it, and once Mab was thrown out…" He shrugged. "I served your mother because of a lie. I'll serve you because I believe you're trying, my lord, and because someone needs to watch your back. Is that acceptable?"

I nodded, listening to Georgie's faint psychic protestations that she was never leaving the ground again. "In that case, there's one thing you can do for me."

"My lord?"

"Call me Coileán. My friends call me by name, and I, um…I would value your friendship."

He briefly regarded me in silence, then said, "And I would gladly give it."

We watched the trio stumble back toward the barn through the lengthening shadows. "So," I said once Georgie's voice had been silenced by distance, "where'd she take you?"

"Home."

"Oh?"

He nodded slowly. "The city…*my* city…is all but buried. But the city built from its bones—you've seen it?"

"A few times. Did you do the tourist thing?"

"All of it," he replied, his face breaking into a wide grin. "There is this vehicle, quite large, horseless—"

"A bus?"

"Yes! All of iron, unfortunately, but the deck is pleasant. And it goes all about the city—the roads, have you ever seen their like? Marvelous things."

I thought of Rome's warren of alleys and side streets, reminded myself that Valerius had never seen a highway, and nodded. "Quite nice."

"And the temples! No...Toula called them something else, but...ah, well, it's the same thing," he said, brushing the matter off with a shrug. "Magnificent. And the art, she took me to this place...oh, *gelato*," he added, interrupting himself. "*Such* an improvement, and it's everywhere! And the lodging house—but I take it you've seen this all before," he said, catching me on the verge of laughter.

Not wanting to offend him, I subdued my mirth. "I was in that realm for many years. The novelty wears off."

"Perhaps," he allowed. "Oh, but Toula—she's amazing. The language, it changed, but she speaks it well enough. And several more besides, she told me...she taught herself Fae, did you know that?"

"Explains the accent."

"Yes, that will take some effort to improve," he said, nodding to himself. "But beyond that, she's brilliant. Why do you two irritate each other? How has she offended?"

"What," I asked, heading back to the palace, "she didn't tease you with every third breath?"

"Not at all," he replied, sounding perplexed. "She was patient, informative...she couldn't have been kinder. Is that not your experience?"

I chuckled and stuffed my hands into my pockets. "Congratulations, you may be the first person ever to see what's under that shell of hers. Well, maybe you and Meggy—"

"Shell?" he echoed.

I turned down the path to the rose hedge and waited until Valerius latched the ornamental gate behind us. "Did Toula tell you much about herself?"

"About her father and the Arcanum, you mean? Yes, she was forthright about everything, though I suspect she doesn't like discussing it."

"Probably not. You know, when we met, she was living

in a shitty little apartment about as far from the Arcanum silo as she could go, and they'd had a bind on her practically from birth. Toula...how to put this...has some issues."

Valerius paused a few feet from me with a strange look on his face, then said, "All of this talk of issues is coming from the man who killed his brother, spent a few centuries avoiding his mother, and got a child on one of Oberon's brood?"

"You forgot providing muscle to fringe priests and running away from Meggy once I knocked her up, but yeah, that's otherwise accurate. I *know* issues, Val."

He nodded and strolled past me down the lane. "As long as we're clear on that point, my lord."

CHAPTER 12

Time, unless it's finally catching up with you, has little meaning in Faerie. Oh, it *passes*, but the days blend together, and they have an annoying habit of varying in length. You can make all the plans you like, but sometimes darkness comes a few hours earlier than you'd anticipated, while other times, you may be drop-dead exhausted and faced with full daylight. As far as I've ever been able to tell, it's the realm's aggravating side effect of being magical ground zero. Granted, in the long-term, the days roughly parallel those of the mortal realm, but on a micro-scale, well, good luck keeping any bi-realm appointments without a proper clock.

Certain older Arcanum texts describe faeries as capricious, in part because they never show up when they're supposed to. That's not entirely fair—sure, faeries are capricious and worse, but it's awfully difficult to coordinate anything when, say, "high noon" is a variable concept.

I'd gotten around this with a clock—a boring, analogue, plastic-housed affair I'd picked up at Walmart for ten dollars and religiously checked against Meggy's stovetop readout when I visited. After several months, I'd begun to relax my vigil—the background magic seemed to have no effect on the little battery-powered motor—but I hid a stash of double-As in my desk so as to be certain I could keep track of the time in Virginia.

As such, I knew exactly when Saturday rolled around, and Sunday after that, and felt the pressing weight of my silent phone. I'd broken down and told Valerius the extent of the situation, and he agreed with Paul that the best course of action was to wait—but then again, he wasn't the one sitting there with a knotted stomach, hoping for a call. And so I tried to keep my mind on other matters that weekend: Aiden's quest to retain his title as Party King of the Nerds, Joey's attempts to cajole Georgie back into the sky, and Valerius's occasional non sequiturs about events that had transpired on his Mediterranean fall break.

On Sunday evening, Grivam sent a request asking for another audience, and, lacking a better plan, I agreed to meet him at a friendlier location than my throne room. There were such things to consider as diplomacy and tact, and making the old fellow totter in a second time for a chat would have been a petty and unnecessary power play. I sent word that I'd see him the next morning and retired early to read an old bargain-bin paperback, trying not to think of Meggy and Stuart extending their stay in Richmond.

As I'd feared, I slept little and fitfully, and I was on my way to my office before dawn, leaving Valerius to decide with the rest of the guards who among them wanted to go for a boat ride with me. I pushed the door open, ticking through a list of back-burner projects and ignoring the nagging voice of the realm—I had no patience for it that morning—and almost jumped when Meggy stood from the couch. While I clutched my chest and shut the door, she gave me a once-over and said, "You too, huh? You look like shit."

"How did you—"

"Toula opened a gate for me. Said it'd be easier than teaching me to do it at, to paraphrase, three in the goddamned morning. So." She crossed her arms and regarded me with grim determination. "I've always liked to make my apologies in person."

"What are you talking—"

"Shut up and let me get this out, okay?" she

interrupted, and sighed. "I'm sorry I hit you. I shouldn't have, it was uncalled for, and I was wrong to do it. In all honesty, I'd probably do it again since you went off the fucking reservation, but anyway...sorry about that."

I waited to be sure she had finished, then replied, "It was entirely warranted. You were defending Stuart."

"No, see, I tried telling myself that for two days, and then I admitted that I was just thoroughly pissed at you. But thanks for the out," she said, and sat back on the couch. "God, I need coffee. You want coffee? Is there a protocol here involving coffee?"

"Do you want me to make it?"

"Nah," she muttered, "I can do this..."

She squished her eyes closed in deep concentration. An instant later, a white mug appeared on the table before her, and when she noticed its presence, she took a test sip and grimaced.

"Not right?"

"Bitter."

"It takes some practice." A second mug appeared beside hers, and after giving it an uncertain appraisal, she tasted. "Columbian, two sugars, right?" I asked.

"Okay," she said reluctantly, "I'll give you that one. So, you going to stand there all day, or are we going to talk like reasonable adults?"

I took the facing couch, produced my own coffee, and stared into its depths. "About Stuart."

"Yeah?"

"I...screwed up."

"Big time."

I looked up to find her watching me, her clean-scrubbed face a careful blank. "And I'm sorry, Meggy. Is he, uh..."

"He's fine, a little bruised. Had something new to tell his buddies at the convention, so you almost did him a favor, I suppose." She drank slowly, letting her eyes wander around the room, then finally met mine again. "I love you, Colin," she murmured. "But I'm not going to go through life walking on eggshells, hoping you don't go nuclear every time something doesn't go your way. Or someone you don't like talks to me. And if what happened last week *ever* happens again, I swear to God, we're through. Do you understand?"

I nodded.

"And can you promise me no repeats?"

"I…I'll do my best. Yes."

Meggy mulled that over, then shrugged. "Well, you can be an all-powerful asshole, or you can be with me. It's your call." She cradled her mug in her hands and scowled at the table. "And I'll do my very best not to hit you again. This makes twice, though, so I suppose I have something to work on."

"Pretty sure I earned it both times—"

"You don't raise your hand to me, I don't raise mine to you," she snapped. "That's basic stuff."

We sat in silence, drinking as if the right thing to say was hidden at the bottom of our cups. When that proved fallacious, at least on my side of the coffee table, I cleared my throat and muttered, "How was Richmond?"

"Weird," Meggy replied, then considered her mug for a moment before sending it back into the ether. "Place was full of nutjobs, and Stuart kept trying to explain the wonders of cryptozoology to me. I'm thirty-six, damn it, I know what the Patterson-Gimlin Film is." She shook her head, dispelling the memory. "And I made it clear to him that he's firmly in the friendzone, now and forever more, amen. What," she asked, seeing my face work, "you think I'm blind or something? He's been hitting on me for the last month! I had the situation well in hand without your help, thanks."

"So you were leading him on, then? To what end?"

"I was letting him down gently, not leading him on," she retorted.

"Then what was Richmond?"

"Common decency. Being neighborly to the new guy in town, the lunatic with no friends and only Eunice for company. He's not so bad when he's not off on a rant," she added. "The trick is getting him to talk about something normal—he's a cat fancier, believe it or not."

"Oh, I believe it. I believe he's over there in his lonely little store with his cats and some Harry Potter replica light-up wand, running around naked and chanting."

"Jerk." She grinned.

"Probably thinks that come the spring equinox, you two can do fertility rituals together as the Goddess and Horned God. It'd be for the greater good, after all."

"You are so full of *shit*," she protested through a wicked smile. "And I mean it, Leffee—I talk to whomever I want to, I go on completely platonic work trips with whomever I want to, and you don't get a vote. Got it?"

We stood, and I pulled her into my arms with little resistance. "Seriously, Meggy? You're going to come into my office, unannounced and uninvited, and threaten me? *Here?*"

"Yup."

Her eyes challenged, and I blinked first. "God, you're gorgeous when you're sleep-deprived."

"Shut up, already," she said, and went in for the kiss.

When we parted, I murmured into her hair, "We should have timed this better, honey. I've got to go."

"Why?" she mumbled, her voice muffled against my chest.

"Got to talk to a merman about a sea monster."

She pulled back just far enough to glare in exasperation. "Okay, that's the weakest excuse I've heard in a long time."

"It's the truth! I promised him we'd talk this morning."

Meggy cocked her head at the window and the moon hanging low in the pale sky. "You know, I don't think you really have to rush. And fancy that, there's a couch conveniently located beside us! How fortuitous indeed!"

I kissed her again, long and deeply. "Aiden might come by."

"Bull. Kid's going to be asleep until noon. Now lock the damn door and show me what you've got."

"Yes, *ma'am*," I replied, and we tumbled onto the sofa together, eager and needy and burning in each other's arms.

It was over all too quickly. We'd barely made it through the preliminaries when someone rapped at the door, and I groaned into the cushions. "Tell him to get lost," Meggy whispered, guiding my face back toward hers. "Come on, I don't smell smoke."

I shifted to the realm's omniscient view and spotted Valerius outside the door, holding my open phone. "I've got to take this," I muttered, sliding off of her, and quickly redressed. "Hold that thought, I'll be right back."

She sighed and sat up, wrapping herself in her sweater while I cracked the door open and poked my head into the hallway. "Problem?"

"It started making noises," Valerius replied, holding the phone out. "And she's most insistent. Is, uh…" He craned his neck to see around me, and his eyes widened in understanding. "*Ah*. I'll come back later—"

"No, let me get this over with," I said, taking the phone from him. "Hello?" I said as I ducked into the hall. "Who is this?"

"Morning, sunshine," the woman on the other end replied, and I wrestled to keep my promise to Meggy.

"Ms. Stowe."

"Eh, call me Vivi," she chirped, obscenely perky for the hour. "And your priest buddy let me borrow his phone, if you were wondering."

"I was about to ask," I muttered, leaning against the wall. "What's the emergency?"

"Nothing *super*-pressing, but I figured I'd catch you

early while you weren't busy."

"The sun isn't even up, and I *am* rather busy."

"Then I'll keep it brief, Mister Buzzkill." I heard the sound of a keyboard on the other end, and my aural intruder cleared her throat. "Okay. So the guy who sets off all my alarms—you remember, I told you about him two games ago? And that reminds me, I didn't see you there last Friday. Lost faith in the Buccaneers already?"

"Can't lose something you never had to begin with, and yes, I remember. What about him?"

"Ooh, you're cranky in the morning." She tapped rapidly, then said, "Right, my mystery man. So there's this weekly after-party on Fridays, yeah? Beer, pot, the usual. Sometimes Hal and I stop by—he's not a stickler, and I don't care what the little dumbasses do as long as no one throws up on me."

I sighed, thinking of Meggy waiting on the other side of the wall. "Was there a point I missed?"

"I'm getting there! Anyway, I saw the guy again at the party last Friday. He rolled up with two cases of Bud, and I got a closer look at him while he was making out with your kid."

"*What?*"

"Thought you'd be interested," she replied with a smirk in her voice. "And my first impression was wrong—he's definitely not a student. I'd say he's college-aged, but he wasn't wearing a sweatshirt or anything, so for all I know, he's waiting tables somewhere in town. Showing up with that much beer, even with the Shop 'N' Save's see-no-evil policy…hell, he's got to be legal. I don't think he's quite my age, but he's probably at least twenty-one."

"And magically gifted?" I pressed, beginning to fret yet again about the integrity of the bind holding Olive's power in check.

"Can't say for sure, Chief," she said, sounding almost apologetic. "I didn't see him do anything, and all I get is a weird feeling—fae, wizard, enchanted, spellbound, or other, don't ask me which. But speaking of that, I meant to ask Rick—there was another new kid there Friday, had this cooler rover following along with him. I didn't get a name, but the defensive line kept calling him 'Octobong.' Makes me all tingly. Know anything?"

"That would be my brother, and if you wouldn't blow his cover, I'd greatly appreciate it."

Vivian perked up. "Oh, *that's* Aiden? Rick mentioned him, but I didn't know he was lurking around. Hey, in all seriousness, if he needs to talk to someone, the Fringe is here. It's what we do. You tell him, okay?"

"I'll pass the message," I replied, "but back to the other—"

"Yeah, that's all I've got," she interrupted. "I wanted to pick your brain."

I turned around as the door creaked open, and Meggy gave me a questioning look. *Just a minute*, I mouthed, then turned my attention back to the phone as Valerius mumbled pleasantries. Catching Meggy's expression, I remembered too late that no one had yet given her Fae, but I figured the two of them could sign without killing each other while I finished with Vivian. "Aiden says he's called G, but that's all he could give me," I told her. "And you said you saw him and…"

She waited while my voice trailed off, then asked, "How much detail do you want, exactly?"

"Broad strokes," I muttered, rubbing my forehead.

"Clothed, but there was some tonsillary exploration going on."

"Great, thanks. I'll look into it," I said, and hung up before she could get another word in.

When I turned back to Meggy and Valerius, they were regarding each other with frustration. Suddenly, he snapped. "Ah. *Buongiorno, signorina. Capisci…no?* No, that doesn't work, either," he mumbled, drumming his fingers against his arm.

"Little souvenir from your holiday?" I asked him in

Fae, then looked at Meggy and shook my head. "There's a linguistic barrier here," I told her, switching tongues once more. "I can fix it for you painlessly, or you can keep letting Val try out his new Italian. Your call."

She eyed him suspiciously. "*That's* Italian?"

"That's Italian by a native speaker of some variant of Latin who's spent two millennia speaking Fae. The syntax and vocabulary come instantaneously, but the accent's on you to figure out. Interested?"

"You know what? Sure." She closed her eyes while I touched her head and concentrated. A few seconds later, she relaxed and asked, "Did it work?"

"That's it, I'm out of ideas," Valerius muttered. "What does she—"

Meggy whipped around and grinned. "Hey, I got that! Oh wow, this is weird," she said, holding her temples. "All right...no one say anything, let me process..."

"It'll pass," I told her, and switched to English once more. "But while things settle, we need to talk about Olive."

"What about her?" she asked, suddenly on edge. "She's fine. Sleeping when I left."

It was painfully obvious by then that I'd blown any chance we'd had of a physical reconciliation. "Let's get out of the hall, and I'll tell you. Valerius," I said, switching yet again, "who's going with me?"

"I am," he replied with a smirk. "And how long can you keep up this back-and-forth, then?"

"Not much longer. Later," I said, and shepherded Meggy back behind closed doors. When we were once more alone, I lowered my voice and told her, "I've got it on good information that Olive's seeing someone."

"O...*kay*," said Meggy, taking a seat on our abandoned couch. "She's sixteen. That's pretty normal."

"Agreed, except there's something magically *off* about him," I continued, sinking down beside her. "And no, I'm not being paranoid—have you met any of the Fringe folk?"

Her forehead wrinkled. "Rick mentioned it…"

"Well, one of them just called to pass along some intel. She's not sure what's wrong with the boy, but something is. Ever hear Olive mention someone named G?"

Meggy shook her head. "No, she's been growing more distant of late…but so what?" she asked, crossing her arms. "She's still bound. If all it took to break the bind was proximity to, you know, you or me or whoever, it wouldn't have lasted a day. Why worry about some kid?"

"For starters, what if he's fae and decides to bring her across?" I said, ticking off a list on my fingers. "That'd break the bind. Or what if he's some sort of wizard, tries to magically enhance her chest or whatever, and figures out there's something already at work on her? And furthermore, he's not even a high school student. My source thinks he's at least twenty-one—"

"Oh no, don't *even* start that," she interrupted, giving me her best look of disbelief.

"He's just old enough to be creepy."

"Says the octo-centenarian."

"Touché," I grunted. "But I'm serious, Meggy—Olive dating anyone unusual isn't likely to end well. Can you make her break it off?"

Her disbelief turned to disdain. "You've heard of *Romeo and Juliet*, I trust? They're all convinced they're living it at that age."

"So…no?"

"Absolutely not. But I'll see if I can weasel anything out of her." She pushed herself off the couch with a little sigh. "G. What kind of a name is *G*?"

"Probably something embarrassing," I said, following her lead. "And since the sun is finally coming up," I added, glancing out the window, "I should probably think about this meeting."

"With a merman."

"I'll prove it! Want to come along?"

Meggy began to speak, but her reply was cut off by a familiar screech as something dark and dragon-shaped flashed by the glass. "Not again," I muttered, climbing out onto the balcony for a better view. "Joey!" I shouted to the dawn. "Hey, Joey! Georgie's loose! *Joey*!"

I scanned the ground for movement, then dropped just in time as Georgie made a low swoop by the palace, covering the balcony with her wing. I jumped back to my feet once she passed and tracked her across the sky, trying to determine her trajectory…

…and then I spotted the figure straddling her back and whooping.

"Holy *hell*," Meggy murmured behind me as she slipped outside. "Is that…"

"Yeah. Dragon. Juvenile dragon."

We stood there in stunned silence until Georgie and Joey were a black smudge on the horizon, and then Meggy whistled softly. "Colin, if it's all the same to you, I'd like to get back to reality now, please."

Having spent most of my childhood by a secluded lake, I'd seldom had cause to acknowledge Faerie's western sea beyond recognizing its existence. It was as nameless as every other physical feature in the realm, but then again, there was no other sea from which it needed to be differentiated. Nor, as far as I'd heard, was there a shore on the other side. Joey had made mention of exploring it—present an American with uncharted wilderness, and he'll do his utmost to rectify the situation—but the thought of sending him out alone, even with a solid craft beneath him, sat uneasily with me. Navigation by Faerie's unfixed stars is impossible, and it wasn't as if Joey had GPS he could rely upon. I didn't entirely like the notion of letting him roam the realm at all, but at least if something went wrong on solid land, he was unlikely to drown before I could reach him.

That outcome wasn't *impossible*, mind you, but I could live with the odds.

But with Joey's exploration limited, I was left to rely on what I knew: the sea was vast and usually placid, and there was a fixed gate to the northern Caribbean several leagues offshore and about a hundred feet down. The gate was modest, wide enough for no more than two people to traverse at once, which kept most of the larger denizens of each realm's seas safely on their proper side. True, there was some bleed-through, but in general, the only beings larger than a tuna to make the passage were the merrow, and then only on rare occasions.

Grivam's talk of a monster in the Keys worried me more than I'd let on to my companions, especially given the merrow's continued presence in Faerie. They hadn't exactly been apex predators here, but they were close to the top of the food chain, and the things in our deeps capable of hunting them were few and well-known. For Grivam, old as he was, to fear a nameless monster led me reluctantly to the conclusion that something had washed into the Gulf from the Gray Lands.

If my internal map of Faerie was rough around the coastline and bled off the paper, my conception of the Gray Lands was a crude circle in black crayon with a big X in the middle of the page. I'd read no firsthand account of the place, presumably because those who ventured over the border often didn't make it back. The long-standing rumor was that Mab had camped there after her expulsion, but no one I knew could prove it, and I hadn't thought to make the enquiry before dispatching her. My limited experience with that realm had taught me only that I didn't like what came out of there and that fighting it on its own turf was next to impossible. Unfortunately, it was looking more and more likely that *someone* was going to have to deal with a beast out of the Gray Lands sooner or later—and I knew that if he could avoid getting his hands dirty, it wasn't going to be Oberon.

The root of the merrow's problem is that both Faerie and the Gray Lands have fixed gates into the mortal realm. Picture a Venn diagram of three circles in which two don't overlap each other, much like the logo of a certain rodent-obsessed animation studio. One can punch open a gate into the Gray Lands from Faerie if one is of a mind, but there's no naturally-occurring connection between the two. The few races in Faerie that originated over there—trolls and dragons come to mind—came here by accident, having first passed through the intermediary realm. Why they stayed is beyond my comprehension, as any power they wielded outside of Faerie is useless here. Magically speaking, Faerie and the Gray Lands are yin and yang. Each produces a type of energy—a magic, if you will—that certain of its natives can manipulate to their own ends. These energies then spill over into the mortal realm, and in miniscule quantities, into the third realm.

Most faeries and wizards sense magic as ribbons of light or flashes of color. The energy that comes out of the Gray Lands has been dubbed "dark magic" by those of us who can't use it because it shows up as patches of shadow. And while there's never enough dark magic in Faerie to cause a problem, both energies flow into the mortal realm to varying degrees, and wizards occasionally run into wandering nightmares and find themselves with their hands full, if not quickly dead. Verified sightings are somewhat rare, but let's just say those monsters in the corners of old maps aren't purely the result of cartographers' fever dreams.

As my boat sped out to our arranged meeting place that morning, I hoped whatever was troubling the merrow would find its way home without my intervention. The last thing the mortals needed was another cryptid to stalk. Florida already had a long-established population of beasts in the Everglades—fur-covered, vaguely hominid, magically unskilled omnivores—but they kept out of sight and had practically gone native. It was the newcomers that worried me, as I'd seen the chaos they could cause.

I had been only two years in Manhattan when rumor started to circulate about a demon down in the Pine Barrens, and the beast ate five clergymen and nearly a dozen soldiers before I cornered it in the woods and fried its head off. The priest I was working with at the time was one of the victims, but the surviving minister, whose Oxford education had done little to prepare him for monsters in the colonies, was shaken enough to follow my instructions and take credit for exorcising the demon back to hell. He went on to have an uneventful career, while I camped out in New Jersey until I found the gate through which the creature had come and did my best to seal it off. And I thought I had succeeded, too, until reports started up again a few decades later. I trekked back into the wilderness, only to find that the gate I'd carefully blocked was wide open, my enchantment long since broken by the constant outflow of dark magic. Apparently, there's a herd of the damn creatures in the Gray Lands, as they continue to make appearances close to that gate.

As Joey had yet to return from the wide blue yonder and Aiden kept moping around the windows, I took him with Valerius and me, hoping the novelty would take his mind off the missing dragon and rider. To my surprise, it seemed to work—Aiden sat near the bow, letting the wind ruffle his unruly hair, and clung to the sides every time we bumped over a low wave. Soon enough, however, we began to slow, and Valerius pointed to a golden light below the surface. "The signal, I think," he said, pulling us around. "Shall I reply?"

"I've got it," I told him, reaching over the side to press my palm against the water. Light streamed down beside the glowing column, and I wiped my hand dry against my trousers. "And now we wait," I explained to Aiden. "You can't rush Griv—"

A familiar gray head broke the surface, and Aiden yelped in surprise. "Young Coileán," said Grivam, pulling himself against the boat. "I trust I've not kept you long."

"Not at all," I replied, grateful for the aborted wait but fearful of what his speed boded. "Grivam, I believe you've met my captain, Valerius. The boy is Aiden, my brother," I continued, nodding to each in turn. "Is their presence agreeable to you?"

His eyes swiveled independently of each other, focusing on the rest of my party. "It does not displease me." He gave Aiden a prolonged stare, then murmured, "Young Aiden...he has not been long in the realm?"

"No," I said, hoping the kid would relax. The merrow were predatory, true, but they didn't usually eat prey as large as we were. "You wanted to discuss the situation?"

He sighed deeply. "I sent an expedition of five back through the gate not two days ago. Only one returned. The beast lurks still." He hooked his elbows over the side, drawing himself higher against the boat. "Your hospitality is appreciated, but I would take my people home."

"I understand."

"Then you will help us?"

"Grivam," I began after a moment's hesitation, but he interrupted me immediately.

"Name your price. Please, your price."

"This isn't a matter of pricing," I said, hearing the desperation in his voice. "Oberon has claimed that territory. If I were to intervene without his permission...we both know that would end poorly."

He reached out and gripped my wrist. "Coileán, it killed my *sons*. Please, I will give you anything you ask. Do anything you ask. Please."

My gut clenched as I glanced down at the webbed fingers cutting off circulation to my hand. "I'll speak to him," I mumbled. "I can't say how quickly he'll see me, but I'll bring this to his attention. That's the best I can do right now. And...my sympathies."

Grivam nodded slowly, then released me and slid back beneath the waves. After a moment of silence, Aiden peeled himself off his bench, looked down into the murky water, then muttered, "So...that went well?"

"Not particularly," I replied, rubbing my wrist. "And now I've got to find an excuse to go back to Florida."

He turned and grinned. "If you need one, I've never been to Disney World."

"Nice try."

"We could make it a bonding experience."

"Aiden," I muttered, shaking my head, "are you familiar with the phrase 'hell on earth'? A fenced enclosure with a million hyped-up children and amusements requiring that you strap yourself into steel contraptions?"

He considered that briefly. "I've heard of a drinking game involving EPCOT. Think about it, eh?"

As the boat turned for home, I mulled over the likelihood of Oberon trying to kill me if I darkened his door yet again. He wouldn't be pleased, no matter why I turned up, but if I could present the issue as a problem to him, he might be willing to listen...

Something swooped low overhead, and I jumped from my reverie at the sound of a splash to port. As I tried to pinpoint the source, Joey's head popped up, and Valerius, who must have spotted him on landing, swung around to retrieve him. "What happened?" I called as we closed the distance. "Did she throw you?"

"Meant to fall!" he yelled back between long strokes. "My legs were cramping, she's tired...thought you wouldn't mind a hitchhiker." He pulled himself over the side and landed in the bottom of the boat, dripping and sunburned but smiling even as he panted. "Morning! I'm starving. Any chance of snacks?"

"You're insane," I replied, producing a towel and chucking it across the boat.

He caught it and began rubbing his hair dry. "Oh, probably. But since this still beats seminary by a substantial margin, I think I'll stay off my meds a while longer. So, why the field trip?"

"Had a little chat with Grivam," I said, smiling to myself as Joey's eyes widened. "You know, Ilunna's probably around if you wanted to see her again."

Joey's frantic glare spoke volumes, but Aiden looked back and forth between us, blind to the subtext. "Is *anyone* going to tell me what's going on?" he protested.

Valerius beckoned him to the back of the boat. "I don't know the specifics," I heard him whisper as Joey blushed furiously, "but I can hazard a strong guess."

CHAPTER 13

The merrow, no matter how unhappy they were with their displacement, were safe for the moment. My more pressing concern was Olive's new suitor, but short of lurking around the Friday night gatherings in hopes of cornering her with her young man, I suspected I wasn't going to get much information by traditional routes. I might have looked into Olive's thoughts, had she not become so adept at avoiding me—something always seemed to come up in her schedule every time I stopped by Meggy's place that fall. For her part, Meggy had cajoled a reluctant admission from Olive that she was *maybe* seeing someone, but that was all. "I can't just pry," Meggy explained when we were alone. "If she thinks I'm pushing, she'll shut me out. We'll all be better off if I keep the lines open and let her know I'm here if she wants to talk."

But seeing as Olive already disliked me, I decided that it couldn't hurt if I pushed my luck.

My chance came in early November, as Rigby's disastrous football season was limping to its playoff-less end. The penultimate match was an away game, but Olive's usual ride had car trouble, meaning she was forced to endure the humiliation of getting a lift from her mother. With no after-party to look forward to, Aiden had bowed out that week, leaving Olive alone in the car with Meggy and me for a terse thirty-minute drive up the coast. She sprawled across the backseat, arms folded and lips tight, and glared at the back of Meggy's head as if daring her to make conversation. Obliging Olive's unspoken demand,

Meggy kept her eyes on the road and the radio on the pop station. My tolerance for whiny teenage chanteurs is abysmal, however, and after listening to ten minutes of nasal drivel on relationship issues the singers couldn't begin to comprehend, I turned in my seat and smiled at my daughter. "So, Olive, I understand you're dating someone."

Fortunately for me, she was still bound and too young to kill with a glance. "Yeah," she muttered, tucking her arms across her tight uniform. "Got a problem with that?"

"No, not at all," I lied. "Who's the lucky fellow?"

"None of your business."

"Olive," Meggy warned.

She looked as if she were witnessing the greatest injustice in the history of the world. "*What?* It's none of his business! I don't have to talk to Colin if I don't want to!"

Meggy exhaled slowly, but I caught her gloved fingers tightening and loosening on the steering wheel as Olive whined. "It wouldn't kill you to be polite, sweetie," she finally replied. "And I'm curious, too. What's his name?"

Olive sat back and scowled at the universe, then muttered under her breath, "G."

Meggy's eyes darted to mine, and I played dumb. "G?" I echoed. "Just G?"

"Yeah. Just G."

"And does he have a last name, this G of yours?"

Her lip rose in a slight snarl. "Does it matter?"

"Actually, yes. I think your mom would feel better to know you weren't dating some sort of transient with an assumed name. I mean, maybe this is me, but you tell me this boy's name is G and only G, and I assume he's either a drug dealer or headlining a drag revue."

At that, she not only rolled her eyes but went so far as to throw her head back and stare at the roof of the car in utter exasperation. "God, you are *so* annoying! Stop trying to be my fucking dad!"

"Olive Marie Horn!" Meggy snapped, glaring over her shoulder. "Language, young lady!"

"He's picking on me again!" she protested. "Make him stop, Mom!"

Meggy grimaced apologetically, and I shrugged and turned back to stare out the windshield. "I'm not trying to make you miserable, Olive," I said, keeping my voice level. "I'm concerned—and your mom is concerned, more importantly—that you're spending time with an older man we've never met."

"Did Aiden squeal about that, too?" she asked in a huff.

"Aiden didn't squeal about anything," I lied again. "He didn't have to. Rigby's not that big, kid, and word gets around. Now, as we hear it, you've been seen with a twenty-something guy no one seems to know. Want to put our minds at ease?"

"I don't give a damn about your peace of mind."

"Your mom's mind, then," I said, touching Meggy's knee before she could fly off the handle. "Details?"

Olive sat silently for a moment, but when no one moved to change the conversation, she sighed and threw up her hands. "He goes to At Com, okay? Is that what you wanted? Can you get out of my personal life now, please?"

"Atlantic Community College," Meggy murmured, and I nodded—the two-year school on the edge of town had been there since the seventies and offered courses mainly in automotive repair and cosmetology. I surmised that G wasn't going to be transferring to Tech anytime soon.

After a few minutes of uncomfortable silence and the radio's half-rapped anthem to secondhand clothing, Meggy asked, "So...any chance you could bring G over for dinner?"

"*Mom!*" Olive wailed, and the subject was quickly dropped.

I should have acted. I should have altered the bind, maybe tampered with Olive's libido or strengthened her inhibitions. I should have followed her invisibly, stalked this G to the end of the earth, squeezed the truth from him, and left him to choke on his own vomit and bile.

But I didn't act. I sat back, trusted that my daughter had a perfectly normal crush on perhaps a low-blooded witch, and left the matter to Meggy's sound discretion. And if that was all we'd faced—a couple of hormonal kids figuring out the basics of coupling—then Meggy's instincts surely would have steered us through Olive's first relationship. Granted, knowing Olive, there would have been shouting matches and tearful accusations, but we'd have come through it in one piece, albeit a little battered.

I wish it'd been that simple, but then I've never had the best of luck.

The final football game of the season was a home match, and I attended so Meggy wouldn't have to suffer alone. Aiden, having by then built three more robotic coolers and worked out a synchronized dance routine for them, shot odd reciprocal hand signs at other boys as we took our seats. The withdrawn child I'd met almost three months before had finally begun to open up, dividing his time between the peace of his workshop and the chaos of Georgie's barn, and now, among his peers, he exhibited a touch of the cockiness common to youths, a subtle swagger that announced his confidence in his social standing. Aiden was never going to be homecoming king or Rigby's starting quarterback—partly due to the fact that he didn't attend the high school, of course—but he'd quickly carved out a niche once he found himself among boys who didn't know or care about his magical ineptitude, but liked the idea of alcohol-themed innovation. He'd styled himself as a nerd with flair, a non-threat who was potentially of use, and while the males accepted his presence, I noticed a few of the female band members looking up and waving as he climbed the stands.

The kid had begun to fill out even as he'd stretched—his cuffs were skimming the tops of his ankles those days, and whatever tasks Joey had given him in the barn had added a little bulk to his arms and chest. He wasn't finished, not by a long shot, but even under the stadium lights, he looked *healthy*, well-fed and slightly tanned. Best of all, I still had no desire to kill him—a remarkable situation, considering his age. The rest of our siblings had avoided him, as far as Valerius knew, and I had to admit that I'd not been the most attentive of guardians, but Aiden and Joey had become fast friends, and Galahad's better bits seemed to be rubbing off on the boy. If Aiden needed a role model, I decided, he could do worse than the dragon-riding lunatic with the arming sword.

We huddled in the bleachers under blankets that night in the cold mist, watching as the beleaguered Buccaneers made their last futile stand. At halftime, the band took the field in ski jackets and fingerless gloves, and even the cheerleaders gave in to their leggings' siren song. I surreptitiously produced bottles of coffee to pass around and thought longingly of the basketball game for which Olive was slated to cheer the following week. Those stands were of the collapsible steel type, but at that moment, I'd have chosen nearly anything over being cold and damp with a sea breeze blowing in. I'd almost drummed up enough resolve to leave the warmth of the huddle for nachos when I caught Olive waving coyly at someone sitting in the first row.

All I could see was the back of his head and part of his jacket, giving me little to work with. The kid was black-haired, perhaps olive-skinned, though it was difficult to tell with the lights. His thin jacket, black and slick, was stretched taut over broad shoulders, and when he raised his hand to wave back at Olive, I saw a heavy golden ring with a green stone—a signet, possibly—covering the lower half of his middle finger.

"Back in a minute," I told Meggy, then strolled down the bleachers as casually as I could, winding a long path toward the concessions building that would take me in front of him. As I passed, I cut my gaze to his face, trying to find meaning in a split-second glance. Blue eyes, deep and heavy-lidded. Pale lips, slightly parted as he ran his tongue back and forth over his top teeth. And...*there*. I didn't have Vivian's strange gift, but something about the boy I assumed to be G made the hair on my neck rise. Before I could look away, he met my eyes, but there was no recognition in his stare, nothing to cause alarm...and yet...

I hurried to purchase my nachos and returned to my seat, then pointed down the bleachers and muttered to Meggy, "G's sitting there. I don't like him."

"Where?" she whispered, and I noticed the gap in the shoulders on the front row an instant before I spotted G standing near the trees behind the goalposts, beckoning. Olive, who was sitting on the end of her bench, stood and headed for the water cooler, but when her continued checks over her shoulder reassured her that she hadn't been noticed, she darted around the field to join him.

"Aiden," I began, but he was already on his feet.

"On it." He jumped the stairs two at a time and jogged toward the trees. I followed his progress, willing him on, but Olive had a significant head start. She ran into G's arms and seemed to say something, but he tightened his grip about her and stared back into the bleachers.

Even from that distance, I knew he was looking for me. I felt it when our eyes met again, and G smiled. And then, in what I can only describe as a flash of black, he and my daughter were gone.

It goes without saying that students disappearing into thin air isn't covered in the Rigby teachers' handbook. The next two hours played out as I could have anticipated they would—the screaming people who insisted they saw something supernatural, the skeptics who chalked it up to a smoke grenade or swamp gas, the rational administrator who alone thought to call in a missing child report—but with the additional wrinkle of Vivian. Five minutes after the football field was swarmed by concerned students and parents, as I was holding Meggy back from the pressing crowd and swearing by any god she liked that I'd find her baby, Vivian popped up beside us, clutching Aiden by the wrist. "I'm getting the kid out of Dodge," she announced. "Safest place for him in this town is Rick's basement—the wards are solid. We'll be there if you need us."

Aiden tried to protest, but I cut him off before he got the chance. "Go with her," I told him. "I need to be here. Rick's a friend, he'll look after you until I can get by. And what sort of wards were we talking about?" I asked Vivian. "I've been down there, and I didn't feel anything."

"That's because you *can't*," she said with a condescending look. "Be safe."

Before I could question her further, she had dragged Aiden into the throng, and I was left with the more immediate task of keeping Meggy somewhere in the neighborhood of calm. She sat on the front row of the bleachers—as far as she'd gotten before I stopped her from rushing the field—and rocked back and forth, her gloves over her mouth and her eyes wide. Eventually, someone made the connection between the missing child and the woman in a state of shock, and I was forced to deal with the police interrogation until Meggy could pull herself together. No, we'd never met the boy. No, we didn't know where they could have gone. No, I wasn't Olive's father, just Ms. Horn's boyfriend. No, we hadn't fought—no more than usual. No, Ms. Horn didn't need an ambulance.

By the time the questions had cycled through and begun to repeat, the crowd on the field had been driven back by Rigby High's security squad, and a roll of yellow tape had been unspooled around the goal area. I told our interviewer that Meggy needed to rest, and after taking Meggy's business card, she allowed us to leave the campus. I took Meggy's keys, helped her into the passenger seat of her car, and started the short drive back to town. Halfway there, Meggy finally stopped rocking, but she stared out the windshield in silence, and I knew better than to continue to offer hollow reassurances that everything would be all right.

Business at Slim's was brisk—the tiki bar lost some of its allure as winter rolled down the coast—but its proprietor caught my eye and beckoned us over as soon as I led Meggy through the door. "Aiden's helping Vivi find the leak in my tap system," he said loudly enough for the patrons near us to hear. "They're in the cellar. You ready to take him home?"

"Yeah, I think we've had enough for one night," I replied, guiding Meggy onto a barstool. "Could I get—"

"I'll take you down to him, one second," he replied, but his hands were already in motion over the shelves, pulling bottles and glassware with a rapidity of which I'd not thought him capable. Within a minute, he plunked a half-full tumbler down in front of Meggy and stooped to look her in the face. "You drink that, okay?" he said gently, pushing it toward her. "It'll help a little."

She lifted it, sniffed, then sipped and winced.

"Burns, I know, but you work on that, and we'll be back in a minute," Slim promised, then lifted the hatch and followed me down. When the trapdoor was closed behind us and the overhead bulb lit, he muttered, "Triple Dark 'N' Stormy, hold the Stormy. Meg's not the type to shoot whisky. Now, you want to compare notes?"

"Where's Aiden?"

"Workshop. I've got solid wards around the place, he's perfectly safe."

"That's what Vivian said," I replied, "but if you've got

wards, then why didn't—"

"They're not to keep *you* out," he murmured, folding his arms. "This may come as a surprise, Colin, but faeries in the basement isn't my worst-case scenario."

"Dare I ask?"

He snorted and turned for the second trapdoor. "If you want to see that girl again, you'd better. From where I'm standing, it looks like you're about to be up to your ass in alligators."

I waited while he opened the door to the workshop, then followed him into the red glow of the sub-basement, where I found Aiden and Vivian playing cards across the long workbench. "We had to do *something*," she said guiltily while Aiden packed the deck away. "You don't get Wi-Fi down here, Rick."

"And what part of this job requires Internet access, pray tell?" he retorted, closing the door behind us with a solid *thud*. "Now, Colin, about your alligators—see that little light over there?" He pointed to a dim blue bulb mounted on a shelf of the far side of the room.

"I thought you only used red light down here," I replied.

"I do. That's an alarm. Flares up if there's a significant disturbance in the background dark magical field within a fifty-mile radius. Dying down now," he explained, sinking onto a folding chair, "but something big happened, and we're still seeing the after-effects. Vivi called me when things went nuts at the game, and I put two and two together." He glanced about the room, then shrugged. "Sorry, man. I'd offer you a seat, but…"

The only empty chair was a folding steel contraption, and I brushed the matter aside. "How the hell are you tracking dark magic events?"

Slim leaned back and folded his hands behind his head. "You're asking me to get into theoretical thaumics, and I don't think you want to sit down here that long."

"Layman's terms?" I asked, leaning against a relatively

clean section of shelving.

He puffed his cheeks, stared at the ceiling as he thought, then exhaled in a noisy rush. "We're not so much detecting dark magic as we are its effect on the regular magic around it. Same principle behind the wards down here—the spell revs up in the presence of a strong dark magic event, detected when the regular magical levels vacillate too much. Keeps anything wielding dark magic out of the hole, but lets schmucks like us right through. Good enough?"

"I suppose," I muttered, wishing Slim had been more generous with the liquor. "So you think the punk who took Olive was using *dark* magic? How? You people can't—"

"Bingo." He sat forward again and leaned over his thighs. "Wizards can't use dark magic. So, with that in mind, do you want to tell me who you pissed off in the Gray Lands?"

"No one! I've had no contact with that realm!"

Slim looked at the others, then at the dimming blue bulb. "Might want to think harder."

Once the initial shock wore off, Meggy proved surprisingly stoic, and she put up no fuss when I insisted she return to Faerie for her own protection. "Just tell me what we need to do," she said, pacing across my office while Aiden watched her march from the safety of the couch. "I'm getting her back, Colin—come hell or high water, I'm getting her back. And don't think you're going to sideline me, either," she added, jabbing her finger in the air as she crisscrossed the rug. "I'm not sitting back and waiting for someone else to bring Olive home. I've waited too damn long already—"

She broke off her rant as Valerius rapped on the door and quickly let himself in. "Your pardon, but they insist," he said, holding the door closed. "I told them this was a terrible time, but they won't be sent away."

"Who?" I asked, topping up my scotch while Meggy's back was turned.

Val cocked his head back at the door. "All five of them," he muttered. "What do you want me to do?"

I glanced at Aiden, who shrugged. "Tonight can't get much worse, can it?" he offered. "Hey, maybe they'll go away if I'm here."

"Or maybe they'll be impossible," I countered, but motioned for Val to admit my siblings and knocked back my liquid patience.

They pushed past him in a clump, talking over each other in an incomprehensible jumble of threats, protestations, and vaguely-worded references to past insults. I waited until the door slammed, then banged my fist on the desk until the cacophony dropped to an irritated susurrus. "I'm busy," I said once I could hear myself think again. "What is it now?"

Ji stepped forward, crossed her bare arms over her tight-laced tunic, and glowered up at me. "This is *your* fault. If you'd brought Moyna home, this would never have happened."

"What are you talking—"

"Word travels," Syral interrupted from the rear of the room, where she had draped herself against Huc's side. The two of them exchanged knowing gazes, and her burgundy lips barely curled as she looked back at me. "Word always travels. So what are you going to do about her?"

I hesitated briefly, examining their faces—Ji's anger, Syral's mocking curiosity, Huc's apathy, Doran's undisguised contempt, and Nanine's unreadable smile—then quietly asked, "Who told you?"

"Does it matter?" Ji spat. "Moyna was *Mother's* little pet, and you had no right—"

"Olive."

Meggy's voice was low and controlled, but it cut

through Ji's intended tirade like a shout. The others turned as one to locate the source, and she stepped away from the wall, clenching and unclenching her fists. "Olive," she repeated. "My daughter's name is *Olive*. Olive Marie Horn. I carried her, I bore her, I named her. And now I'm going to find her. So unless you idiots have anything useful to add, *get out*."

The five of them gawked, momentarily speechless, before Ji recovered her voice. "Who do you think you are?" she demanded, pulling herself to her full, albeit limited, height as her voice shrilled. "Who do you think you *are*, dog? Who are you to speak to me—"

I saw the bolt leave Ji's hand and knew I couldn't stop it in time. Before I could cry out, however, Meggy had thrown up a decent shield, and the energy dissipated into the corners of the room.

"Who am I?" she asked as Ji scowled in confusion. "I'm Olive's mother. But you," she said, drawing her hands together as if packing an invisible snowball, "can call me Lady Meghan."

My sister had three hundred years on Meggy, but Meggy had surprise on her side. She twisted her hands, releasing the force she'd built up between her palms, and threw Ji halfway across the room and into an end table. Ji yelped on impact and stared at the ceiling, dazed with the blow, and Meggy readied another blast. "What was that about your mama's pets?" she asked, closing the distance between them. "Go on, say it again! *Say it*, damn you! Say it!"

Before she could reach Ji, Syral smoothly inserted herself into Meggy's path and held up her open palms. "My dear little one," she murmured, "stop and think about what you're doing."

Meggy stood there, eyes narrowed, teeth bared, breathing in furious gasps, then seemed to realize she was surrounded. Her muscles were still tight, but her hands dropped, releasing her built-up ammunition. "You knew," she muttered, looking at each of them in turn. "You knew she had my daughter, and you did nothing."

"And if you would fight someone over that," Syral replied, "you should in fairness fight everyone who came to court in the last decade. Moyna was known to all."

"*Olive!*"

"Very well, Olive," she soothed. "You're angry, I can see that. But child, is this the way you want to die?"

"That's enough," I interjected, pulling Meggy back to my side before the situation could deteriorate further. "No one's dying today. And get up, Ji," I snapped, "you're not even bleeding."

Doran sprawled across the empty sofa and smirked at the room. "So, you've elevated your whore, Coileán? Feeling generous, or was she being difficult?"

I gripped Meggy's wrist and felt her trembling with rage. "Meghan is Oberon's youngest," I told him, fighting the urge to make him join Ji on the rug. "She is not my *whore*. And you'll excuse us for a minute," I said, ripping open a gate to my chambers, then led Meggy through and closed the way before the others could complain.

When we were alone, I pulled her against me and held her while the worst of her shaking subsided. "It's all right, it's over," I murmured, patting her curls. "Stand down, honey, you can't win that one."

She looked up at me and shook her head. "She *knew*. That bitch knew—"

"They *all* knew. And you're not going to get a second cheap shot in, so please don't try to kill my sister again. I appreciate the effort, but that's not even close to a fair fight."

Meggy closed her eyes and held on until her breathing slowed to normal. "Sometimes it's really bad," she finally mumbled.

"What is?"

"The rage. I get so angry...everything with Olive, you know, and the first time I ended up here, and then they look at me like that..." She tightened her grip around my chest. "You're not the only one with a temper. It didn't use to be like this, but lately..."

Her voice drifted off, and I rubbed her back. "Started after Olive came home, didn't it?"

"Mm-hmm. Teenager in the house. Guess the hormones are contagious," she joked weakly.

"It's not hormones. That bind that had been on you—this is only a guess, but I think it might have been dampening more than your talent."

She pulled away and blew her hair out of her eyes. "You think this is a faerie thing?"

"Seems like it. I mean, you'd have never pulled something like I just witnessed when I first knew you, and there *were* hormones back then."

Meggy mulled that over, then sat on the edge of my bed and frowned in thought. "When you lost it with Stuart—"

"Exactly." I saw the flash of panic cross her face and quickly added, "It doesn't always happen like that. I don't get homicidal road rage, right? Just sometimes...someone pushes me too far, and then it's either hold on as hard as I can or ride it out. It gets easier to control, I promise it does," I said, sitting beside her. "But while you're getting yourself sorted, I'm going to have to ask that you refrain from making attempts on my siblings. There are five of them, and I can't be everywhere at once."

"Six," she corrected. "You're forgetting Aiden."

"Aiden can't remotely set you on fire, but yeah, please don't kill the little guy."

We sat in unsettled silence for a time, and then Meggy murmured, "I really was going to hurt her."

"I know."

"Shit," she sighed. "What I said about you and me and Stuart—I feel a *teensy* bit hypocritical right now."

"Don't. You're still adjusting..."

She looked at me incredulously. "Colin, I just tried to

kill your sister. You don't even seem disturbed, and I don't know what I'm supposed to do with that."

"I love you," I said, and kissed her forehead. "Ji's a rock in my shoe, and I wouldn't exactly mourn her passing. And besides, I didn't think you'd actually pull it off," I added, nudging her in the shoulder. "She's ten times your age, Meggy. But in all honesty, that was impressive. Toula's not a bad teacher."

She gave me a half-smile. "I can't think it and do it yet. Not for the big stuff," she clarified. "She's been trying to wean me off the gestures, but they *work*."

"Wizards gesture all the time," I said, shrugging. "It's about the mindset. If interpretive dance puts you in the proper frame of mind, then dance on."

"Yeah, but I shouldn't have to."

"Cut yourself some slack! Moon and stars, you've been at this game, what, eight months? If anyone should be embarrassed here, it's Ji. Speaking of whom," I muttered, rising from the bed. "Coming back with me? I need to make sure Aiden's still in one piece."

She smirked as she pushed herself to her feet. "I guess I can behave."

"I'm not asking you to *behave*, my lady—I just don't want you to commit suicide by faerie." I started to open the gate, then paused. "And nice one, Lady Meghan."

"Sorry," she muttered.

"For what? It's your title, do with it what you will. Although," I said, rubbing my neck, "*technically* speaking, you know you were born into Oberon's court, yes? He hasn't let any of his people return to Faerie since he split. You being here…he might not like it."

"Well, then, you can both get over yourselves, because as far as I'm concerned, I'm a free agent. Now, are you going to talk politics all night, or are we going to find Olive?"

"Yes, ma'am," I replied, and opened the gate back to my office. When we were through and the gate closed once more, I looked about the room, saw no corpses, and nodded. "Right. The situation is as follows: Olive is probably in the Gray Lands or in the custody of something out of the Gray Lands. Assuming she's in that realm, my hands are somewhat tied. Suggestions?"

"You can't leave her!" Ji protested, pressing a bag of ice to the back of her head. "And muzzle your dog, Coileán," she added, sparing a glare for Meggy.

I perched on the corner of my desk. "Talk about the mother of my child in that fashion again, and I'll throw you through the wall and feed what's left of you to the dragon out back. Is that perfectly clear?"

Ji began to respond, saw that I was in earnest, and quickly shut her mouth.

"She has a point," said Doran as he examined his fingernails. "If you leave Moyna in the Gray Lands, then you've proven yourself weak to the court." His dark eyes—Aiden's eyes, but narrower—rose briefly to mine in challenge. "Of course, I don't know how you propose to fight properly in that hell. Your problem, I suppose, dear brother."

Aiden looked around the room, puzzled, then lifted his finger. "Sorry, what's the problem?"

Doran snorted and continued to gaze at me. "Going to send the mongrel in as bait?"

"*The mongrel* asked a simple question," Aiden retorted, staring at Doran until he reluctantly glanced in Aiden's direction. "What, scared to cross your own borders?"

"Allow me," said Syral, interjecting before another fight could break out. "There's virtually no magic in the Gray Lands," she explained, leaning over the back of Aiden's couch to address him. "Anyone who chose to fight there would have a significant disadvantage. Quite possibly a fatal disadvantage, I would think."

Doran's expression had shifted into an enigmatic quasi-smile, and I contemplated how lovely it would feel to throttle him. "Even if I punched a gate open from here," I told Aiden, "there's too much dark magic in that realm. Whatever flowed out of Faerie would meet a reverse flow out of the Gray Lands—ten feet inside the border, I doubt you'd be able to draw on enough magic to work a glamour, let alone anything defensive."

Aiden's brows knit. "So why not carry it over with you? Pipe it in and up the flow rate rather than rely on whatever's passively coming through the gate?"

The rest of our siblings chuckled, and I shook my head. "The last person who knew how to store and transport magic was Simon Magus, and he's been gone a long time, kid."

He looked at me quizzically, then stood and glanced around the room until he settled on a carved wooden box on a side table, an old tea chest I'd liked and never had the heart to discard. With a little grunt, he carried it to the coffee table, lifted the lid, and took a deep breath.

"Aiden?" I asked, but he shook his head.

"Don't. Let me concentrate. I've never done this with an audience," he mumbled, closing his eyes. His hands spread apart, and then, ever so slowly, they came toward each other again, twitching as if straining against a great weight. Nanine gasped softly, and the others pushed closer, watching as Aiden turned his palms down over the box, then snapped the lid closed. When he opened his eyes again, he was flushed and sweating, but he grinned. "See? That's the only thing I've ever been able to do. I can't use magic, but I can push it around."

"What did you—"

"Are you *blind*?" Ji snarled.

Beside me, Meggy snapped her fingers, then hefted the box off the table. "Actually, he is," she told Ji, and pressed the chest into my arms. "Go on, take a whiff."

Puzzled, I cracked the lid, then coughed at the overwhelming stench of concentrated magic, a sensation greatly akin to pouring citronella straight up my nose. "How?" I managed to hack once I could breathe again.

My brother fidgeted under the room's incredulous eyes. "I don't know, you push it where you want it to go. Like cupping your hands in the pool…" He paused, waiting for the recognition that didn't come. "You…can't do that?"

"*No one* can do that," said Huc as I fell into another coughing fit and slammed the chest closed. "Magic isn't portable—you can't pack a little backup supply and carry it about with you."

"Except that's what the Arcanum did," I said, putting the odiferous box on my desk for safekeeping. "And that's how we opened the gate again last spring—we used relics from the Great War." The younger of the bunch frowned, and I explained, "Inter-arcana conflict about a thousand years back. A wizard called Simon Magus figured out how to store and transport magic, but they've never been able to replicate his results." I peered down at Aiden, who had taken his seat and seemed to be attempting to shrink into himself. "Does Greg know you can do that?"

He shook his head. "I'm not *doing* anything. I push it back and forth, make the colors move around, when I'm trying to think. It's like doodling, I guess."

"*Doodling?*"

"Clears my head," he mumbled. "Something to do with my hands. I didn't know—"

"Aiden," I interrupted, sliding onto the coffee table in front of him, "that's like getting bored with transcription and drawing the *Mona Lisa* in the margin."

He hadn't been so miserably uncomfortable since our first meeting. "I thought everyone can do that. I mean, you know, people *do* things with magic—I poke at it."

I gripped his arms and waited until he met my eyes. "If Greg had the first inkling that you were capable of what you just did," I said quietly, "he'd have never let you out of his sight. Your 'doodling' borders on the miraculous. Honestly," I said, releasing him, "I've never known a wizard who could do that."

"Simon Magus—"

"Could have had someone like you working behind the scenes. He comes off as insufferable in his writings—I wouldn't be surprised if he'd taken the credit for a witch-blood's work."

Behind me, Doran's robes rustled as he shifted on the couch. "Well, then, I suppose your troubles are over. Let the mongrel pack a bag for you, and go find Moyna."

"Whoa, wait a minute, don't put this on me," Aiden hurriedly interjected. "I just mess around with this—if you want a reliable backup source of magic, I'm going to need specs and time. How much does it take to power one of those fireballs, anyway?"

The others looked at him blankly, and I replied, "I don't think anyone's ever tried to quantify magic with a unit."

"Then we'll have to experiment and figure it out," he countered, "because if you make me guess at it, you'll probably end up flat or crispy or what have you."

"Timeframe?"

"At least a few days. I'll work as fast as I can, Coileán, but this is new to me…"

I looked over my shoulder at Meggy, who waited beside the tea chest. She nodded in acquiescence, but her arms were tightly crossed, and her jaw had clenched. "All right," I sighed. "Do what you can, as quickly as you can. I'll give you whatever assistance you require."

Aiden rose to leave, but before he could slip out, Doran said, "That's all? You're going to leave the girl to languish in the Gray Lands until the mongrel thinks the time is right?"

At that, Aiden stopped and fixed Doran with a withering look. "First, the name's Aiden, not 'the mongrel.' You're old, not senile. Secondly, there's no point in starting a firefight without a loaded gun. Everything I've heard so far has suggested that going over there would be suicidal. Third, we don't even know that Olive's in the Gray Lands. She could be anywhere."

"And whoever took her surely had a reason," Meggy added. "There's bound to be a ransom note coming, right?"

"Exactly," said Aiden. "And finally, I don't see *you* leaping into action," he told Doran. "You're not too busy to rescue your niece, are you? Got any plans this weekend?"

The room fell silent, and I watched my siblings' eyes swivel to catch Doran's reaction. After a tense moment, he blinked slowly and murmured, "You presume, mongrel."

"And maybe I'm imagining things, but it sounds to me like you're trying to get Coileán killed."

It was subtle, but I caught the flash of something shifting in Doran's eyes. "Why would I want to kill Coileán?" he retorted. "And leave Moyna with the throne? A mere *child*? The girl amuses me," he said, pushing himself off the sofa, "but not so greatly that I would venture into the Gray Lands on her behalf. Then again," he added, giving me a pointed look, "I'm neither her father nor her king, am I?"

"No, you're not," Meggy interrupted, "so I suggest you get out of here and let these two get to work."

He smirked back at her. "Moyna's mother, did you say? Your concern for her welfare is overwhelming."

She stepped away from the desk but held herself in check. "No one wants her back more than I do. As soon as we've got a location and a power source, I'll be the first one through the gate. But I'm not pushing *him* into a suicide mission," she continued, pointing at me, "and if he doesn't think it's even remotely safe to jump into the Gray Lands right now, I'll trust him."

"I'd expect nothing less from his whore," Doran replied with a smile. Before he had time to make his exit, however, an invisible blow struck him full in the chest, and he reeled and collapsed onto the couch.

I jumped up in the sudden tumult and spotted Valerius, who still stood by the door, silent and scowling—but his nod, almost imperceptible, told me what I needed to know. With Doran incapacitated and wheezing, I was able to shoo my siblings out, leaving me once more alone with my captain, Meggy, and Aiden, who seemed wary of further attack. "Nicely timed," I told Val, running my hands through my hair in hopes of staving off the headache that threatened.

He grunted, then inclined his head toward Meggy. "Toula speaks well of you, my lady. It was my pleasure."

CHAPTER 14

Although I am, admittedly, a man of considerable talent, very little of that talent extends to the sciences. Don't get me wrong, I appreciate discoveries like microwave ovens and the heliocentric model as much as the next fellow, but I've no patience for the process of trial and error that leads to progress. Some enjoy poking at things to figure out how they work and how to improve them, but I'd rather wait and be handed the best possible product, preferably with a thin instruction manual and a tech support number.

Aiden, however, was a poker, a fiddler, a builder, and a taker of copious notes, which drove me to the brink of madness that weekend. How much magic did it take to power a low-level enchantment? How much to construct a glamour? A shield? How was something unitless to be quantified? How well did magic compress? Like a liquid? Like a gas? How did its density affect its usability? Did magic behave differently under pressure? Did it have mass? And what about my fighting style? On average, how many shots would I take per minute? Per incident? With what sort of shielding? What was he overlooking?

I sat in a chair beside Aiden's long desk, well out of the way of the metallic litter of his robotics projects, and tried to respond to his peppering of questions. When he reached a point of satisfaction, he would pause, experiment, take more notes, and then resume the interview. Once Aiden reached his preliminary conclusions about me, he dragged Meggy in for comparison, then Valerius, all the while oscillating between a notepad and his laptop. He fell asleep the first night over his desk, pen in hand, muttering about flow regulation, and Meggy covered him with a quilt and kicked everyone out. The next morning, she roused him at dawn, forced cereal and black coffee down his throat, and took my vacated chair as his first guinea pig of the day.

At least she was staying busy. Meggy tried to project serenity, but I could feel the nervous energy radiating off of her, and I knew from her constant shifting beside me the night before that she hadn't slept. I could do nothing to speed along Olive's rescue, but I kept the coffee warm.

Aiden continued to crunch his numbers long into Sunday night, while I slipped back and forth to Meggy's apartment, looking for any indication that Olive's captor was trying to make contact. The house remained dark and untouched, however, as did the school and the football field. Aside from the police tape that still fluttered around the trees behind the end zone, there was no sign that anything unusual had happened at all. Slim reported a quiet radar, as did Vivian, who loitered in his bar that weekend, watching the windows while she played with her glasses. The administration, she informed me, was treating Olive as a runway, not an abductee—pyrotechnic work to create a distraction, a quick getaway through the woods with her boyfriend, and no blame at all on the Rigby board members' heads.

And then, as I was beginning to wonder whether I'd ever see a list of demands, my phone rang early Monday morning.

I'd been in my office, poring over the few texts I'd found in Mother's library that offered guidance to the Gray Lands, when I heard my homemade cell phone break into its familiar tinny fugue. To my surprise, the little readout stated Unknown Number, and I tapped the line open, thoroughly perplexed. "Hello?"

"You're awake. Good," said a voice I recognized an instant later as Oberon's. "There seems to be a large sea serpent menacing my island."

"Shit," I muttered, pressing my eyes closed. "I meant to tell you about that. The merrow have been here since September—"

"I don't give a damn about the merrow. There's a sea serpent sitting twenty yards offshore. What do you want to do about it?"

"Me?" I asked, more confused than ever. "I thought that was your turf. And this really isn't a good time, my daughter's been kidnapped—"

"Well, she's riding the goddamned snake," he retorted, "and she's demanding that you show yourself. So I thought I'd do you a favor and let you give me a hand with this before I blow them both to dust. Interested?"

"On my way," I said, ripping open a gate to Aiden's room. "Five minutes. And how the hell did you get this number?"

"*Magic.*"

"Seriously."

He sighed deeply. "The realm still likes me, so yes, magic. Now hurry up before I change my mind. If she comes ashore, she's fair game."

The connection broke, and I ran into the middle of what appeared to be a shielding experiment with Valerius and Meggy. "Olive's outside of Oberon's bar on top of a sea monster, let's go," I said, closing the gate. "Meggy, if you're coming, you'll want shoes. Val, are you in?"

"Of course," he replied, hastily retrieving his sword from the corner.

"Excellent. I want you in the van with me if this turns physical. Meggy—"

"Give me two minutes," said Joey, who popped out of the shadows with a plate of eggs and toast, "and I'll have Georgie saddled and ready."

"Joey," I protested, "you're not bringing a dragon to *Florida.*"

"It's East Rock! And you said there's a monster. What's

Georgie going to hurt, huh?"

"What about you?"

"What *about* me?" he echoed. "Val?"

The captain glanced up from buckling his sword belt. "I'll shield him as I can, Coileán. This is the beast that was harrying the merrow?"

"I think so," I muttered.

"Then the more hands, the better the odds. If we're lucky, Georgie will figure out fire breathing while we're there."

"If we're *lucky*?"

"Couldn't hurt," said Joey, putting the remains of his breakfast on the desk. "Meet you out back," he added, and dashed out the door.

When his footsteps died away, Valerius straightened his tunic and quietly said, "The boy has something of the warrior in him. I'd counsel you to employ it."

"Against a sea serpent?" I replied, waiting as Meggy tied her sneakers.

"Fighting dragonback? Why not? The aerial advantage—"

"Ready," Meggy interrupted, heading for the door. "Argue later. Daylight's burning."

We were halfway down the hall when I noticed that Aiden was jogging after us. "Oh no, not *you*," I said, catching him before he could reach the staircase. "You stay here, kid."

"But I can help!" he said as Meggy and Val came to a halt. "Maybe you'll need some magic pushed around."

"Not in that realm, I won't."

"Iron stuff?"

"Unlikely," I said, taking hold of his shoulders. "Stay here, be safe. I can't promise you protection if things go upside-down over there."

But Aiden's chin rose in defiance. "I want to come."

"You're in no way prepared for a situation like this, and you're running on caffeine. No." I looked at the others, but found similarly odd expressions on their faces. "Come on, you're not serious," I said. "He's *fifteen*."

"I was armed at fifteen," Valerius replied. "The boy's growing up. If he'll bear the risk, let him."

"An unprotected witch-blood?" I shot back. "He's a liability—"

"Catch," Val interrupted, pulling his sword from his belt and tossing it past me. Aiden fumbled as he grabbed the hilt, but he quickly righted his grip. "Joey's not been my only pupil," the captain explained, producing an identical sword for himself. "Give him a chance."

I looked back and forth between armed and hopeful Aiden, stoic Valerius, and Meggy, who tapped her foot and cocked her head toward the door. "Please don't get yourself eaten," I muttered, then followed Meggy down the stairs and out to rendezvous with my would-be dragon rider.

We made a motley crew when we landed outside Red's in the cool dawn. Valerius, immediately tense, assessed our surroundings, while Meggy hung back, gawked at the water, and muttered, "Oh, my God, what is *that*?"

Joey, who had led leery Georgie through the gate, dropped the reins and scrambled onto her back. "Trouble," he replied, stroking the dragon's neck to calm her.

I caught a flash of the maille he'd thrown on under his jacket and felt marginally better about his chances. "Stay back until we know what we're up against," I ordered, then spotted Oberon strolling down the beach to meet us. "And keep her well in hand, yes?"

I don't like it.

The psychic intrusion caught me off-guard for a second, and Meggy nearly jumped, but the others, who had spent considerable time at the barn in recent weeks, remained unfazed. "It's all right," Aiden soothed, patting

Georgie's flank. "We don't like it, either."

Her red eyes narrowed to slits as she contemplated the brown-scaled neck rising fifty feet out of the sea. *It smells wrong. Bad. Everything smells wrong...*

"Different realm, sweetie, nothing to worry about," said Joey. "Just smells a little different—"

No. She bobbed her head slowly side to side, sensing something I couldn't detect, then declared, *Feels different.*

"Less magic here," Joey explained.

And something...else. Her nostrils flared as she sniffed the breeze. *Can't name it.*

"Worry about that later," I said, then left the huddle to meet Oberon on the beach. "Any casualties?" I called to him as I approached.

"Nah, I dropped them all in a bar on Key West when that thing came up to play," he called back, casually shoving his hands into the pockets of his board shorts. "Dead customers are bad for business. Nice lizard you have there. Overgrown iguana?"

I glanced over my shoulder at the distressed Georgie, who had sunk to the sand and curled her tail around her nose. "She's young."

"Obviously. *That* isn't," he said, pointing to the serpent in the shallows. "Want to tell me how your little darling acquired that particular pet?"

"Wasn't our doing. Like I said, she was kidnapped last Friday—"

"I wouldn't be so sure about that," he interrupted. "Either the 'kidnapping' was staged or the girl's deep in the throes of Stockholm syndrome by now. Ah," he said, looking past me, "and this must be Meggy. Couldn't keep one little girl under control, dear?"

She stopped beside me, gave him a sneering once-over, then snorted. "Ed Hardy? That's the best you could do?"

"Fashion is a fickle thing," he replied with a little shrug. "Your mother didn't seem to mind, but then again, she didn't keep her own clothes on for very long."

"Son of a *bitch*…"

I grabbed Meggy around the waist before she could lunge at him, and Oberon stepped back a pace, grinning as she cursed him with every profane syllable in her vocabulary. "Feisty, isn't she?" he said to me, raising his voice to be heard over her outburst. "Good luck, Coileán. Poor choice with that one. The girl's no better," he continued, cutting his eyes to the snake. "There's a fair bit of Titania in her, I'd wager. What was your plan, again?"

I waited until Meggy, red-faced and nearly crying, ran out of steam, then muttered, "It's been a long weekend. Don't provoke her."

"And miss the entertainment?" he replied. "Besides, how better to get acquainted with my daughter than to learn what drives her to madness?"

Meggy spat in the sand, then shook me off and brushed her curls from her face. "You're disgusting," she told him, "you raped my mother, and you have the audacity to call me your daughter?"

Oberon remained unflappable. "I wouldn't call it rape, little one. She was more than willing."

"I'm not stupid, and I know how enchantment works," she retorted. "She still blames herself for getting drunk that night. Mom wouldn't have cheated on Dad."

"Wouldn't she?" His unreadable smile broadened as Meggy's face shifted ever closer to purple. "A little alcohol, a little suggestion…child, she did nothing against her will. I didn't have to force her."

Meggy's blue eyes blazed. "A married, Catholic, mother of two? You didn't force her?"

At that, he actually laughed. "I've had Catholics, single, married, and sworn to celibacy. As did *your* mother, boy," he added, smirking at me. "Religion-driven declarations of chastity seldom overcome lust, but that's a conversation for another day." He cocked his thumb at the serpent and said, "Get your child under control and off my island, or she's dead."

"Gee, thanks, that's big of you," said Meggy, stomping past him toward the water. "Either make yourself useful or get lost, asshole. Olive!" she shouted into the wind. "Olive, for the love of God, *get off that thing!*"

Oberon's face slowly swiveled toward mine. "You know," he said softly, "I could kill her right now for that insolence. I probably should. But then I recall that you have to put up with that, every single day, and I feel all warm and tingly inside."

I stood there, watching Meggy's hair bounce as she picked up speed, then wheeled on Oberon, grabbed him by the T-shirt, and employed the two inches I had on him to their full advantage. "Touch one of mine," I said, pulling him close enough to smell the beer on his breath, "and I will destroy you. If I have to lead an army onto this damn island, I'll do it. And by the time I get to you, if you're not already dead, I'll drag you off, bleeding and begging for mercy, lock you in an iron box, and wall you up so your screams don't disturb me. Got it?"

He smiled in the face of my fury. "Big words."

"Try me."

He yanked himself free of my grip and smoothed his shirt against his tanned chest. "Perhaps I will. Perhaps someday, when you're ready—"

"Damn it, Colin," Meggy yelled from the high-tide line, "get over here and help me!"

Oberon practically beamed. "That's my girl!" he crowed, and his cackling laughter followed me as I ran to see what had become of Olive.

I can state with confidence that staring up at a dripping sea serpent whose RV-sized skull is rearing roughly four stories above yours doesn't rank highly on anyone's bucket list.

Our party, joined by Oberon—out of curiosity, I can only imagine—gathered at the water's edge and waited while the beast swam closer. Even from a distance, I could pick out the little figure sitting cross-legged on its flat head, which gradually resolved into my daughter, now wearing a black catsuit of the type one might find in a collection of better dominatrix attire. When the snake had closed to within ten yards, she stood and spread her hands, which burst into green flame. "You thought you could chain *me?*" she bellowed down at us in Fae. "I am the Lady Moyna, daughter of the queen, and *I will not be bound!*"

Meggy looked stricken, and I squeezed her hand before stepping out from the line. "Come down here, Oli— Moyna," I said, trying to toe the tonal line between no-nonsense and reasonable. "We need to talk."

"*Murderer!*" she screamed, then leapt into the air as the snake's head plummeted toward me, mouth open and fangs extended. I felt Val's shield form as I threw a wall of pure force at the monster, and the snake rebounded as if it had struck concrete, hissing and suddenly minus a tooth. The broken fang fell into the water a few feet offshore and bobbed in the chop, and Moyna landed back on her snake, furious but controlled.

"Let's talk about this," I tried again once she had ceased to hover. "You're outnumbered, Moyna. You can't win like that, and nothing good ever comes from giant snakes. Come on, now, let's be rational."

But she shook her head. "Come down?" she mocked. "Why, so you can bind me again? You took away my memories, my mind—"

"Because you asked Mother to execute me! What was I supposed to do, throw you in a cell and lose the key? I tried to give you the life you should have had!"

Moyna laughed incredulously. "So you cast me out of Faerie and dump me in Rigby? Take away my power? My...my soul?" she sputtered. "You killed my mother, and you expect me to play your little game without complaint? *No!*" She stamped her foot, and the wounded snake winced. "I'm not your pawn, Ironhand, and I'm not your plaything!"

"Please, Olive," Meggy begged, "just come down—"

"*Moyna!*" she screamed. "I am Moyna, you stupid cow! Olive is *dead!*"

Oberon whistled softly and looked out at the sunrise. "If you're wise, boy, you'll kill her now. Save yourself the trouble."

Before I could rebuke him again, Aiden kicked off his shoes and waded into the surf. "Hey, Moyna!" he yelled up at her, cupping his hands into a makeshift megaphone. "It's Aiden! Remember me?"

She peered over the side of her mount and wrinkled her nose. "Robot Boy? One of his minions, are you?"

"Not exactly. I'm, uh...I'm your uncle. Surprise," he said with a shrug. "And one hundred percent grade-A witch-blood." He held up his empty hands, then pulled Val's sword from his belt and tossed it back onto the sand. "I'm unarmed."

"Aiden, get back here!" I began, but Val gripped my arm to stay me and shook his head.

My brother continued, heedless of my order. "You're angry. You have every right to be," he called. "I'd be angry, too, if someone killed my mom in front of me."

"I *didn't* kill her," I muttered to no one in particular.

Joey glanced down from his saddle. "Dude," he whispered, "I think you're getting into technicalities at this point."

"The thing is," said Aiden, ignoring the chatter behind him, "we've got to figure out how to make this right. Now, I know you think you're in a Mexican standoff, but Moyna, they've matched you in oversized reptiles and beaten you in numbers. You want to get in a firefight with two kings? Oberon's not going to lose any sleep if he kills you, and you're pushing Coileán into a corner." He paused, letting that sink in, then said, "If I come out to you—just me, unarmed, no tricks—could we talk?"

She planted her hands on her hips and stared down at

him, puzzling out her circumstances. "In good faith?"

"Absolutely," said Aiden. "And look," he added, pushing up his sleeves and lifting his shirt, "nothing hiding, nothing strapped on. We can talk about what you want, okay? Maybe you can work something out."

"This is a terrible idea," Meggy muttered.

"Just a minute," I yelled, and beckoned Aiden out from the water. He marched back up the beach, his jeans soaked to mid-calf and wicking higher by the minute, and looked at me enquiringly. I waited until he was close, then bent to his ear and said, "If you go out past a certain radius, I can't protect you. She's raging right now, and I don't know what she has on her mind—she's repelling me." I glanced at Val, who nodded. "Repelling all of us. You go out there, and you're a sitting duck."

"Do you have a better idea?" he replied.

"*I* do," said Meggy, joining the huddle. "Bind Olive again, take down the snake when she's safe, and we'll deal with the repercussions later. You're not going to reason with her like this. Listen to me, Colin," she insisted, "I'm the one who's lived with her, and I've seen her moods. She's close to impossible when she's angry—there's no sense in trying diplomacy until she's calmed down."

I cut my eyes to the waiting monster, which had drifted away from the shore while we debated, then back to Meggy. "I don't trust myself to bind her like this. The first one obviously failed—"

"What about him?" she interrupted, nodding to Oberon, who was now nursing a cup of coffee and enjoying the sunrise from a wooden beach chair. "We know he's good at it," she added bitterly.

"You want to entrust *Oberon* with her safety right now? Bastard's got an itchy trigger finger, Meggy."

She huffed in frustration. "Okay, what about knocking her out? You kept her unconscious while I recouped last spring."

"No, Toula did, but I could replicate the effect…"

"And if you do that," said Aiden, "she'll never trust you again. I wouldn't." Meggy and I wheeled on him, and he stared impassively back at us. "Look, I'm not saying she's right, but you guys screwed with her head for the last eight months. I'd be pissed if I were in her shoes, and that's not counting whatever you did to Titania."

"I *defended* myself," I shot back. "And I shouldn't have to justify that to—"

"I'm not asking you to justify it," he said. "Not to me, anyway. But look, I get it, you tried to find a solution to a bad situation, and now it's biting you in the ass. You want to make things right with Moyna? Start by acknowledging that she's got a legitimate grievance or two, stop treating her like she's throwing a tantrum, and try to negotiate a cease-fire." He pointed to the distant snake and added, "Her fight isn't with me. I'm the least threatening person on this island, and she knows it—what's it going to hurt if I try to talk her down?"

I looked at Meggy, whose pursed lips silently said enough, then sighed and raised my hands in surrender. "Don't get hurt."

"That's the goal," he replied, heading for the water. "Got a boat or something handy?"

"How about this?" I muttered, gesturing to the sea. With a moment's work, a sandbar rose out of the water in a beeline for Moyna. "Have you gone far enough?" I called out to her.

"Suffices!" she called back.

With a last smile of reassurance, Aiden stepped out onto the sandbar and made his steady way toward Moyna, who had paused perhaps fifty yards offshore. He walked carefully, testing for boggy patches, and held his hands out to prove to her he was unarmed. After a tense few minutes, he reached the end of the bridge and waited. The serpent's head descended to the sea, and Moyna stepped to the edge, beckoning for Aiden to join her. He scrambled up the snake, and the head rose again, cutting off Aiden's escape route.

"Oh, look," said Oberon, still sipping his coffee, "she's taken her first hostage. Delightful."

"We don't know that," I began, but he chuckled into his mug.

"The boy's helpless, and he's obviously of some value to you," he said, sparing me a glance. "Sentimental value, I suppose. A mongrel's not good for anything else."

"Except the mongrel who killed Titania, of course," I retorted.

"And hi, there," said Joey, waving down at us. "Yoo-hoo, guy on dragon checking in. You're looking at your backup plan."

"Yeah, sorry," Meggy mumbled, "but that's not reassuring."

Valerius, who had been observing the negotiations in silence, abruptly wheeled about and grabbed my shoulder. "Gate opening," was all he had time to say before a short brunette in jeans and a purple peacoat sprinted through onto the beach. She looked around wildly, spotted Aiden in the distance, and dashed for the makeshift land bridge.

"Hey! *Hey*!" she yelled between ragged breaths. "Let him go! You let him go right now!"

"Uh…who the hell is *that*?" said Meggy.

I ran to the gate as it started to close, just in time to see Greg watching with his arms folded on the other side. "What's going on?" I demanded.

He cut his eyes to the sea monster. "Could ask the same thing, old timer, but I guess I'll get an earful later," he replied, and the gate vanished.

In the meantime, the runner on the bridge had pulled something from inside her coat. I feared she was carrying a gun until the suddenly sparking tip gave it away as a wand, which made the situation infinitely worse. "Let him go!" she continued to yell with the breath she could spare. "You want to fight someone, fight me! He's just a mongrel, let him go!"

Georgie shifted her weight as she readied for flight, and Joey asked, "Want me to break this up?"

"Hold for now," I said, groaning inside as the pieces fell into place.

Moyna looked over the side of her snake, spotted the wizard on the bridge, then sent her ride back to sea level once more. "You would fight me?" she asked in the faint drawl she'd picked up in Virginia, her voice echoing over the waves as it rose. "*Me*? Do you know who I *am*?"

The wizard stepped into a combat stance. "Yeah. You're a bitch with a giant snake who's threatening my little brother," she shouted back.

"I am the Lady Moyna of the queen's court, idiot!"

"Okay, fine," said the wizard. "You're still the bitch with the giant snake who's threatening my little brother. Let him go."

I couldn't see Moyna's expression from the beach, but I could hear the contempt in her reply. "He came freely. You have no right—"

"The wand says I do," she interrupted, flinging a thin bolt of lightning into the sea. "Aiden, get your ass off the snake, *now*."

He slipped closer to the side of the beast's head and held up his hands. "It's okay, we're just talking," he said, looking back and forth between the girls as if unsure whom to placate. "I'm fine. Everything's fine."

"The hell it's fine! Get out of here!" the wizard snapped. "Are you friggin' *stupid*?" She extended her wand arm as if wielding a foil, and her open coat flapped around her in the wind. "Let him go," she told Moyna, "or so help me, I'll blow you to kingdom come."

Moyna cocked her head, giving the wizard a close look, then grabbed Aiden's wrist and pulled him off the snake with her. They landed at the foot of the sandbar, and the snake's head rose above them, casting the three into its shadow. "I don't like threats," Moyna said, then shouted incomprehensibly at the snake, which reared and plunged to strike the wizard, snapping her into its mouth before she had a chance to fight back.

"And that's my cue," said Joey as Aiden screamed. "Come on, girl, let's do it," he muttered, rubbing Georgie's neck, and she lumbered down the beach, broke into a near-gallop, and rose with surprising grace. Georgie circled once, testing the wind, then started a sudden dive toward the end of the sandbar.

Meggy, who had been momentarily frozen with shock when the wizard was eaten alive, grabbed my arm. "Get them out of there! Olive's going to kill them, she's lost it, get them back—"

The rest of her frantic plea was cut off by the ripping, squelching blast of the snake's head exploding outward from the spark of the swallowed wizard's wand.

I had time to see Georgie pull up and out of the way before I grabbed Meggy and flung her to the sand, then threw myself atop her ahead of the rain of raw meat and bone shrapnel. When the patter of gore against my shield ceased, I pushed myself upright, pulled her back to her feet, and ran for the sandbar as the headless neck swayed and spurted.

Replaying that moment in distant retrospection, I can't help but cringe. There was no need to run like a madman—a second's effort would have sufficiently warped reality to put me at the end of the sandbar, right where Aiden and Moyna had been. But I *was* a madman that morning, and when reason failed, only my legs remembered what to do.

People talk of time slowing in moments of crisis, but I'm not so sure. It wasn't time that changed as I sprinted down the packed sand toward the dying serpent, throwing up intermittent shields against the bright blood spraying above me and bellowing my brother's name. Rather, it was my mind that malfunctioned as it attempted to process too many simultaneous stimuli—the sand, the sea, the massive splash as the snake gave up the ghost and sank into the water, and the overwhelming, racing thoughts: *Aiden's dead. I sent my defenseless baby brother to his death. Moyna's gone. What's this relief? Am I wishing her dead? I'm a terrible father. I've become Mother. Meggy will never forgive me. Aiden, where's Aiden?*

And then, like headlights through the fog, I heard Georgie's thoughts interrupt mine: *Got him!*

I looked up and nearly wept with relief. Georgie was hovering—or the closest thing to it, frantically beating her wings to maintain an approximate location—while Joey, who had one arm wrapped around Aiden's chest, was thumping his back as the boy coughed and retched seawater. "One down, going in!" Joey yelled over Georgie's flapping. "I don't see the other two, and she can't carry four!"

I waved him on and resumed my race for the end of the sandbar. One of the snake's dark coils had fallen across the path, and I vaulted it, fearing what I'd find on the other side.

But there was nothing to find—sand, sea, a faint indication of the corpse below the surface, but no trace of the wizard or Moyna. I stopped and planted my hands on my thighs, catching my breath as I scanned the water for signs of life. For a moment, all I could hear was the blood pounding in my ears, and then something splashed behind me.

It was the wizard. Soaked, scowling, and streaked with bits of the snake that were never meant to see daylight, she kicked toward the sandbar, swimming awkwardly with one hand. The other towed Moyna, who half-floated behind her, limp as a raft of kelp. As I watched, the girl reached the sandbar, dragged her unconscious prize onto dry land, then stuffed her wand into the back of her pants and knelt over Moyna. "Breathing," she announced a few seconds later, wiping at a bleeding cut on my daughter's forehead. "Concussion must have knocked her out. You want her or what?"

"I'll...I'll handle this from here," I replied, thrown by

her perfunctory assessment. "Are you al—"

"The *fuck* were you thinking?" she snapped as she found her feet. "How the hell did Aiden get out here? Did no one bother telling you he's a damn mongrel, or was your head too far up your ass to see that he's got no talent whatsoever?"

I floated Moyna a few feet above the ground and glanced over the wizard's shoulder as Joey and Georgie landed on the sandbar. "Helen Carver, I presume."

"Damn straight. Where's my brother?"

"He's resting," said Joey, and Helen, who had been too preoccupied to notice the incoming dragon, spun around and yelped. "He's awake, just got a little water up his nose," he soothed. "I think he's got a few broken ribs, though, and he's worried sick about you—want a lift?" he asked, patting Georgie's side.

Helen took a retreating step toward me, then seemed to accept the fact that she was caught between two things that upset her and chose the lesser evil. "Sure," she muttered, and let Joey pull her onto the dragon's back. "Does this thing come with seatbelts?"

You smell awful, Georgie thought, unable to understand the wizard's complaints, and took off before Helen could change her mind and disembark.

Left alone with Moyna, I sighed, blasted a hole through the snake bits blocking my path, and made my way back to shore, dissolving the sandbar behind me.

CHAPTER 15

"**He**'s coming home with me, and that's final."

"Ms. Carver," I sighed, rubbing my head to distract me from the morning's headache—which, by then, had become the afternoon's headache—"that is entirely up to him, and he's not going anywhere until he's whole."

"Mom's been putting him back together for years!" she protested, slamming her fist on my desk. "She knows what goes where! Why are you being so damn *difficult?*"

I cracked my eyes open, found her leaning over the desk in an obvious attempt at dominance, and decided I didn't have one more fight in me at that moment. "Aiden is here because he wants to be here," I said quietly, resuming my massage. "And the last time I took him back to your little bunker, your parents locked him out. So tell me, Ms. Carver, what's changed?"

She stiffened and withdrew slightly from my personal space. "They didn't say—"

"They told you about him, didn't they?"

"The grand magus did." Her chin rose as her jaw clenched. "I let him know when I was coming home for Thanksgiving break—he'd promised to work with me on this defensive matrix...never mind," she muttered, remembering her audience. "He wrote me back and said we needed to talk before I came home, and that my folks weren't to know about it. Hence the five a.m. meeting. I thought he wanted to chat about the succession again, but he told me what had happened to Aiden."

"What did he say?"

Helen folded her arms and rested her hip against the desk, staring out the window at the perpetually blooming rose garden. "Told me the truth. Aiden's a mongrel, Mom's not his mother. Said you were holding him over here."

"Did Greg bother telling you I'm trying to help him?" I asked, looking at her until she turned to glare at me again. "Did he tell you Aiden spent most of last year in his bedroom out of fear for his safety? Did he tell you what happened to the poor kid once you left?"

"Stop it."

"Well, did he?"

"What was I supposed to do?" she exclaimed. "Take him with me, plunk him in some public school in Nashville, hide him in my dorm? He'd have been miserable with me."

"I don't know, he speaks of you fondly enough. Good old Hel who always looked out for him." I watched her face work for a few seconds, then said, "I'm not trying to make you feel guilty. You're entitled to an education, and congratulations to you for escaping the silo. Daylight must be such a novel sensation."

"Yeah, laugh it up," she muttered. "I've heard all the Mole People jokes before. But look, I know the truth about Aiden now, and if he's really fighting with Mom and Dad…well, it wouldn't be that hard to get an off-campus apartment, not at the start of the semester. He could live with me…he's too young for a full-time job," she said, working it out as she spoke, "but if he took the SAT, he could start school by this time next year. Especially if I'm there to keep an eye on him. Problem solved."

"And for now? You can't bring him back to the silo."

"If our parents are being difficult…I *suppose* we could do the holidays in the dorms," she said, frowning into the corner. "Not ideal, but…but you have no right to keep him here," she continued with renewed indignation, finding her message once more. "I'm his *sister*, I'll take care of him."

I studied her for a moment in silence, then murmured, "Greg didn't tell you who Aiden's mother was, did he?"

"Given that he's here, I'd assume one of your people. I made the grand magus open a gate to Aiden before he got into the details—the Arcanum keeps blood samples around for location purposes," she explained. "He said he'd had the tracking spell going for days. Led me right to him. What were you doing with him, anyway? Sending a mongrel up against a faerie? What's that, some sort of sick joke?"

"He was trying to help me...*diffuse*...a situation," I said. "And he might have done it, had you not butted in and started sparking." I stood and headed past her to my bar. "Aiden's my brother."

"*What?*"

"He's as much my blood as he is yours," I continued, reaching for the scotch. "And as such, I also have a vested interest in his well-being. If you'd like to sit down, the couches aren't booby-trapped." She looked about uncertainly, finally shaken, and slunk to a free seat as I poured a neat double. "What's your poison?"

"Vodka tonic," she mumbled, staring into space.

"Oh, good. I was afraid you were going to name something pink in the martini family." I fixed her drink and carried them to the coffee table, then sat across from her. "Ms. Carver," I said as she took a cautious sip, "I'm not holding Aiden captive. If he wants to go, it's his right. If he wants to stay, he's welcome. I'm trying to help him."

"By getting him killed?" she retorted, slamming her glass to the table as her thoughts snapped back into focus. "He's a kid! He's helpless—"

"And he's trying to stand on his own feet. We were right there—it's not as if I let him go without backup. I mean, yes, he's *young*," I said, swirling my scotch, "but you've got to give him room to be a man."

She sat back and crossed her arms. "I'd rather him be

alive and hating me than dead as a result of half-cocked self-actualization. He's a fifteen-year-old mongrel. You let him square off again a faerie with a giant *snake*. Now, which of us is the responsible adult here?"

"Says the child who can't legally purchase her vodka."

"Bite me," she huffed. "All right. You're telling me my kid brother is a high lord, is that it?"

"Quick on the draw, aren't you?"

Her dark eyes narrowed in exasperation. "We do learn *something* of the courts, you realize."

"Not nearly enough." As her brows knit, I sipped my drink, then said calmly, "You entered the realm without an express invitation or any guarantee of safe passage. You and your little stick are now in my office, defying me to my face. Has Greg taught you nothing about, oh, propriety or self-preservation?" I smirked as she began to pale, then shook my head. "Relax, kid, you're in no immediate danger. If I'd thought you a legitimate threat, you'd be dead by now."

I had to give her credit—the girl kept her composure remarkably well. "You're not going to bully me into abandoning Aiden," she said. "He's my responsibility."

"You're tenacious, and I admire that, but the decision is Aiden's, not yours. Nor mine, for that matter." While she was preoccupied with finding a rebuttal, I glanced beneath the surface of her thoughts and drank in silence.

Finally, she said, "He needs to be around people his own age. Or hell, people *my* age. Maybe he's not emotionally ready for college—I don't know—but he could be learning something useful, meeting people, figuring out what he's going to do with his life. I can help him."

"Sure. And in a couple of years, you'll go back to Montana and prepare to take the reins from Greg, and Aiden will be on his own. You can't take him back to the silo with you," I continued, watching her mouth tighten. "Boy's a mongrel, right? Word's bound to get around eventually. So you're going to be grand magus before long, and Aiden will live out his days working a nine-to-five, maybe going to Fringe support meetings—"

"To what?"

"Exactly. He'll have nothing to do with the Arcanum, and he'll resent all of you for the rest of his life because he's seen behind the curtain, he knows what's really out there, and it's been snatched away. So maybe he'll meet that nice girl and settle down," I said, speeding up to deny the wizard her opening, "and he'll tell her he's an orphan, because how else would he explain his family? Maybe he'll have those two and a half kids and a Lab, and maybe they'll be perfectly mundane, and no one will ever know Daddy's little secret. Of course," I said, leaning toward her, "you and I will be watching his every move for the next seventy-odd years, since he'll be the perfect target. Your little brother, *my* little brother, and as you said, helpless. Easy pickings." I paused, letting that sink in. "If that's what he wants, so be it. But if he wants to stay here and see if something rubs off on him, then I'm not going to kick him out just because you think he needs to get on with his life."

She sipped her drink in silence for a long moment, then put it down and murmured, "You can't keep him safe here."

"At least as safe as you can over there," I countered. "Really, sending him off to battle his niece is only an occasional event. He spends most of his time either playing with his robots or hanging around with Joey."

"Who?"

"The fellow with the dragon."

"Oh, right," she muttered. "That's *so* reassuring."

"He's twenty-five, he's responsible enough. And like it or not, Aiden seems happy."

She sighed and scowled at the carpet. "So how am I supposed to tell Mom and Dad that I left him here with you?"

"Honestly?" I finished my scotch, and the dirty glass vanished. "Perhaps I'm mistaken, but the impression I've gotten thus far is that you may be the one person in that hole who gives a damn. Well, maybe your mother, too," I amended. "*Maybe* Greg. But I can't see your father shedding many tears if Aiden were to drop off the face of the earth. Can you?" She struggled for a response, and I said, "Ms. Carver, I know you're concerned. The extent of your concern is admirable. The fact that you would take on an angry faerie and something out of the Gray Lands out of concern for Aiden is also admirable, even if it makes *me* concerned for your overall sanity. But you didn't do this to Aiden," I continued quietly. "You didn't make him like this, you didn't 'hog' the talent. And you can't protect him forever. Maybe I can."

She looked up, the light of challenge glowing once more in her eyes. "I'm stronger than you think."

"I don't doubt that you're strong, but let's be realistic about this. Which of us is better equipped?"

Her hand snaked behind her coat and emerged with her wand as she went to her feet. "I'm not some pushover witch," she insisted, slipping behind the couch. "I don't even need the wand half the time. I can hold my own, and as for Aiden—"

"Oh, you can hold your own, can you?" I echoed, chuckling. "I'm sure you're quite formidable against your peers, but do you think—"

A sudden bolt of force from the wand cut me off, and I shielded, deflecting it to dissipate harmlessly near the ceiling. "You really want to rumble?" I asked her incredulously. "You and me, here, now?"

She gritted her teeth and nodded, wand at the ready.

"All right, then," I said, spreading my arms, "take your best shot, kid."

And she did. The blast that flew from the tip of her wand put her warning shot to shame, but I concentrated on my shield and held her at bay. She danced around the room, trying to get around the shield, but I'd been in enough fights with wizards to anticipate her choreography—the Arcanum, grown fat and lazy, hadn't developed any new fighting techniques in centuries. I let her go on the offensive for a few minutes, giving her time to wear herself out, then dropped my shield and grabbed her in an invisible chokehold. An instant later, she was flat against the ceiling, coughing against the pressure on her trachea and kicking at nothing.

"Drop the stick," I murmured as she purpled.

She resisted as long as she could, then let her wand fall to the rug. I picked it up, turned it over in my hands, then dropped her back to the ground, jerking her to a stop an instant before she hit the floor. "Nice construction," I said, studying the decorative flourishes carved into her wand as she wheezed at my feet. "Obviously not a witch's tool. I assume Rick made this?"

She looked up at me, eyes watering, and struggled for breath. "You...cheat..."

"Cheat?" I laughed, tossing the wand back to her. "Hardly. *That's* how you wield magic, Ms. Carver." I squatted down, watching her rub her bruising throat. "I may be new to this job, but I'm still a king. Certain power comes with the throne. If I wanted you dead, little girl, I'd have stopped your heart before you got your hand on that pretty wand of yours. Consider this a lesson," I added, standing once more, "and tell your teachers they've been remiss in their instruction."

When her gasping calmed, she tucked the wand away and pushed herself from the floor, red-faced and disheveled but seemingly in control. A peek below her surface revealed the storm within, however—anger and humiliation raging against the knowledge that she was, for once, impotent—and I stepped away, giving her a bit of breathing room. "That was, perhaps, uncalled for," I said, leaning against the bar. "Are you hurt?"

"Fine," she croaked, absently massaging her neck.

I watched her return to her seat, then offered, "Greg wouldn't have fared any better, you know." Her head shot up, and I thought I detected a flash of surprise beneath her façade. "It's the truth—he's powerful for what he is, but we're playing in different leagues, so to speak. All things considered, you handled yourself well," I continued, pouring a fresh drink. "I'm sure you're a match for any wizard, Ms. Carver, and your training is evident. Stop doubting yourself."

Her eyes widened. "How did—"

"Fae. Refill?" I asked, tipping the open bottle toward her. She nodded, and I whipped up a second vodka tonic, going heavy on the vodka to assuage my sudden guilt at her bruises. "Greg hasn't been grand magus this long due to brute strength," I told her as I headed for the couch. "Half of his power comes from understanding and working around his limitations. Get that part down, and you'll be his equal. Until then, try to remember that cockiness gets you killed, kid."

She waited as I drank, then mumbled, "I thought…you know, we've, uh…"

"The Arcanum has killed faeries in the past?" I finished for her. "Yes, I'm well aware. Been on the target end of that a few times," I added, smiling to myself to see her squirm. "But they seldom send a lone wizard to do the job—that's nearly always suicidal. You have better success in groups, and if you're wise, you'll forget the sticks entirely." The wizard frowned, and I explained, "I smell magic. Your wands reek of it. More importantly, the odds of besting a faerie in a contest of magic are slim—you're better served with a knife."

"A knife," she echoed doubtfully.

"Yeah. Knife, sword, something sharp and iron-based. A gun's not a bad backup, but they're easy enough to jam. Hell, a bag of ball bearings and a slingshot would be a better idea than waving a stick around and hoping for the best. Trust me," I said, lifting my glass, "if you want the job done, you go armed with iron. Silver's effective but impractical as a true weapon. Too soft."

She bit her lip as she mulled this over. "And you're telling me this because…"

"Because it might save your life someday," I replied, turning the empty glass back to dust, "and because Aiden, at least, would mourn your passing. But seriously, when you see him next, do impress upon Greg the fact that you thought you could take me on by yourself. He'll have a heart attack, but at least he'll know where your education is lacking." I watched her as she sipped her drink and noticed again the angry discolorations around her throat. "Neck still sore?"

"It'll be fine."

"I can dull the pain for you, if you'd like," I said, then caught her expression and offered, "Or Toula—she's down the hall, and it's not as if she's doing much until Aiden wakes."

The girl snorted and massaged her neck. "Yeah, like I'm going to let Toula Pavli come near me with a wand."

"You make it sound like she's Wizard Hitler. I'm fairly sure she's not doing anything to harm Aiden."

"Ever heard of Apollonios Pavli?" she retorted.

"Does she behave like her father?" I countered. "Come to think of it, if we're going by that logic, does your brother behave like Titania?"

"That's not—"

"That's *exactly* the same comparison," I said, cutting her protest short. "Toula isn't a mass murderer, and Aiden isn't Mother. Trust me on that one," I muttered, "I knew her." She continued to regard me uneasily, and I sighed. "Look, Ms. Carver, we may as well try to be civil for Aiden's sake. Especially if Greg's tapped you for—"

"Helen."

I paused, thrown by the interruption. "Come again?"

"Helen," she repeated. "I suppose, if we're going to be dealing with each other…I'm Helen."

"As you like," I said with a nod. "Coileán. Or Colin, one's as good as the other." I waited, studying her inscrutable expression, then quietly told her, "I'm not the enemy, you know. Greg and I have managed to stay on speaking terms thus far. I just want what's best for Aiden."

"So do I," she began, but whatever followed slipped past me as the realm, which had been quietly complaining ever since I'd had the audacity to let Toula and Helen into Faerie, sent up an excited shout. I cried aloud and grabbed my temples with the volume of the realm's joy, and I felt Helen's hand on my shoulder an instant later. "What's wrong?" she asked through the internal clamor. "Are you all right? What's happening?"

Before I could answer, the door flew open and Oberon strolled in, still sporting his board shorts and faded flip-flops. "Sounds like someone missed me," he said, rubbing one ear. "Do hope I'm not interrupting."

I forced myself off the couch and slid in front of the wizard, blocking her in case of sudden enchantment. "What are you doing here?" I demanded as the ringing in my head began to subside.

He spread his hands and smirked. "Am I not allowed to see my dear granddaughter? You *did* bring her back here, I take it." He glanced around my office and gave it a cursory nod. "Bit more subdued than your mother's style. She'd have hated what you've done with the place."

"Stay away from her."

Oberon rolled his eyes and sighed. "I'm not here to kill her—unless you've reconsidered? No?" My glare was as good as an answer, and he shrugged. "All right, but it's your funeral, boy. As long as you're keeping her alive, I thought I might offer some assistance."

That set off every alarm, though I tried to keep my face still. "Meaning?"

"Meaning you obviously can't construct a bind to save your life. I'll bind her for you, do it properly this time. As long as you keep her from returning to Faerie, it should hold."

He had a point, but I knew well enough not to leap into a bargain blind. "What's in it for you, then?"

"Aside from protecting my investments against marauding children and their pet snakes? Entertainment. You, my idiot daughter, and little Mordred, trying to make a family if it kills you. Believe me, Coileán," he said with a cold smile, "I'm willing to play the long game."

"And what's that?" I snapped. "Sit back and wait until we implode?"

"Precisely." An open bottle of Corona appeared in his hand, and he took a long swig. "This little fantasy you've concocted can't last," he said, wiping his mouth. "The girl's a walking bomb. If you had even the most common of sense, you'd realize that, but you don't, and there's no convincing fools of their foolishness. And so I'll be in the wings until you see the light or she destroys you, whichever comes first." He raised his bottle in a mocking salute. "Sentiment's going to be your downfall, you know. And what's that, a pet wizard?" he added, glancing around me at Helen.

She stepped forward, head high but wand tucked away. "Not pet," she replied in badly accented Fae. "You—"

"I'll handle this," I interrupted, trying to push her back to relative safety, but Oberon chuckled.

"Go on, let the little thing speak for herself," he said, grinning as the girl tried to keep up. "What does one do with a pet wizard, anyway?"

I glanced pointedly at Helen, who thought for a moment, then folded her arms and cleared her throat. "Lord Oberon," she said, resorting to English, "I know you understand me perfectly well, and so I'll save us the time. I am no one's *pet*, I am a guest, and I assume you're making Lord Coileán cross for the sheer pleasure of provoking him. As we've all had a long day, and as I can only suppose you came alone, might I humbly suggest you cut it the hell out?"

Oberon, taken aback, gawked at Helen in sudden silence, and I fought hard to control my laughter. "What she said," I told him, cocking my head at the annoyed wizard. "If you want to take a stab at binding Moyna, go ahead, but I'll not suffer insults to the girl."

He looked back and forth between us, studying the situation, then seemed to come to an internal resolution and drank again. "You're hopeless, boy," he said as he brushed past Valerius and into the corridor, "but yes, I think I'll have a bit of fun."

Helen and I stood there as his footsteps died away, and I realized my muscles had reflexively tightened and forced them to unclench. When I was sure he was out of earshot, I muttered to her, "Don't do that again, okay?"

"I'm really not in the mood for any more bullshit right now," she replied, then finished her drink in one long sip. "And I've had two of those in under an hour, so that could be exacerbating the problem."

"Would you like to be sober?"

"No, and don't try to mess with my head," she said, sliding out of my reach. "This is a no-enchantment zone," she added, prodding her chest with two fingers. "Are we clear on that?"

"Crystal, but if you're going to be lurking around here, you might want the language."

"Not today." She frowned at the room, then plopped back onto the couch, covered her face with her palms, and groaned. "Shit, I can't go home like this."

"You're not *that* wasted," I replied, sitting beside her. "Believe me, Greg's seen worse."

"No, I mean everything with Aiden—I can't *leave* him. For God's sake," she said, looking up at me, "he's unconscious, you've got *Pavli* allegedly putting him back together, and he's in the middle of friggin' Faerie. I can't leave him like this."

"Well, I've got matters to address, and I'm not leaving you unattended in my office," I said. "Want a room? I'll send someone to fetch you when he wakes."

"No," she muttered, and stood once more. "I need to get out of here. Need to walk. Think."

I caught her before she reached the door. "The gardens are out back," I offered. "And Joey should be around—he knows the place reasonably well. Do you want a guide?"

Helen shrugged and brushed her hair from her face. "This day's not going to get any weirder. Bring on Dragon Boy."

I had to hand it to Toula—the woman was more adept with technical magic than most of the magi, grand or otherwise, I'd ever known. A lifetime of working around the limitations of her bind had forced her to perfect the finer nuances of spellwork that so many wizards ignored. When bound, she had been skilled, albeit frustrated. Freed and in her full power, though, she was a force to be respected—a fact I didn't treat lightly. It was one thing to find myself nominally in charge of a court—I thought I knew enough by then to stay one step ahead of the average faerie—but quite another to be confronted with an atypical witch-blood with the skill and the chutzpah to wander into the realm whenever she pleased.

Fortunately for me, Toula seemed to have decided that we could be pals.

Valerius had thought to fetch her once I'd herded or dragged our crew back through the gate, and whether because he'd been the one to ask or because he let slip that Meggy was almost in hysterics, she hopped out of bed, threw an oft-washed D.C. sweatshirt on over her boxers, and assumed control of the situation while I tried to simultaneously calm Meggy and pacify Helen. By the time I'd coaxed Meggy into a dark room and nudged her into sleep, Toula had banished Joey and Georgie to the barn to decompress, worked a spell over Moyna to keep her unconscious, moved Aiden into his room to begin fusing his ribs back together, and told her brother, in no uncertain terms, to keep Helen out of her hair while she worked. With Helen finally out of my way, I had time to check on Toula's progress.

I caught her slipping out of Aiden's room as I rounded the corner to find her. "Sleeping," she whispered, latching the door. "He'll be good as new when he wakes. Maybe a little sore, but that's why we have Tylenol." She wiped her hands against each other as if brushing off the etheric traces of her spell. "Sent Carver home?"

"Sent her outside," I replied, following Toula down the hall to the bedroom where I'd left Meggy. "Oberon's here to bind Moyna."

"Oh, goody," she muttered, then cracked the door open, listened to the silence, and shut it with a nod. "Still out. Let them both sleep it off—it's not going to hurt them, and quite honestly, I'd rather deal with this situation without asking Meggy to make any decisions."

She headed for the stairwell, aiming for the secure underground room where we'd moved Moyna, and I trailed at her heels. "Meggy has a right—"

"Meggy is a mess," Toula interrupted, lighting the spiral staircase with a flick of her fingers as pair of glowing orbs manifested above her. "I say this with love, but you and I both know she's going to be useless in a crisis involving that girl. Better to do what needs to be done and ask forgiveness later."

"We're not killing her."

She stopped and looked at me with horror. "Of course we aren't killing her! Damn, Gramps, let's ease up on the psychopathy, okay? I was thinking, you know, a bind and some therapy, and you're all the way off the cliff…"

"Long day," I muttered, pushing past her down the stairs. "And what sort of therapy would you recommend, hmm? I can't really see the three of us in family counseling."

"Not as such, but if you got some sort of mediator,

tried to talk it out with her—"

It was my turn to stop and stare. "She wants me dead. By now, I'm sure she wants Meggy dead, too. How am I supposed to talk sense into *that*?"

Toula shrugged. "Start with a decent bind, I guess, and see where it goes once she wears herself out." She hesitated, then said, "You really thought of killing her? Your own kid?"

"It was Oberon's idea."

She muttered under her breath—I caught only the words *faerie* and *lunatic*—and we descended the rest of the way into the cool darkness of the cellar in silence. Her roving light joined us an instant later, throwing the barred doors of Mother's storage rooms—and Oberon—into sudden relief.

He leaned against the moist stone wall, arms folded, and blinked rapidly at the change in light. "You could have warned me about that," he said, his voice echoing off the vaulted ceiling.

"You're lurking in my basement," I replied, and he straightened as I headed past him toward Moyna's holding cell. "I don't lurk in your basement, do I?"

"I don't *have* a basement. And you've found another pet witch?" he asked, deigning to notice Toula. "What are you doing, breeding them?"

"Can it, Red," Toula muttered over the slap of her flip-flops on the flagstones. "Be useful or be gone."

I smelled the change as it happened, but Toula was quicker on the draw and threw up a shield against the bolt of force that flew from Oberon's palm. "Cute," she said, straining slightly as the attack subsided, then dropped her shield, cupped her hands together, and blasted back at him with a ringing cry of, "*Lorem!*"

Surprised for the second time that afternoon, Oberon failed to prepare for the counter-attack and was thrown headfirst into the wall by the strength of Toula's spell. He sank to the floor with a groan, and by the time he'd realized what had happened and why his head was pounding, she was shielded again and primed. He slowly picked himself up, patted the back of his head for injury, then looked at me in confusion.

"Perfect witch-blood," I explained, hoping he hadn't had a concussion. "You remember Toula, right?"

He watched her for a moment as his eyes recalled how to focus, then gingerly nodded.

"Great," she said, smirking at his dazed discomfort. "No more cheap shots, eh?"

Oberon stumbled away from the wall, giving her a significant berth, then peered at me and muttered, "How?"

"Mab, a wizard, and a ton of dumb luck," I replied. "And I'd prefer not to find out exactly what she's capable of while we're all down here together, so how about not making this difficult for once?"

"She *hit* me," he said, nearly whining in his disbelief.

"She's quick on the draw—and again, she's my guest. Try that again if you want a fight."

His green eyes narrowed. "Your mother wouldn't have permitted her pets to so insult me, boy."

"You may have noticed by now that I'm not my mother," I said, and stopped before Moyna's door. "How are we proceeding?"

"Well," said Toula, drawing up beside me, "I can keep her unconscious indefinitely. There's plenty here to feed the spell, and the work's solid, if I do say so myself. If you want to bind her, you can do so with the spell still intact, but I'd feel more comfortable being on hand to patch it as needed. Large-scale enchantment plus large-scale spellwork…"

The end of that thought didn't need to be vocalized. "Agreed. What do you need from me?"

"Just be nearby in case I need to amp up the juice. I'd rather not be rebuilding and feeding all at once." She looked around me at Oberon, who glared sullenly back at her. "You're doing the bind, I understand?"

"Perhaps."

Toula huffed in exasperation. "Yes or no, it's that simple. Or did I hurt your little feelings?"

"Don't even think it," I snapped, seeing his hand flinch, then gave Toula a look that I hoped properly conveyed the gravity of the situation. She stepped back a pace and raised her palms in surrender, and I turned my attention to Oberon. "You're right," I told him, "your binds are better than mine. Will you do it?"

He stood there, regarding us both in stony silence, then shrugged as if nothing were amiss. "Of course my binds are better than yours, boy," he replied, pushing the door open. "Do you have any idea how much practice I've had?"

"I don't really want to think about it," I muttered to no one, but followed him into the room.

My daughter lay motionless atop a plush bed in her windowless cell. I assumed the bed and its rose-print linens were a product of Toula's imagination, as the ensemble was nothing if not out of place in that dank hole. I'd thrown up wards around the cellar to keep Moyna in, but Toula had taken it a step further, crafting her own brand of wards around the walls and door of the room, and my skin tingled as I passed through them. The little orbs followed Toula, giving me a clearer view of Moyna's pale face, her salt-stiffened tresses, and the myriad bruises on her bare arms from impact with the flying gore and the water. In the poor light, she could have been a corpse— but on closer inspection, her thin chest rose and fell in a slow rhythm, and enough color suffused her cheeks to give me confidence that she lived yet.

"Are you *certain* about this?" Oberon asked, pulling me back from her bedside. "It would be a moment's work—"

"Don't hurt her."

He sighed. "If she harms my people or my property, I'll hold you fully responsible."

"If you bind her properly," I countered, "she won't be

able to harm you."

After a moment's contemplation, he allowed, "I suppose that's fair," then stepped closer to the bed. "Next question: keep her memory intact?"

"No."

"*Yes*," Toula insisted, planting her fists on her hips when we turned to her. "Seriously? We're having this debate? How well did that memory wipe work last time?"

"It only failed because the bind failed," I protested. "And need I remind you that she—"

"Wants to dance atop your grave, I know, I know. But how do you expect this mess to get any better if you don't even try? You've got her at your mercy—treat her with a modicum of respect, have the decency to leave her with her own mind, and work with her. Rewriting her memory again is tantamount to slapping a band-aid on a septic wound and hoping for the best."

"Or," Oberon said quietly, "you could take the advice of the most experienced person in this room. Your decision, Coileán."

I moved to Moyna's side and looked down at my child, who was still and dirty and frowning ever so slightly in her sleep. There was so much of Mother—and, I realized uncomfortably, of Aiden—in her features, but there was also a shadow of Meggy across her face, something I recognized yet couldn't quite pinpoint.

She had her mother's eyes, I recalled. If they opened, I would see Meggy's pale blue eyes staring back at me, hating me, fearing me...

I almost touched her hand, but I hesitated, suddenly—irrationally—afraid of breaking the spell holding her in check.

"All right, Toula," I said, stepping out of the way, "we'll leave Moyna intact. But you're going to have to explain why to Meggy when this is all said and done."

"If she ever wants Olive," she replied, pushing up her sweatshirt's sleeves, "she's going to have to trust me and

make peace with Moyna. Now get back and let me work."
She waited until I'd retreated to the door, then nodded at
Oberon. "Whenever you're ready, bub."

CHAPTER 16

Aiden woke at dawn, whole and hale—if a little discolored and smelling of salt—and wandered down to my preferred dining room to ask about pancakes and his sister. I summoned an aide to handle the former—my attempts at pancakes usually ended up rubbery, for some reason—and turned to the realm for assistance with the latter. The familiar voice in my head, which had mellowed in its disappointment at Oberon's departure, directed me toward the barn, and I forewent the walk in favor of the faster rip-open-the-fabric-of-space method upon which I'd recently come to rely.

The interior of the barn was still shaded from the weak light, but Georgie's red eyes opened as I slipped into the main room—which, I noticed with faint trepidation, had been expanded in recent days. The dragonet stretched her front legs and refolded her wings, then rested her head on her feet and blinked slowly. *Breakfast?* she asked, sounding hopeful.

"There's a flock out there with your name on it," I whispered back to her, stepping around a waist-high pile of her cold leavings. "Go do some damage."

Not anymore.

"What do you mean?" I asked, glancing at the open doors, then realized that something seemed amiss in the barn—a certain lack of bleating. "Where are they?"

Georgie's thought was colored by a faint sheen of guilt. *I got hungry last night.*

I could only goggle at her. "You ate the *entire* flock?"

Wrapping her tail around her, she explained, *Couldn't sleep. Sheep helped.*

"Why couldn't you sleep? What's the matter?"

The tip of her tail twitched as it slid over her nose. *Bad dream.*

"A bad dream," I repeated, leaning against a stack of hay bales. "You had a bad dream, and you stress-ate twenty-odd sheep? Is that right?"

Yes?

I sighed and waved at the empty pasture, and the familiar bleating once more filled the air. "That's forty, Georgie. *Forty.* Try to give them time to reproduce between meals, all right?"

She stared through the doors at the pasture, seemingly uncertain of whether it was safe to unwrap herself and rise, but her stomach rumbled audibly, and with another snort, she climbed to her feet and plodded out to kill her meal, screeching at the sunrise for good measure. I shook my head, tried to ignore my terrified creations' frantic bleats, and climbed the wooden staircase to the loft—once a little room under the eaves, and now a pleasant nook roughly halfway up the enlarged barn. I supposed Joey had worked with Val to customize his space—I couldn't fathom where else he'd have come up with taupe paint, light-blocking curtains, sword hooks, and, I noticed to my amusement, a large bathroom with a claw-footed soaking tub. The place was rustic but still on the respectable end of bachelor pads, even if everything smelled slightly of charred mutton and dragon dung.

As my eyes adjusted, I picked out two figures in the room, one buried beneath the blankets on the bed, and the other sprawled on the couch across the loft. A closer inspection of the couch revealed a tuft of blond hair peeking from beneath the quilt—Joey, I presumed. The smaller lump on the bed appeared to be a brunette, and the purple coat discarded at the foot lent credence to my supposition that I'd found Helen. I shook her shoulder and stepped back as she muttered and sat up, scowling at the gloom and clasping the burgundy comforter to her chest. "Wha?" she mumbled, then noticed me, remembered where she was, and clutched the blanket more tightly. "*Jesus*," she hissed, suddenly awake, "a little privacy?"

"Aiden was asking for you," I whispered, mindful of Joey sleeping behind me. "I thought you'd want to know." I paused, took in the details of the room, then smirked at the girl in the bed. "Sorry, am I interrupting something?"

Helen snatched her discarded clothing off the rug and slipped back beneath the blankets. "You know, there's a reason he's sleeping on that side of the room. *Some* guys are gentlemen."

"And then there's me," I replied, lifting her bra off the floor with one finger. "Missing this?" Her hand darted out from under the covers and yanked it back, and I chuckled as the bed creaked with her awkward attempt at modesty. "You're telling me you spent all night out here with these two, and nothing at all untoward happened?"

A moment later, she emerged from the bedding, disheveled but clothed, and tucked her wand back into her pants as she scoured Joey's dresser for his hairbrush. "And why would anything untoward have happened?" she asked, yanking the brush through her thick rat's nest. "We toured, we talked, he cooked, I slept. Not everyone has the libido of a sixteen-year-old boy."

"He took a vow of celibacy once—did he mention that?"

"Briefly." She winced at a bad tangle, then gave in, waved her wand at her head, and waited as her hair returned to smooth and straight. "We didn't exactly dwell on it. The priesthood's more than a chronic lack of sex."

"So he told you about seminary?" I asked as she pulled her coat on.

"Yep. He told me how he got here."

"Told you about the mermaid?"

Helen's dark brow arched. "Actually, yes. He said he figured you'd tell me eventually anyway. To each his own," she added, shoving her feet into her tennis shoes. "Now, where've you hidden Aiden this time?"

Helen's face broadcast her relief at seeing Aiden sitting up and stuffing himself, but to her chagrin, he refused to leave with her. "I'd get in the way in Nashville," he said between bites of bacon. "And things are good here...unless you want me gone?" he asked me, abruptly unsure of himself.

"Nothing of the sort," I replied, reaching for the coffee.

"Okay, good." He started mopping up the remaining syrup with whatever food was most readily at hand. "So I'm staying here, then," he told his sister. "Thanks for the offer, but I'm fine where I am."

"Aid," she protested, "do you hear yourself? This is *Faerie*! It's dangerous, I can't leave you on your own!"

He cut his eyes to me and shrugged. "I'm not on my own. Coileán's all right."

"High praise," I muttered into my mug.

Aiden grinned and continued his quest to scrub every atom of syrup from the china. "You don't have to worry about me," he said to Helen as he worked. "Go on, go do your finals or whatever, and...uh..." He hesitated, then looked up at her and mumbled, "When you go home, tell Mom I'm okay, will you? I'd tell her myself, but...you know."

She slid into the chair beside him and gripped his shoulder. "Come back with me. I'll talk to the grand magus, and we'll get everything straightened out. You don't have to do this—"

"I *want* to do this."

Flummoxed, she fumbled for a response for a moment, then tried again with intensified fervor. "Just listen to me, okay? Listen to the sister who loves you, Aiden," she said, taking his chin in hand and steering his face toward hers. "If you stay here, you're turning your back on all of us. All of the Arcanum, everyone you've ever known, everything that's ever mattered. Is that what you really want?" She took his free hand and squeezed it so hard her fingers whitened. "Come with me. Let me get you back into school, get you a job, whatever you want to do. We'll do it together, okay? You and me, Aid, like always."

He sat there in miserable silence, then dropped the last of his pancakes, wiped his hand clean, and stared at the nothingness over his plate. "I'm not turning my back on you, Hel," he said softly. "I wouldn't do that."

"But you are."

"No, I'm *not*," he insisted, and when he looked up again, his eyes were moist. "All of you turned your backs on me. Dad, Mom, the grand magus…all of you. And now you want me to go home and pretend like everything's great? Like I don't know they look at me like I'm nothing? Go back and be the dud again, stay out of the way until someone needs a punching bag? *That's* what you think I should do?" he asked, his voice rising. "You don't know what it's like! You'll *never* know what it's like!"

"You think they respect you any more over here?" she retorted. "They *kill* mongrels! They're a bunch of crazy—"

"No one's broken my face lately! Or my arms!"

"Then what the hell do you call yesterday?"

"I was trying to help!"

"You could have been killed!"

"It was going along fine until *you* butted in!" He snatched his hand away from her and pushed back from the table. "Go home, Hel. You don't get it, you don't want to get it, so go home."

"Aid, wait," she pleaded as he stormed out of the room, but the slamming door was his only reply.

And so we sat in awkward silence, Helen and I, as the grandfather clock ticked and I drank my coffee, until she broke down, covered her face, and sobbed.

By the time she pulled herself back together, I'd finished my drink and taken Aiden's vacated chair. "Are you giving up on him?" I asked, passing her a clean napkin.

She swiped at her eyes and shook her head.

"Good. Stay as long as you like." Before she could protest, I touched her temple and pressed Fae into her mind. "Sorry about that, but you may need it. Oh, and for the record," I said over her sniffles, "we don't kill all our mongrels. And you might want to have a chat with Toula before you go. You know, get someone else's perspective on growing up in that silo of yours. I'm sure she has stories. Then again," I said, rising from the table, "you're going to be grand magus, so why should the miserable childhoods of a couple of mongrels trouble you?"

I headed for the door, intending to leave her to her thoughts, but I paused when she mumbled, "Witch-blood."

"Good girl," I said, and took my leave.

On waking, Meggy had been too preoccupied with our daughter's welfare and whereabouts over the past few days to debate about the ethics of binds and memory wipes, and she brushed me off when I tried to broach the subject. "I need to be sure she's all right," she said, heading for the cellar, "and then we can talk about you doing things to her behind my back."

"Toula agreed," I began, but she cut me off with a finger to my chest.

"You're her *father*. I'm her *mother*. Toula doesn't get a vote as far as Olive's concerned."

I bit my tongue, praying to any conveniently listening deities for patience, then made another attempt as she walked away. "If you're going down now, at least take Val with you."

Meggy turned again, exasperated. "Colin, I may be new to this, but I'm fairly certain that I can handle one bound teenager by myself."

"If it doesn't hold—"

"Then I'm sure you'll know soon enough. Let me deal with Olive," she ordered, and I watched from the top of the stairs as she made her rapid descent into darkness.

At a loss for a better idea, I wandered over to Val's quarters—the man was owed many days off by then—where I found him busied with breakfast preparations. Catching me let myself in, he raised a finger to his lips, then glanced at the corner of the room, where Toula was snoring on a cot. "Problem?" he whispered, abandoning the bread he'd been prodding to rise.

"Up for a ride?" I asked.

Shortly thereafter, with food and a note left for Toula, we set out alone in my boat for the spot where Grivam and I had last parted. As Val brought us to a standstill, I stretched out my hand and signaled, hoping the merrow wouldn't keep me waiting long. Fortune decided to cut me a break, however, and within five minutes, Grivam pulled himself up against the side of the craft. "I assume that was for me," he said, his black eyes squinting in the sunlight as he dripped. "What news, Coileán?"

I pivoted in the boat to face the old merrow, careful to avoid the puddle forming beneath him. "The creature's dead. You should be able to go home in safety."

It was difficult to read his expression in his natural form, but I thought Grivam seemed more resigned than pleased at the tidings. "That is good," he said, "and I will trouble you no longer." He hesitated, then asked, "The favor I promised you...have you decided yet what you would ask of me?"

"Not at this time."

He nodded in understanding. "Then should that time come, you know where to find me. Farewell," he said, and disappeared without another word.

I stood and leaned over the side, watching the water for a trace of his passage, but the merrow have nearly perfected the art of going unnoticed, and my vigil proved fruitless. My task accomplished, Val turned our prow back toward shore, and I settled in for a pleasant trip—until, that was, my phone rang.

"I hate this thing," I muttered, pulling it from my pocket, then saw Meggy's name on the screen and felt my stomach knot as I took the call. "Any luck?"

Her voice was strained on the other end. "She won't talk to me. Just sits there and stares."

"Catatonic?" I asked, fearful that Oberon had slipped a little something extra into the bind.

"No, stubborn. Won't eat, won't speak, doesn't even react when I touch her..." She paused, and I heard her exhale slowly. "You said her memory is intact?"

"Yeah," I said, raising my voice to be heard over the wind.

"So she knows what we've done to her since March."

"I would assume so."

Meggy said nothing for the space of a long breath, then mumbled, "I want her back."

"In what—"

"I want her *back*," she insisted. "I want my Olive back. Bring her back to me."

I wished then, more than ever, that I'd left the phone at home. "Meggy, I—"

"Please, Colin. She hates me, she won't even acknowledge me," she said in a rush, "and I can't get through to her. Give me back my baby, okay? Give me my Olive. That's all I want, just my Olive, and we'll go home. Just like it was before..."

Whatever was to follow dissolved into tears, and my heart broke anew as she cried. "I'll be back soon, and we can talk about this," I said, but when that garnered no coherent response, I ended the call and put the phone away.

From the rear of the boat, Valerius asked, "Do you want a quicker arrival? It's no trouble—"

"No, but thank you." I hunched over and rested my head on my palms. "How am I supposed to tell Meggy that altering Moyna's memory again might not be the best idea?"

"Was that rhetorical, or did you want advice?"

I sat up and looked back to find him leaning against the wall of the canopied pilothouse. "Go ahead."

Val folded his bare arms and nodded curtly. "Do the right thing."

"For whom?"

"There's no 'for whom' in this—there is only the right thing." I looked at him blankly, and his eyebrow rose. "If I may be so bold, Coileán, I've known Lady Moyna much longer than you have. She can be somewhat prickly."

"Tell me something I didn't know."

His smirk spoke volumes. "But for good or ill, she is what she is. Her mother may prefer her more...well, *malleable*, I suppose...but that's not Moyna. That's a girl with Moyna's face and someone else's mind, and the Moyna I know—the Moyna who gets her way—won't sit by and let herself be mentally neutered forever." He stepped back behind the steering console and made a few fine adjustments in light of the shifting wind. "A bind is a complex piece of enchantment, you know."

"Oberon's more than proficient."

"I'm not saying he isn't. But making a bind and keeping it intact are two different matters. You...haven't had much cause to experiment with this, have you?" he added, sounding as though he already knew the answer.

"Not exactly," I admitted.

Valerius grunted and set the controls, then took a seat on the bench beside mine. "Any piece of magic— enchantment, spellcraft, what have you—is a disruption to the natural order of things, yes? You're forcing your will on the universe. If you're not careful, if you're sloppy, then wards fall, shields fail...you know this, my lord."

I nodded. "Of course."

"Well, complicate that by trying to enchant someone sensitive enough to fight back. I'm not speaking of throwing fire or lightning—I mean the more subtle works, binds and the like. The average mortal is powerless, but binding, say, another faerie..." He shifted his weight, cocked his head toward the climbing sun, then shielded his eyes from the glare. "Toula's bind would have failed years ago if she hadn't accepted it—I think she was so desperate to win the Arcanum's favor that she allowed that spell to stand, flawed as it was. Perhaps Lady Meghan would have broken her own bind, too, had she known she had the power. But *Moyna*..." Val whistled low. "She knows her power, and she's not going to accept this quietly—consciously or not, she's fighting against that bind."

I thought back over the past months and winced. "She never liked me, not from day one. I thought it was because I was dating her mother, but even with the memories I gave her, she was having trouble with Meggy by the end..."

"Fighting," he repeated. "Now, whatever Oberon did to her this time is assumedly strong, but that doesn't mean it's infallible."

"You think she's going to break it herself?"

"I think anything's possible with enough time. And should I be correct about this, what happens when it fails?" Val watched me wrestle for a moment, then said, "You have a stopgap in place, but it's not a permanent solution. I'd advise you to either find a way to dissuade Moyna from outright patricide or eliminate her."

"*Eliminate!*"

"Those are the only logical solutions," he replied, unfazed by my outburst. "And you'd be wise to remember that she favors her grandmother." He stood and returned to his post, but added, "I understand that your lover might prefer a different short-term solution, but she doesn't yet understand the long game. By now, I would hope you do."

I sighed and rose to join him at the back of the boat.

"You want to tell Meggy she's not getting her little girl back, Valerius?"

"If you insist, but since I'm not the one sleeping with her, perhaps the news should come from you. She's going to blame you, no matter who bears the tidings, but at least she won't think you a coward if you're upfront with her."

I looked out to sea, watching the waves glint as we flew by. "That's what two thousand years gets you? Clarity?"

"In certain respects. In others, I muddle through as well as the next man." He waited until I turned around, then said, "I spoke because I was asked to do so, and my advice is yours to leave or take. Whatever you choose to do, you'll hear no protest from me."

"No," I muttered, "but Georgie might."

He smiled at that. "She's a nosy little thing, isn't she?"

By the time we reached the shore—and Val, bless him, took the scenic route—I'd made up my mind to do what was in Moyna's best interest, as sick as the thought made me. Meggy would rage, and I doubted she'd be quick to forgive me, but I mused that if I could keep our daughter in Faerie—imprisoned or free, but always bound—and gradually show her I wasn't the enemy, perhaps she would come around. That would satisfy my siblings, I reasoned— Moyna without magic was still a return of their plaything—and maybe it would help me build rapport with them as well. Ji, at least, would likely be warmer toward me for bringing Moyna home.

My resolution firmed as Val and I stepped through the gate back to my office, but it faltered immediately upon seeing Meggy's puffy face. She had curled up on one of the couches with a cup of tea, and she hugged her knees against the sudden wind as I closed the gate behind us. "Honey," I began, but she shook her head to silence me.

"Still won't talk. Aiden tried. Joey tried. The little wizard girl, what's-her-name, she tried. Nothing." She uncurled and wrapped her hands around her mug. "I told Toula she could try if she wanted to, but I don't know how that's going."

Val perked up at the news. "So Toula is there now?"

"I don't know," she said dully. "Doesn't really matter, does it?"

"It might," I interjected, settling down beside Meggy and waving my hand over the coffee table. The realm was happy to oblige, and a picture appeared in the air before us, a security-camera view of Moyna's cell.

Meggy sat up and gaped. "How did—"

"Realm likes me. Shh," I said, motioning the volume up, then heard slapping footsteps crescendo outside the frame. "She's on her way in."

A few seconds later, Toula passed through the security wards, still sporting her sweatshirt and flip-flops. "Hey, there," she said in her odd version of Fae, addressing the motionless figure sitting cross-legged at the foot of the bed. "I don't think we've been introduced. Toula Pavli." She extended her hand, but Moyna gave no flicker of recognition, and she aborted the gesture. "So, Moyna," she said, waving a folding chair into existence and making herself comfortable, "I understand you're not in the mood for small talk right now. That's fine, you don't have to say anything. I just wanted to tell you a little bit about your mom and dad."

I couldn't tell if Moyna's expression changed, but Toula, seemingly nonplussed, settled back into her new seat and crossed her legs. "Let's get something out of the way to begin with: I killed Titania."

Moyna twitched at that, and Toula nodded. "Not your father, not your mother. Little old me." She waited, but Moyna was once again a statue. "You were there, sweetheart, I know you saw it go down. Maybe you want to blame Colin—and you wouldn't be alone in that, trust me—but it's not fair to drop that solely on him. He didn't come back to Faerie to kill her, you know."

Silence fell over the room for a solid minute, until finally, almost inaudibly, Moyna murmured, "Then why?"

"To rescue you and your mom. She was almost dead when we found her, did you know that? Titania was letting her starve in the dark." Toula shook her head as if to dispel the memory. "Think what you will about her, but Megs is a friend of mine. All she ever wanted was to find her stolen baby. That'd be you, incidentally," she added, raising her chin toward the bed. "She never did a damn thing to Titania, and that old hag locked her up to starve. I don't know," she said, fixing her eyes on Moyna, "maybe things are different here, but back home, if you starve a *dog*, you get prosecuted for cruelty."

Moyna maintained her silence, and Toula shrugged. "But back to my point—Colin was ready to trade himself for the two of you. That's what Titania was after, you know," she said, bouncing her sandal up and down on her foot. "Megs was collateral, and you were the bait. She wanted him back. She might have gotten him, too, if you hadn't suggested execution. Maybe it's a quirk about Joey and me, but we take it kind of personally when people are killed right in front of us—and you've got to admit that Robin had a *nasty* end."

"Mother was protecting me. She loved me," Moyna whispered.

At that, Toula threw back her head and laughed. "Bullshit," she chuckled, and Moyna flinched. "Kid, you were the means to an end, nothing more. I'm sorry to be blunt, and I know you don't want to hear this, but it's the truth. You know what Colin was worried about, all that time after the realm sealed?" she continued, leaning toward Moyna. "He was panicking about Meggy, sure, but he was also afraid that Titania would be upset that you'd come without him and kill you out of spite. *That's* what drove him—not killing her, but rescuing you. Now, you want to talk about this like an adult, or are you going to keep pouting like a toddler? Ball's in your court, babe."

By then, Moyna had abandoned all traces of her feigned apathy. "And what do you know?" she spat back at Toula. "Mother didn't love me? Moon and stars, how could *you* presume to know the first thing about that?" she said, then laughed bitterly. "So, to be clear: Mother cared nothing for me, but she gave me the world. Coileán and his whore 'love' me, so they bind me—*again*—and lock me in this stinking hole. Is that what you're telling me?"

"Pretty much," said Toula, impassive in the face of Moyna's anger. "Looks bad, I know, but Moyna, I've got a few years and a hell of a lot of experience on you."

"Don't you mean *Olive*?" she smirked.

"No. You want to be Moyna, so be Moyna. Names bring a lot of baggage with them—believe me, I get it," she muttered. "I'm not trying to make you someone you're obviously not."

That seemed to mollify the girl for the moment, and she shifted backward on the bed, moving out of Toula's space. "Fine. But don't sit there and tell me they love me. If this is their idea of love," she said, glaring at the damp walls, "then I'll take whatever you think Mother felt for me any day."

Toula absently cracked her knuckles. "I think we can agree that this is about as far from ideal as it gets, yeah?"

"Are you going to help me?"

"I'm going to try, but first, I want you to understand something." With a little grunt, she pushed herself out of her chair and moved to the bed, the better to stand over Moyna. "You think you have it bad?" she asked quietly. "My mother didn't want me for *me*. She got pregnant in order to have another experimental pawn, and my father decided to go along with it because he thought I might be a get-out-of-jail-free card. I failed on that count," she added, folding her arms. "So since my mom couldn't be bothered to raise me and my dad was incarcerated, I was raised in the Arcanum silo among people who'd just as soon have seen me dead because of the shit my dad pulled.

I got passed around a lot," she murmured. "Got a lot of side looks when folks didn't know I was on to them. Got my share of abuse, got the hell out of there as soon as I could. Long story short, I was never loved. I've never *been* loved."

I cut my eyes to Valerius, who stood in the corner of my office, silently watching. He'd adopted a stance nearly identical to his sister's, down to the wrinkle between his brows, but there was something different and unreadable in his eyes.

"Now," Toula continued, pinning Moyna to the bed with her stare, "your parents are about as far from perfect as they come, but they're trying to do right by you. This— all of this," she said, twirling one finger to encompass the room—"was the absolute best idea they could come up with in these circumstances, seeing as you tried to kill that wizard. That's Aiden's sister, by the way, so yeah, maybe not the smartest move on your part, but whatever, you're angry, I get that. Anyway, they want to work something out with you, maybe some deal whereby you get to leave the cellar and don't immediately try to kill anyone."

"And the bind comes off?" Moyna muttered.

"Not right away. Think of this as probation."

The girl huffed and glowered at the wall. "If they're going to keep me bound, why not be merciful and kill me?"

"Speaking as someone who spent the first thirty-five years of her life mostly bound, I do sympathize," said Toula, and Moyna whipped her head back around in surprise. "Yeah, you heard me—I got to grow up with a bind on because dear old Daddy went on a killing spree and my darling, absentee mother was *Mab*." She smiled grimly as the shock on Moyna's face deepened. "Oh, yes, little lady, I'm messed up in ways you can't imagine. We're not so different in that regard, I suppose," she added, watching the girl try to shift her expression back to neutral. "But enough about me. Look, Moyna, I might not know

Colin all that well, but I've known Meggy for years. *She never gave up on you*," she said, slowing for emphasis. "Meggy didn't have a fucking *clue* where you'd gone or even if you were still alive, and she kept hoping. She kept trying. That woman would die for you, and if that isn't love, I don't know what is."

"So torturing me?" Moyna retorted. "This is love, then?"

"They're not torturing you, they're trying to keep everyone safe while you get your head on straight." Toula stepped back and found her chair again. "The bind's a precaution for them while you're still feeling stabby, and it's a safeguard for you. I mean, going with some punk you barely know into the Gray Lands?" she asked incredulously. "Sure, your brain is still developing, but come on, that's a textbook stupid idea."

"He loves me," she mumbled.

"If he's what I think he is, then I strongly doubt it." She paused, waiting while Moyna's face shifted through half a dozen expressions, then lowered her voice and said, "I know this is tough, and no one wants to feel like a fool, but Titania didn't love you. She *couldn't*. Hell," she muttered, "Oberon's your damn grandfather, and his great idea was to kill you and be done with it. Don't you get it?" she said, staring Moyna in the eye. "Full fae can't love. You know that, right?"

Moyna stared back at her, biting her lip, then pulled her knees to her chest. "She loved me," she whispered in the gloom.

But Toula shook her head. "All that hurt you're feeling right now, all that anger…you loved Titania. I get it, it's okay. That's the closest thing to a mom you've had, and I…well, I'm sorry that we had to do what we did. For you, I mean. I'm not—you know, never mind." She flicked her hand at the air as if brushing a fly from her face. "The important thing, honey, is she never loved you. She may have treated you well, but you were a means to an end."

Seeing Moyna continue to retract into herself, Toula stood once more and, after a moment's hesitation, sat beside her on the bed. "Those two out there, you may hate their guts right now, but they love you, kid. This so-called torture is a way they can avoid locking you up or worse. They're doing the best they can. Work with us, hmm? Stop trying to kill them, and they'll take the bind off. Easy."

They sat there together, neither moving, while Moyna mulled this over. I was beginning to think she had reverted to her earlier tactic of ignoring anything that displeased her when she glanced at Toula, rested her cheek on her knees, and mumbled, "I'm thirsty."

Meggy let out her held breath beside me, and I reached over to squeeze her hand.

"No problem," said Toula with a snap of her fingers. An empty glass appeared between them on the bed, and she asked, "Water? Juice? Something stronger?"

"Root beer," Moyna said in a half-whisper, and the glass filled as she watched. She snatched it up and gulped it down, and Toula refilled it twice until Moyna put it aside and stifled a belch. "Anything to eat, or are they starving me, too?" she asked.

A familiar flat box manifested beside her, and she yanked the lid open to get at the pizza within. Toula took a piece once Moyna had a slice in each hand and ate slowly, biding her time while the girl gorged herself. Moyna chewed ravenously and licked her fingers clean, then went back for seconds and thirds. Within minutes, the box was empty but for a fragment of gnawed crust, and Toula sent the mess back into the ether. "So," she said, handing Moyna a paper napkin, "who's this G character, anyway?"

Moyna hesitated, but her full stomach seemed to have mellowed her mood toward Toula, and she flopped back on the bed with a little sigh. "He's my boyfriend. My lover."

Toula sprawled beside her, propping her head on her hand. "Uh-huh. And what would you know about taking a lover, little miss?"

She looked over and rolled her eyes. "I'm not a *child*, you know."

"Didn't say you were—just trying to figure out where you two stand. Now, I'm at a loss here," she said, scooting closer and lowering her voice. "How the heck did you meet up with a guy from the Gray Lands?"

Moyna's eyes narrowed. "I didn't say—"

"You didn't have to. There was a spike in dark magic when you disappeared with him, and when you surfaced again, you had your snake, and we all know *that* wasn't native to the mortal realm. Obviously, he took you into the Gray Lands—that would kill the bind on you, even if he weren't strong enough to do it on his own—so what gives? What's a nice girl like you doing with a guy like that, hmm?"

Her lips began to curl. "You think I'm a nice girl, do you?"

"Figure of speech."

That earned a proper smile, and Moyna rested her head on her arms. "G found me at one of the football parties. Told me I was special, I had a secret. He promised to help me figure it out. We talk all the time..." Her voice drifted off, and she turned back to Toula. "He showed me magic again, made me start to remember. Helped me fight the bind. He's incredible."

"I bet," she said, managing to sound sincere. "What's G short for?"

"Why do you ask?"

"Just curious. If someone introduces himself by a weird nickname, I have to assume there's a terrible name behind it."

"That's not what I meant," she replied, rolling over and propping herself up to match Toula's position. "You said Mab was your mother, yes? She was G's, too. You don't know him?"

Meggy hissed sharply beside me, but Toula kept her

composure. "I've met exactly one of my siblings," she said, "so no, I don't know him. And now I'm really curious," she added in a tone promising conspiracy. "How bad *is* his name?"

"Not that bad," said Moyna. "Geheret."

"Geheret," she repeated, rolling it around in her mouth. "Well, not great, but I've heard worse—there are some fantastically bad family names floating around the Arcanum," she confided. "How old is he?"

"Little older than me."

"Gotcha. But I'm still wondering what a guy out of the Gray Lands was doing in Rigby, of all places."

Moyna's eyes, suddenly shifty, narrowed in thought as she considered Toula. "If I told you," she finally replied, "and if the information proved useful, what would be in it for me?"

Toula, to her credit, displayed a remarkable talent for maintaining a poker face. "I suppose," she said with deliberate slowness, "that if it were sufficiently interesting, and if you gave it of your own free will, the powers keeping you bound might consider loosening their hold on you. That's not a guarantee," she stressed, "but I'd put in a good word for you."

"And you have Coileán's ear?"

"As much as anyone does."

After weighing this information, Moyna seemed to come to a resolution and sat up on the bed. When Toula followed suit, she leaned closer and murmured, "G told me this once we were safe in the Gray Lands. A few months ago, one of my uncles came to him with a proposition." Her pale eyebrow arched, and Toula nodded in understanding. "If G got me out of the picture," she continued, "then once Coileán was removed, the new king would be generous and remember G's friendship."

"And let him into Faerie?"

"Perhaps. He'd at least have recognition of his court." She watched Toula's face for a clue, then gave up and pressed on. "But once G met me, he couldn't go through with it. He loves me. So the plan changed, you see."

"Oh?"

She nodded emphatically. "We were going to do it together, G and me. Take out Coileán, and the court would be mine. We could have ruled together," she said, sounding almost wistful. "But since I suppose I'm to be kept prisoner here…"

"You may as well save yourself?" Toula suggested.

"Yes, that. And change the plan." Moyna straightened and clasped her hands in her lap. "Overthrowing Coileán would be difficult in my present circumstances. But if he should know who's plotting against him, perhaps he'd be willing to work with G. We'd be doing him a favor, after all."

I had to strain to hear their conversation over the rush of blood pounding in my ears, but Toula was serenity personified. "Makes sense," she told Moyna. "So it was your uncle, you said?"

"Doran," I muttered. "I knew I couldn't trust him, I knew—"

"That's what G told me," Moyna replied, oblivious to my mounting rage. "Huc."

I never saw how Toula's visit ended. Shocked, furious, and fighting a rising wave of paranoia, I cut the feed, picked up my coffee table, and threw it against the wall, where it exploded into splinters. Meggy remained in the safety of the couch, sitting silently as I paced the office and railed against my siblings with every profane term I'd accumulated in eight centuries. Even Valerius kept his distance—I caught him out of the corner of my eye as I made my circuit, poised against the wall with all the subtlety of a compressed spring and shifting his gaze between Meggy and me.

A few laps later, I realized he had readied himself to

jump to Meggy's aid—and that the look on her face was not shock, but fear.

I forced myself to end the march and breathed until the red in my vision cleared. "I'm sorry," I heard myself mumble as I surveyed the damage: the broken table, the shards of porcelain vase mixed in with the rubble, the chips in the stone. "I don't...I..."

"Want a drink?" she asked quietly.

"No." I pushed my hair from my eyes and sat opposite her, ignoring the space the table had recently occupied between us. "My entire family wants me dead. Johnnie isn't going to fix *that*."

"All she said was Huc—"

"Who isn't acting alone." I held up my hand and started counting off my fingers. "The only one of them who stands to immediately gain if Moyna and I are gone is Doran, who'd inherit. There's no reason for Huc to plot against us unless Doran's promised him a substantial reward...and he probably doesn't breathe unless Syral knows and approves," I continued, pushing three fingers to one side. "Doran and Syral have been at each other's throat—or at least have pretended to be at each other's throat," I admitted, "for months, and Ji and Nanine have partly taken sides. The odds of them being left out of this little conspiracy are slim to none."

"Which leaves Aiden," Meggy pointed out.

"All right, one. And *his* sister probably wants me dead by now, too, not to mention my damn daughter." I slumped back against the couch and closed my eyes, hoping the oncoming headache would subside on its own. "Of course, that's assuming Moyna's telling the truth about this cretin."

"So find out. Pick her brain and be sure."

Surprised at the sudden coolness in her tone, I looked at Meggy and found her cheeks blazing. "And if she is?"

When she spoke again, her voice was velvet flowing over stone. "Then you kill them. Slowly. Painfully. You bind them and throw them in a pit together, and when there's only one left, you leave him there with the corpses until he starves. *That* is what you do with them."

Words failed me as I gawked at the unknown creature wearing Meggy's face, but I managed to cobble together a response a moment later. "I can't execute them. The realm—"

"They tried to kill my daughter," she interrupted, implacable as an oncoming glacier. "I don't give a damn how the realm feels about it. Get rid of them and do it now, or so help me, I'll do it myself."

"Meggy," I said, trying to find something familiar in her eyes, "do you hear yourself? Remember Stuart? You said—"

"I know what I said," she snapped, rising from the couch. "And if you love me, you'll protect our child."

I winced when the door slammed behind her, then looked to Val for a rational voice. "What am I supposed to do?" I asked. "Tell me there's an option besides fratricide."

A knock at the door cut short his reply, and he opened it to reveal Toula on the threshold. "Hey, sorry to interrupt," she began, letting herself in, "but I got Moyna to talk, and she told me something you need to hear—"

Before she could launch into a recap of what I'd witnessed, Val embraced her, whispered something in her ear, and let himself out of the room. When the latch clicked behind him, I studied Toula, who absently rubbed her arm as if trying to comprehend the sudden physical contact. "What was that all about?" I asked.

"I...don't know," she mumbled, then noticed the broken table and knick-knacks. "What the hell happened in here?"

"I watched your conversation," I confessed, waving the table back into shape. "Lost my temper, needed something convenient to punch."

"Ah. Makes sense." Her mouth twitched, and the wall repaired itself. "Did Val listen in, too?"

"Yeah." When that merited no further response, I turned and saw an odd sheen in her eyes. "Something wrong? Besides my homicidal clan, I mean."

Toula's hand returned to its place on her arm, and she bit her lip for the space of a few breaths before she spoke. "He told me I'm loved," she said, sounding perplexed. "Why would he say that?"

"Perhaps you are."

She stood there, holding herself through her sweatshirt, then nodded. "Excuse me," she said, turning for the door. "I need to have a word with my brother. Do me a favor and butt out of this one, okay?"

"No problem there," I replied, but I felt the walls begin to close in once I was left to consider my options in uneasy solitude.

CHAPTER 17

As I'd anticipated, Moyna was none too pleased when I darkened her door that evening. "I assume Toula relayed my message?" she asked, trying to sound imperious and disdainful but achieving only petulant.

"She did." I stepped through the wards, concentrated, and began my quick examination of Moyna's mind.

She jerked and rubbed her temples, but bound, she couldn't keep me out of her head. "Oh, so you're the thought police now, too?" she snapped once I'd withdrawn. "You don't believe me?"

I blinked hard, trying to clear the images I'd seen. "Now I do," I muttered, and retreated through the door.

Moyna ran after me, but she bounced off the wards holding her prisoner. "What about the bind?" she yelled, her voice echoing off the cellar walls. "Toula said you'd take it off!"

I stopped a few paces from the door and turned to face her frantic eyes. "She made no such promise, and you know that," I replied. "While I appreciate your help, Moyna, I also know I can't trust you. Stand there and tell me to my face that you wouldn't go after Meggy or me as soon as I took the bind off. Go on, do it if you can." She remained sullenly silent, and I shrugged. "I'm willing to work with you," I continued, approaching the invisible fence. "I *want* to work with you. But letting you go now is out of the question."

"You're afraid of me," she challenged.

"No, but I respect what you're capable of."

She stepped back and hugged herself, but her reply was defiant. "So that's it, then? I'm to stay down here until I crack and run to the bosom of my loving family?"

"Not exactly. I'd prefer to move you upstairs," I said, leaning against the door frame. "Make you comfortable. You could have your old suite back, if you'd like."

Moyna seemed unimpressed by my largesse. "A gilded cage is still a cage, Coileán."

I decided to let the slight go unnoted. "But surely it beats a dungeon. Come upstairs, see some daylight, perhaps realize someday that I'm not the worst thing that ever happened to you. Or would you prefer to return to Rigby?"

Her lip rose in a little snarl. "You expect me to go back to that hellhole and pretend like nothing's amiss? Back to geometry and the pep squad, is that the plan?"

"Just an option, in case you decide you can't stand the sight of me."

After mulling this over, she muttered, "A valid point. And would that be with my memory intact, or were you thinking of raping my mind again?"

I sighed, forcing my blood pressure down. "You've a flare for the dramatic, haven't you?"

"Ever had *your* memory wiped?" she retorted.

"Get a few more years on you, and you'd be grateful for selective erasure." I stuffed my hands in my pockets and watched my daughter boil with the righteous indignation of long-suffering youth. "Tell you what," I said, "if you go back, you go back as you are. No further binds, no wipes, no false memories, just you and Meggy and high school and all that jazz. Tell whomever you like about Faerie—no one except Wizard Stu will believe you." She twitched, and I took advantage of the momentary crack in the dike. "Stuart's the only guy in that town without a Fringe connection who's a big enough nutjob to believe in faeries—and if you want to convince him, you'll have to shrink a few feet and sprout wings, so good luck with that. I mean," I continued, taking secret pleasure in her agitation, "you're bound, so you're not going to be able to *prove* anything. Start raving about magic, and your little friends will think you've lost your damn mind."

"They're not my *friends*," she muttered.

"Your merry band of streetwalkers, then. Go back, and you'll be keeping a low profile unless you plan to start brewing potions with Stewie and his cats. That's your choice."

Moyna stared at me as if she could make my head explode through ocular pressure alone, then flounced across the room and jumped onto the foot of her bed with an exaggerated sigh. "You're an impossible bastard, you know that?"

"So I've been told. But think about it, let me know. We'll get you moved upstairs tonight, if you'd like."

"Can't get much worse," she sniffed, glaring at the damp walls. "I assume I'm not to have free run of the palace, then?"

"Not yet. Be a good girl and we'll see."

"Bastard," she repeated. "And what do you plan to do about Huc, hmm?" she called after me as I turned to go. "You know I'm not lying. Can he get through these wards?"

I thought I might be imagining it, but I could almost detect a trace of fear in her tone. "They won't bother you," I said stiffly, hoping she'd drop the issue.

But Moyna was nothing if not difficult. "Oh, really? You plan to bind them, too? If not, I'm unprotected, I'm defenseless—"

"I said they won't bother you." I glanced at her over my shoulder, trying to decipher her expression. "Like it or not, you're my daughter, and I *will* protect you."

I was halfway to the staircase when her voice echoed around the cellar: "Do you love me, Ironhand?"

The mocking reverberations died away, and I gritted my teeth to stop the lie that would prove I still understood the terms of the great social contract. "I'm trying," I said, and when no new insult was forthcoming, I took my hasty leave.

Darkness fell early that evening—I had no interest in staying the daylight, in any case—and I tasked my guard with seeing to Moyna's re-housing. Working in tandem, Valerius and Toula crafted a fresh, doubly-secure ward system around my daughter's rooms, but I didn't press them for details of its construction. When I last saw them that night, they were making fine tweaks to the magic in the walls, working back to back in comfortable silence, and I found myself envying the apparent ease of their relationship. They had been acquainted a bare month, and yet there they worked, anticipating each other's movements and speaking quietly in the indecipherable code of the technically skilled.

Meggy had locked herself in my room, and having no desire to thrust myself into a fight, I stationed a pair of guards at the door for her safety and turned my steps toward the barn. Halfway through the rose garden, I looked up at a passing shadow that blotted out the crescent moon, then traced Georgie's descent to a skidding halt outside the sheep pen. By the time I picked my way down the path, Joey had slid off and was holding his hand up toward his passenger. "All clear, no droppings," he said, oblivious to my presence. "Just kick your leg over and slide off—Georgie's not going anywhere."

Make it quick, the dragon thought. *I'm hungry.*

The passenger—Helen, I realized, catching the silhouette of her long hair as it bounced behind her on her descent—grabbed Joey's hands and let him swing her to the ground. He promptly released his hold, and she patted her tangles into a closer approximation of presentable as Georgie lumbered off to terrorize the flock. "Okay, you were right," I heard her tell him, half-laughing as Georgie's swishing tail almost knocked Joey off his feet. "That's a pretty incredible ride. And she really doesn't mind?"

Joey waited while the chorus of bleats rose and fell, then said, "Nah. Georgie and me...it's kind of hard to explain, but she's my best girl. Aren't you the best?" he called to the gorging lizard in Fae.

Georgie glanced up, her red eyes flashing in the dim moonlight as her muzzle dripped. *You know it.*

"And that's kind of, uh...gross," Helen remarked as the sounds of breaking bone and slurping flesh intensified.

Joey shrugged. "Circle of life, *amiga*. She's got to eat."

"Yeah, but...you know, never mind," she sighed, shaking her head. "I used to feed the corn snake frozen mice in high school bio, and that was disgusting, too." She moved into Joey's orbit with effortless grace, standing close enough to him to let his body block the worst of the night wind. "It got chilly, huh?"

"Yeah," he said, stamping his feet, then hooked his arm around hers. "Come on, we'll go warm up—I've got some soup to reheat in the loft, and I'm pretty sure Aiden left his Wii out here."

I lurked by the hedge, watching in the shadows until they disappeared, arm in arm, and then I heard a soft thought from the far side of the pasture: *I see you.*

"Shh," I whispered to the night.

Georgie snorted and continued to feast. *What are you doing over there?*

"Spying."

Why?

"Because I want to give them a moment's privacy."

But you aren't, she pointed out.

"The illusion of privacy, then." I slid out of the garden and hiked through the tall grass to the fence. "What were they up to, anyway?"

The dragon tossed a chunk of raw sheep into the air and snapped it from its descending arc. *Talking. Too much talking. If they're going to mate, they should do it already.*

"Mate?" I chuckled. "What do *you* know about mating, little one?"

Enough, she replied, nonplussed. *I asked Joey about my mother, and then I asked about my father, and then he told me about mating. I knew some of it already, but what he said made sense.*

"You…knew already? How?"

The question seemed to confuse her. *I just know. Don't you? It's not complicated, if you need to me to tell—*

"No, no, I'm, uh…I'm well informed," I said in a rush, hoping to cut her off before she could elaborate. "Anyway, Joey and Helen aren't going to mate. They barely know each other."

So? She sounded legitimately perplexed. *Male, female, compatibility, no competition…*

"Georgie," I said, leaning over the fence to be better heard, "it's not that simple. She's not going to be here long."

And?

"And she's a few years younger than he is." This failed to change the dragon's bemused thoughts, so I tried, "She's a wizard and Aiden's sister, and he's a lunatic with a sword and a gig in Faerie. There are…complications."

Like what? she asked, bending back to the meal at hand. *How long does mating take for you, anyway? They mate, she leaves, who cares?*

"Human mating isn't that simple," I began, but paused at the sound of footsteps approaching behind me. When I turned, I found myself staring down the barrel of a flashlight, which clicked off as I winced in pain.

"Sorry," said Aiden, sidling up to the fence. "Who's mating?"

Georgie raised her head and cut her eyes to mine. I was no expert on draconic moods—and my temporarily shot night vision limited what little I could see of her expression—but I hastened to fill the void before she could try to be helpful. "No one. What are you doing out here?"

He waved the darkened flashlight toward the barn. "Figured Hel was around. Joey told me he was going to keep an eye on her, and…" His thought died unfinished as something clicked into place, and he cleared his throat. "Okay, please don't tell me that what I think is happening is happening."

"Leftovers and video games."

"Thank God." Aiden exhaled in a loud rush and slumped against the fence. "I don't need that right now, I *really* don't need that right now."

He seemed simultaneously older and younger in that moment, wise to the ways of the world yet somewhat squeamish about the details. "I thought you liked Joey," I teased.

"I do," he replied, shaking his head. "But that's my *sister*."

"Your point?"

"My point is that if she's going to fool around, I'd rather not know about it. Or think about it. Can we change the subject, please?"

"Have you two come to terms?"

"Not exactly," he said with a soft sigh. "I, um…I've been avoiding her all day."

I nodded toward the warm lights of the barn loft. "Well, kid, now's your chance," I began, then sobered, feeling my guts clench for the hundredth time that day as my thoughts circled back to Moyna. "Seriously, go to the barn and stay there," I said quietly. "I'm going to post a guard, and if anything seems amiss tonight, go with Helen. I'll come for you when it's safe."

Aiden's eyes went wide. "What's wrong?"

Briefly, I considered keeping him in the dark, but I decided forewarning was better than false reassurances. "I have it on decent information that our siblings are conspiring against me, and no, I'm not paranoid," I murmured, bending to his ear. "They sent someone after Moyna, and with you around…"

I didn't need to finish the thought. Aiden nodded curtly, then turned his troubled gaze back on the barn. "Do they know?"

"No. Are you armed?"

"Nope."

"Come with me, then." I opened a gate into his room, and Aiden followed me through into the debris field. "Is there a projectile weapon in here?" I asked as I turned the lamps on from the safety of my relatively clean patch of floor.

He skirted a few half-finished projects and the remnants of the past weekend's experimentation, then plucked a piece of white PVC pipe from the rubble. "Could be. I need you to stretch this."

"To what dimensions?"

"Just a minute, I'll sketch it out," he muttered, reaching for a battered notepad. "And I'll need propane. How much time can you spare?"

"Whatever you require," I replied, trying to make sense of his frantic scribbling. "What are you—"

"Spud gun loaded with grapeshot." He made a few more flourishes to his diagram, then ripped the paper loose and passed it to me. "The pipe's the barrel. I'll need a few specific fittings—don't worry, I'll draw them," he said, returning to his work, "and a tank of propane. Oh, and a small lighter would be *great*. Any chance you've got a Bic?"

"I…think I can rig something up."

"Good. And I'm going to need to melt this down," he continued, approaching with a handful of scrap metal, "so if you could get a fire going, that would be most helpful."

I'd observed Joey's process, his quick but methodical construction methods and contemplative moments of double-checking his design. Aiden, on the other hand, moved in a quiet, barely controlled frenzy, running back and forth between the gun on his workbench and the brazier with its bowl of molten steel. One moment, he was fitting a valve, and the next, he was pouring another batch into the molds I'd made to his specifications, filling the spheroid forms with glowing metal and plunging them into ice water. The resultant balls, he muttered in passing, were bound to be brittle, but he almost considered shrapnel a plus. "I'm not trying to shoot these through anyone," he said, plucking the dripping pellets from their ice bath. "I'm trying to give my target a nasty burn. A swarm of wasps may not kill you, but you'd probably wish you were dead, right?"

After an hour or so of crafting and tweaking, Aiden packed his gun full of pellets, tucked the canister of propane under his arm, and smiled grimly. "Faerie deterrent is a go."

"Unless they see you first," I reminded him, opening a gate back to the barn. "Stay low near a window, be on guard, and shoot quickly. You'll probably only get one round off, so if it comes to that, make it count and get the hell out of here." I followed him into the pasture and considered the bulk of the barn, black against the night sky but for the single light in the loft. "I could put up wards around this place," I mused, "but it'd take time and draw attention…"

"Leave it to me," he replied, and I considered my little brother, standing there with the barrel of his gun resting on his shoulder, his arms tensed, his face somehow older in an unnamable way. The sheep bleated, Georgie grunted from the depths of the barn, and I fought the sudden urge to rip open a gate to Greg's office and shove the kid through, back to a place where broken bones could be easily mended and hurt feelings shoved under metaphoric rugs.

But I couldn't do that to him, and so I bade him a quiet good night and good luck.

Aiden made his way across the hard-packed practice

yard toward the resting dragon, and I contemplated the freewheeling stars, trying to augur the time until my siblings grew wise to the fact that their plan had gone awry. Surely, I told myself, no one would act before the dawn.

But dawn came, and they were nowhere to be found.

I couldn't entirely blame the realm for failing to notify me—if anything, the intrusive consciousness seemed perplexed that I was upset at its oversight. Faerie was happy to feed me information *when asked*, but I had made no request concerning my family. To the realm, they were fixtures, nothing more—certainly nothing warranting the excitement of Oberon's return or the anxiety of Toula's visits. Mother's children had come and gone for centuries, and the realm assigned this particular mass outing little importance.

By contrast, I was ready to throw the realm into lockdown and warn Greg to shore up his defenses. If the five of them weren't in Faerie, I reasoned, then they had to be hiding in the mortal realm, and that meant the Arcanum was a likely target. Surely they wouldn't go after Oberon, but burrowing wizards were fair game. That also meant that I couldn't in good conscience let Meggy or Helen go back, not when a sibling of mine could be *anywhere*.

Despite the earlier oversight, the realm was perfectly willing to inform me that Aiden was asleep in the barn, and so I opened a gate straight into the loft, where I found myself on the receiving end of Aiden's new toy. I threw up my hands reflexively, and Joey, whose dark circles spoke of a long vigil, lowered the barrel. "Warning is always appreciated," he said, putting the gun on the ground. "Especially with that little pep talk you gave Aiden last night. What's the situation?"

"He filled you in, I take it."

Joey nodded at the two lumps beneath the blankets on

his bed and couch. "First watch, second watch. I've been supervising. And the situation is?"

I told him what had transpired as the Carvers woke, and then I repeated the news a few minutes later in my office when Meggy and Toula demanded answers. "And so no one is going anywhere," I concluded to the assembled, "until they're located. Any questions?"

Helen raised her finger. "You can't just keep us here."

"That wasn't a question."

"And this isn't a request," she replied. "If there's a potential scenario in which the Arcanum is at risk, my place is on the front lines."

"She's got a point," Toula added. "Lord knows Greg could use the help, and I'm not willing to hunker down and leave them hanging."

"I'm taking my daughter home," said Meggy, her voice soft but firm. "She's missed three days of school already."

I looked around my office at the faces ringing me, feeling rather like an asylum warden. "Did nothing I said make sense to anyone? They're after me, they're after Moyna, they're on the loose—"

"They're just *missing*," Meggy protested, "and you're basing all of the rest off of something that bastard told Olive."

"She believes it."

"She's sixteen and disturbed," she retorted. "I wouldn't make any snap decisions based on her best judgment." Squaring her shoulders and pulling herself to her full five and half feet, she said, "I've been through hell since Friday night. I want my bed, I want my shop, and I'm pretty sure all the leftovers in my fridge have turned by now. We're going home."

"Meggy," I began, but caught the look in her eye and stopped. *Do you remember our deal?* she seemed to ask. *We do this as equals, or we don't do it at all.*

I gritted my teeth, knowing I wasn't going to win this without a show of force. "If you go back," I muttered, "I can't protect you from here."

"And I'll drag them back over at the first sign of trouble," Toula offered. "Heck, Megs, I'll even sleep over for a few nights if you want—just like the old days, huh? You, me, Lifetime Original Movies, our favorite men?"

She flashed a wry smile. "Ben and Jerry."

"My main squeezes. Come on," she said, taking Meggy's hands, "let me crash with you until things settle down. Maybe *he'll* stay out of your hair if he knows I'm lurking, eh?"

"Possibly," I allowed, realizing the gift she was offering us. "And if you go to Rigby," I told Toula, "you're bound to meet the incredible Stuart the White."

"Stuart the what?"

"He fancies himself a white wizard. I'm sure you'll have *loads* to talk about."

"Oh, hell," she laughed, "I'm in. Okay, Megs?"

Meggy nodded and squeezed Toula's hands, and with a parting glance of understanding for me, Toula led her off to gather her things and break the news to Moyna. When the door had closed behind them, Helen cocked her thumb at the garden window and said, "My stuff's still in the barn. I'll be out of here shortly." Aiden began to protest, but she cut him off with a raised hand. "*You* stay put, bud. And you," she added, turning to Joey, "had better take care of him, got it?"

"And who's going to take care of you?" he countered.

"I can manage myself. Help me pack?" she asked, opening a gate to the barn loft with a gesture.

Joey followed her through, and I caught Aiden's mistrustful look as the gate closed. "She doesn't have anything out there, does she?" I murmured.

"No," he said stiffly, "she does not."

"Then, if I may offer a suggestion," Valerius interjected, "give them a moment of peace. Nothing out there requires your presence."

Aiden scowled at the air where the gate had been, then

rolled his eyes and headed for the door. "He'd better not be kissing my sister," he muttered as he let himself out.

When he'd stomped off to his room, Val cleared his throat and folded his arms. "Will you satisfy my curiosity, Coileán?"

"If I can," I replied, returning to my desk and the pile of neglected grievance petitions. "What's on your mind?"

"Meggy and Toula…"

He left the question unasked, and I shrugged. "Toula says nothing ever came of it. I don't think she's Meggy's preference. Why?"

"Just checking," he replied, showing himself out. "I've seen my share of jealousy-fueled fights in this realm, and I'd rather hoped to avoid one between the two of you."

I chuckled and plucked the first letter off the pile— anything to keep my mind off the immediate problem of my missing siblings. "You think it'd be a contest?"

That gave him pause. "I don't know," he finally admitted, "and I don't want to find out."

CHAPTER 18

The trouble with having an admittedly awesome level of power in Faerie was adjusting to the limitations of trying to wield it outside the realm. Within its bounds, there was little the realm wouldn't do for me—if I'd wanted to watch random strangers bathing on a continual feed, the realm would have been happy to link me into its omniscient view, no questions asked. Finding someone hiding within Faerie was as simple as directing the realm to provide his coordinates. Once beyond the borders, however, I found myself somewhat hamstrung, as my continual mental companion was as clueless about the mortal realm as any tourist dumped in a foreign country without a guidebook. Power was great, but I needed information, and for that, I realized I'd have to consult a local.

And so I found myself standing on the faded welcome mat outside Vivi Stowe's apartment door in tiny Skipton Thursday morning, shivering in the November predawn and silently cursing the complex's architect, who had designed her building as a perfect funnel for the northerly wind. A wrinkled neon green flyer for a pet-sitting service ripped free of her neighbor's door and skittered off into oblivion, and I jabbed my gloved finger against the doorbell, halfway hoping the lady of the house was sleeping over at her boyfriend's place.

Two minutes later, after a muffled shout to wait just a second and the sleepy cursing of one ripped from the warmth of bed and thrust straight into a shin-targeting table, the door flew open, and Vivi squinted blearily up at me from the threshold. I wasn't sure what was most striking about her—the way one side of her hair seemed to defy gravity as it rose from her scalp in a mess of black frizz, while the rest hung limply to her shoulders; her glasses, which perched on her upturned nose at a good twenty-degree pitch from horizontal; or her nightgown, an oversized gray T-shirt sporting a wash-faded picture of Daisy Duck, which had probably seen better decades. She blinked a few times as if trying to draw sense from the scene before her, then muttered, "The hell?"

"May I come in?"

"Sure. Whatever." She slipped back a step, giving me room to squeeze past her, then latched the door and shook with the change in temperature. "You know it's, like, five a.m., right? And I was up *really* late—"

"Would coffee make you happier?"

"Couldn't hurt," she grumped, plopping into a rattan basket chair. Her bare feet kicked out as she landed on the flat pink cushion, and she stared at me with deep suspicion. "Any leads on the dark magic situation?"

I plied her with a trio of doppios, which she knocked back like a frat boy at happy hour, and told her what had transpired since the previous Friday night. As the caffeine began to take effect—I was mildly disturbed to witness how well she handled six shots of espresso—Vivi tucked her legs up beneath her, straightened her glasses, and drummed her fingers on the rim of the chair. "So you're telling me we've got five rogue faeries to worry about, is that it?" she said. "Five rogue faeries who are probably running scared, ergo, who are more dangerous than usual? Well, *shit*." Her fingertip percussion intensified as she considered the ramifications. "Any chance of getting help from Oberon?"

"I hope it doesn't come to that," I replied, stacking her spent cups in a tiny pyramid on her coffee table, a wobbly IKEA special. "The Arcanum's been notified—I assume I'll hear from Greg if they come sniffing around. But I don't have Mother's old spy network in place, and I've got no idea where they might be hiding."

"And so you came to me," she concluded, "because you need boots on the ground, and because if you'd gone to Rick at this hour, he'd have ripped you a new one with a broken longneck. Gotcha." After a moment of rocking false starts, she managed to extricate herself from her chair and disappeared down the short hallway leading to her bedroom. "Back in a minute," she called before she shut her door.

"What're you—"

The door creaked open again as I spoke, and she interrupted, "If I'm going to be drafted into this nonsense, I'm damn well going to be drafted with my pants on. Now hold your horses. Sheesh," she muttered, and the door slammed.

And so I waited on the futon with my own cup of coffee while my unwilling hostess located a pair of trousers, and I began to see the wisdom in Mother's absolute intolerance for disrespect.

A few minutes later, sporting jeans and having thrown a moth-eaten brown sweater on over her nightshirt—and still having neglected her disastrous hair—Vivi reappeared with a slim laptop and slid onto the futon beside me. Without preamble, she lifted the lid, tapped out a series of passwords, and made a black box fill most of the screen. "What's that?" I enquired.

"Working," she mumbled, typing a long string of gibberish. The black box began to fill with aqua-colored text in neat rows, then green text, and finally, after a bit of quiet profanity and an apparent do-over, red text. Vivi sat back, and the machine chirped, its picture dissolving into a full-screen video of her face. There was a camera somewhere in the screen's casing, I realized, as Vivi finally noticed her coiffure and hastily finger-combed it into surrender. "All right," she told me, looking up from her makeshift mirror, "just stay quiet while I log into the network, okay? I don't want to spook anyone."

I nodded and scooted to the far side of the futon, and she made a few more taps. A red light illuminated at the top of the screen, and with a little *ding*, she was in. "This is Monkey, repeat, this is Monkey," she said to the computer. "Who's up?"

A miniature picture popped up on the right-hand margin of Vivi's screen, revealing a middle-aged woman with a fat, sweater-clad dachshund sprawled across her lap. "Good morning, Vivian," she said in the perfectly polished tones of a BBC presenter. "Aren't we up early today."

"Morning, Butterfly," she replied, straightening her posture. "Still morning on your side of the pond, yeah?"

"Unless my watch deceives me." She paused as another pair of screens chimed in—two young men, one a pale Australian with a prominent eyebrow ring, the other a South African with close-cropped hair, sporting a pencil behind his ear. "Insomnia?" the Brit asked. "Or have we located Bigfoot yet and called it a night?"

All four shared a laugh at that one, and another trio of headshots flashed onto Vivi's computer. "Not this time, I'm afraid," she said, sobering as her screen continued to fill. "We've been asked for a favor. More like a BOLO and report, really."

The South African pulled his pencil loose and tapped it against his desk. "Arcanum business?"

"Court, actually," she said, and paused as a few of her listeners muttered. "I wouldn't bring it up if I hadn't seen a dark magic spike here last week," she continued over the susurrus. "Situation's bad news. We're not being asked to do anything active—just keep an ear to the ground and let me know if something seems off. And my contact would be *most* grateful," she said, keeping her eyes firmly on the screen. "Is anyone willing? I can send the details around if I've got volunteers…"

The others hesitated, and then, one by one, they began to nod and murmur assent—all but the Brit, who peered back at Vivi and asked, "Who's your contact?"

Without warning, she reached across the futon, grabbed me by the arm, and pulled as she turned the computer around. "Coileán, my posse. Posse, Coileán. Want to fill them in, or should I do the honors?"

One of the little screens flickered to black, but the other Fringe members, perhaps too startled to leave, simply stared.

"Uh…good morning," I said, trying to think on my feet. "I'm…well, I'm pretty desperate right now," I admitted. "I don't know what your going rate is—"

"We work pro bono…my lord," said the Australian, flashing a set of extensive tattoos as he rolled up his sleeves. "Pro *bono*. For the greater good. Can't be bought."

"I understand."

"And if we assist you," the South African added, "then you would be in the Fringe's debt, yes?"

"Correct."

He slipped his pencil back into place and leaned toward his camera, his dark eyes boring into mine. "And what sort of guarantee would we have that you would honor that obligation?"

Before I could say something stupid, Vivi pivoted the computer back to her. "His word's good, I'll vouch for him," she said. "Slim trusts him."

This revelation gave the others pause, and a teenage blonde with a pronounced Parisian accent moved closer to the screen. "The Fatman?" she asked. "You mean the Fatman?"

"I mean Slim's had him down in the workshop and everywhere else. Coileán's not going to weasel out of this one," she said, then gave me a pointed look out of the corner of her eye. I nodded, and she relaxed. "So, who's interested?"

Ten minutes later, I'd produced pictures of my siblings from memory, and Vivi had scanned them into her computer. She was sending off a dossier to the rest of her people when I asked, "Fatman?"

"Fatman Slim," she replied, not looking up from her work. "We choose our own code names for the network. Rick said it was easy to remember—folks in the Fringe have been calling him Slim for years. Where did you think that nickname started?" she said, flashing a brief smirk. "There's enough fae blood in this group to make assholery an expected work hazard. You know how it is."

Fae blood or not, there was also a degree of honor among the Fringe. For the next three days, I received a morning call from Vivian, who had insisted that I leave her with a direct-line phone of her own before I escaped her apartment. There was no useful information to relay, she told me, but the fact that this was the sum of twenty other reports was far more useful than she thought. The dearth of worldwide sightings didn't tell me where my siblings were, but they did tell me where my siblings *weren't*, which was curious.

They weren't in Rigby—or, in all probability, in coastal Virginia—that much was clear. Slim was a contact point and information clearinghouse, a hub for the East Coast Fringe community, and if someone had seen something amiss, he would have been among the first to know. This, at least, gave me some peace of mind: if they weren't near Rigby, then Meggy and Moyna were probably safe for the time being, especially with Toula babysitting.

They also weren't near an Arcanum installation. I'd notified Greg, who, after offering a halfhearted apology for Helen's behavior, had promised to pass along anything of note. The last thing the Arcanum needed was a firefight on its turf, after all. But the line had remained silent, giving me further pins to pull from my mental map.

Nor, I assumed, had they gone to Oberon. He'd have nothing to gain by sheltering them, and I couldn't very well see them switching court allegiance, which would mean renouncing the titles they so dearly prized. Surely Oberon would alert me if they were getting on his nerves, I reasoned, which left only a few places they might be.

I'd gone to bed Sunday night, confident that the noose was tightening and that one of the five would slip up soon. Five faeries on the run, none of whom had spent any considerable time in the mortal realm—and certainly not in the last hundred years—could hardly stay hidden more than a few days without leaving some telltale sign of their whereabouts. But as dawn broke, I woke in a cold sweat, having realized that I'd left one major variable out of my calculations: what if they'd run to the Gray Lands?

The notion was silly, I told myself as I sat there in the twilight with a racing heart. They'd be defenseless in the Gray Lands. Even if they'd forged some pact with this Geheret, how much protection could he offer them? I had no inkling of who was running the court after Mab's death—Geheret, for all I knew—but even if he were, and even if he'd promised them sanctuary, what good was his word? They'd have to be desperate to take that risk...

Then again, given what I was considering doing to them when I found them, perhaps certain risks were worth taking. But the *Gray Lands*?

Trying to put the matter from my mind, I rose, told Valerius through the door that I'd be in the bath if the end of the world commenced, and began to soak and steam away the nightmare thought. I'd almost dozed off again when an insistent pounding on the bathroom door made me jerk awake, and I unlatched it remotely, preparing to offer my guard clarification about what Armageddon and Ragnarök actually entailed.

But it was Meggy who burst onto the marble floor and skidded to a stop against the long vanity, and I knew, even as the reprimand died on my lips, that I should listen to my subconscious more often.

The few days since their return to Rigby had been tense, but they could have been worse. With Toula hanging around, Meggy reverted to her habits of years past and subsisted largely off of pizza and ice cream, augmented with occasional bags of veggie chips to mollify her nagging inner mother. Toula, who had no such hardwired matriarchal guilt, was only too happy to keep the pies and pints coming. The two of them binged in multiple senses, gorging themselves on junk food, polishing off a few bottles of wine, and entertaining themselves with bad, yet quotable, films. While they lounged in the main room, Moyna locked herself in her bedroom, emerging only to skulk into the kitchen for provisions. The girl was plainly unhappy, but she was in no mood to talk to Meggy, and Meggy, mindful of the precariousness of the situation, gave Moyna her space and left a box of pink-frosted cupcakes outside her bedroom door as a peace offering. The gesture hadn't made Moyna any more sociable, but the cupcakes had disappeared into her room, and the empty plastic shell was later discovered in the kitchen garbage can.

By Friday, Meggy and Toula had worked out a cover story and called the high school to report that Olive was safe and sound. "Sneaky kids and a smoke grenade," Meggy lied to the principal when she phoned that morning. "Olive called me from Myrtle Beach when they ran out of money and he sneaked off... Yes, *Myrtle Beach*. I just got back from picking her up." She and the principal had clucked into their phones in shared understanding, and with Meggy's insistence that the whole thing was a silly mistake and wouldn't happen again, the principal decided no further punishment was warranted. Meggy had then broken the news to Moyna that she'd be returning to school the following Monday—spoken through the door, of course—and had received a soft groan for her pains.

Just to be on the safe side, Toula put a temporary ward around the building that would block Moyna's unauthorized egress. Neither woman thought she would seriously attempt escape—"She wants that bind off, and no one else around here can do it for her," Toula explained, trying to reassure Meggy—but the action still sat uneasily with them. Meggy didn't want to make Moyna a prisoner in her own home, but she rationalized that house arrest and mandatory education was preferable to an extended stay in my cellar.

Still, she opted to play it safe and informed Moyna she'd be driving her to school Monday morning. "It's supposed to be fifty and breezy again," she told Moyna through her locked door. "Better than standing in the wind, waiting for the bus, am I right?"

Moyna hadn't replied, as both knew the answer to that question: better always to suffer in the elements than suffer the indignity of being chauffeured by a parent. But she also knew better than to protest, and so she emerged on Monday at seven-thirty, attired barely on the proper side of the dress code and carrying her bag for cheerleading practice. "Keeping up appearances," she'd muttered as she slunk to the car behind Meggy. "Assuming they haven't kicked me off the squad yet."

Meggy had slid behind the wheel and cranked the heater. "You don't have to keep cheering if you don't want to," she said, watching Moyna in the rearview mirror. "We're not going to force you. If you want to do nothing but go to school and come home, that's fine."

Moyna had sighed at that and rolled her eyes—Meggy's eyes, merely younger and fringed with spider lashes. "I suppose I should do *something* so as to keep me from killing myself."

"Keep that up," Meggy had cautioned as she backed onto the street, "and you're going to be spending some quality time with the guidance counselor."

The ride had been brief and silent but for the rumble of the engine and the crunch as the tires turned onto the school's gravel-covered driveway, which was being repaved before winter. "Have a good day," Meggy told Moyna as she pulled up in front of the building, a few car lengths past the front door. "And I know you don't believe it, but I do love you."

Moyna had climbed out without a word, and Meggy had watched through the rearview mirror as she shouldered her bags and headed for the entrance. Before she reached the stairs, however, she stopped on the sidewalk and waited as someone—a boy, Meggy presumed—in an oversized burgundy sweatshirt jogged up to her. His hood was pulled low over his face, obscuring the details, but Moyna seemed to recognize him and dropped her bags to run into his arms. He hugged her tightly, and Meggy was beginning to allow herself the tiniest hope for the rest of the school year when the boy gestured, opening a gate. "No!" she shouted, fumbling for the seatbelt buckle with gloved hands, but as she watched, trapped in her seat, he released Moyna and stepped through the hole in reality, and Moyna, with a smirk and a mocking wave at Meggy's car, ran after him.

By the time Meggy had relayed the news to me, I was almost dressed and awake enough to know I needed to take the situation in hand. "We're going to find her," I said, holding Meggy by the arms to steady her. "It's obvious where they've gone. I'll warn Greg and Oberon in case she tries anything stupid again, and then we'll figure—"

My phone began to play its canned fugue before I could finish, and I retrieved it from the counter, thinking black thoughts about technological development. "*Yes?*"

"Hey," Toula drawled, "we've got a little situation here. Where's Megs?"

"With me. Moyna's run off with Geheret again, can this wait?"

"Mm. Nope." I heard a door slam and the lock turn. "There's a couple of things coming down the alley, Colin.

You need to get over here."

"*Things?* What things?" I asked, reaching for my loafers.

"I don't know what you'd call them. They're big," she replied, and I understood then why her voice sounded off—she was trying to keep herself calm. "One's yellow, one's kind of beigy-brown, and I think the best descriptor for them is 'chitinous.' So how about doing me a favor and getting the hell over here, huh?"

"On my way," I said, and the line went dead as I shoved my shoes on and opened a gate back to Rigby. "Stay here, stay safe," I told Meggy. "I'm going to go fight some..."—I grasped for a noun, then gave up—"*things* with Toula. Tell Val what's going on," I added, then slipped into Meggy's apartment bedroom and closed the gate before she could follow me. A moment's search produced Toula, who was standing by the kitchen door, having transformed the frosted panes into clear—and, I hoped, bulletproof—glass. "Where are they?" I whispered.

She beckoned me closer with a cocked finger, then tapped the glass. "Thing One, Thing Two. I was going to go with Ugly and Uglier, but I couldn't decide which was which." Stepping back from the door to give me a better look at the monstrosities lurching down the road behind Meggy's building, she muttered, "What're we dealing with, Gramps?"

The things I saw out the window looked rather like the mutant love child of a wolf and a praying mantis, albeit blown up to gargantuan proportions. They were perhaps twenty feet tall and slender, their long torsos covered with patchy, sickly-hued fur, and they crept forward on four insect-like legs. The remaining pair of legs was raised like pincered arms, and their heads, bald and terminating in fanged mouths, swiveled back and forth as if scenting the breeze.

"I've got nothing," I said, "but I'm guessing Gray Lands."

"Magical?"

"Doubt it—have you seen the teeth on those things?"

"I discount nothing without proof," she replied, and pushed up her sleeves. "Okay, I take beige, you take yellow?"

"You have a plan?" I asked, flipping the brass turn bolt.

"I was thinking something along the lines of 'kill it with fire,' but if you've got a better idea…"

"No, that works," I replied, and stepped out onto the landing. By the time I'd navigated the stairway debris to the ground, the creatures had noticed me and picked up speed. Foregoing a shield, I summoned what magic I could from around me—I'd gotten so *spoiled* in Faerie—and threw it at my target as a bolt of plasma. The beast wasn't quick enough to duck, and it shrieked with pain when the shot burned a hole through its thorax. Before it could recover, Toula aimed a rapid stream of fireballs at its partner, blinding it and burning its legs in short order. With the backup distracted, I finished off the first, abandoning the artillery in favor of reaching in and stopping the thing's heart from a distance. It took some work to penetrate the film of dark magic clinging to the creature, but the thing wasn't properly shielded, and so giving its heart a lethal squeeze was simpler than it had any right to be. When the beast fell, taking out a section of Meggy's neighbor's wooden fence in its descent, I looked over and saw that Toula had made similarly quick work of the other, and we stood together in the driveway, catching our breath as we surveyed the damage.

"Allow me," she finally said, and snapped. The corpses burst into flame, and before I could stop it, the fire had begun moving through the downed fence as well. Toula muttered a brief, profanity-laced incantation, and both the fence and corpses vanished, leaving nothing but twin pools of dark ichor and holes in the sod where the fence posts had stood.

She cleared her throat and nodded to the yard. "You want to…"

A duplicate fence appeared, and I brushed off my hands. "Well," I began, "that wasn't too tough—"

A screech echoed down the alley behind us, and we turned to see another four of the beasts skittering up the street. "Oh, come *on*," Toula groaned, throwing up a shield. "Okay, new plan: I'll take care of these," she said, raising her voice over their excited hunting cries, "and you get the targets evacuated."

"Meggy's already safe!" I yelled back, sending a quick volley of fireballs into the pack to slow them. "We need to—"

"Anyone Fringe needs to get out of town!" she protested. "Get Rick!"

Before I could reply, I heard a high-pitched scream to my right, and I spun around to find Mrs. Cooper standing beside Meggy's back staircase, still clad in her bathrobe and clutching her hands to her mouth. "Hold them off," I told Toula, then sprinted toward my former neighbor. "Time for a field trip!" I said to her, trying to distract her from the monsters closing on Toula, then grabbed her by the arm and dragged her back to the main street.

By the time we reached the front of the building, the initial shock had begun to fade, and Mrs. Cooper dug in her heels. "What on earth are *those*?" she demanded, pulling back against my insistent tug. "I…I never—"

I stopped trying to motivate her through force and grabbed her shoulders as I stooped to look her in the eye. "They're dangerous," I said as quietly as I could over their shrieks of pain—Toula's aim was fantastic. "And there may be more, so I'm getting you out of here for the time being. All right?"

She cringed at the rasping death cry behind her. "Where are we going? My pocketbook's in the kitchen—"

"You don't need it. I'm taking you home with me." With that, I opened a gate in the middle of the street, ignoring the lone passing driver, who gawked, then burned rubber as one of the giant lupine mantises crashed into the flagpole of the little veterans' memorial park. "Go through," I told her. "It doesn't hurt, and you'll be safe. Stay in my office until I get back, okay?"

But she pursed her lips and shook her head so vehemently that her spray-locked blonde waves actually moved. "I can't leave Stuart, he's all I've got."

"You're at the epicenter of this," I protested, but she was having none of it.

"If there are monsters on the rampage in Rigby, then my idiot grandnephew is going to get in the middle of it," she insisted. "He thinks he's a *wizard*. Colin, dear, I appreciate the offer, but I can't leave him here alone to get"—she flinched as another beast fell on top of its companion, impaling itself on the flagpole on the way down—"eaten. Or squished. Or worse. Someone has to try to talk sense into him."

I started to argue with her, then gave up and tried another tactic. "Where's he hiding now?"

"Probably at his shop," she said, then swallowed hard as the latest corpse slid down the pole in a streak of black. "It's about three miles down the road, after you cross the square. The old knitting shop—you know, Mrs. Amari's place, she always had the obese calico in the window?"

I knew it, and I also knew that Eunice Cooper, the most prim and unflappable of Rigby's old biddies, was on the verge of full-blown panic. If I was going to keep her with me, the last thing she needed at that moment was superfluous magic. "Sure," I said, pivoting her so as to block the sight of the carnage down the road, and waved the gate closed. "You know, I think Meggy left her car at the high school—can we take the Continental?"

"Of course," she replied, letting me guide her across the street to her garage, but froze at the median. "Oh, gracious," she exclaimed, remembering her attire, "I can't go out like *this*! My face—"

"Is perfectly lovely," I interrupted, pulling her out of the light morning traffic, then raised my voice over the sounds of squealing brakes and screaming hell-beasts. "You're an absolute picture, don't change a thing. Keys?"

"Oh, *you*," she said, swatting me on the arm, but let me lead her inside to the car. "The keys are on the hook in the kitchen—there's a big ring, you can't miss it. Shall I—"

"Just stay where you are," I said, imagining a pair of gardening gloves into reality. I didn't fully trust them, but under the circumstances, I couldn't be picky. I ran up the stairs to the apartment above Mrs. Cooper's teahouse, then pushed the door open and flicked on the lights. The place was immaculate as ever, covered in doilies and yellowing lace, and it took only a second's search to locate the painted wooden key rack nailed to the wall beside the dining nook. It was incongruous with the rest of the Victorian finery, a colorful cutout of a farmhouse overlaid with a sloppily painted Home Is Where The Heart Is motto, but the center hook bore the promised key ring, which wouldn't have seemed out of place on a warden's belt. I grabbed it, then tossed it from hand to hand as I ran back to the garage in case my gloves failed. Mrs. Cooper picked the correct key from the dozens available and unlocked the car, and I sped out onto the street, swerving to miss the head of the third fallen creature.

Mrs. Cooper peered out the window through her bifocals. "How many—"

"Toula was up against four, last I checked," I replied, ignoring the stop sign at the empty intersection. "And she's about to have company," I muttered, and pointed to a shape moving against the sunrise. "Shit, how many *are* there?"

"Where are they coming from?"

"Gray Lands, I think."

"No, *where* are they coming from? How are they getting in?"

I cut my eyes to her, saw that a touch of the mad sheen had left her face, and breathed slightly more easily. "Someone's opened a gate, but I'll be damned if I know where. Slim might have an idea—"

"Who?"

"Slim. Uh…Rick Matherson? Runs the bar downtown?"

"Oh. *Him*." Her distaste couldn't have been more evident if she'd taken out a flashing billboard. "What on earth would he—"

"He's got toys in his basement that I can't even operate," I said, then had an idea. "Okay, change of plans: we'll go by Slim's and see what he's got to offer, then we'll pick Stuart up."

"Toys?" she echoed, pulling her robe more tightly over her bosom. "And dear, I don't mean to be a backseat driver, but you're supposed to yield—"

"As far as I'm concerned, the guy trying to stop the giant monsters has right-of-way," I replied. "And this thing's a tank. What's the vintage, 1970?"

"It's a '68, and I'd rather you didn't total it. Now, what toys?"

I slowed a notch as we approached Rigby's modest town square—largely a repository for its churches and the police station—then picked up speed again when it was apparent that the two cops nominally on duty were still eating breakfast elsewhere. "Slim does piecework for the Arcanum," I explained. "He's not a wizard, but given the circumstances, he'll do."

After a few turns, I pulled Mrs. Cooper's land yacht into the line of empty spaces in front of Slim's, then hopped out and was pounding on the locked door before I noticed that my passenger was slumped down in her seat. "Come on, Eunice!" I yelled at the car. "I'm not letting you out of my sight!"

She hesitated, then opened the door and approached the bar with as much dignity as she could muster in her nightclothes. "Perhaps he's not home," she whispered, slinking close to the building as if she might fade into the brick.

"Oh, he's home—he's probably just sleeping. *Slim!*" I bellowed at the door, then sighed, pulled out my phone, and tried to recall the bar's main line.

"Can't you just...*you know?*" Mrs. Cooper asked, but I shook my head.

"Place is protected. Warded," I said, pressing my free hand against the invisible barrier I felt hugging the building like a skin. Certain perks came with being the Arcanum's go-to craftsman, and while I could have punched my way through Slim's defenses, something told me I'd regret that decision. "I assume it goes down during business hours. And...yes, that's it."

I tapped out the last few digits and waited, hearing the faint ringing through the windowless door, until Slim opened the line and grunted, "What?"

"Evacuating. There's things running around here out of the Gray Lands, and I'm getting you out before I go searching for the gate, so put your pants on. Oh, and if you've got any sort of detector for dark magic flow—"

"Damn it, Leffee," he muttered, and the springs of his mattress creaked. "The hell have you done now?"

"Hard to believe, I know, but this one's not my fault." I waited, listening to the sounds of faint cursing as Slim groggily fumbled for his clothing, then added, "We're in a bit of a time crunch, so how about hurrying it up?"

"How about not waking me in the middle of my night?"

"*Monsters!*" I shouted into the phone. "There are *monsters* in this town, Toula's killing some as we speak, and you're holding up the parade. Move it!"

Some sliver of my disquietude seemed to penetrate his sleep fog, as Slim's profanity picked up in tempo and clarity. By the time I heard him stomping down the stairs to the bar level, he could have given sailors everywhere a master class, and Mrs. Cooper was shielding her face from the street, lest any of her acquaintances witness her humiliation. He unlocked and threw open the door, pressed his palm against a plaque on the wall—the trigger for the wards, I gathered—and beckoned us in with a toss of his head. "Get in here while I get my gear out of the hole," he said, slamming the door behind us and reactivating the wards, "and stay away from the windows. Try not to use magic," he added as he hurried behind the bar and opened the trapdoor. "They can smell it, zero in on it."

"How do you—"

"Got a look out the window while I was finding my shirt. Arcanum calls them 'insectiform canids,' which goes to show you how shitty the Arcanum's biology department is. Fringe just calls them 'scent hounds.' And come on, give me a hand," he ordered, beginning his descent. "Ma'am, I don't know why he's dragged you into this," he called over his shoulder to Mrs. Cooper, "but if you could use a stiff one, help yourself. Won't be a minute."

She peered down the hole while I felt my way off the staircase. "The name's Eunice Cooper. And you must be…"

"It's on the door."

"Pleasure to make your acquaintance, Mr. Slim," she replied, her voice echoing faintly around the basement.

"You're a very polite liar," he called back. "Go on and hit the top shelf. Back in a jiffy."

Five minutes later, we climbed out of the hole, our arms laden with jars and boxes and sacks whose contents I couldn't begin to name, only to find Mrs. Cooper sitting on a barstool, nursing what appeared to be a rose-colored Sprite. Slim dropped his load and shook his head as he closed the trap door again. "There's thirty-year-old hooch over there," he said, gesturing toward the mirrored shelves behind the bar, "and you make yourself a fucking Shirley Temple?" Mrs. Cooper cleared her throat, and Slim's eyebrow rose. "Language?"

"If you don't mind," she replied, then bit her maraschino cherry from its stem.

I began to tell her that Slim's jar of cherries might be nearly as old as some of his better whiskies, then thought better of it. "Is this everything?" I asked him. "Nothing upstairs to transport?"

"Nah, this is the worst of it," he said, swinging his bags onto his broad back. "To the car?"

"To the car," I agreed. "Mrs. Cooper, if you want to take that with you—"

She looked horrified at the thought. "Really, Mr. Leffee," she said, putting the half-emptied glass in the bar sink, "I'm not going to *drink* in my Conti. Not with the way you drive, at least. What if that spilled, hmm?" she continued, trailing us out the door. "I'd never get the stain out of the floormat…"

Her voice rose to a squeak at the sight of a pair of the scent hounds, which were sniffing around the bank's sidewalk strip of bushes, a halfhearted attempt at downtown beautification. "*Fuck*," Slim muttered, and I fumbled with the keys until I found the one that unlatched the trunk. "No magic, no sudden moves," he murmured, carefully raising the trunk lid. "Be slow and deliberate, and they might not notice you. Start throwing lightning bolts, and they *will* smell it."

I carefully shed my burden into the back of the Continental, then eased around the car and caught Mrs. Cooper's arm. "Hey, Eunice," I said softly, following her wide eyes to the defoliation of the garden's holly hedge. "Come on, honey, we've got to go."

She remained frozen a moment longer, and I was about to pick her up and shove her into the backseat when she thawed enough to remember the car behind her. She slipped in, and when Slim was secured in the front passenger seat, I stepped out from the safety of the building, took a deep breath, and focused. In seconds, both beasts were shrieking, and then they collapsed into the middle of the road, taking out a memorial bench and a Dumpster on their way down.

I jumped into the car, which Slim had already cranked, and backed furiously, keeping one eye on the mirrors in case of latecomers. "What did I say about no magic?" Slim shouted, pounding the dashboard for good measure. "What was *that?*"

"That was getting rid of the witnesses," I replied, "and creating a distraction while we leave the scene."

"That's also going to lead any of those things in a five-mile radius downtown!"

"Details," I muttered, checking behind me again. "Mrs. Cooper, are you still with us?"

She turned and spotted the next monster tuning on to Jefferson at the same time I did. "Drive faster, dear, won't you?"

I didn't need the encouragement. As a police siren several blocks behind me began to wail, I sped through Rigby, weaving around the occasional car in my way. Few of the downtown shops opened before ten, a small mercy that allowed me to do fifty in twenty-five zones without great risk of vehicular manslaughter, even when keeping one eye fixed on the rearview mirror. Mrs. Cooper, who was still staring out the back window, began to hyperventilate, and Slim reached toward the backseat to pat her knee. "Hey. Hey, there. Eunice, was it?" he said with forced cheeriness. "Eunice, can you talk to me for a second?"

She turned, momentarily distracted from the chaos behind us, and I saw her chest heaving under her pink robe. "Yeah, that's it," Slim coaxed. "I thought you looked familiar. You're on the historic preservation board, aren't you? Saved the old Henley warehouse, yeah?"

Something seemed to click, and she nodded. "Oh, yes, the warehouse. There's a developer on board, you know, and she's gung-ho to turn the place into condominiums. Dora Ness, she's out of Richmond, and she says that young people want to live in places like that. Something about exposed brick."

A beast screeched, and Mrs. Cooper shuddered as her head swiveled toward the sound.

"Sure, sure, the kids love old brick," said Slim, keeping his grip on her knee as I swerved around a garbage truck. "Old brick and bad fedoras and shitty beer—guess taste comes with age, am I right? Eunice?"

She glanced back at him and nodded distractedly. "Yes. Age, yes."

"Eunice?" he said as she checked again for pursuers. "Hey, Eunice, I need you to talk to me, okay? Come on, hon, focus here—"

I whipped the car into a parking space in front of The Endless Knot, cutting Slim's exhortations short as he was thrown about the car. "Sorry, man," I said, tossing him the keys, then climbed out and pulled Mrs. Cooper from the back. "Get inside," I told her, speaking as if she'd gone deaf. "Go find Stuart. Stay in there. Yes?"

Her eyes kept darting back toward the center of town, but she understood well enough to aim her footsteps at the shop's front door and ring the after-hours bell. Less than a minute later, as Slim and I were unloading the trunk, the door cracked open, and Stuart's thin face appeared from the gloom. "Auntie Eunice!" he exclaimed. "Good heavens, this is no place for you to..."

His voice trailed off as we locked eyes, and I threw another bag onto my shoulders as Slim slammed the trunk. "Get her in the damn building!" I yelled over a fresh screech—and, if my ears weren't deceiving me, a *closer* screech. "She's going to pass out, Stu, get her in there!"

"It's *Stuart*," he said icily, but he shepherded Mrs. Cooper off the sidewalk.

By the time he'd situated her on a folding chair—he'd set up a makeshift tearoom in the corner of the shop, from the looks of things, though I doubted he was brewing up anything Mrs. Cooper would have recognized—Slim and I had pushed our way inside and locked the door. "Plan?" Slim puffed as he dropped his load onto the wooden floor.

I paused, taking stock of the company, the pile of expensive arcane tools on the ground, and the patchouli-scented store full of useless crap. "That depends. Want to help me find the open gate?"

"Not really." He planted his palms on his thighs and caught his breath, then straightened with a bit of effort and brushed his limp hair from his face. "But I suppose someone's got to do it, right? The *kaiju* aren't going to waltz on home by themselves."

"That's the spirit," I muttered, clapping him on the shoulder. "And as for those two, once they're safe—"

"And Vivi."

"What?"

"Vivi," he repeated, wincing at the sudden sound of squealing brakes and crumpling metal in the near distance. "I'm not leaving her in danger."

"She's in *Skipton*," I protested. "She's out of the way."

"We don't know that." He pulled a late-model phone from his pocket and swiped at the screen until it began to squawk. "Hey, lady, you all right?" he said, giving the phone another tap.

The squawking sharpened and crescendoed into Vivi's shout as the speakerphone engaged. "Something just walked by the complex, and I do *not* know what it was, and I think an ambulance went by—"

"It's okay," he said, using the same quasi-hypnotic tone he'd deployed with Mrs. Cooper. "Listen, Vivi, we're evacuating until this clears. Party at Colin's. He's standing right here with me."

"I'm going to make a gate to your place," I said to the outstretched phone. "Five minutes. Take whatever you need and can carry."

"*What?*" she said. "No, I…no! Hell, no! There's a monster headed toward Rigby—"

"He's got friends," Slim interrupted, "and they're already here. Time to split."

"What about Hal?" she demanded.

I closed my eyes and sighed. "Shit. Boyfriend."

Slim covered the phone and muttered, "Can he come, too?"

Evidently, he hadn't muffled his voice enough, as Vivi hissed, "*He doesn't know!* I haven't told him about the Fringe! I can't…I can't leave…"

Her voice died as a deeper voice mumbled something in the background, and Slim winced. "Sleepover?" he whispered.

"Sounds like it," I said, then took the phone from him and held it close. "Vivian, listen to me. I'm coming for you, and that's final. Get dressed." I handed Slim the phone again as she tried to protest, then looked around the shop, saw that Mrs. Cooper was still conscious, and nodded. "Right, then. You two," I said to the pair by the artificial ficus, "time to go. Slim and I will take care of the cleanup."

But Stuart—who, I noticed, had shoved a braided silver circlet down over his messy locks—shook his head and pushed up the sleeves of his sweatshirt, revealing metal bracelets studded with stones and carved-rune charms. "This is no time for civilian heroics," he said, then pointed to a steel circle set into the floor tiles. "You two take Auntie Eunice and sit in the circle. I'll activate it when you're inside—it'll protect you from evil—and then I'll see to the…whatever…out there. Never fear."

"Oh, my God," Slim groaned, smacking his forehead with the heel of his hand. "He's serious. Colin, he's *serious*."

I took a deep breath, reminding myself that Stuart, delusional though he might be, was primed and willing to take on a monster. "First," I told him, pointing to the ring in the floor, "protective circles only work if they're unobstructed. You've broken it with those tables," I explained, gesturing to the displays of crystals and mass-produced carvings of fertility deities that crossed the metal line. "Second, you've got to have wards already in place to make a circle like that useful, which I can almost guarantee you don't. Third, I don't have time to get a proper ward system going before our little friends find us, so why don't we do this my way, hmm?"

That pulled the wind from his sails, but only for a beat. "And what would you know about protective circles?" he snapped as he straightened his headband. "Excuse me, but which of us is the wizard, here?"

"That would be neither of us," I replied, tracing a rip in reality with my finger. Stuart gaped and fell back a few steps, and I widened the gate to reveal my sunlit office. "But since *I'm* a king of fucking Faerie and *you're* the idiot wearing *Lord of the Rings* props, how about you help Eunice out of her chair and go hang out at my place? We'll be along soon. Try not to break anything, won't you?"

I should have known better than to expect compliance from Stuart the White. He opened and shut his mouth like a landed fish for only a few seconds before recovering sufficiently to duck around the tables and pull a crooked, two-foot branch from behind the cash register. The stick had a chunk of quartz tied to the tip with a leather thong, and I realized what it was supposed to be just as Stuart aimed his homemade wand at my chest and shouted an incantation in badly-pronounced Latin. Slim rolled his eyes, and I stood there quietly, making a point of examining my cuticles, until Stuart ran out of steam. "'I banish you, evil spirit'? That's the best you can do?" I asked as he shook his wand—whether for emphasis or to be sure it was turned on, I couldn't tell. "And I don't mean to be picky, since you're the obvious wizard and all, but you invoked the Goddess, God, several archangels, and Baphomet all in one spell. *Baphomet?* Look, we can debate this later, but I'm fairly sure that Uriel and Baphomet cancel each other out, theologically speaking."

He stared at the useless wand, then at me, then back at the wand. "I...but that..."

"Where'd you get the spell?"

"Benjamin the Celestial. My mentor," he mumbled,

furiously tapping the crystal against his palm like a broken remote control. "That's an incredibly potent invocation against malevolent spirit beings—"

"Do I *look* like a spirit to you, genius?"

The reality of the situation finally clicked with Stuart, and he gave up on coaxing magic from his branch in favor of the equally useless tactic of running into his protective circle and shouting more Latin as he spun about with his fingers splayed. By then, Mrs. Cooper had taken enough of a breather to sort out the more pressing issues of the morning, and she rose and joined Slim and me as we watched Stuart make himself dizzy. Giving my arm a soft pat, she muttered, "I'm so sorry for the trouble, dear."

"Oh, no trouble," I said, raising my voice as a pair of screeches echoed down the street. "But they're going to be here soon—if they're looking for magic, *that's* the jackpot," I added, cocking my head toward the open gate. "Time to get you out of here."

She looked doubtfully at Stuart, who continued to chant nonsense. "You'll send him along?"

"Soon as I can." Catching movement from the corner of my eye, I glanced back at the gate and spotted Val standing on the far side, arms folded and eyebrow arched. "Everything all right?" I asked him.

He shrugged. "Relatively speaking. What's happened? And what's he doing?" he asked, squinting at Stuart's gyrations.

"It's under control. Take care of this one for me—she's had a rough morning." With that, I cupped Mrs. Cooper's face in my hands, switched languages again, and murmured, "This won't hurt."

"You're sure?" she asked, wide-eyed and lightly trembling. "You're *quite* sure about that?"

"Positive," I said, then made the linguistic addition to her mind before she could press for details. She flinched and frowned, surprised at the sensation, and I released her. "Think of it as a built-in translator," I told her in Fae.

"Ready to go?"

She nodded. "Be safe, dear, and…"—her brow knit as she heard herself—"and be…wait, now…I don't—"

"Val will explain," I interrupted, nudging her toward the gate.

My captain extended his hand to her and flashed an almost pants-charming smile, breaking through her sudden confusion. "This way, dear lady, it's quite safe…ah, watch the step," he said, catching her before she could stumble on my rug. "There, now, nothing to it. Have a seat, that's a good girl…"

Mrs. Cooper let him escort her to a couch as she stared at him, her dark eyes enormous behind her glasses. "I hate to be a bother, young man," she asked softly, "but is there any chance you could spare a cup of tea?"

Val looked back through the gate at me and mouthed, *Young man?*

"Ask the kitchen, they know where my tea things are, and behave yourself," I told him, then closed the gate as the screeches neared. "All right," I said, turning to Slim, "we've got to move. I don't trust the structural integrity of this dump enough to let those things fall on it."

"Back in the car?" he asked, pulling a bag from the floor.

"No, let's take this shindig to Vivi's. Might draw the riffraff out of town, at any rate." I began to open a new gate, then paused, remembering the third member of our trio. "We're evacuating," I told Stuart, who had ceased his spinning to gawk at the place where the first gate had been. "You're coming with us. Is there anything you can't leave here? I'm sure the cats will look after themselves."

He whipped his head from side to side in vehement negation. "I don't know who you are or what sort of trickery this is, but a wizard of the Mid-Atlantic Circle doesn't run away from danger! I am a sworn defender of the Light—"

"Oh, for the love of God," Slim muttered, dropping his

bag, then marched across the unwarded circle and dragged Stuart out by his ear. "You don't know the first thing about spellcraft," he said over Stuart's yelped protestations, "you don't know the first thing about magic, and here's a little life tip." He tossed Stuart at my feet with surprising gusto—but then again, Slim had always served as his own bar security. "If a faerie lord tells you it's time to evacuate," he snapped as Stuart scrambled back to his feet, "then it's time to friggin' *evacuate*."

"A wizard does not evacuate," Stuart sniffed with as much dignity as he could muster in sweats and a cockeyed headband. "A wizard fights evil when called upon to do so. He does not run from danger when innocents are—"

Slim grabbed his shoulders and gave him a brusque shake. "Listen to me, moron," he said in a low rush, "you don't know *shit* about wizards. My mother's a wizard. My grandparents were wizards. I grew up with more wizards than I knew what to do with, okay? *And wizards know when to run.*"

Stuart pulled himself free of Slim's grip and straightened his sweatshirt. "Oh, so you're a wizard, now? And *he's* a fairy?" he said, glaring at us in turn. "I see no wands, I see no wings."

One of our pursuers screeched about a block away, and yet another car smashed into something solid as a fresh siren kicked off. "Did you see me make that little gate thing?" I asked him, then levitated Slim's pile of gear with a glance as I opened the new gate to Vivi's apartment. "That's what magic looks like, kid. Well, and *this*," I added, patting my youthful face. "Left the glamour off this morning. But you know, there's a better time for this discussion," I said, then grabbed his arm and yanked him into the next town.

The first person I spotted in the apartment wasn't Vivi, but rather a bull-necked redhead whose Rigby Buccaneers

T-shirt barely stretched to cover his sculpted chest and biceps. He had armed himself with a serrated kitchen knife, which he held at an awkward angle as he emerged from the hallway into the main room. I gathered from his unease that he would rather have tackled us than gone for the stabbing approach, but at that moment, I was in the mood for neither and simply threw him against the wall. "Hi," I said, releasing Stuart as I remotely forced our would-be assailant's fingers to curl away from his weapon. He thrashed, kicking dents into the plaster, but I'd pinned him securely, and he stared back at me as his knife fell, panicking but trying not to show it. "I'm Coileán," I continued, nudging the knife out of the way with my toe. "You must be Hal."

"How," he began in a squeak, then cleared his throat and tried again. "How do you know who—"

"Go Bucs," I muttered, then noticed Vivi peeking out of her bedroom. "Gate's open, and it's going to draw them here. You need to move," I called to her. Her mouth tightened, and I caught a glimpse of the tangled emotions raging in her mind before I turned back to Hal. "Let me explain what's going on, Coach," I told him. "And I'll make this as straightforward as possible. Magic is real. You're getting a taste of it right now, in fact. I happen to be rather skilled with it, which you may also have gathered from your current predicament. Ms. Stowe has assisted me in several matters with her paranormal research, and since there are an unknown number of, for lack of a better term, hell-beasts on the rampage in Rigby at the moment, I'm taking her to safety. You're welcome to come along. Interested?"

He hung there, digesting what I'd said, then nodded.

"Great." I lowered him to the carpet and cut my eyes to Vivi, who continued to goggle from her hiding place. "Come on out, kid, we don't have much time."

She slipped through the door and skulked past me to join her boyfriend, who pulled her to his side and wrapped one of his thick arms around her protectively. "This won't hurt," I said for his benefit, opening another gate to my office, then peeked through and spotted Mrs. Cooper on the couch with a laden tea tray set before her. She was back in her element, a teacup in one hand and a saucer in the other, and she looked my way at the sudden noise.

"There you are!" she called, lifting her teacup in greeting. "This is lovely! Where's Stuart?" she asked, craning her neck for a better view of my side of the gate.

"With me. I'll send him soon," I said, then stepped aside and swept my arm in invitation. "Ms. Stowe. And, uh…"

"Perryman," said Hal, keeping his grip on Vivi as they headed for the gate. "Henry Perryman." He paused on the threshold, gave me one last uneasy look, then let his girlfriend lead him over the border.

Before they could have second thoughts, I closed the portal and regarded the others. "All right, that's everyone but Toula, and she's a big girl. Find the rift?"

"Ahead of you," said Slim as he pulled a little box free from one of his bags. Lifting the lid, he revealed a notched green disc that wobbled for a few seconds until it settled with its notch pointing north. "Dark magic detector," he explained. "Points toward the area of highest concentration, which has to mean the gate. When we find it, can you close it?"

I thought, with a sick feeling, of my misadventures in the Pine Barrens. "Working assumption is yes," I replied, then turned to Stuart, who'd had a moment for the cogs to spin into place. "All right, Merlin, decision time. Would you rather be safe or be of use?"

Stuart stared mournfully back at me, looking rather like I'd just told him the truth about Santa Claus. "You *can't* be a fairy," he mumbled. "My research…all of my study…my *work*…"

Slim started muttering curses, but I kept my attention on the ersatz wizard, who had rapidly descended into the throes of an existential crisis. "Hate to break this to you," I said, "but tiny girls with wings, dancing on flowers? Not even close. I'm not a skeptic," I told him, closing the distance between us, "I'm the genuine article. And there are monsters on the loose, and Olive's missing again, and I don't have time to argue with you today. You can either go to safety with Eunice or see what magic can actually do. Your choice."

He swallowed hard, but he held my gaze. "I'm a wizard," he whispered. "I took vows. And I do not run."

"So be it." I grabbed a long, highly carved wooden rod from Slim's stash and examined its markings. "Is this what I think it is?"

"Dud Defender," said Slim with a curt nod. "And she's fully loaded and on a hair trigger, so watch where the hell you're pointing that, thanks."

"Huh?" Stuart mumbled, staring as the rod's runes began to glow orange under my hand.

"My favorite boomstick," Slim explained, gingerly taking it from me and passing it to Stuart. "Designed for the magically inept. It's point-and-think thaumaturgy—ensorcelled and preloaded with fireballs."

He watched the rod light up, testing his grip, then aimed it at Vivi's living-room window and the trash compactor beyond. "So how does this—" was as far as he made it before the window, the compactor, and the Toyota behind the compactor exploded in a blast of glass, metal, and garbage.

When the debris finished pattering off my shield, I rose from my defensive crouch and turned to find Stuart frozen where he stood, his eyes bugging from his skull as he surveyed the smoking damage. Slim grunted, shook the glass shards from his hair, and thumped Stuart's rigid back. "Boomstick," he muttered. "Hair trigger. Pay attention."

I stepped to the wall and waved the window whole, began piecing the compactor back together, then saw the first of the beasts come striding into the complex parking lot and hoped the owner of the totaled car had decent coverage. "Party time," I said, heading for the door with Slim on my heels. "Stay low. I'll shield you when I can, but try to stay out of the blast radius while you get a heading on that thing."

"I've got a heading," he replied, following me down the concrete staircase, "but I don't have a distance. Want me to hotwire a ride?"

"Could you? I'd really rather not try to enchant steel on top of everything else today."

"Give me about five minutes' coverage and see." He glanced over his shoulder at Stuart, who was following at a safe distance, holding the rod between finger and thumb. "You break my stick, man, and I'm going to be pissed," he warned.

"I'm not accustomed to this type of magic," Stuart protested.

"You're not accustomed to magic, period." Slim pressed himself against the breezeway wall, then slammed Stuart against the brick beside him with one meaty arm. "Aim for the heads."

"What h—oh, my God," he whispered as the beast came into view. "What is *that*…"

"And don't hit Colin," Slim added, then puffed toward the parking lot and an old Cadillac sedan.

I studied the newcomer: perhaps a hair smaller than the ones I'd already dispatched that morning, but still massive and skittering toward us. I began to ask Stuart in jest if he'd like the first crack at it, but before I could form the words, he was running toward the creature with Slim's glowing rod extended, screaming like a madman. The beast bellowed its hunting call just as the first fireballs tore through its waving neck and thorax. Its cry choked in its torn throat and faltered, and after another few shots, six more cars joined the Toyota as insurance claims.

When the thing ceased twitching, I sloshed through the spreading puddle of ichor and carefully pried the rod from

Stuart's hand as he shouted incoherent challenges at the corpse. "Maybe I should hold on to this for a while," I said, glancing at the darkened runes to see how much of a charge the rod still held. "Safekeeping, you know," I added, raising my voice over the blaring car alarms. "Uh…good first effort, a little sloppy in the execution, but all things considered…Stu. Stu, hey, it's dead, you can stop yelling now."

It took a hard shake to snap him out of it, and he looked around with wild eyes as a few of Vivi's neighbors began to emerge from their apartments. "Where's my wand?" he cried, suddenly realizing his hand was empty. "I had…where did…"

I held it up and took a step back. "You're trigger-happy right now. Calm down, kid, deep breaths." I surveyed the growing crowd and groaned to myself. At that moment, I couldn't have cared less if anyone saw me go to work—I just didn't want to deal with the mess of casualties. Throwing caution aside, I dissolved the beast into dust, then killed the car alarms with a snap. My loafers were stained, I vaguely realized, but decided that all things considered, the condition of my footwear was the least of my concerns. Turning to face the huddled crowd, I shoved the rod into my belt and held up my hands for quiet. "There's been a freak meteorological event," I said when I had their attention. "Lightning strike, microburst, whatever." The clear sky proved me a liar, but the mortals were too spooked to notice. "And it appears this large tree fell on your cars," I continued, willing an ancient oak into existence to fit the multi-car depression the fallen beast had left behind. "You should probably call your adjustors this afternoon when the weather clears."

An elderly man in a gray cardigan finally looked to the heavens and frowned. "I didn't see any storm," he muttered, scowling at the sun. "And whatever it was, it's passed now—"

He was cut short by an all-too-familiar screech, and we

turned as one to see another monster galloping toward us. This one, however, seemed distracted. It waved its arms around its bucking head as it ran as if trying to shake something off, and as I squinted, a black form came into focus, something dark and vaguely humanoid that was clinging to the creature's neck. As the crowd began to scream and rushed for shelter, the beast shrieked again, then flung the irritant from its body. The dark form tucked and rolled, landed in a stumbling run, then whipped around and shot twin jets of white flame from its hands, turning its former mount into a yowling bonfire. After a few long seconds, it died and fell, taking out a garage and the maintenance golf cart on its way down.

The rider brushed off its palms and strolled toward me, and I recognized Toula beneath heavy black streaks of gore. "Hey!" she yelled, wagging her finger at me. "Way to leave me with the cleanup! Were you planning to help today, or were you going to sit this one out?" As she closed, she noticed the clump of residents cowering in the breezeway and offered a little wave. "Hi, folks. Sorry about the mess. Uh…maybe don't go to Rigby right now, okay? You know, in fact, you should probably go back into your apartments and draw the blinds until this is over."

Most didn't need to be told twice. The observant senior blinked at Toula a few times, considered the monster two buildings over, then nodded and retreated without another word. By the time his door slammed, Slim had coaxed the hotwired car to life, and I gave Toula a pointed once-over. "We're about to liberate someone's car, and you're going to *wreck* the interior if you get in like that."

"Shove it, Gramps," she muttered, but willed herself clean as she brushed past me and into the front seat.

Slim had already laid claim to the wheel, and as I dragged Stuart into the back, Slim passed his box to Toula and pointed to the notch. "Keep us on the right track," he ordered, then drove off at a respectable forty, staying well clear of the police cars that sped by us, heading toward

Rigby and the discomfiting cloud of smoke rising over the trees.

Perhaps because the universe has a sense of humor, the gate into the Gray Lands was hovering over a vacant lot behind a Walmart on the far side of Skipton. By the time Slim parked, the last of the pack seemed to have come through, as a glance through the gate revealed nothing but a wasteland of brown grass beneath a sky of slate. While Toula and Slim checked our surroundings for signs of monsters—not a difficult task, I imagine, as it wasn't as if they could *hide*—I stood at the edge of the gate, reading and re-reading the words burned into the short grass on the other side. I saw Stuart approach from the corner of my eye, but I ignored him until he knelt and reached through the gate to run his finger over the blackened swirls. "What's that?" he asked, brushing the dirt off his sweatpants as he stood.

"A message."

"Yeah?" He peered at the writing again. "I don't recognize the runes—"

"It's not a runic system, it's Fae. And it's for me." I stepped back from the gate, and the stench of the outflow—to my senses, a smell much like formaldehyde overlaid with strong notes of gardenia—began to diffuse with distance. "Time to seal this off," I said, then waved Stuart away while I opened a gate to my office facing the gate to the wilderness.

My guests on the other side—Mrs. Cooper, Vivi, her perplexed beau, and now Meggy—were still congregating around the tea tray. "Any sign of her?" Meggy called through the opening, rising from the couch for a better look. "Have you found her yet?"

"I think so," I called back, and as Stuart waved to reassure his great-aunt that he was still very much alive and whole, I began to weave a plug for the first gate. My technical skill had improved in the years since my failed attempt in New Jersey, but more importantly, with the outflow from Faerie pressing back against the outflow of dark magic, I had far more raw power than I'd had the first time around, and the enchantment I worked was *solid*. It wouldn't hold forever—not against a continual battering of dark magic—but I assumed it would hold long enough for the natural barrier between the realms to regrow itself, a sort of magical bandage over the wound. Ten minutes later, as the first screeches began to echo across the superstore's parking lot, I finished sealing the breach, then turned my attention to the waiting spectators. "Just a bit of cleanup to finish," I explained. "We'll be with you shortly."

I returned to the street, where Slim and Toula stood at the ready and Stuart anxiously flexed his fingers. "Here, Stu," I said, passing him the rod as what turned out to be the last three beasts standing came running down the highway, accompanied by a chorus of squealing tires and smashing cars. "Knock yourself out. Slim, get out of here, you've done enough."

He retreated to the gate without protest, and Toula pushed up her sleeves. "When we're finished here," she said, "we should probably go back to Rigby and repair the damage."

"And how do you see that going over?" I retorted. "'Oh, hello,'" I minced in a falsetto, "'don't mind me, I'm just your friendly neighborhood wizard!'"

"I could do it," said Stuart, flinching as the nearest of the things kicked a stalled SUV out of its way. "I've held myself out as a wizard—what if you did it and I took the credit?"

Toula looked incredulously at Stuart. "*You're* a wizard?"

"In a manner of speaking, yes," he muttered.

"In a manner that counts, no," I replied. "Toula, this is the Stuart I told you about. And Stu, given that anyone in Rigby with more than two brain cells knows you can't actually do magic, no, I really don't think we need to make an effort to disprove that. Let it lie."

Toula waited until the hunting calls had subsided, then said, "Ten to one someone blames it all on swamp gas. Ready, boys?" she asked, and her hands sparked to life.

I made the three final corpses disappear—we were right there, after all, and they were blocking traffic—and closed the gate once Toula and Stuart were through, the former tired and once again ichor-streaked, the latter vibrating with adrenaline like he'd grabbed a live wire. Meggy ran to me and seized my arms before I could so much as pour a drink. "Olive. *Where is Olive?*"

"Gray Lands," I said, sliding from her grip, and headed for the bar. "As assumed. She left me a note." I selected a bottle of whisky older than any of my company, then poured liberally and took it in one long shot. "Burned it in the grass at the gate," I continued, coughing with the alcohol. "Considerate of her, I suppose."

Meggy's face hardened. "How do you know—"

"It was her?" I finished. "I can't be sure, but '*Find me, Ironhand*' seems like a giveaway." I considered the open bottle, then the ring of eyes watching me for direction, and shrugged. "So, who else needs a drink?"

CHAPTER 19

Doris, High Keeper of the Parish Payroll, was less than impressed to see me again when I strode into Sacred Heart's office that afternoon. "Father Paul," I said, even as her pink lips moved into a tight line. "Is he in?"

"I'm sorry," she replied, offering a fair impression of a smile, "but Father's with the bishop right now. They're not to be disturbed—"

I brushed past her toward the hallway of offices, and she rose and shouted after me, "Hey! I said he's with the *bishop*! You can't go back there!"

"Watch me," I muttered, pounding on Paul's office door even as I heard Doris scrambling for the telephone. "Paul!" I called through the thick wood. "Problem!"

A moment later, the door cracked open, and Paul peeked out into the hall. "What's up?" he asked. "I'm guessing this can't wait."

"Long story short, you're at risk, and I'd like to evacuate you for the time being."

His brow rose and wrinkled. "*Evacuate*? From Virginia?"

"From this realm."

"Who is it, Paul?" asked a deep voice from inside the office, and the priest opened the door to reveal his middle-aged superior, who half-rose from his armchair for a better look. "Oh…hello, son," said the bishop, noticing me, "is everything all right? Do you need some help? Social services is on the other side of the building—"

"Uh, Nick," Paul interrupted, absently rubbing the

back of his neck, "this is my associate. You know. My *associate.*"

"Oh," he replied, and then mumbled, "*Oh*," again as the light of recognition dawned in his face. "This, um...*this is—*"

"Yes."

The bishop stood, but he kept his chair between us. "I...was expecting someone—"

"Older?" I volunteered. "I'm eight hundred and twelve, and we can discuss this later. Paul, have you seen any news out of Rigby this morning?" I asked, ignoring the flabbergasted bishop.

"No." He folded his arms. "No, I've not even checked my e-mail today...why, did something happen?"

"See for yourself."

With a brief flash of impatience for my evasiveness, he beckoned me into the office, then flipped open the laptop on his desk, shoved a pair of reading glasses into position, and began his work. I'd just taken up a comfortable spot on the wall when he exclaimed, "Good Lord, what the hell is *that?*"

"Mantis wolf thingy?"

He looked up over the screen and nodded. "What have you done?"

"Stopped them, actually. We were able to do a little cleanup, but you forget how many damn cameras there are nowadays." I shrugged against the plaster. "Look, Paul, I think our daughter's out to get Meggy and me. Those things didn't show up in Rigby by chance, you know. I've already pulled a few people over for safekeeping until we settle this. Even Greg's offering help, but—"

The priest pushed his glasses down his nose. "You think I'm in danger?"

"The day I first took Moyna to her mother, I told her where I'd gotten the information. She might not remember you, but if she does, and if she's trying to get to me..."

I left the thought unfinished, and Paul snapped his

computer closed. "Do we have a time frame?" he asked, then bent with a grunt to pull a well-worn duffel bag from beneath his desk.

"Not as such, but hopefully not long. And you really don't need holy water, man."

"One can never be too careful," he replied, slinging the bag onto his shoulder, then turned to the nervous bishop. "If Colin says it's time, then it's time," he told his guest. "Sorry to cut this short, Nick. I'll call you when I return."

Before the bishop could raise a fuss, I opened the gate, and Paul stepped through without a backward glance. I followed him, and Doris barged into the office in time to see me close the rift behind us.

Even with all that followed, I look back sometimes on her puffy face and its perfectly round *O* of shock, and I laugh.

On my return, I found that my office was no longer quite as I'd left it. There were more couches, for one, and they had been rearranged into a semicircle around what appeared to be Meggy's television, which had somehow been mounted on the stone wall. Its power and cable cords disappeared into a micro-gate below it, and I recognized the Virginia Beach morning news team on the screen, all looking slightly ashen and worse for wear. I supposed they had been held over past noon, as the station appeared to have forsaken its daily schedule in favor of continual coverage from Rigby. I heard snippets of commentary as I surveyed the laden buffet table and collection of dirty glasses on the bar—*explosion, chemical agent, hallucinogenic, terrorist.* Catching me standing by the door, Slim hurried over and murmured, "We've got people in D.C. running interference on the media snoops. It helps that they're more willing to believe that al-Qaeda is sending suicide bombers to a little beach town than they are that we were attacked by monsters from somewhere outside the known universe."

"Militants are easier to work with than Cthulhu," I replied, then nodded to Paul, who looked about the room with wide eyes. "Rick Matherson, Paul McGill."

"Slim," Rick amended, gripping the priest's hand. "I'm his bartender."

"Exorcist," Paul replied, giving Slim a careful look. "I knew he had a thirst, but—"

"And I'm also a crafter for the Arcanum."

"Ah, gotcha. And Joseph!" he called, releasing Slim to meet Joey's embrace. "My goodness, son, look at you," he said when he pulled back, then held the younger man at arm's length. "When were you planning on a haircut, eh?"

Joey ran one hand through his admittedly shaggy scruff and grinned. "Eventually. Here, Father, look outside," he said, leading the priest toward the window. "There's someone I want you to meet..."

I turned around until I spotted Valerius, who remained on guard near the door, silently watching my guests come to terms with the situation. "How bad are things?" I muttered once he was within earshot.

Val sighed quietly as he made his calculations. "Lady Meghan remains inconsolable," he began, cutting his eyes to the central couch and the small knot of people glued to the television. "Toula has been with her of late, but..."

"But it's not Olive?"

"Precisely. And the other woman, Eunice—she's been a calming influence, I believe. How do you—"

"Former neighbor," I replied. "Meggy's current neighbor. Once bested Robin and some of his people with a steel kettle."

Val grimaced at that. "Good to know. And her companion, the one with the, uh...circlet?"

I followed his finger to the far corner of the room, where Stuart had taken up a position on a lonely window seat and stared out at the garden. "He's had a difficult morning."

"He's also had three glasses of wine."

"*Very* difficult." I saw Aiden approach Joey and Paul—and on his heels, Helen. "When did she—"

"Shortly after you left," said Val, following the direction of my stare. "Toula departed to update the grand magus about the situation, if I recall correctly, and Helen returned with her. Under the circumstances, I thought it prudent not to make a scene."

"Good choice." I glanced around again, taking a mental headcount, and came up short. "The last two, Vivi and Hal...where did they go?"

My captain tapped the door behind him. "It seems she thought the time was right for a private talk. I don't know the topic." His eyes narrowed, and he lowered his voice. "She understood me. I know she did—her eyes gave her away—but she's feigning ignorance. Why?"

"Because her parents are half fae," I replied quietly, "and he doesn't know that yet."

Val's confusion deepened. "And she is—"

"Mortal, as far as anyone knows. No talent whatsoever. Works with Slim," I added, nodding to my bartender—who, perhaps for lack of a better idea, had fallen into old habits and taken up a place behind my bar. "He's the Arcanum's go-to craftsman. Witch-blood."

"And you trust him?"

"As much as I do anyone. Toula's quite fond of him," I said, watching Joey lead his old mentor to the bar. Paul's face had become animated, and though I couldn't make out his words over the general babble and the blaring television, I surmised that Georgie had made camp in the garden. "You heard about the message?" I muttered, looking back at Val.

He nodded. "A challenge. And, I would assume, a trap. You can't win in the Gray Lands, Coileán."

"Unless," I replied, glancing at Aiden and his sister, "I can bring the magic with me."

Val studied them for a moment in silence, then

muttered, "He's very young."

"I'm aware of that. He has the ability—"

"You're certain?"

"I've seen it! *You've* seen it. Why the sudden doubt?"

"I don't doubt, I just..." Val struggled before managing, "I fear that you'll ask too much of him, and he won't want to disappoint you. That's all." He paused to watch Aiden again. "The boy has a gift, yes, but what does it cost him to employ it? My concern," he hastened, seeing my eyes shift back to my brother, "is that if you try to storm the Gray Lands, Lord Aiden will either injure himself or fail when his strength leaves him. He's never been tested in conditions like these, has he?"

He was right, and my guts clenched. "He's our only conduit. No one else can pack the stuff."

"I know. But I..." His thought ended abruptly, and Val took a deep breath. "My lord, may I be perfectly frank?"

"Please," I replied, fighting my rising sense of dread.

"Let Moyna go," he murmured, barely louder than a whisper. "Let the lords and ladies go. Fight them later if they show their faces, but for now, let them go."

"Val," I protested, "I can't just—"

"Is it worth the risk?" he pressed, drawing closer to me in his urgency. "I assume the plan is as before—Lord Aiden packs the magic, the rest of us at arms, yes? But who goes on this mission? You and me? Lady Meghan? My sister? And all for what, to drag Moyna back and imprison her until she learns to tolerate her jailers? Is *that* worth the risk?" My face began to work, and he sighed. "Coileán, I realize she's your daughter. I understand the delicacy of your arrangement with Lady Meghan. But this is a fool's fight. Take my advice, withdraw and wait, and the enemy will tire and come to you. Moyna is many things, but she is not patient."

"I know, and you're probably right," I admitted, "but Meggy—"

"Is also very young."

"And is likely to go after Moyna herself if I don't help her," I retorted. "She wouldn't last five minutes in a real fight, even if she had a source of magic. I can't let her do that alone."

He regarded me sadly. "You love her, boy."

"I do."

"And that," he said, shaking his head, "is the problem."

Half an hour later, Meggy took my decision not to immediately charge into the Gray Lands about as well as I'd anticipated. "You don't know she's the one who left you the message!" she protested, shouting over the continual Rigby coverage. "It could have been anyone! And there's no telling what that Geheret kid is doing to her while we're twiddling our thumbs—"

"Probably nothing," I replied, fighting to keep my temper in check in the face of her angry tears. "She went willingly, didn't she?"

She sputtered, then spat, "That is my *baby*! You can help me, or you can get out of my way. What's it going to be?"

"That's not your baby," said Toula. Meggy wheeled on her, fists half-raised, but Toula held her ground. "Megs, honey, I know you don't want to hear this, but Monya hasn't been a baby in a long time. Whatever she might have been…that's gone. You don't grow up at Titania's feet and come away unchanged. Come on," she said, reaching out to take hold of Meggy's taut arms, "I sat there with you all weekend, and I know what hatred looks like. You're not going to win this one."

Mrs. Cooper, who had made camp one couch to the left, nodded emphatically. "I could have told you months ago that Olive was trouble waiting to happen," she interjected. "It's nothing you did, dear—there's no fixing some children. And once you realize that, you can either keep fighting a losing battle, or you can stand back, admit you did your best, and let go."

But Meggy was unappeased, and she pushed Toula aside to glare at me. "I thought you loved me, Colin," she said, her voice trembling with rage. "You told me you loved me."

"I do, Me—"

"Then *bring her home*! Why are you stalling? We can get her…"

I looked from my furious girlfriend's swollen eyes to Toula, who stood behind her with tight lips and folded arms. "Not tonight," I said quietly. Meggy began to yell a reply, but I held up my hands and spoke over her. "I'm concerned, too, but I'm not going to ask my people to face unnecessary risks every time Moyna runs away. We'll get her when we're prepared."

"Aiden's had time to run his numbers! We know where she is! There's no need to wait, and if he finds out what she told us…" She clenched and unclenched her fists in her distress. "He's going to kill her this time, I know he is, and you won't get her back. Why won't you get my baby back?"

I tried to placate her. "It's just like last time. We have a better shot of making it back in one piece if we put a plan in place, and I don't want to lose you because we were rash. Give me the night at least, let me get organized, and then we'll see about Moyna. I promise you, Meggy, we're going to find her. Give me time."

She stared at me, silently accusing me of an unknown multitude of sins, then swiped at her eyes and raised her chin. "You're a coward," she said, taking care with every syllable, "and you're cruel. Just like your mother."

"Meggy, please," I tried, reaching for her, but she swatted my hand aside and brushed past me. After screwing her eyes closed in concentration, she ripped open a small gate onto a familiar sunlit shore. Val moved to grab her, but I held him back and shook my head, and Meggy left without another word.

When she had put a few yards between us without looking back, I closed the gate and looked at my silent companions. "An aide will take you to your rooms," I muttered, wrestling against the urge to punch a hole in the nearest convenient wall. "For your safety, please remain within the palace. Val, Toula, Helen, Aiden, Joey…if you'd stay for a time, I'd appreciate it."

The other six filed out—Hal, who'd returned shortly before, had his arm around Vivi—and when the door latched behind them, I sank onto a convenient couch and buried my head in my hands. "Someone tell me how to fix this," I mumbled into my palms. "Anyone. Suggestions."

"Correct me if I'm wrong," said Joey, "but did Meggy just go to Red's?"

"Yes."

"And we can all guess how well that's going to play out," Toula sighed, flopping onto the cushion beside me. "Oberon's not going to help her."

"Hell, he might kill her for bothering him," I said, pressing on my eyes to distract me from the building headache. "Harshing his vibe or whatever. Do people still say that?"

"We get the gist." Toula patted my back until I uncovered my face. "Pull it together, Gramps," she said, not unkindly. "It ain't over until the dust settles. Now, do we have a plan, or are we going to sit around and nurse hurt feelings all evening?"

I turned to look at Aiden, who nodded. "I've been going over my data," he said, shoving his hands into his pockets. "Got some sense of how much juice you need."

"And?"

"And," he muttered, "I don't think I can pack it for you. You need too much, and I can't manually compress magic past a certain density. That said," he hastened, "I've got an idea."

"A feasible idea?" Val asked.

"Depends on how good your aim is," he retorted, then

looked back at me. "If you were to open a gate into the Gray Lands, could you zero in on a target over there? Say, Moyna?"

"A moving gate," muttered Val. "Yes, it's *possible*…"

"Then once you get close to her, you go through," Aiden continued. "I stay on the edge and keep pumping magic across. Kind of like a fire hose, see?"

I looked at the others, who began to slowly nod. "It's risky," said Toula, "but with a little practice…how fast can you pump? You can actually pull off Simon Magus's trick?"

"So I've been told, but I don't know what my rate is," he replied with a one-shouldered shrug. "If I could have time to get my feet wet, so to speak…"

Helen's eyes narrowed, but she kept her peace, and I stood. "You'll have all the time I can give you," I told Aiden. "Tell me what you need."

What Aiden needed, he explained, was a space devoid of magic. "I need a clean slate for testing purposes," he said, sketching a cube in a little notebook he'd pulled from his back pocket. "Someone goes in"—a stick figure appeared in the box he'd drawn—"and I stand at the door, pumping." He added a second stick figure, then lines radiating from the figure into the box. Clearly, Aiden was never going to be an artist, but I nodded along. "The guy inside cranks up the enchantment," he continued, "and that way, we can tell whether I'm getting enough power to him. See?"

The trick, then, was finding an equivalent of Aiden's magic-less cube. For that, Val came to my assistance and led me to Mother's "special" prison cells, which I'd given serious thought to incinerating. Ignoring my discomfort—fifty years of solitary confinement is an eternity, regardless of whether one is mortal or fae—he described the wards around the rooms that prevented large-scale enchantment.

"Prisoners can feed themselves, remove waste—"

"Writing material," I muttered.

"Small comforts," he agreed. "But the wards block most magic, so anything larger than that is impossible."

"Kindly refrain from reminding me, hmm?" I pressed my palm against the invisible barrier and felt the wards hum. "It's a starting point."

I had to give Mother credit—she'd constructed her wards well, and they took my additions with little trouble. By the end of the dinner hour, when Aiden came around to check on me with an enormous sandwich in hand, I'd strengthened the wards to not only block magic, but also to actively repulse it. The wards extended backward in a tunnel from the door, culminating in a hole that was roughly the size of my brother. As he could actually see what I'd been doing by touch and smell, he directed the fine-tuning, then stepped into the breach and tested himself against the wards. After a few preliminary thrusts at thin air, he wiped his brow and stepped out of the unseen tunnel. "It'll do," he declared, then took half my sandwich back and devoured it in three bites. "What?" he asked when he caught my incredulous stare. "This is hungry work, you know!"

"That was the size of your face."

"I'm *fifteen*," he protested. "And growing, theoretically, so if it's not in someone else's mouth already, it's fair game."

Over the long night, Aiden demonstrated the true depths of his stomach, downing at least half a dozen more sandwiches before dawn. Helen kept him plied with snacks while Val, Toula, and I took turns in the cell—the wards of which, for safety's sake, I'd rebuilt with two-hour time-out locks to prevent anyone being trapped inside. There was by necessity a limit to the types of large enchantments one could pull off in a small room, but the hours the three of us spent in practice gave us an idea of what it would be like to pull magic from a concentrated source—and it gave

Aiden a sense of how hard he had to work. By breakfast, the boy's shirt was soaked through under the arms and down his back, and his sweaty hair had dried against his scalp in uneven clumps. He swore he was feeling fine, but his face had flushed crimson, and he fell asleep on his crooked arm at the breakfast table.

Helen pushed his plate out of the way and gave the rest of us a stern look, but she didn't chide us over his snores. Someone had to keep the gate open and protect Aiden, and Helen had volunteered for—nay, insisted on—the job. She was as culpable as we were by her participation, but she made her dislike of the plan abundantly clear, even in her silence.

I didn't appreciate Helen's quiet condemnation, but I had to give the wizard credit for sticking around. Though Greg had offered me access to the Arcanum's library, he had refused to cross into the Gray Lands, citing the high risk and his age. He and I both knew better than to ask for assistance from the Inner Council in a court matter. Helen was under no obligation to help, and I suspected that given his druthers, Greg would have kept her out of Faerie. But however much Helen disapproved of my existence, she wasn't about to leave Aiden's safety in my hands—which, all things considered, was a wise move. And while she seemed less reluctant to entrust our brother to Joey, he would be unavailable when the time came. "Georgie is willing to go," he told us, "and I've got a halfway decent sword. We're not going to do anyone any good if we stay on this side of the gate and supervise."

As Aiden slept it off, the five of us who were still conscious discussed strategy over coffee, trying to find ways to maximize the limited power he was able to give us. Slim joined us in his frayed bathrobe, as did Vivi, who slipped in, helped herself to the remains of the bacon, and periodically offered suggestions. "A focus array would be useful," Toula told her after her fourth idea had been shot down, "but only if we had time to plant and power it, and if I could get those two to learn some damn spellcraft," she added, cocking her head to Val and me. "Arcanum tools aren't going to be particularly helpful in this situation."

"Excuse me," someone drawled from the back of the dining room, and I turned to find Vivi's boyfriend on the threshold, still wearing his Buccaneers T-shirt but somewhat worse for the night. "Uh…hey," he said quietly, suddenly finding himself the center of attention. "Sorry. Don't mean to interrupt, but, uh…the wizard guy, Stuart? He's been chanting or something for the last two hours, and I don't know what's going on, and if someone could maybe give it to me in English around here, that would be *really* great."

Vivi winced and sank lower in her chair, and I stood. "Chanting, Mr. Perryman?"

He seemed relieved to recognize words once more. "Yeah, chanting, sounds like. I mean, I've only heard it through the wall," he added, "but we're right next door, and he was doing this yodeling thing around dawn. You heard it, right, babe?" he asked, glancing around the table to find his girlfriend.

"Ululation," she confirmed. "I couldn't make out what he was saying, but given the quality of his Latin, I'm not surprised." Slim snorted, and Toula muttered a quick translation for Val, who seemed pained at the news. "The Mid-Atlantic Circle goes all in for ritual," Vivi continued, "so he's probably trying to harness the power of the sun or some shit like that."

"And since he's a wizard…" said Hal, letting the thought hang.

I shook my head. "He's a wizard in his own eyes and a nutbag with a crystal collection in everyone else's. If it makes him feel better to do his thing…well, it's keeping him out of trouble."

Hal folded his arms and frowned at the room for a long moment, then sighed. "Okay, now, let me get this straight." He started pointing at us in turn and muttered, "Faerie, faerie, witch-faerie-something, my girlfriend, who still has some explaining to do, the guy who keeps carding my players, witch, sleeping kid I don't know, and dude with a dragon?"

"Witch-blood," Toula corrected. "Sleeping kid is, too. And before she gets offended," she added, cutting her eyes across the table to Helen, "'wizard' is the gender-neutral term. A witch is a mostly useless wizard, and calling someone like *Helen* a witch is, you know, like suggesting the valedictorian is in special ed." Helen grinned at that, and Toula dipped her chin in recognition before turning back to the coach. "Of course, given the circumstances, I don't think anyone's going to be too offended if you get the details confused. Bagel?"

"Yeah, sure," he mumbled, pulling up the empty chair beside Vivi as Toula floated a platter of breads to his end of the table. "I, uh…just checking, but this isn't some convoluted dream, is it?"

"Afraid not, but we hope to have you home safely in the near future," she replied, giving him a surprisingly reassuring smile. "In the meantime, try to relax—you're not going to be battling warlocks or anything. Think of this as an early Thanksgiving break, huh?"

Hal split a bagel and reached for the jam. "We've got a game Saturday week," he said morosely. "There's a championship thing Thanksgiving weekend. The boys need practice—"

"*Championship?*" I exclaimed, leaning past Toula to see his face. "I thought Rigby wasn't going to the playoffs! Have you won at all this season?"

"Once, and there's a game for the two bottom teams so no one feels left out…" He paused, shook his head, and leaned around the others to better see me. "And how the hell would you know how we've played?"

"I suffered through most of your games because until she decided to run off to the damn Gray Lands and sic monsters on your town, my daughter was cheering for the high school."

His eyes widened, and he dropped the jam spoon to the tablecloth. "*Who?*"

"Olive Horn? Blonde?"

"She's *yours?*"

"Genetically," I muttered, leaving Vivi to fill in the gaps at her discretion. "Joey, remind me to check on Eunice and Paul," I said, and he raised a thumb as he continued to shovel eggs down his throat. "Helen, let's get Aiden to bed, and then I'd appreciate it if you could see what Greg might be holding back—if he's got anything in his storerooms that can amplify magic, now would be the time to share. The easier we can make this on Aiden, the better," I added, and she nodded emphatically. "And Toula—"

That was as far as I got before a gate ripped open and Oberon stormed through, dragging Meggy by the arm. "Have you misplaced something?" he asked, tossing her toward the table, then noticed the spread and helped himself to a muffin. "Really, Coileán, you *must* take better care of your pets."

Val was on his feet, but I had eyes only for Meggy, who had landed against the edge of the table and was covering the left side of her face. "Let me see," I said, crouching beside her, but she kept her eye covered and pushed me away. Once I'd moved out of striking distance, she revealed a small gash across her eyebrow, and her fingertips came away bloody.

Taking advantage of the opening, Toula gave me a glare that demanded compliance and slipped between us. "Look here," she soothed, taking hold of Meggy's chin, "you're leaking. Let me fix it, hmm?"

Meggy silently acquiesced, and while Toula was busy, I rose to face Oberon, who was watching with obvious pleasure as he ate. "Is there some reason you couldn't have just sent her on her way?" I asked, feeling my arms begin to tighten.

He rolled his eyes and took another bite. "Annoyed me all evening," he said, spewing bran crumbs. "Wouldn't go away. Also took up real estate at the bar and didn't buy anything."

"As if that matters to you," I snapped, exasperated.

Oberon shrugged. "Sets a bad example for the actual customers," he replied, then wiped his mouth and dropped the wrapper onto the tablecloth. "Anyway, as I told her *repeatedly*"—he glowered at the top of Meggy's head, but received only Toula's snarl for his trouble—"this isn't my problem. I offered you wise counsel a week ago, and you ignored me. This mess is your own creation, Coileán, not mine."

It's difficult on the best of days to take any man wearing board shorts and flip-flops seriously, but I heard the impatience in Oberon's voice and opted not to provoke him. "All right, understood," I said, holding up my hands. "Meggy's had a rough week. She won't trouble you further."

The look Meggy gave me should have been lethal, but Oberon seemed mollified. "See that she doesn't," he said, producing for himself a Bloody Mary as he sprawled across an open chair. "So, storming the ramparts, are we, or have you found a little sense by now?" He sipped, looked around the table, and smirked. "What's the term, 'cannon fodder'? The witch I understand," he added, tilting his drink toward Helen, "but what's the rest of the riffraff doing here?"

I prayed to whatever might have been listening that Vivi kept her mouth shut. "Acquaintances of mine," I said as neutrally as possible. "Didn't want to see them get eaten when the rampage started."

"Considerate, I suppose." He finished the rest of his cocktail in one long slurp, then destroyed the evidence and stood. "Well, this has been entertaining as always, but I really must—"

The door across the room cracked open, and one of my aides poked her head in. "My lord?" she murmured. "Lord Doran has returned."

Oberon chuckled and shook his head, and I fought for serenity. "Alone?"

"Yes, my lord." She hesitated, catching sight of my company, then added, "He says he brings a message."

I looked at Val and Toula, who gave me identical tight-lipped glances, then back at the aide. "Show him to the throne room. I'll be along shortly."

Doran, as usual, erred on the side of opulence in his dress. The robe he sported that morning must have weighed ten pounds, a fur-trimmed cloth-of-gold number with a train, all studded with miniscule diamonds that glittered in the sunlight. He had set a golden circlet on his brow, the gaudier cousin to Stuart's headwear, and the theme continued into his suit and even his shoes, soft leather pumps with short, gold-plated heels. Doran seemed calculatingly unaware of the fact that he cast dancing diamonds of light on every wall he passed, but Liberace would have drooled.

I had opted for a white Oxford with jeans and loafers, if for no other reason than to make him twitch.

"Doran," I sighed, taking the throne, "I'd been wondering when you'd crawl out of your hole. To what do I owe the singular pleasure of seeing your face again?"

He held himself in check—whether because he had noticed Val beside me and Toula in the gallery with Helen and Meggy or because Oberon was leaning against the wall, smirking through a cloud of reflected diamonds, I couldn't tell. "I bring a message from Lord Geheret," he said stiffly. "Will you hear it?"

"*Lord* Geheret, is it?" I replied, crossing my legs. "What, you're his errand boy now? You decided that taking orders from some punk in the Gray Lands was preferable to living under my rule?"

"Will you hear it, yes or no?"

"Oh, I'll hear it," I said, glancing at the door as Joey led Aiden, who was half-sleepwalking, to a back bench. "I just question your choices. Proceed."

Doran straightened to his full height and produced a paper from his pocket. "My lord says that the creatures he released into that hamlet you so fancy were only a taste of his power. Also, he has the girl, and his patience is wearing thin."

"Oh, really?" I said, keeping my tone level. "And here I thought they were madly in love."

My brother's lip rose into a brief sneer. "Lord Geheret has suffered her presence long enough."

"Then he should return her and go about his business, shouldn't he?"

"Much simpler to kill her."

I watched Toula clamp down on Meggy's shoulder before Meggy could leap from her seat. "Perhaps," I said, examining my knuckles. "By your presence here, I assume he'd consider a trade."

"I bring his terms."

Across the room, Oberon crossed his arms and muttered, "Oh, this should be good."

Doran ignored him. "My lord's terms are as follows: you will abdicate. You will leave this realm, and you will allow yourself to be bound. If these terms are met, Moyna will be returned to you."

I let him stand there and stew while I looked at Meggy, who was nodding, then at Aiden, who was shaking his head. "Tell me, Doran," I said quietly, "do you take me for a fool?"

"These are the terms I was giv—"

"The terms are no terms at all. If I abdicate—Oberon, is that even possible?"

"I suppose," he called back, shrugging his bare shoulders. "Never given it serious consideration. The realm wouldn't like it."

"Tell me something new." The little voice in my head hadn't shut up about Helen and Slim's presence, and it wasn't coy about its displeasure with Doran. There was a stink about him, I realized, recognizing the odor of dark magic. The snakes had escaped to the Gray Lands after all, and against all good sense. "Well, then," I said, turning back to Doran, "let's assume that the realm allows me to step down. That puts Moyna on the throne."

"She would resign and be bound as well," he replied, sounding bored.

"Mm. Assuming she wasn't killed the moment I couldn't do anything about it, yes? And, for that matter, if I were to agree to Geheret's terms, what would stop him from, oh, killing me in my sleep?"

Doran's mouth barely twitched. "That is beyond the scope of the agreement."

I leaned forward and steepled my fingers. "I see. But let me be quite sure I understand your lord's proposal: I'm bound, Moyna is bound, Meggy…"

He followed my stare back to Meggy, who was straining against Toula's arm to rise. "She's of no concern."

"All right. So you're saying that we'll be left to our own devices in the mortal realm? That I'm to simply trust that Geheret won't send someone to pay us a visit?"

Finally, Doran allowed himself to smile. "Trust is an integral part of any deal, brother. But my lord is being more than generous," he said, sweeping his arm toward Meggy. "Isn't that what you want? You and your whore and the brat, a perfect little family. Isn't that worth more to you than mere power?"

"Perhaps it would be if your scenario didn't have more holes than a rusting sieve," I retorted. "The instant I can't hold Moyna, she'll be gone. And knowing her, she'll find a way back into Faerie, the bind will break…"

"And Lord Geheret would kill her for reneging on the

agreement," he concluded. "But he could do what you did to her before—give her a new name, a new set of memories. Take any trace of Mother out of her mind. You could be her darling father, just like you wanted."

"Except for the tiny matter of my age. Without magic, without glamour, a twenty-something raising a teenager? Not remotely likely."

"There are ways around that," said Doran, his voice soft and low. "A little something extra worked into the bind to age you."

"And eventually kill me, I suppose?"

"A small price to pay for your family, wouldn't you say?"

I looked out once more at the room, picking at the holes in the tapestry Doran was weaving. The largest was the most evident: no matter what sort of happy story he told, he and I both knew that Geheret would kill me as soon as it was convenient. I'd probably never see Moyna again, and Meggy…well, if I was gone, she was as good as dead. Her father would never protect her, and she wasn't yet a force to be reckoned with in terms of magical talent. Val might be all right, and Toula would always have her Arcanum connections…

But then there was Aiden.

The Arcanum would never protect him against a court onslaught—not a witch-blood, not even with his gifts—and without them, he would be helpless.

I met his weary eyes across the throne room and saw the fear there—but fear for himself or for Moyna or me, I could not tell.

Before I could glance at his thoughts, Meggy broke free of Toula's grip and jumped onto the bench. "Take the deal!" she cried as Toula latched on to her leg. "Colin, you have to, they're going to kill her! Please!" Her voice rose with her panic. "Don't let them kill her! *Don't let them kill my baby!*"

Meggy's face was terrible, red and wet with frantic

tears, her curls wild from the night on the beach. And in that moment, the truth sounded like a trumpet in my mind: it was up to me to save her and her baby.

When I glanced at Doran again, his smile spoke of victory. "Well?" he said. "My lord is not a patient man. What should I tell—"

That was as far as he made it before the double gunshots echoed around the ceiling arches. Hal dropped immediately, pulling Vivi under him, and even Oberon fell back against the wall—but then I saw Joey calmly walking up the aisle with a pistol in his right hand, his left locked about his wrist to steady his aim. Doran fell to his knees and fumbled at his tunic, which was beginning to turn reddish-black around his heart. He stared up at me, his dark eyes flickering between pain and confusion, and when he tried to speak, blood dripped onto his chin.

Vaguely, I realized that Val had moved into a defensive stance beside me, but Joey paused beside my bleeding brother and kicked him onto his back. "Special ammunition," he murmured in his weirdly accented Fae, pinning Doran with his foot and the barrel of the gun. "Little something whipped up for me. The rounds in this baby are mostly steel." He bent closer as Doran began to gasp. "And since my aim is pretty true, I'm guessing they're lodged somewhere in your chest right now." Doran's face contorted, but Joey pressed the muzzle of the gun against his cheek until he screamed with the burn. "You try anything, and I'll make it hurt worse."

When Joey pulled the gun away, Doran's face was blistered and smoking. "Who...you..." he tried, coughing up bright blood with every word. "Who...you think..."

"Who do I think I am?" Joey replied, keeping the pistol trained on Doran's chest. "I am Joseph Percival Bolin. The dragon rider. The knight of the red cross. And this is your chance to beg for mercy."

Doran looked at me imploringly, but I sat silent and frozen, and Joey shifted his grip on the handle. "I'm not a patient man, you little bastard. Now *beg*."

My brother was heaving to draw breath, but he managed to gurgle, "Please."

Joey nodded once, curtly, then bent down and fired a third round between Doran's eyes. He died almost instantly, and Joey stepped off of him, staring at the corpse as if to be sure it was cooling. Before he could holster his gun, however, a wall of force flung him into the stone wall beside me, and behind it was Meggy, screaming as she readied the fire in her hands.

Joey lived that morning only thanks to Toula's reflexes. Before Meggy could throw the building fireball, Toula appeared at her side and tackled her to floor, shouting for her to be still. To my surprise, Helen ran up the aisle behind her and straight to Joey—though not before looking over her shoulder and telling Aiden to stay the hell back. She dropped to her knees beside him, laid him flat, and began patting his cheeks, trying to keep him conscious.

I stood as if in a trance, looking from the battered seminarian to my dead brother, to Toula, who had by then wrestled Meggy into a headlock and shoved her into enchanted sleep, and I heard Oberon start to laugh. Softly and slowly, as Doran's blood congealed and Helen ripped Joey's shirt open to look for damage, he laughed and laughed.

CHAPTER 20

Later that morning, as Helen mended Joey's cracked ribs and Meggy lingered on in forced sleep, Oberon found me in my office with Toula and brushed in past Val. "You knew he was going to kill you," he said by way of greeting. "I mean, it was obvious. You didn't seriously consider it, did you?"

I shook my head and poured myself another three fingers of bourbon—a raw spirit, briefly aged and still tasting strongly of corn and ethanol, which was what I needed then. "If he'd actually been able to deliver on those promises…"

Oberon grunted and flopped onto the couch beside Toula, then propped his sandals on the coffee table. "He'd still have killed you. And I doubt he could have fully bound you, anyway, let alone throw in an expiration date." I frowned, and he explained, "You're too old, boy. Take aside what Faerie gives you, and you're still too strong. Those binds work on the young—your little girlfriend should know," he added with a smirk, "but for someone with a few centuries on him? Good luck crafting something permanent. No, he'd only have weakened you, but he'd kill you long before you realized he couldn't do anything in the long term."

"Unless he's ancient," Toula countered.

"He would have to be older than I am," said Oberon, "and if he's of Mab, that's impossible." His hand suddenly held a sweating bottle of beer, and he drank with relish. "Mab was the eldest of us, but only by a year or so. This

Geheret probably hasn't seen a millennium." His glance shifted to Toula, and he added, "Brothers are such fun, aren't they?"

"Mab may have birthed me," she muttered in reply, "but I'm under no obligation to claim the rest of her children. Present company excepted," she said, lifting her eyes to Val, who remained on guard at the door.

Oberon looked curiously at my captain, then drank again. "Ah, right," he said when he came up for air. "I'd forgotten about that one. Finally figured it out, did you, boy?" he called toward the door. "How long did it take?"

Val remained unruffled by the taunting. "Geheret's lineage is no concern of mine, my lord," he said, keeping his eyes on the window.

I studied his profile, noting the way he ground his teeth as he avoided directly watching us. "Something's troubling you, Val."

His dark eyes flicked to mine, then back to the window. "Nothing unexpected. Would you hear my counsel?"

"Gladly," I sighed into my bourbon.

"If you can't be dissuaded from charging into the Gray Lands, then take action as soon as Joey's whole. Strike while Geheret is still uncertain of Doran's whereabouts. He'll be less likely to raise his defenses if he thinks you're considering his 'offer.'"

"That was my thought, too. But only once Joey's healed and rested, and Aiden needs sleep as well." I considered my drink for a moment, then asked Toula, "How long can you keep Meggy down?"

"As long as we need," she said, giving me a strange look. "She may be fighting it, but she's too weak to break it, especially if I keep checking my work. That said," she mused, "the longer I keep this up, the more pissed she's going to be when she wakes. What did you have in mind?"

"We do this without her," I said, and downed my drink.

Toula waited while I poured another refill, then said,

"She'd never forgive you."

"I know."

"And that's *her* child's life on the line. Moyna may be a pain in the ass, but by God, she's Meggy's pain in the ass. If something were to go wrong…"

She let the unspoken linger, and I broke the silence when the alcohol burn had faded. "I don't feel confident about this," I said slowly. "At all. For all we know, Moyna doesn't wish to be rescued, and she'll fight us every step of the way. I don't like trusting Aiden for ammunition. I don't like the fact that Joey's probably going to get blasted off his lizard before she makes her first attack, and I *really* don't like the fact that the rest of my siblings are waiting there for me. We're pumping magic in," I continued, staring into my glass. "What would stop them from using it, too? Or any of Mab's court, any of them old enough to remember Faerie—we're practically tossing them swords."

"Are you moping, or do you have a better idea?" asked Oberon.

"No and no," I muttered, "and what are you still doing here? You made your point—Meggy's not going to trouble you. Go home."

He chuckled as he leaned into the cushions, and one sandal began to flap back and forth against his tanned foot. "Go back and miss this little debacle? Why would I do that?"

"Well, then," Toula interrupted, "as long as you're hanging out, maybe you could, oh, I don't know, *give us a damn hand.*"

Oberon grinned—a genuine smile, which somehow made it all the more unsettling. "And *there's* the Mab I remember. Nice to see at least one of you got something of her," he said, turning again to look at Val. "It's difficult to say whether a half-breed will be of any use at all, you know. Mortal blood so often seems to water everything down beyond recognition. You're…*weaker*," he said, pausing to take a drink and fix me with a calculated stare.

"Slower. Consumed with trivialities—affections, sentimentality. It's a wonder you accomplish anything, truly it is."

Toula propped her head on her arm and snorted. "You done, bub?"

"For the nonce. But here, Coileán, a gift," he continued, gesturing to me with his bottle. "You want good counsel, boy? Leave the brat where she is. Either Geheret will take care of the matter for you or she'll crawl back tuck-tailed and you can show her a taste of your dear mother's hospitality."

I shrugged, ignoring the bait. "And as for Meggy?"

He finished his beer, and the bottle vanished. "To hell with her. Let her sleep until the end of time, for all it concerns me. Just keep her off my island."

It was Val's turn to grunt—softly, almost imperceptibly—but Toula, who had listened impassively, shared little of her brother's reservation. "Meanwhile, in the land of Working with the Variables You've Got, your advice is bullshit. I'm going to go wake Megs while there's still a chance she'll speak to me after this, and we're going to get Moyna back once everyone's in one piece again. And if you'd like to help save your granddaughter from probable peril, well, I'm sure no one would stand in your way."

Oberon turned to me with a smirk. "She has a tongue, doesn't she? Shall I silence it for you? I'm feeling unusually generous today."

From the corner of my eye, I watched Val disappear and instantly flicker back into existence behind Oberon, poised and waiting for a word.

"Toula is my guest," I told Oberon. "You are not. Remember that."

He laughed in mockery, and I picked up my glass from its resting place, ignoring him. "As soon as Aiden and Joey are ready," I muttered, cutting my eyes to Val and Toula in turn. "But to be frank, getting Moyna back alive can't be our first priority." The others regarded me in silence, and I drank to quiet the part of me that sat in condemnation of the whole.

Toula was right: I couldn't in good conscience keep Meggy asleep until the deed was done, one way or another, and so I asked Toula to bring her back gently. Meggy had come around by late afternoon, and the realm warned me just before she stormed into my office, dirty and seething. "How dare you," was all she said before she slammed the door behind her.

Meggy wasn't shouting, but I understood the murderous look in her eye far too well. "You were going to kill him," I said, gesturing to the couches in invitation. "I couldn't let you do that."

She ignored my offer and remained standing, arms akimbo and voice rising. "That was our chance to get Olive back, and he shot the messenger!"

I sighed and rubbed my forehead. "That offer was nothing but a lie. He was never going to return her."

"You don't know that! You *can't*!"

"I can, and I do." I looked up at her over my desk, watching her face redden. "Honey, if I thought for a second that I could have gotten her back that way—and kept us all alive in the aftermath—I'd have taken the deal."

She regarded me in angry silence, then shook her head and took a seat. "You can believe any lie if you tell yourself it's the truth often enough, can't you?" I said nothing, and she stared at the wall and muttered, "How is he?"

"On the mend. He should be well by dinner, and once Aiden's ready, we'll make the assault." After a moment's hesitation to test her mood, I rose and took the opposite couch, but Meggy wouldn't look at me. "I don't want you going along—and listen to me first," I added in a rush as her mouth opened. "Val, Toula, and I practiced last night. We're going to have Helen at the gate with Aiden, and

Joey and Georgie are going to try an aerial attack. You haven't tested yourself with the setup, and…" I chose my words carefully, watching her eyes narrow. "Meggy, you're not strong enough. You're young, you're still getting your footing—"

"And Toula's not?" she retorted.

"Toula is a lucky freak of nature, and she has her Arcanum training to guide her," I replied. "If all she does over there is cast spells, we'll still be in a decent position. But there's so much you don't know yet, and in a situation like this…I'm sorry, but you'd do more harm than good."

She held her hands a few inches apart and waited while a spark appeared. I watched the little fire grow between her palms for a solid half-minute until it approximated a decent missile, and she snapped, "You think I can't handle myself? You think I'm *weak*?"

My shield manifested well before her ragged fireball hit, and as I lowered it, I instantly produced twin spheres of blue flame in my open hands. "Can you shield?" I asked her, letting each swell to the size of a basketball. Meggy nodded, but I felt the lie in her thoughts and extinguished my ammunition. "You're not safe, and you're not going."

"That's not your decision."

"Actually, yes, it is."

Her eyes rolled to the ceiling. "Going to pull rank on me, Colin? *Really?*"

"I will if it means keeping you in one piece."

She pushed herself off the couch and glowered down at me. "I don't need you to protect me. I'm not a child, and the sooner you get that through your head, the better off we'll both be. I'm going after Olive, end of discussion."

"Meggy—"

"*End of discussion.*" She crossed her arms and studied the tapestry behind my head while I tried to formulate an argument that wouldn't make matters worse. Just as I thought I'd found a way in, she muttered, "I think we need a break."

That took me by surprise, and my planned remarks fell apart as I scrambled for an answer. "What sort of break?" was all I managed.

"We need to see other people. Colin, I..." Meggy hugged herself more tightly and again refused to meet my eyes. "As soon as I've got Olive safe with me again, I'm selling the store and moving back to Phoenix. Maybe there's still time for me to mend fences with my family, you know? In any case, I'm getting us out of this game."

"What *game*?"

"This. All of this. I, uh...I'm not sure what I want yet, but I know it's not here."

"All right..."

She forced herself to face me. "And it's not with you. I'm sorry, but...I don't think this is going to work."

I stared back at her, flabbergasted and feeling rather like I'd been punched in the stomach, simultaneously shocked and sick. "Meggy, honey, you've had a long week and—"

"And I've had time to think. I had plenty of time while you two were holding me down today. I had time last night when Oberon refused to talk to me. I had time all weekend when my daughter wouldn't speak to me." She sighed deeply and looked away, but her eyes remained dry. "If you love me—if you *ever* loved me—then bring Olive back. Bind her, take her memories away, do whatever you have to do, but bring my Olive back. We're going to start over, just the two of us. Like it was supposed to be."

My chest clenched. "And in a few years, when she's on her own and realizes she isn't normal? What then?"

"She won't as long as I keep a glamour on us both."

"Eventually—"

She brushed me aside. "Yes, yes, *eventually*, but not for years—and by then, everything will be all right again between us."

"Meggy," I began, then paused with the words still on my tongue, unspoken: *this is a terrible idea.* "Meggy...I love you. You know I love you."

"See, that's the problem—you don't." Meggy moved around to the back of the couch, widening the moat of furniture between us. "Maybe you loved me at twenty. We both know you lusted after me," she added with a shrug. "But *me*, now—Colin, I'm not that girl you knew in Coleridge. I haven't been that girl in a long time, and you…you show up again and act like nothing's changed," she said, picking up speed, "like I've been frozen all this time, waiting for you to waltz back into my life. Well, I haven't been frozen, you know? I've grown *up*," she added, punctuating the declaration with raised brows. "And you're not good for me."

I sat there, telling myself I should stand, at least to lessen the feeling that I was being lectured like a foolish child, but I couldn't seem to will my legs into action. "You said you loved me," I mumbled, hearing how pathetic that sounded even as the words spilled out. "You said…I thought you said—"

"I thought I did. Maybe I'm also pretty good at lying to myself," she said softly. "I mean, yeah, I *wanted* you, but I *needed* Jack. Understand?"

"No, I—"

"Jack was good for me," she pressed on before I could finish. "Solid. Normal. He would have been a good father."

"Maybe if he weren't dead," I shot back, too angry to worry about delicacy.

The attack fizzled. "I never said he was the brightest, but…" She frowned at the middle distance, putting form to her thoughts, then said, "Jack didn't have all the answers. Neither did I. But you…hell, you don't know what you're doing half the damn time, but you act like you do. And if I disagree, well, it's 'run along and play, little girl, let the grownups talk.' I mean, for crying out loud," she said, sounding more annoyed by the second, "you still call me Meggy like I'm in grade school. My own *mother* calls me Meg by now."

She shook her head brusquely, then watched for a moment while I floundered for a reply. "I want an equal," she continued. "A partner. And we can lie to ourselves about it as hard as we might, but we're never going to get to that point. I tried, Colin," she continued, gripping the back of the couch. "And we had some fun, didn't we?" she asked with a lame half-smile. "The last few months were nice, more or less—and don't get me wrong, you're not half bad in the sack. But that's not enough. I…" She paused to draw and release a long breath. "I don't want you to protect me, I don't want you to hold my hand and save me from myself and everything else, I don't want the rage and the politics and the monsters—I just want Olive back, and I want you to let me figure life out on my own. Okay?"

No, I should have said, *that's not okay, I love you, I want you, I need you, tell me how to make it better, I'm sorry, I'll do better, I'll be better.*

But the old rage was building, the blinding, burning anger, and I heard myself mutter, "Okay," as I pushed myself off the couch.

"Maybe…you know, down the line," she said, offering the lie of hope. "Give me a few years. Let's see how things go with Olive."

"Okay, Meg. If that's what you want."

She released her hold on the couch and stepped back a pace as her brows drew together. "Are you, uh…are you all right?"

I was keeping myself in check only through total concentration, but somehow, I felt a faint pressure in my palms, more annoyance than pain. Glancing down, I saw that my hands had clenched into white-knuckled fists, and that my nails, short and dull as they were, had ripped open half-moon gashes in my skin. I watched the bloody trickles merge and begin to drip off my wrists with complete detachment, as if contemplating a tastefully subdued wound in a painting, then lifted my gaze to Meggy and saw the uncertainty in her eyes.

"Please leave," I said, fighting the growing pressure in my head.

She hesitated briefly. "I know my timing sucks, but there's really no good time for a conversation like—"

"*GO!*"

Meggy jumped as if I'd struck her, but she composed herself and jutted her chin. "Oh, that's really mature. Going to throw a tantrum?"

By then, even the discomfort in my hands had faded beside the fire burning through me. "Meg," I said through gritted teeth, "if you do not leave, I will not be responsible for what happens."

She opened her mouth, but whatever she was planning to say died unuttered. I have no idea what I looked like in that moment, but I saw fear and anger and hurt crossing and re-crossing her face in waves, and for once, I made no move to comfort her. Her mouth snapped closed, and she left me without another word.

And when the pounding in my ears grew louder than her running footsteps, I ripped open a gate and stormed into the wilderness before I killed someone.

For all its inhabitants' squabbling over choice bits of land, Faerie is overwhelmingly a wild place, a land of jagged mountains and tangled forests and wide savannahs and deep valleys where the days are short and the moon rises late. Any of this land could be magically terraformed, but few put in the effort, preferring to spend their time fighting with their neighbors and jockeying for position in the ancient social webs I'll probably never fully comprehend. But the general apathy for expansion left me with a high, bare-topped range perhaps a hundred miles to the northeast of my palace, a perfect place to throw fire and shatter boulders until my rage was spent.

I don't remember much about that afternoon besides the overwhelming need to destroy. If there was a sunset, I can't say; a thunderstorm kicked up at some point, perhaps the first in centuries—perhaps the first ever, given Faerie's typical weather patterns—and whether I triggered it unconsciously or the realm just tried to contain the ring of burning debris with which I'd surrounded myself, I may never know. But at some point that night, as lightning flickered in the east, I heard the deep thump of giant wings beating and looked up through the pouring rain as Georgie came in for a landing. She gripped the wet rock like a pro, then looked over her shoulder as the figure astride her back slipped off and made his way toward my circle of fire with the awkward gait of one who's ridden hard and long and still feels a beast beneath him. The man's features resolved into Joey's—his light hair slicked black with the rain that beaded on his leather motorcycle jacket, his brown eyes squinting against the firelight and the blowing storm, his broad hands open and empty, held out for balance on the slick stone. I watched as he crossed the ruined pass between us, and then he paused outside the fire and regarded me as I shook inside my makeshift fortress, spent and soaked and chilling.

Joey shoved his hands into his jacket and made a face. "Chicks, man."

I don't know when—or if—I opened the ring for him. He may have simply stridden through the fire, too drenched to burn. But my next memory is of the smell of the wet leather against my face and Joey's arms holding me up, and I was shaking with something that wasn't the cold.

I wept on that mountain as I hadn't wept in lifetimes, and when I was empty and numb, Joey was still patting my back as Étaín had done when I was young and overwhelmed, offering nothing but silent support. When my breathing slowed, I pulled away from him and extinguished the blaze, too drained at that moment to even be ashamed of my show of weakness. Joey waited while I pulled myself together and the rain began to slack off, and then I turned to him with a sigh. "Word spread already, I take it."

"Val might have mentioned something to a few select individuals," he replied, brushing the rain from his face. "I thought you might want some company."

"Feeling particularly suicidal, were we?"

"Nope. But I *do* remember bits and pieces of the two-day bender I went on with my freshman roommates after my high-school girlfriend, who I was pretty much convinced I was going to marry, decided she loved someone else. And no," he added with a smirk, "she didn't drive me into the arms of Mother Church. She did drive me to blacking out in my own vomit on the bathroom floor of the one bar in town that would serve minors—which was about as classy a joint as it sounds. I mean, yeah, technically, the blackout was my own damn fault," he allowed, "but I wouldn't have been slamming shots of Jose Cuervo if I hadn't thought my life was over. Oh, and once I woke up," he continued, rolling his eyes, "by which I mean once my buddies rolled me out of my puke so I wouldn't choke to death and I came to enough to figure out how to stand again, I picked a fight with a linebacker who was slightly less inebriated and ended up at University Health with three broken ribs, a dislocated shoulder, and a blood-alcohol level approaching point-two-five."

"You came all this way to get me drunk?"

"Nah, I figured you could handle that on your own. Just thought you might need someone to pull you off the bathroom floor."

"Yeah," I muttered, feeling pain begin to return to my wounded hands. "Yeah, I suppose. Thanks, kid."

"No sweat." He kept his distance, as if the last few minutes had never passed between us. "Coming home tonight?"

I looked around at what little I could see in the dark of my burned and blasted surroundings. "I probably should, shouldn't I?"

"I think I speak for all of us involved in this Gray Lands excursion when I say I'd feel better if you were rested and on your game when we get there." He adjusted his jacket, dumping a little puddle that had pooled in a deep wrinkle. "And I know this horse is long since out of the barn, but is there any chance you could whip up an umbrella?"

Within a minute, the rain had petered out to a thick mist, which even then was beginning to break into patches of stars overhead. "Will that do?"

"That was my other suggestion," he replied, then cocked his head toward the waiting dragon. "Georgie says she can carry two if you want to go the long way back."

"No need." I stood there for a moment, dripping in the dissipating fog, then recalled where I'd last seen Joey. "How are the ribs?"

"Good as new," he said, sounding nonplussed. "Remind me to list Helen and Toula as my primary care providers on my company insurance, eh?" He smiled briefly at his own joke, and then, sobering, he asked, "Are we okay?"

"We?"

"You and me. After…you know?"

"Doran?" I finished for him. "Yes." I took a few steps toward the drop and stared out at the night-shrouded peaks rising below us, trying not to see my brother choking on blood at my feet. "Why'd you do it, Joey?"

"Because I knew you couldn't, and it needed to be done. Someone had to handle it." I heard his boots slap the rock behind me as he joined me at the end of the ledge. "If I screwed up, I'm really sorry, but I thought—"

"You were right."

"Oh. Good," he sighed.

"Have you talked to Paul yet?"

Joey whistled low. "I think he's still trying to decide whether that warrants penance."

"I'll put in a good word for you, if it'll help."

"Thanks, but last time I checked, you don't get a vote in this." He put his hands in his jacket pockets again and took his place beside me, saying nothing as the fog rolled out.

After a time, I cleared my throat and turned back from the edge. "So, Joseph *Percival* Bolin? Did I hear you properly?"

"Yeah," he mumbled. "Got a little carried away, there."

"You realize you're giving Toula fodder, yes?"

"Well, my goal at this point is to make it through the entire Round Table with her," he replied, following me back toward Georgie. "And before you ask, no, it's not a family name—my parents are *deeply* into the Faire circuit."

"You poor bastard. Though I suppose there are worse options in the canon…" I paused, reviewing that morning once more, then glanced up at Joey. "'Knight of the red cross'?"

If there had been sufficient light, I'm sure his face would have been scarlet. "It's the only surcoat I have left," he said, rubbing his neck. "After I started seminary, I got rid of some of my gear…it kind of seemed appropriate to keep that one, but…look, I got carried away, all right? Heat of the moment and all."

I chuckled and gripped his shoulder through his wet coat. "Tell me, Joey, by chance, have you read any Spenser?"

"Yeah, that one wasn't lost on me, either."

"Just making sure." I opened a gate to the barn and waved Georgie through, and she happily lumbered off to slaughter her dinner. "So where did you get the gun?"

Joey waited until I'd closed the gate behind us. "Helen made it for me. Said if I was going to be looking after Aiden, she wanted me to do it properly. Is that, uh—"

"Keep it close." I gave his shoulder a final squeeze, then set off alone toward the lights of my palace, trying and failing to think of anything but my Meggy.

Meg, now. And no longer mine.

CHAPTER 21

I passed the long night alone, sitting on the edge of my unused bed and mulling over all the ways Meggy might have a change of heart. She was worried over Moyna, I told myself; she was over-stressed and under-slept and perhaps not thinking clearly. Yes, I could have been more sensitive with her—given what her father had done to her, surely Meggy didn't appreciate it when Toula overpowered her, and I should have woken her sooner. Maybe if I'd reprimanded Toula...or Joey...

But as dawn broke, I admitted to myself that letting Meggy kill Joey wouldn't have made her love me. I'd stopped her, protected her, kept that death from her conscience—and still, she wanted out. She didn't love me anymore. Maybe she never had.

No, something in me insisted, that couldn't be true— I'd loved her, she'd loved me, and *she* was the one who had dreamed of us making a little family together. We'd been so happy that summer, Meggy and me, and I'd do anything to please her, she knew that...

...and she still didn't love me.

My Meggy didn't love me.

And so I sat there as the sunlight began its slow stretch across the rug, holding my head in my hands and wondering where I'd gone so horribly wrong. When I closed my eyes, I saw her standing there, twenty-one and still all limbs and soft curves, her blue eyes bright and smiling, her unruly curls tamed into a ponytail that bounced with each flick of her head, her shorts teasingly brief, her pink T-shirt thinned to translucence by laundering. The clothing faded away into a cheap black bikini, and as the light faded, I felt her soft lips on mine, tasted salt on her skin and beer in her mouth, heard the ocean's ceaseless pounding behind us and a gull crying as it passed overhead. The sun had set, her clothes had been tossed away, and she arched her back and gasped as I moved in her, moved with her, letting the waves set the tempo. I saw her chipped red fingernails disappear into the towel as she clutched handfuls to steady herself—and then she was beside me, chilling in the breeze and curling against me for warmth, her hair spreading on the rumpled towel like a living thing, quivering to its own secret rhythm.

I held her there, deep in my mind, and then I looked upon the orange sunrise and let the memory go.

Meggy didn't love me, and I had to face her once again.

I sent word to the others to meet me at the barn, as there was no convenient place in the palace to open a dragon-sized rip in the fabric of the world. By the time I'd dressed and pushed thoughts of the previous day to a dark corner of my mind, the sun was decently high, and Val was waiting in the corridor with half a dozen guards. "Change of plans?" I asked, surprised to find him accompanied.

The squad fell in against the far wall, giving me space to maneuver, and Val stepped aside to allow me passage. "A precaution," he said quietly, taking up his usual position to my left. "Lord Oberon remains in the realm."

I felt him glance at my thoughts just as I made the same examination of his, and he nodded, satisfied that we'd reached one conclusion. I didn't trust Oberon—I'd have been a fool to trust him, in truth—but I couldn't cast him out of Faerie. The realm was only too happy to have him back, as it continued to remind me whenever I crossed his path. But Oberon had made it clear that he wasn't going to help us, meaning that while I took the plunge into the Gray Lands, he'd be waiting on the safe side of the gate, assumedly watching the fun with a beer in his hand. I wouldn't have put it past him to enchant himself a box of popcorn.

And with me on the far side and only Helen holding the gate open, what was to stop him from subduing her and closing the gate? With the connection cut, we'd run out of magic in minutes, and then we'd be at the mercy of whatever we found in the other realm, unable to open an escape route. In other words, we'd probably be dead.

I had run that scenario once I'd forced myself to put my moping on hold. Assuming something in the Gray Lands dispatched me and Geheret killed Moyna, the court would then fall to Syral, Mother's eldest surviving child—but given Doran's little performance, Syral and the other three were probably guests of Geheret's, and what would stop him from clearing them from the picture as well? With all of them dead, there would be only one of Mother's children still alive to inherit: Aiden, trapped in Faerie at Oberon's mercy, who assuredly would not live long. I didn't know what would happen when Aiden fell— maybe the realm would choose one of Mother's grandchildren, or maybe it would give up—but in any case, my court would be in chaos, and Oberon, if he moved quickly, could do as he pleased.

There was no telling what Oberon, reigning King of the Keys, really wanted—and in retrospect, I'm not sure if Oberon even knew at that time—but I wasn't going to give him an opportunity to figure it out in my absence.

It seemed Val and I weren't the only ones with reservations, as my entourage nearly stumbled over Vivi on the way downstairs. I didn't know where she had acquired a skintight pair of jeans and a plaid flannel shirt in the last two days, but I strongly suspected Toula's involvement. "Morning, Chief," she said, hoisting herself off the middle of the staircase. "Got a second?"

I glanced back at my security, then at Vivi. "I'm on my way to a rendezvous—"

"Yeah, I know, everyone's waiting, and Hal's down there geeking out over the dragon. Walk and talk?" A shrug satisfied her, and she slipped into the pack to my right as we descended. "So, while the hospitality's been lovely, and I do thank you for trying to cover for me with the boy, I think it's time we bounced."

I nodded, squinting into the morning light as we passed onto the back terrace. "Bounced where, pray tell? You're not going back to Rigby until this is settled."

"Says who?"

"Say I, and if that's not good enough, says Slim and Toula and anyone else with half a brain. I'm not dropping you off until I'm satisfied that you're not going to get eaten in your sleep, understood?"

Vivi huffed and kicked at a chip of rock, sending it skittering across the flagstones. "All right, then, if you're going to be difficult, how about taking me to my parents' place?"

I had to think for a second. "Alaska, right?"

"Yeah, they're about an hour south of Denali—the park border, not the mountain," she explained. "Not many neighbors. If it'll make you feel better, I'll stay off the Fringe network until you surface again."

"You really want to go to Alaska in *November*?"

It was Vivi's turn to shrug. "I'm expected for Thanksgiving."

"Thanksgiving," I said doubtfully.

She nodded. "Family's been doing it for a while—it's an excuse for Mom to get us all under one roof and tell us we're not eating enough. If I'm in a week early, they're not going to be upset. Hell, two of my brothers still hang around there. So how about doing me a favor and letting me clear out with Hal?"

We were approaching the rose garden, and I paused in the pathway to study her face. There was no need to look at her thoughts—I spotted the fear beneath Vivi's superficially placid countenance. Annoying as she could be, the girl was far from stupid.

"I assume you intend this exit as a precaution," I murmured, bending close to her.

My breath had fogged her glasses, and she pulled them off to clean them before she replied. "Should things not go according to plan"—she popped them back into place and fiddled with the frame until they were roughly straight— "I'd rather not be stranded here, hoping *someone* allows me to leave. Yeah?"

The fact that she was willing to take her boyfriend— the man who until recently hadn't even known about the Fringe—home to meet her parents told me everything I needed to know about her state of mind. "Yeah," I said. "Do you suppose they'd mind having a few additional houseguests?"

Her eyes narrowed. "How many additional houseguests?"

"Besides you two? I was thinking of four."

She considered this briefly, then nodded. "Shouldn't be a problem unless Father P has some objection to sharing quarters with a bunch of faeries. He didn't seem too keen on my paranormal investigators, you know."

"Oh, don't worry about Paul," I said, pushing open the gate to the garden. "I broke him in years ago. *Hard.*"

It cheered me to find that Oberon had apparently opted not to see me off, but I worked quickly in case he changed his mind. Leaving the guards outside the barn and Georgie blocking the staircase, I sent Vivi and Hal up to Joey's quarters in the loft and herded Eunice, Paul, and Slim up the stairs behind them. True to form, Stuart gave me a moment's trouble—"I told you, a wizard doesn't *run,*" he protested when I explained the change of plans—but Toula countered with a palm full of fire and a pointed look, and he scurried off after the rest of the pack. When he had gone, I looked about until I spotted Meggy, who had laid claim to a seat atop a stack of hay bales in the far corner of the barn and was speaking to no one. She kept her eyes on me as I approached but otherwise gave no acknowledgement of my presence, and I fought to push thoughts of the previous day back into the shadows for a more opportune time. "You don't have to talk to me," I told her, keeping my voice low so as not to echo around the barn, "just listen. I think we may have a safe house for the Rigby crowd until this blows over. Go with them."

She shook her head in silence.

"Meg," I tried, "I can't protect you."

She continued to stare down at me, and I'd just accepted that all I was going to get from her that morning was the silent treatment when she muttered, "I told you, I don't want protection. I'm going after my daughter, and so help me God, you're not going to stop me. Is that clear?"

"Please, Meggy. Don't do this."

But she had said her piece and would offer nothing further, and I headed for the loft and my little group of refugees. Briefly, I mulled over the notion of compelling her to leave—overpowering her would have been a moment's work, perhaps another forced sleep or enchanted paralysis—but I abandoned the idea as ludicrous before I hit the staircase. If I wanted Meggy back, I had to respect her judgment. If all went well and she had a little while to come to her senses, then maybe…

Toula ran up and grabbed my wrist before I reached the second stair. "Tell me she's leaving," she whispered, cutting her eyes to Meggy on her perch.

"You want to reason with her?"

"She's not speaking to me. Come on, get her out of here."

I pulled free of her grip and shook my head. "Her decision. If she changes her mind, let me know," I said, and marched upstairs to face the winter.

Take someone with a hefty dose of fae blood and set him loose in the mortal realm to fend for himself. Odds are, he'll do one of two things: either try to blend into his surroundings and keep a low profile or say to hell with subtlety, build a seaside mansion, and procure a sports car. I'd chosen the former route, more or less, while Robin had opted for opulence and a steady supply of pretty, flexible guests. From the looks of things through the gate, the Stowes were more in line with my school of thought, with the exception of their ice- and snow-free driveway, an impossibility without magic in light of the two-foot drifts and fifteen-mile-per-hour wind. Aside from that little convenience, however, the homestead looked remarkably mundane, a modest ranch house with faded vinyl siding and deep blue shutters, all bathed in the bright white glare of a security light. Whatever piece of enchantment was keeping the driveway clear had also been extended to the curving concrete path across the snow-covered lawn and the front stoop, which was bedecked with a broad welcome mat decorated with palm trees.

I stood at the gate, which I'd guided into place with the picture in Vivi's mind, and shivered with the sudden nighttime cold as little puffs of snow began to blow through onto Joey's rug. "Think anyone's awake?" I asked Vivi, who was turning up her collar beside me. "It's a little early…"

"Someone's *always* awake," she replied, then stepped through and promptly sank in a drift to mid-thigh. Cursing my directional abilities—"You just couldn't park the gate on the driveway, could you?" she yelled over her shoulder—she slogged through the snow until she reached the cleared walk, then stomped her shoes clean, brushed the worst of the clinging mess from her wet jeans, and ran to the front door. She didn't bother knocking, but simply placed her hand on one of the door's painted panels and waited until the latch clicked open. By then, Hal and I had crossed the snow to join her—I'd foregone the ice bath in favor of melting a path across the yard, and he followed behind me—but we remained on the stoop while she pushed her way into the house. "Mom? Dad?" she called in perfectly accented Fae as she crossed the threshold. "It's me! Anyone around?"

As the door fully swung open, revealing a foyer the size of a modest ballroom lit with softly glowing brass wall sconces, Hal fell back a pace and muttered, "Whoa."

"Keep it together," I told him, watching the last of the snow drop from Vivi's clothing onto the polished hardwood. "Exterior glamour. It's not going to hurt you."

"She didn't mention that her parents live in a friggin' TARDIS," he replied, but found his spine again and straightened his T-shirt as we waited in the cold. "What do you suppose happens when the neighbors try to borrow sugar, huh?"

I glanced around at the empty night and silent road running behind the gate. "What neighbors? They probably protect their privacy—"

"Vivian?" a female voice called from within the camouflaged château, and a petite brunette who could have been Vivi's sister appeared from a side hallway, clutching her fuzzy white robe closed at her breast. "Oh, child!" she exclaimed, catching sight of Vivi in her wet, underdressed splendor, and threw herself onto the girl. "I thought you were dead, why didn't you call, it's been all over the news," she chided in a rush as she pulled Vivi into a crushing embrace. "We've been *so* worried—I kept telling your father we needed to check on you, but—"

Her breath caught as she turned to the open door and spotted the two of us standing there, waiting. "Mrs. Stowe," I said, watching as she pivoted Vivi out of my line of fire, "I'm sorry to trouble you, but Vivi and I thought she would be safer with you for the time being."

She pulled back slightly from her daughter, just enough to catch Vivi's wide-eyed nod, then released her and tightened her robe belt. "Lord Coileán," she replied stiffly, keeping Vivi behind her, "I...I don't know what my daughter has done, but—"

"Hey, Mom? Mom," Vivi interrupted, tugging on her mother's sleeve as she stepped out from behind her impromptu shield. "It's all right, we're cool. He got me out of Skipton when the monsters came through."

"Cool?" she echoed incredulously, wheeling on Vivi and jabbing one finger in my direction. "*That* is a high lord, no one is 'cool' with high lords, and certainly not—"

"I mean her no harm," I said, cutting the panicked chastisement short. "The Fringe recently assisted me—if anything, I'm still in your daughter's debt."

That caught her attention, but she remained flummoxed as she looked back and forth between us. Finally, she managed, "I don't...my lord, I fail to understand—"

"Told you not to underestimate us," said Vivi, flashing her mother a toothy smile, then deftly swapped places with her to serve as a buffer. "Long story short," she said, holding up her hands for quiet, "little trouble in Faerie, *he* still thinks something could be lurking back in Virginia, so I was wondering if I could crash here for a few days with a few, uh...friends. Pretty please?"

Mrs. Stowe peered at Vivi, then finally noticed the man standing beside me, who had given up on his stoic act and was rubbing his bare arms. "Is that..."

Vivi turned, following her glance, and nodded. "Mom," she said, effortlessly switching tongues, "this is Hal."

Whatever reservations Vivi's mother had about my presence were thrown aside as she ran for the door in a sudden maternal flurry. "Oh, you poor dear, you're *freezing!*" she cried, dragging Hal into the house. "Where is your coat, young man? And your boots? And—goodness, child, don't they sell gloves down south? Come in, come in," she insisted, then glanced toward the wall as a fireplace blazed to life. "Stay there, thaw," she said, parking him beside the mantel, "and Vivi—ah, Rufus," she called as a dark-haired man popped his head out from a door off the foyer, "go to the kitchen, bring the soup, I liked that batch. Hurry, now."

Rufus squinted at the sudden commotion, then spotted Vivi and beamed, instructions forgotten. "Hey, the princess is back!" he cried, throwing her into a headlock before she could slip away, then ground his knuckles against her skull as she protested the mistreatment. "What happened? Mother's been frantic—"

"Soup!" Mrs. Stowe ordered.

He released his squirming sister with an impatient grunt. "Hope you're in the mood for caribou."

"It's for him," she replied, nodding toward her uneasy beau, who had inched closer to the fire while Vivi was being manhandled.

Rufus's eyes flew open. "You told him?"

"Coileán kind of dropped in on us," she said, cocking her thumb at the open front door, and grinned as Rufus froze in his tracks. "It's okay, he's with me," she said with nonchalance, then pushed him toward another door. "Shoo. And hey, Chief," she added, looking back my way, "if you want to come in out of the cold, I'm sure Mom won't mind."

Mrs. Stowe nodded hesitantly, and I closed the door behind me, shutting out the freezing wind. "I won't trouble you long," I said, catching sight of a fair-haired man jogging down a distant hallway. Physically, he could have been Rufus's brother, but Vivi's eyes lit up when she turned and saw him coming.

"Dad!" she cried, waving from the foyer. "It's all right! I'm alive! And I brought Hal, so be nice!"

He disappeared in his tracks and reappeared an instant later beside Vivi, bathrobe flapping and long arms reaching out to envelop her. When he broke away, his face was red and wet, and he swiped at it with his sleeve to hide the evidence. "We were so *worried*—"

"Martin," his wife murmured, "guests."

At that, he looked up from his daughter to find Hal huddled by the fire and me standing by the door, then made a face remarkably similar to his son's recent expression of shock. "My lord, I…we've done nothing—"

"Save it," Vivi interrupted, stepping away from her frightened parents. "Like I was telling Mom, Skipton might not be the safest right now, there's a little issue in Faerie that I'll tell you about once I'm dry—ooh, thank you, don't mind if I do," she said, snatching one of the steaming bowls from her brother's hands as he reappeared in the foyer—"but Hal and I need somewhere to land for a few days, and I've got four other folks waiting who could really use a bed, and everyone's harmless, even the guy who thinks he's Gandalf. Please?"

The elder Stowes looked at each other uncertainly, but Rufus, who by then had thrust the remainder of his burden into Hal's hands, broke the silence. "Aw, come on," he told his parents, "if they can put up with Vivi, surely they can't be *that* bad. And what did you do," he asked her, giving her attire a quick sneer, "rob a lumberjack?"

"Jealous?" she replied with a smirk, and joined Hal by the fire. "It's *en vogue*."

He headed for the door, retorting, "Just tell me you didn't pay actual money for that," then added a quick, "Sorry, coming around," as he sidestepped me and opened the door. "Hello!" he yelled across the yard, waving at the gate and the four anxious people waiting on the far side. "Come in, it's frozen! Oh, wait—don't do that alone, let me help," he added, then darted out across the lawn as Eunice took a tottering first step back into the realm.

I shook my head and joined Vivi, who was shoveling stew into her mouth like she hadn't seen a meal in a week. "See where you get it," I said, glancing at the open door.

Unlike the rest of the room, Vivi seemed completely at ease. "Yeah, Rufe and I can be pretty effective when we work together. I mean, I'm his favorite sister, after all."

"You're his *only* sister," said another male voice, and

Vivi raised her spoon in salute to the blond in black sweatpants who had appeared beside her parents. "And what's all this about?"

"I'm sorry, sweetie, did we wake you?" she said with a malicious grin. "Does someone need a beauty nap?"

He began to counter, took a second look at me, and promptly shut his mouth.

Vivi watched his surprise register and chuckled. "That's my youngest older brother, Harry," she told Hal. "Rufe's the next one up the line," she added as he slowly walked back inside with Eunice on his arm. "I don't know where the other guys are, but they should be here in a few days."

Hal had begun to relax fractionally as he thawed. "You three are close?"

"Eh, relatively," she replied, tucking back into her breakfast. "We're the youngest of the bunch. Sibling alliances and all that. Not that I'm much good in a fight," she admitted with a shrug, "and Harry's still pretty useless, all things considered, but for Rufe...well, you've got ten older brothers, you take what you can get, know what I mean?"

"*Ten?*" he echoed, clutching his bowl. "You...wait, how many—"

"I'm the youngest of thirteen," she said, giving his back a solid thump. "Only girl, and from the looks of it, the only one lacking in the fae genes department, so the boys...you know, they're either beating me up or defending my honor with extreme prejudice. But don't worry, I already told the family all about you," she chirped, then yelled across the room over the din of the incoming arrivals, "Hey, Lothario, she's too young for you! Mitts off!"

Rufus, who was still holding Eunice's arm, waved dismissively at his sister. "There is no rule against assisting a lady, you little vagrant."

Hal's grip on his soup tightened as he looked from Rufus's smooth face to Eunice's wrinkles and helmet of frosted hair. "Too young?" he muttered.

"He's eighty-nine," Vivi explained.

"*Ninety*, thank you, and his hearing is excellent," Rufus replied. "And I'm still waiting on your birthday gift."

"Keep pestering me about it and you'll get an Erector Set."

"Deluxe, I trust."

Vivi stuck out her tongue and turned to her unsettled boyfriend. "Just ignore him when he's being a jackass. It works for me."

"Ninety?" he said, blinking rapidly.

She glanced at me, rolled her eyes, and wrapped her free arm around Hal's waist. "Harry's only forty-seven, if that'll make you any happier. Come on, I'll show you my room."

As she dragged him off into the depths of the mansion, I surveyed the foyer. Paul had cornered Martin and flashed his warmest professional smile as he made the rapid introductions. Across the room, Slim had taken Mrs. Stowe's hand with a cheery, "So nice to see you again, Rohese, lovely place you've got here, sorry about the intrusion," while Stuart turned in a slow circle, gawking at the ceiling fresco with his mouth open. I traded glances with Eunice, who nodded and held up crossed fingers, then saw myself out into the cold. Vivi could handle the explanations without my assistance, and I sincerely doubted that the Stowes were sorry to see the door latch behind me. For all of my promises of goodwill, there was no getting around the fact that my encounters with members of Oberon's court had a history of going south.

When I descended from the loft, I found Oberon waiting in the barn, stroking Georgie's neck as Joey glared from the shadows. "I thought perhaps you'd reconsidered," he said, giving the dragon a final pat. "Pity."

"Something I can do for you?" I muttered, brushing

past him toward the sunlight as the last stray flakes in my hair melted and dripped onto my collar.

"Me? No, I'm just enjoying the morning," he replied, sounding almost chummy. "Pleasant day, warm breeze— it's giving Florida a run for its money. One does tend to forget after a long absence—"

"You can talk about the weather later," Toula interrupted, pressing a plastic compass into my hand. "Going to need a blood sample, Gramps. Prick and stick."

"Do *what?*" I asked, turning the compass around and over in search of a hint.

Helen had followed on Toula's heels and cut in before she could get snippy. "Unless you've got a map of the Gray Lands hiding around here somewhere, Toula and I thought we could use a tracker to find Moyna. A blood sample would give us a vertical trace, yeah? Well, if we tie the trace to the compass, we can use it to zero in on her. Open a gate and keep it slightly unstable so we can move it until we get close to the target."

"I mean," Toula added, "the alternative is to randomly choose locations and hope we find her someday. Your call."

I began to agree, but before I could do so, Meggy swooped in and snatched the compass from my hand. "Would you *give* me that?" she snapped, casting baleful looks at Helen and Toula, then produced a short brass blade from nothing and sliced open her palm. "There," she said, wiping the welling blood on the plastic casing, "like I told you five minutes ago, I'll do it. Stop wasting time."

With a strained sigh, Helen plucked up the bloodied compass between finger and thumb. "And like I told you five minutes ago, you're useless for this."

"I am her *mother*—"

"Big damn deal," the wizard muttered as she traced runes in the air over the compass. A few seconds later, the needle began to spin, then pointed straight to Oberon. "Vertical traces go in both directions," she explained, tossing the compass back to Meggy. "It's going to point to the most proximate living match to you, up or down your family tree, which would currently be your *father*—unless, of course, you wanted to step out of the realm for a bit?" she added, turning to Oberon. He folded his bare arms and grinned, and Helen beckoned to Toula with a muttered, "Hit me again, Pavli."

A second compass, twin to the first but clean, appeared in Toula's hand, and I produced a blade and did my part without being asked. Helen repeated the spell, but when she ceased her casting, the needle spun about in a slow circle as if scanning for a signal. "Bingo," said Toula, then looked up and did a quick head count. "Helen, Aiden, Val, Megs, Gramps, *Percival*"—she flashed Joey a mischievous grin—"and Godzilla. That it?"

I'm Georgie.

"She knows, she's just being Toula," said Joey, tightening the dragon's chest strap. Georgie must have replied directly to him, as he began to chuckle at nothing and hoisted himself onto her back.

"And your…reinforcements?" asked Oberon, cocking his head at the tense knot of guards circled around Val.

"In case anything tries to slip through behind us," I said.

We regarded each other, both very much aware of the lie, but he merely smiled. "Good boy," he replied, then strolled toward a rudimentary bench outside the barn. I assumed the attempt at furniture was Joey's handiwork—it was little more than a glorified sawhorse—but as Oberon approached, it morphed into a bright green Adirondack with a built-in cup holder. He flopped down, suddenly equipped with an oversized Bloody Mary, and stretched his legs. "Go, if you're going," he said, waving us on with the unburdened hand. "I don't like to wait for my entertainment."

"Ass," Aiden whispered behind me, and I nodded as I steered him into position to my right. "Compass?"

"Check," said Helen, falling in line beside our brother. "You drive, I'll navigate. Aid?"

He squeezed her hand and took a deep breath.

"First priority," I said, giving my team one last inspection, "is to make it back alive. Everything else is secondary. Is that understood?" My eyes passed over their faces, then lingered on Meggy, who had reverted to her earlier stubborn silence. "I'm sorry, Meg," I mumbled, but her expression remained fixed, and I turned away.

Closing my eyes, I imagined the skin of the world around me stretched taut like cellophane—and then, with a bolt of focused will, I ripped it open.

CHAPTER 22

Picture the confluence of two powerful rivers, one fresh, the other brackish. If the conditions are right, the two streams will barely mix, and for a time, they'll continue their journey downstream flowing one beside or beneath the other, separated by a barrier of their own creation. Such is the example generally used to approximate the conditions if a gate were opened from Faerie directly into the Gray Lands—theoretical conditions, certainly, as no one would be so stupid as to make the attempt.

I can state now that this is utter bunk. The theoretical streams run along peacefully together, but the real streams—magic and dark magic, each trying to flow through the hole—run straight into each other at the confluence point. For anyone sensitive to magic and foolish enough to stand in front of such a gate, it's rather like being blasted before and behind with fire hoses.

Etheric Theory 101: magic and dark magic do not play nicely together. The one place they naturally mix is the mortal realm, whose border is pocked with gates of varying degrees of permanence. If the power balance in that realm favors magic, it's only because we've punched more holes through and maintained them better than our Gray Lands counterparts, who tend to create gates only when needed and let them close of their own accord. The Arcanum, which knows damn well what comes out of the Gray Lands, has also done its part over the years to seal off most of the breaches. As a result, while there is a low level of dark magic in the mortal realm, it's overcome by the background magic flowing out of Faerie. This imbalance lets us maintain the status quo—apply sufficiently concentrated magic to a Gray Lands gate and hold it in place, and eventually, the border will scab over. After all, although the barriers between the realms can be penetrated, their default state is to be…well, *barriers*. The force that seals the mortal realm off is tough and resilient, and given enough time, it can be healed.

When a gate appears between the mortal realm and one of the others, the etheric flow only goes in one direction. But double that flow, force magic and dark magic to interact at high pressure along the skin of the realms, and even the toughest border can tear.

The hole I'd created was rapidly widening of its own accord, and I struggled to tame the gate before it irreparably destroyed the border. "Aiden," I yelled, aching with the strain, "any time now!"

A heartbeat later, the fire hose behind me intensified, and the surge of magic flowed around me and against its counterforce, driving the incoming dark magic a precious few inches back from the gate. Pinned no longer, I stabilized the gate and shrank it to a circle a few feet across, then looked out onto the formless plain on the other side.

Faerie's not exactly a riot of color—think of what would result if the English countryside had a child with San Diego that had a fetish for architectural novelty—but what I've seen of the Gray Lands makes it look like a kaleidoscopic acid trip by comparison. The other realm can charitably be described as having a neutral palate, one dominated by shadow and mist in fact and in coloration. My gate revealed little of the landing site, largely because I'd opened it into a thick fog, but I saw below us more of the brown grass I'd seen through the last gate, so at least we were over land. "Got a heading?" I asked Helen.

"Just a minute," she muttered, and I glanced over to find her standing behind Aiden with her eyes scrunched closed and her palms held out toward the hole. Her lips moved silently, and I could feel something subtly modulating in the enchantment I'd created to hold the gate open. Before I could make enquiries, Toula gripped my shoulder to get my attention and shook her head.

"She's shoring it up," she whispered. "Putting supports in place."

"It's stable—"

"For you, for now. Helen can't hold it on her own." She double-tapped my temple and arched her brow. "Think about it. You've got enough trouble feeding a spell—imagine the reverse. She's crafting around the gate so that once you're distracted, the whole thing won't come crashing down around her. See?"

"Wizards," I sighed.

"That particular wizard is our ticket home, so watch it, bub." Toula stepped back, surveyed the spell I couldn't see, then joined Helen and extended two fingers. "Looks solid, but I can move some of the stress around," she murmured as her hand twitched from side to side. Helen nodded, too focused on her work to do more, and Aiden sweat as he continued to push magic against the tide.

With progress momentarily stymied, I watched the fog roil and listened for wildlife. Nothing the size of the giant mantis creatures could have squeezed through the gate, but I knew there were other nasty surprises on the other side—smaller, but no more pleasant—and kept vigil. So hard was I straining to hear footsteps that I jumped a few minutes later when Toula grabbed my arm to let me know the spell was complete. "Easy," she soothed, then beckoned Helen up to the hole with a low, "Okay, Carver, you know what to do."

Apparently satisfied that she wasn't about to lose a limb due to gate collapse, Helen stuck her hand holding the ensorcelled compass through the rift, being careful to keep it within the pool of magic Aiden had pushed through. I saw the needle slow in its continual revolution, then turn about in the other direction and point to the northeast. "We've got a heading," she said. "Shoot for two o'clock and go straight until I tell you otherwise."

I did a quick calculation based on our proximity to the ground and the height of the Gray Lands natives I'd seen, then raised the gate about twenty feet into the air. The fog remained solid at that height, but without the ground against which to orient ourselves, I was flying blind. "Does that thing give any indication as to distance?" I asked Helen.

"I'm working with a compass, not a GPS system," she replied, her eyes flicking impatiently to mine. "How long can you hold this open?"

"As long as it takes."

She glanced over her shoulder at pale-faced Aiden, and her mouth tightened. "Just hit the gas, all right?"

I spun the little gate until the needle lined up with north, then began to push it through the mist. When we didn't immediately run into anything solid, I picked up speed and kept an eye on the shaking needle in Helen's outstretched hand. I didn't know where we were going, but if the compass had a target, then Moyna was still alive.

If the girl lived, then I could send her off with Meggy, bound and none the wiser.

And if Meggy were happy again, then maybe she would come back to me.

It took nearly two grueling hours to break through the fog. My waiting team was tense, Helen's arm ached, my head wanted to split with the strain of guiding an open gate, and poor Aiden stood behind us in silent concentration, not even opening his eyes when Joey stepped forward every so often to wipe off the boy's dripping face and maneuver a straw between his lips. Oberon made a point of loudly yawning every quarter-hour or so and taking occasional walks around the sheep pen, but I had nothing to spare for him. The needle was the only indication that our course was true, and by then, I'd begun to question its conclusions...

...and then, without warning, the fog broke.

I stopped the gate to survey the world on the other side, a black-sand desert studded with the trunks of twisted, blasted trees, and turned my eyes to the domed stone fortress rising from the horizon ahead. "Helen?"

She glanced down at the compass and nodded. "We may have a winner. See what I see?"

Her hand dipped slightly, and I noticed the dark dots moving around the fortress's base. "Guards."

"Uh-huh. Going to have to fight our way through?"

"Maybe," I muttered, but pushed the gate forward again at a crawl. "Let me circle and see if that's really the target. Keep the compass steady."

I can only imagine what Geheret's troops thought when they spotted us looping the gate around his stronghold. Given the angle—I kept us high for a reason—I doubt they could see me, which means all they probably saw was a circle of light and a disembodied arm flying above their heads.

This may explain much of the preliminary shrieking. Magic allows us to perform wonders and miracles, but still, there are moments that make even the acclimated step back and do a double-take.

From what I could see of them, the creatures below us weren't the kind to scare easily. There were humanoid in the sense that they had a pair each of arms and legs and a single head—never something to be taken for granted—but their arms were long, almost simian, and thick with muscle. The rest of their physique was buff but proportional, giving them the general appearance of television wrestlers...well, if said wrestlers were part orangutan, dark green, and sported leather armor. A few looked skyward as they ran for shelter, giving us a decent view of their faces.

"Cyclopean," said Helen. "And the needle isn't budging—she's in there."

"You sound disappointed," I replied as she retracted her arm for landing.

Helen began massaging feeling back into her wrist. "Cyclops are *easy*. One shot to blind them, and the rest is a matter of cleanup."

"Oh, really? And how many cyclops have you killed in your extensive career?"

"Well, none yet," she admitted, "but in theory—"

"Forget theory. In *fact*, this is the damn Gray Lands, and you're to take nothing for granted, understood? For all you know, those things are magical. Dark magical. *Darkly* magical. Whatever," I muttered, too preoccupied with maneuvering the gate to worry about semantics.

"Not running away like that, they're not," she replied with a smirk in her voice.

By then, I'd descended to perhaps ten feet off the ground, and so I was at the perfect height to see a pair of massive doors open in the side of the fortress and another pack of guards run out to greet us, hauling with them what appeared to be a sharpened battering ram. "The hell is that thing?" I asked, briefly wondering if most of the guards' brain function was dedicated to their large eyes, but just then, the tip of the log began to glow bright blue.

"*Down!*" Toula shouted, shoving Helen and me away from the gate as she threw up a shield like a bubble being blown through the opening. The battering ram sparked and flared, and her shield glowed with zigzagging cracks as it absorbed the monstrous blast of dark magic that had been shot our way.

"That's a *wand*," Helen whispered as she stared out through the clearing shield. "Holy—"

"That's not a wand, that's a bazooka," I replied, peering over Toula's taut shoulders as the guards recharged.

Toula didn't take her eyes off the shield. "The word you're both looking for is *rod*. A wand can't store pre-cast spells. My guess is that they can't actually use dark magic, so the boss gave them a glorified Dud Defender. Shit, incoming..."

She grunted with the strain of holding the shield against the next hit, and Aiden yelped behind us. I turned to find him on his knees, squeezing his eyes closed and rocking back and forth. "Aiden? How're you holding up?" I asked, hoping his sister was too distracted to see him in that state.

He pressed his palms to his temples and winced as Toula tightened her shield, but managed to mumble, "Hurry."

Locked in a standoff with our power source fading, I decided to try a new tactic. "Change of plans," I said, shooing Helen away from the gate, then beckoned Joey and his mount to the front line. "Toula, how much time do we have before the next blast?"

"Maybe ten seconds, why?"

"Once you block, get out of the way. Joey, you're up."

He was already climbing onto Georgie's shoulders. "Going to have to widen the gate, boss."

"Understood. Take out what you can..."

The blast came, and Toula and Aiden cried out in synchronization as her shield flashed. The instant the last of the shot was deflected, she darted out of the way, taking her shield with her as I tore the rip open. "Now!" I yelled, throwing myself to the side just before Georgie galloped through and spread her wings.

For the second time that morning, the cyclopean guards began to shriek, but they never had a chance to summon backup. Georgie had taken them by surprise, and rather than wait for the rod to finish recharging, they dropped it and dashed for cover. I heard Joey shout, his commands made incomprehensible by distance and the chaos on the other side, and then I saw Georgie dive for the back of the running pack. An instant later, she snapped the nearest guard up, tossed him into the air, and swallowed him headfirst. Joey patted her neck and squeezed his knees, urging her on, but she paused in midair, hovering with an odd expression on her face.

"What's wrong?" I called through the gate. "Stuck going down?"

"She needs to burp," he yelled back over the rush of her beating wings. "It's all right, this happens, it's only a little gas—"

The dragon opened her mouth and belched forth a fat jet of flame, charring three of the guards in their tracks. She snapped her mouth closed and looked back at Joey, visibly perplexed.

"*Do it again!*" Toula screamed through the gate, cupping her hands around her mouth to be heard. "*Do that again, Georgie! Good girl!*"

Georgie turned to us at the sound of Toula's voice, then dipped her head and wheeled on the retreating guards. With a screech, she dropped toward the pack, took a deep breath, and incinerated the lot before they reached the open doors. As her last casualties screamed and flailed, she executed a neat two-point landing, daintily folded her wings, and went in for a snack.

With the guards dispatched, I lowered the gate to ground level and nodded to Helen. "Ready?"

"Ready," she confirmed, then closed her eyes. Aiden hissed behind her as she powered her magical scaffolding, but he made no complaint.

"How do you feel?" I asked, slowly withdrawing myself from the gate.

"Like Atlas," she said through gritted teeth. "Do me a favor and hurry it up, okay?"

"You've got it."

Helen grabbed my arm before I could move out of range. "I'm trusting you," she said, tightening her vise grip. "Aid is trusting you. He can't do this forever."

"Understood." She released me, and I beckoned to the

others. With a last worried glance at my brother, who still rocked and held his head, I stepped through into the Gray Lands and immediately began to shiver.

The black-sand desert in which we'd landed was nearly freezing and, at least to me, reeked of floral formaldehyde. I coughed, gagging with the stench, then jogged across the waste to rendezvous with Joey and Georgie. "Cold enough for you?" I called up to him—his windbreaker seemed insufficient for the climate—but he shook his head.

"Flak jacket helps," he replied, punching his chest to demonstrate. "It's not great insulation, but I'm okay."

"Where the hell did you get a flak jacket?"

He unzipped his windbreaker, revealing both the black vest beneath it and the strap of a gun holster—his backup weapon, I assumed. "Helen's pretty handy. And Georgie's heating up like an electric blanket right now," he added, patting the dragon's flank, "so huddle up if you can't hack it."

For some reason, the idea of standing beside a dragon who was busy swallowing charred corpses didn't strike me as wise, and the rest of our party seemed to share the sentiment. We stood close to each other, listening for an approaching army, while Helen worked out the steering controls on the gate and slid in behind us. As the outflow of magic began to reach us, I produced a leather jacket and gloves, while Toula opted for a puffy black coat. "What?" she said, catching Val's look of incredulity. "It's warm! There's no rule against being warm!"

"You look like a burned marshmallow," said Meggy, now sporting a thick sweater and boots.

"Oh, so *now* you're talking to me?" she retorted.

Meggy shrugged and lifted her chin toward the open doors. "Were you planning to wait for an escort, or can we storm the damn castle now?"

A hissing rush of flame interrupted her, and we turned to find Georgie looking around at the glass-studded sand in consternation. *All gone?*

"There's probably more inside," said Joey. "You, uh…you don't have to *eat* them all, hon. We only need to get past them."

But I'm hungry, she pointed out, *and if they're dead anyway, why can't I?*

"How are you hungry? You had, like, ten sheep for breakfast."

She lifted her front leg and touched her belly with her foot. *Everything's hot inside. Makes me hungry.*

"Dual metabolism," said Toula. "Has to be…dark magic triggers fire production, fire speeds up the metabolic processes…"

But Val, who had kept one eye on the doors, interrupted Toula's hypothesizing. "Next wave," he said, pushing up his tunic's thin sleeves as a horde of sword-wielding cyclops rushed out of the citadel. "Georgie, whenever you're ready…"

She wheeled about at the sound of their war shrieks, wide-eyed and spread-winged, then leapt and began to belch death from above.

As the vanguard burned and the sand melted, I looked back through the gate at Aiden, whose condition remained unchanged. "Let them finish their sweep," I said to the others, raising my voice over the cries of the dying. "That's not drawing on magic. Pick off the survivors when they finish." A few of the guards had the bright last-ditch idea to throw their swords at Georgie, but Joey kept her out of range, even as she continued to insist that the food was getting cold. "We've got to stay close to the gate to make this work, so no one wander off, yes?" I continued. "Like we practiced."

Val and Toula nodded, and Meggy reluctantly stepped nearer to our pack.

The brightest of the guards had now turned tail and were running for the doors, and Val charged in their direction with a bronze sword in his hand, skirting their smoldering comrades. The rest of us followed ahead of the gate, and Toula and I took shots at our left and right flanks, keeping Meggy safely between us whether she liked it or not. We passed Joey, who yelled over the snapping and snuffling of Georgie's feast, "We'll be right there! She's tanking up!" Spotting a survivor, he leapt off her back, unsheathed his sword, and started stabbing the dying—whether as an act of mercy or to hasten the cleanup process, I couldn't say, though he seemed unmoved by the carnage around him.

It doesn't take an expert in draconic behavior to understand that one does not come between a hungry dragon and her food, and so we pressed on through the unmanned doors without our flamethrower.

The best approximation I can give for Geheret's stronghold is a domed stadium. Mind you, that's a rough visual at best; the place was several times wider than the largest stadium I'd ever seen, and the walls were composed of solid black rock, broken only by occasional view slits. It appeared rather like Geheret had simply smoothed and hollowed out a mountain instead of taking the time to design his own fortress from scratch, but whatever process he had employed, the end result was impressively forbidding. The Gray Lands were overcast to begin with, but the light inside the wide, high-ceilinged hallway we found beyond the doors was dim and torch-made—or at least it was until Helen parked the gate behind us like a spotlight, giving me a clear view of the bodies strewn in Val's wake. He was still engaged with a pair of guards, pitting reinforced bronze against steel, and I dispatched both with a pair of fireballs to save him the exertion.

Seeing them burn and drop to the stone floor, Val turned to me with a look of mild annoyance and wiped his sword clean on his pants. "I *had* them, Coileán."

"And if there's a prize for body count," Toula snapped, "I'm pretty sure the lizard's going to win it. Shall we?"

With the immediate threat neutralized, I took stock of our situation. The hallway curved to either side—a ring giving passage around the fortress, I surmised. Perhaps this was only the first of a series of concentric halls. If Geheret placed his quarters at the center—logically, the safest place—then surely he would have staggered the doors leading inside from the hallways, thereby preventing an invading enemy from running through the main gates and straight to him.

Toula, who had taken the compass from Helen, pointed it toward the rock wall ahead of us and snorted. "She's straight through there," she said, "so who has a preference as to left or right?"

"Why bother?" Meggy interjected. "Just blast a hole through! It can't be that hard," she muttered, then screwed up her face as she began to conjure a fireball between her hands.

Val pressed his palm against the inner wall, barely flinching when Meggy's fireball bounced harmlessly off the stone. "Warded," he said after a moment's examination. "Difficult to see it, but there is a system in place. I don't know how strong the enchantment is."

"And I can't access it," Toula added, touching her fingertips to the rock. "If we were dealing with magic, I could pull up the architecture and see how it's assembled, but with *dark* magic…" She shrugged and turned away from the wall. "Best I can tell you is that it's warded. I don't know what it would take to bust a hole in that."

I met Meggy's glare, then looked behind me at Helen and Aiden, both of whom were straining to maintain the status quo. "Left it is," I said, turning around as Joey and Georgie lumbered into the building. "Cleanup complete?"

Georgie stifled a burp, and a plume of gray smoke shot out her nostrils. *Better.*

"Great. Can you take the lead? I'll shield you," I offered, seeing Joey's uncertainty. "But if you see something moving up ahead…char it."

The dragon's mouth opened slightly, revealing interlocking rows of dagger teeth, and I realized with mild trepidation that she was smiling.

I can say now from experience that in a low-magic situation, you could do far worse than leading with a flamethrower. While the rest of us hung back, using as little magic as we could to take the pressure off of Aiden, Georgie happily flambéed anything that crossed her path as we progressed around the outer ring of the fortress. Her fire seemed unlimited, as did her appetite—our progress was slowed not so much by the security forces as by Georgie's insistence that she be allowed to eat her kills. Joey and Val did their best to speed things along, running out once her initial blast was over to dispatch anything left standing, but Meggy tensed impatiently every time we stopped for a snack.

As slow as our progress was, at least Moyna wasn't moving. Toula continued to take compass readings, and the needle, without fail, pointed toward the center of the complex. "Maybe she's imprisoned," she postulated during a pit stop. "Or maybe that's where Geheret keeps his official space. Or both—we don't know how deep this thing goes." She pivoted the compass up and down the wall, but the reading remained unchanged. "Moyna could be ten levels down, for all we know."

"Olive."

Toula sighed and turned to face Meggy, who lurked against the outer wall with her arms folded. "*Moyna*. Calling the sky green isn't going to make it so." Meggy began to protest, but Toula held up her hand and shook her head. "You know I love you, Megs," she said, "but if you think this is going to end in happily ever after for you two, you're deluding yourself."

"We just need time," she countered. "A fresh start, a clean slate, whatever you want to call it. I'm going to make this work."

Toula began to respond, but her mouth snapped closed, and she shook her head. "We're not having this discussion right now. I'm only warning you not to get your hopes up, that's all." She glanced back through the gate at Helen's taut face, then pointed to the path ahead. "Let's find the door and get through this damn thing."

"And hope no one sends out anything capable of enchantment—"

"Damn it, don't jinx us!" she cried, socking me in the arm. "You keep that bad juju to yourself, you hear me?"

"Hey, guys," Joey called from the front, "I think we've got something!"

Toula gave me a last warning glare before jogging up to inspect his find. "Door," she confirmed, then called up a preemptive fireball and kicked it open. "Another hall. I think it's empty, but…"

Before she could finish, Georgie gently nosed her out of the way, then torched the inner corridor in both directions. When the fire died, she paused, sniffed deeply, then reported, *Nothing. It's empty.*

"Don't sound so disappointed," Toula muttered, opening the other half of the double door to give the dragon entrance. "How many have you eaten today, anyway?"

I didn't know I was supposed to be counting, she replied, pushing past Toula. *And this is hungry work. If you'd rather do it, you're welcome to take a turn.*

"Easy," said Joey, patting Georgie's flank until her thoughts grew less sharp. "We're all a little stressed, sweetie, you aren't doing anything wrong—"

Before he could finish, she turned sharply at the sound of footfalls on the stone and roasted a trio of newcomers. "Wait, don't eat them," I ordered, closing my eyes until the afterimage of the fire faded, then skirted Georgie to take stock of her newest kills. The corpses were smaller than the others and binocular, but what had caught my eye was the flash of armor in the firelight—*bronze* armor, I saw on closer inspection, heavily decorated and unscratched where it hadn't melted.

"Ceremonial," said Val, confirming my suspicion as he squatted beside me. "They weren't warriors, not wearing *that*." He stood and peered at the bodies, then stiffened and beckoned to Joey. "Sword, please."

Frowning, Joey flipped his blade and offered Val the handle, but Val pointed to the relatively unburned—and seemingly human—face of the farthest corpse. "See if he's sensitive," he said, stepping away from Joey's sword, and watched as Joey pressed the flat of the blade against the corpse's cheek. It began to blister on contact, and Val nodded. "I thought that face was familiar," he muttered, turning back to me. "One of Mab's favorites."

"All right, go on," I said, patting Georgie's neck, and she bent to the task of prying the meat from its armor. "Fae guards are useless without magic," I said to Val, "so what do you think he's doing, sending cannon fodder? Something to stall us while he prepares his real defenses?"

"Maybe more." Val waited until Toula slid past Georgie's thrashing tail, then said, "That wasn't just a favorite of hers—that was a favorite *son*. I can't identify the other two," he added, cutting his eyes to the half-eaten remains, "but I wouldn't be surprised if they were more of the same."

"Eliminating the competition," Toula mumbled, looking away as Georgie noisily finished her meal. "But if he's Mab's son…Val, you didn't know Geheret before the court was expelled, did you?"

"No, and that troubles me." He folded his arms and looked around our little circle. "Assuming Geheret spoke the truth when he said he was Mab's, he's not her eldest. *He* was older," he said, cocking his head toward the ruined armor. "So why is Geheret leading the court? What does he have that his siblings don't?"

"He's native," I said. "Has to be. We know he can use

dark magic, so Mab…"

I left the thought unfinished, and Val grimaced. "Perhaps, but…I've taken *interesting* partners," he said, looking mildly embarrassed, "but there are limits."

Joey patted his shoulder. "Merrow club. I feel you, man."

"This is all charming," said Meggy, storming down the corridor, "but you can relive your conquests together once Olive's safe. Get a move on."

Startled, Georgie trotted after her, and Toula rolled her eyes. "She's going to get herself killed," she said, following the dragon's twitching tail.

I ran ahead and joined Meggy, but she ignored me until I pulled her back. "Let Georgie take point," I said before she could protest, then released her. Meggy's lips tightened, but she fell into step behind Georgie, saying nothing and tapping her foot every time the dragon stopped to clean up after herself. I let her stew in silence, but I kept looking back through the gate, wondering how much Aiden had left to give.

It took us another half hour of slow progress to make the second door, which opened into a nearly emptied armory. No one paused to remark on the scene; Meggy was almost beside herself with the goal so close, and the rest of us knew too well that an armory without armor wasn't a good sign. Joey snagged a helmet in passing, a battered steel bucket with an eye slit, but discarded it when he found it far too massive for his head. I didn't want think about the dimensions of the creature that would require such equipment, and Joey, to his credit, didn't speculate.

Walking in the gate's glow, we passed through a long string of curved storerooms, one filled with black barrels, another with unlabeled sacks, a third with rolled bedding and piles of boots. The ceilings remained high enough to allow Georgie passage, and I assumed we were still on the ground level of the complex, but *where*, precisely, we were, I couldn't say. We had turned left at each door—had we yet rounded the fortress? Had we made it halfway? Without windows or landmarks, our only guides were Joey's watch and the damned compass, which continued to direct our steps inward.

And we hadn't seen a soul in several rooms, which gave me pause. Georgie had killed perhaps a score—all fae—in the second ring, but this section seemed abandoned, and the only sounds around us were our own. A glance at Val's thoughts affirmed my strengthening conclusion that the mass of Geheret's forces would be waiting with their lord—and if they were wise, in a room too small for Georgie's bulk.

At least the absence of guards allowed us to pick up our pace. Meggy surely would have been running if not for our light limitations, but we managed a respectable speed and ran into the third door after a twenty-minute march. The next ring, largely communal living quarters for several thousand men, took us a quarter of an hour to escape, while the next, consisting of at least an abandoned kitchen and infirmary, ate another ten minutes. There was no protest from the gate, but Helen was red-faced and sweating, and Aiden knelt behind her with his forehead in the grass, silently shaking. I wanted to call it off—I *should* have called it off—but Meggy continued her charge through the empty tunnels, and I knew she would never voluntarily return without her daughter.

Our daughter, I reminded myself more than once, but as uncomfortable as it was to admit the truth to myself, Moyna's safety worried me far less than Aiden's. She had run willingly back into the Gray Lands with the rest of our idiotic kin—Aiden was just trying to be useful, and I'd put him on the front lines of a battle he had no business fighting. Helen didn't have to remind me of the precariousness of the situation—her face spoke volumes every time I looked back into Faerie.

Not until we breached the sixth ring did the scenery truly change. The place was still as atmospherically lit as a high-end haunted house, but the stone floor gave way to tile, a continual mosaic of blacks and reds and golds like swirling fire. The walls were decorated with long hangings of a similar theme, abstract tapestries that padded the rock between torch sconces. This ring was narrower, too, wide enough for four of us or one juvenile dragon to pass, and the omnipresent smell of dark magic seemed disproportionally concentrated.

"Antechamber?" Toula whispered, looking left and right at the empty corridor.

"Possibly." I pressed my ear to the inner wall, but pulled away before I could hear anything when the power driving the wards sent me into a coughing fit. "We're approaching *something*," I said between hacking breaths. "The ward system—"

Before I could finish, a gate opened to either side of us, vomiting Geheret's soldiers into the hallway and cutting off our escape through any door but back into Faerie. Georgie hissed and bared her teeth, but Joey, who had climbed into his saddle when the rifts appeared, managed to hold her before she could loose her fire. I looked at the well-armed soldiers to my left and right, whose steel armor gleamed in the torches' glow, and lowered my hands. "I've come for a word with your lord," I said, raising my voice above the clatter of shifting plate and maille. "And I will not be denied. Tell him to show himself."

One of the soldiers, who sported a golden breastplate and helm—another of Mab's refugees, I assumed— stepped out of the pack and stood with his hand on his sword's hilt. "My lord awaits within," he said in perfect Fae. "If you've tired of your fun, boy, he will deign to speak with you."

I surveyed the amassed troops, unsure of the common tongue of the realm or how many faeries were among their number, then opted for the only choice with a chance of privacy. "Joey, come down here," I said, forcing myself to think in English. When he'd dismounted and edged his way past the guards to my side, I muttered, "If this goes south, Val may not leave me—I don't know his mind that well. Toula can fend for herself. But I expect you to get Meggy out of here by any means necessary, is that understood? By the hair, kicking and screaming, I don't care—just keep her safe if something happens to me."

He nodded, but replied in kind, "If something happens to you, won't the court go to Moyna?"

"That's my fear."

"Even if she's on this side of the gate?"

"Your point?"

"Well," he said, folding his arms, "assuming she's over here at the time, she's not going to get the boost you did until she's in a realm with actual *magic* in it, right? So if she's technically the queen but she's hanging out with all of her aunts and uncles over here, and none of them has anything to enchant with, what's to stop them from whacking her, too?"

I considered the picture he was painting, then looked at Meggy, who stared at the troops in silent defiance.

"If I fall," I said, "get Meggy out of here and close the gate. Save Toula and Val if you can. Whichever of Mother's spawn makes it back to Faerie can have the damn throne."

Joey nodded again. "And if, I don't know, this is one big trap to wipe all of you out at once?"

"You think I haven't thought of that, kid?"

"Just putting it out there."

I sighed quietly and glanced at the nearest soldiers, but saw no sign that our conversation had been overheard or understood. "Playing at hypotheticals, the throne should descend to Aiden. And if that should happen—"

"He wouldn't be safe anywhere."

I gripped his arm and bent close to his face. "Joey, if you bear me any friendship at all, save Meggy. And if you would grant my last request, protect my brother while you can."

"You got it, boss."

I released him and waited until he was mounted once more, then turned to Geheret's messenger. "Take me to him," I said, returning to Fae. "And if you get any creative ideas, my associate will ask his *draconic* associate to roast you alive, which she will do gladly. So for your continued safety, I'd suggest you be quick and try not to look delicious."

Too late.

Joey patted Georgie and smiled in the darkness as he whispered, "Atta girl."

But the messenger seemed unfazed by my blustering. "Understood," he replied as he turned to go, then paused and looked back at me. "I almost forgot," he said, raising a finger. "The gate remains here. My lord insists upon security, and seeing the damage you've already inflicted…"

He smiled, and I met Val and Toula's uneasy glances. "Very well," I said, and followed the messenger through the press of soldiers as the comforting smell of magic faded to nothingness.

CHAPTER 23

I realize it seems imprudent to allow oneself to be led by a heavily-armed escort to a meeting with someone who's made little secret of the fact that he'd like one dead, but I was running out of options. As I passed between the ranks, trying to find a workaround for my collapsing battle plan, I took stock of the weapons we had left. Val was armed, but bronze on steel was far from a sure thing. Joey still wore his sword—the fae troops who moved too close to his left side quickly gave him room—but despite the boy's skill, he wasn't going to be able to make much of a dent in the forces around us by himself. Georgie, of course, was a walking tank of combustible goodies, but even with a tough hide for protection, no dragon is completely impervious to pointy objects. Meggy had come empty-handed, as had I, and if Toula had hidden a weapon on her person, I had yet to see it.

Yes, I admitted to myself, this was far from the best possible scenario, especially considering the squadron of Geheret's soldiers left behind to guard the gate. It was taking all of Helen's resources and concentration to keep the rift open—if she gave the soldiers cause to attack her, she might be able to defend herself, but at the cost of the gate. I hoped the few guards Val had left on our side had the sense to cover Helen, but by then, we had progressed around the curving wall, and the gate was lost to my sight.

I forced myself to stop catastrophizing about what might be happening at the border and concentrated on the moment, looking for weaknesses in the horde around us.

True, we were well flanked, and I strongly suspected that leaving without an audience was no longer an option at that point, but the soldiers did not seem to be operating as a unified force. I could pick out individual squadrons by their leaders' more impressive helmets, and it was almost immediately apparent that the squads had formed along clear lines: there were squads in bronze and squads in steel, but none with a mix of armor. The fae forces were as disadvantaged as we were in terms of magic, and their armor made them obvious targets. Suppose, in a mêlée situation, I were able to take a sword from one of the guards—I could hold my own in hand-to-hand combat, I reasoned, though surely I'd rusted in the last couple of centuries from lack of practice. But swordplay was like riding a bicycle, and given a chance to limber up and let the muscle memory engage...

I was jolted from my thoughts when the messenger grabbed me by the arm and steered me toward a pair of enormous, finely wrought iron doors. "Don't be clever, boy," he murmured, waiting as a guard opened the way, then half-shoved me into Geheret's throne room, the nucleus of the citadel.

As throne rooms went, it erred on the side of grandiosity with a hint of hollowed-out volcano lair. The omnipresent black stone walls curved into a high dome through which sourceless light somehow filtered, augmenting the wall torches and the ornamental braziers placed at regular intervals about the room. A thick red and black carpet, twin to the tile floor in the corridor, muffled our footsteps as we were escorted—none too gently—toward the throne, a jagged stone chair that rose from the floor perhaps six or seven feet, high enough to give its occupant a commanding view of anything around him of roughly humanoid form. Atop it, across a seat large enough for three, sprawled Geheret—and at its base, in chairs made miniature by comparison, sat my family.

My siblings' faces were composed, masks of calm

disinterest, but Moyna's rouged lips curled into a smirk when the doors closed behind us.

I pushed the messenger off of me and started toward them, conscious of the eyes of the guards and the curious who stood around our little knot. "Geheret!" I called to him as I marched up the rug, willing confidence into my voice. "I believe you have something of mine."

Slowly, he straightened his pose, brushed his dark hair from his face, and glanced idly at the signet ring gleaming on his hand. "You've accepted my offer, then? I admit, I had expected Doran to return with the news of your—"

"Unfortunately, he's been terminally delayed," I interrupted, cutting my eyes to Syral in time to catch her flinch. "And no, I do not accept your *offer*. But as I was informed that you were preparing to kill my daughter, I thought I might stop by and see if you could be dissuaded. It seemed only proper, after all."

Suddenly uncertain, Moyna glanced at her companions, but if she had expected to find reassurance in their stoicism, she was disappointed. "Kill me?" she said imperiously, rising from her seat, but her face betrayed her sudden doubt. "Oh, Coileán, you *are* a fool."

From the corner of my eye, I saw Meggy began to dart forward, but I threw out my arm to stop her from running to her daughter's side. "Am I? And what use are you to Geheret, pray tell?"

"His lover," she retorted, taking an extra moment to stare at her mother, who sputtered beside me. "And his greatest ally." Her voice strengthened as she began to recover her slipped footing. "You're looking at the newest queen of Faerie," she continued, spreading her hands— and giving the rest of the room an excellent view of her deep blue corset and its corresponding accessory that might, in some distant realm, be considered a skirt. "And when I rule Mother's court, Geheret's people will be welcomed home."

I surveyed the crowd, picking out the clumps of faeries

among the natives. "Really? They're going to abandon Geheret and follow you, is that the plan?"

"Of course not, imbecile. His court will coexist with mine—"

"Oh, so he's going to join you in Faerie, then? The once place where he has absolutely no power?" The troubled expression flitted across her face once more, and I folded my arms as Moyna tried to make the pieces fit together. "Mother may never have mentioned this to you, but the realm is picky," I explained. "It doesn't complain about anyone from our courts, and it accepts some mortals, but with one exception, it is *not* fond of Mab's children. I assume the same could be said for what's left of her court."

A few of the faeries in the gallery began to mutter amongst themselves, and I looked up at Geheret, who was observing Moyna and me with the same attention one might devote to a fish tank. "So since we're all present, let's be honest," I said to him. "You've got no more use for Moyna than you would for any of my idiot kin, and you've got them in a conveniently difficult position," I continued, pointing to the row of chairs at the foot of the throne. "But if you think Faerie is going to welcome you home, you're bound to be disappointed. It was sorely displeased to see your mother, as I recall. So what do you want?"

He sat back and leaned on an armrest, propping his cheek on two fingers as he looked down at me. "Unity." I frowned, and he chuckled at my bemusement. "One realm, united under my rule. A noble goal, don't you think? No more infighting, no more petty bickering, no vigilantes with iron bars"—he grinned knowingly at that—"and no more of this 'courts' nonsense. There will be one court and one realm—mine."

"You…propose to destroy the others?"

"Not destroy, no," he replied, sounding almost bored. "I'll simply break down the barriers, flood the mortal realm with power, and take what I will."

"Aren't you forgetting—"

"No. Either Faerie will join me, or I'll seal it off permanently. Mother had the secret—why shouldn't I replicate it?" Geheret shrugged and swung one foot against the throne. "You've yet to enquire about my father, Coileán. Aren't you at least curious?"

I could sense Georgie growing restless behind me and wondered what she was seeing. "I assume he was native to this realm," I replied, trying to match his affected ennui. "Given your proficiency with dark magic. You can't actually use magic, can you? The two can't coexist."

Geheret examined his ring once more. "Magic is inconsequential. And no, to answer your question, I cannot—my father's gift is simply too powerful." He breathed lightly on the ring, then began polishing it against his violet robe. "I was sired by this realm," he said casually. "Not by a native—by the *realm*. Did you think Faerie was unique in having a consciousness?" he asked, smiling at my surprise. "I know quite well that she wasn't pleased with my mother. So once you and the brat are out of the way," he continued, ignoring Moyna's shocked stare, "and I choose which among your brother and sisters pleases me best as a puppet lord, I'll give Oberon my terms: join me, bow to me, or be severed." He sat up and leaned forward to better see my face. "And if you think the souls of our realms are invincible, I have a few lessons I could teach you. But since I'm going to kill you, there's really no point, is there?"

I stood there before the throne, speechless and trying to understand what Geheret was telling me, when my nose insisted that I pay it heed. It twitched in sudden stimulation, but I pushed its message to the back of my thoughts as I strove to save my skin.

"Why kill me?" I asked him, vying for time. "You need a go-between? Faerie knows me—I could treat with Oberon on your behalf. Keep Moyna here to ensure my reliability," I suggested. "If I break my word to you, kill her."

He seemed to mull that over for a moment while my silent siblings looked on uneasily. "An idea," he finally declared, "but impractical. Far easier to kill the two of you, keep your lovely sister by my side," he said, pointing down to Syral, "and send another in her stead. I get my envoy, and the true heir never receives Faerie's gift."

"You think that will buy your envoy's loyalty?" I retorted with a laugh. "Sure, keep Syral and send Nanine. If Syral never properly inherits, then all Nanine has to do is wait for you to kill the other three, and the power's hers. You can't buy a faerie's good behavior by appealing to her familial bonds—I tell you in truth that none of those four gives a damn if the others live or die. *I'm* the exception," I continued, moving toward the throne. "Make my daughter your hostage, if it soothes your mind, and let me help you."

Before he could respond, Meggy grabbed my arm and hissed, "We are *not* leaving her here."

If she had intended the message only for me, she failed, and Geheret laughed briefly as he leaned over the edge of his seat to look at her. "You'd rather see her dead than a hostage? That can be arranged, but your choice surprises me."

I wanted to talk Meggy down, but ignoring my nose was no longer working. When I surrendered and acquiesced to its demands, it alerted me to the familiar odor of citronella, faint but swelling.

Magic.

"And anyway," Geheret continued, turning his attention back to me, "I don't trust you. They call you the Ironhand, don't they? A traitor to your own kind. Why should I bother with you?"

"Because," I replied, trying to surreptitiously pinpoint the source of the sudden magic flow, "I love my daughter, and I won't do anything to bring her to harm."

Geheret studied my face as he paused to consider this, then shook his head and murmured, "I don't believe you."

I never had a chance to defend myself. The ear-splitting crack of shattering rock boomed around the throne room, and I turned around in time to see a door-sized chunk of the well-warded wall disintegrate. Through the cloud of dust stepped Oberon, still sporting his shorts and sandals but as peeved as I'd ever seen him. Behind him, barely visible through the haze, was a circle of light marking the gate, and a torrent of magic poured through the breach toward us.

An instant later, Geheret had found his feet and was pointing at the intruder in flabbergasted alarm. He shouted something unintelligible to me—I'd never learned the tongue of the Gray Lands, after all—but before he could speak more than a few words, Oberon reared back and flung a blast of magic straight at the throne.

I was aware of only two things in that moment: Aiden screaming behind me, and Geheret screaming before me— the one in agony from the power Oberon demanded of him, the other wailing as his body tried and failed to patch the foot-wide hole that had been punched through his chest.

As Aiden continued to howl in pain, Geheret stared at the room with an expression of deep confusion on his face, then pitched forward and fell to the foot of the throne, narrowly missing Huc's head. And as Geheret breathed his last, a voice in the corner of the room cried out in a high, inhuman screech that crescendoed over the sudden cacophony of the assembled.

It was too much to process simultaneously, and I looked dumbly around the room, seeing nothing but the terrified crowd and unable to decide how that fact should make me feel. Seconds after Geheret's death finally registered, Oberon appeared beside me, gave me a brisk shake, and pointed at the empty throne. "When your opponent begins to soliloquize, *shoot him*," he barked.

"How much more basic does it get, boy?"

I blinked, attempting to connect the shapes I was seeing with the sounds and the smells and the deep sense that I needed to be taking action in some way—and then, as if a switch had been flipped, reality returned to me. "How did you get in here? The wards—"

"Broke through, didn't I?"

"Moon and stars," I breathed, "Aiden—"

"Looks all right to me," he interrupted, glancing over his shoulder at my sobbing brother. "May have an interesting headache after this," he allowed, "but see, he's alive."

I squinted at the gate, trying to make out the shapes behind Helen's tense body. "The guards…where are the guards?"

Oberon grunted. "They seemed confused about my intentions, so I was forced to incapacitate them. Oh, don't look so panicked," he snapped, "they'll wake soon enough."

I was dimly aware that Val and Toula had set up a shield network around us, and that Joey, apparently having decided that all bets were off, was bellowing atop the dragon as she incinerated a dozen men. My siblings hadn't moved, nor had Moyna, who stared down at Geheret's body with her hands over her mouth.

"Glad you changed your mind," I said, squeezing Oberon's bare shoulder. "Thank you."

He shrugged me off with a snort. "I didn't. *She* insisted. And stay behind the shields, you little idiot," he said as he grabbed Meggy's arm, nearly jerking her off her feet as she tried to run for the throne. "Or better yet, go back through the gate. You're getting in my way."

Meggy snarled, but as I moved between them, someone deep in the crowd began to shout, and the rest of the room quickly fell silent. Georgie looked around in confusion, and I held Meggy away from the throne with one arm and watched for a clue until the throng parted, revealing a slim figure in steel plate who was walking our way. It paused a few yards from us, then removed its helmet, revealing a visage that would pass for human only under significant glamour. The being was cerulean and hairless, and each of its solid black eyes was accompanied by a pair of lesser eyes extending toward its temples, giving it a vaguely arachnid appearance. Its ears were small and slightly pointed, as were the teeth it revealed when it addressed us in perfect, if heavily accented, Fae. "I am Nath," it said, pausing to breathe deeply through its nasal slits while the dome echoed its words. When the reverberation subsided, it closed its eyes, and its armor dissolved into a flowing white robe, a more refined adaptation of Geheret's bloodstained outerwear. "I am Nath," it repeated, looking at us once more, "and I am my father's chosen."

Oberon regarded Nath in perplexed silence, and so I took the lead. "My, uh...lady?" I guessed—Nath's voice sounded somewhat feminine, but the shape visible under its robe offered no hint as to gender.

Nath's head bobbed. "'Lady' is sufficiently close," it—*she*—replied. "Lords of Faerie, do you desire war?"

"No. With your leave, I'll take my daughter and trouble you no longer."

"A moment," she said, then looked about her as if seeing the citadel for the first time. Four of her eyes squinted closed, and in the space of a long exhalation, the rock around us vanished, leaving the entire company standing in the black sand beneath the realm's slate-hued sky. Before my eyes finished adjusting to the light, the temperature had risen at least thirty degrees, making my jacket unnecessary and at least lessening half-dressed Oberon's discomfort. The bottom of Nath's robe shifted, and I saw her long toes digging down into the sand as she smiled. "I have been entombed alive too long," she murmured, catching my eyes, then raised her arms into the air as a wide circle of silver-leafed trees rose from the wasteland around us. Another tree began to sprout at the circle's heart, but twisted itself into a generously-proportioned throne of black wood overhung by a living canopy. The crowd parted for its new queen as Nath climbed the three short steps to the throne and seated herself without further ceremony. "Now," she said, beckoning to Oberon and me, "we may treat."

"After you," he muttered.

I led the way across the expanse, skirting Geheret's body and ignoring my siblings, who had congregated in a little knot beside the corpse. "Lady Nath," I began, pausing a respectful distance from the throne, "I want only what is mine."

She cocked her head and gestured toward Moyna. "If I am not mistaken, the child came of her own accord."

"And as you are aware, she is a child."

"And foolish, yes. Though I have no such excuse for the others," she added, glancing at my siblings. "Still, the girl is of no use to me, and I have nothing to gain by holding her captive. I return her to you willingly, Lord Coileán, and suggest that you guard her better in the future."

"Thank you," I replied, feeling my gut begin to unclench for the first time in days.

"But there is one other matter to address," Nath continued, looking at Oberon and me in turn. "Although I suppose I should thank you, I find my brother is dead at your hand. Compensation is owed."

I looked to Oberon for a cue, but he remained stone-faced. "What did you have in mind?"

Nath turned most of her eyes on Geheret's body for a moment, then flicked her hand in the air as if halfheartedly trying to hail a cab. The corpse exploded in black flame, and Moyna screamed and fell backward in her effort to escape the fire. "When Geheret's mother came into this realm," said Nath, "my father favored her, and though she was powerless, he saw to her needs. Geheret was the only fruit of their union—I am younger, and as you may have deduced," she added, flashing what appeared to be a wry grin, "I am not of Mab's line."

"I hadn't noticed," I replied, earning a wider smile from the throne.

"Her people began as refugees in this realm, but they have since aspired to dominion," she continued, cutting her eyes to the little knots of fae troops scattered around her. "They have no place here. I would see them gone from our lands."

I overheard snatches of worried conversation around the circle but kept my attention on Nath. "You would have us...repatriate them?"

"If you like," she said with a light shrug. "In truth, it makes little difference to me. I banish them now and henceforth," she said, raising her voice, then spoke in the realm's tongue—repeating herself, I assumed, given the cheer the non-fae set up immediately thereafter. "For compensation," she said to me, "I would ask that you allow them the use of your gate. What you do with them after they have left me is none of my concern."

"Gladly," I told her, but caught Oberon's eye and added, "If you would excuse us for a moment to discuss the logistics?" Nath nodded and bent to speak to a pair of steel-helmed soldiers at her left hand, and I pulled Oberon aside. "Do you want them?"

"Me?" he muttered. "What am I to do with them? They're Mab's people—if you think they're going to swear allegiance to either of us, you're a bigger fool than you seem." He straightened, seeing something over my shoulder, then beckoned as one of the fae soldiers approached. "Come to talk defection, Kiet?" he asked as the soldier tucked his helmet under his arm.

"Lord Oberon. Lord...Coileán," he managed with obvious distaste. "I can't claim to speak for all, but you know as well as I do that a peaceful merger is impossible at this time."

"I was just explaining the facts of life to the boy," Oberon replied. "What do you suggest?"

Kiet—who, if known to Oberon, had to be some centuries my senior—rubbed his nose in thought. "A third court—"

"Out of the question. The realm won't have it."

He grunted. "I'd feared as much."

"How many of Mab's children remain?"

At that, Kiet cocked an eyebrow. "Excluding the ones slaughtered this day? To my knowledge, one—assuming she is who I think she is, my lords."

We followed his gaze to Toula, who was simultaneously defending the gate and keeping Meggy away from Moyna. "She is," I said quietly. "Would you like a word with her?"

Kiet nodded, and I caught Toula's eye and beckoned for her to join us. She jogged over, frowning, and I pulled her into the huddle. "This is Fotoula Pavli," I said, ignoring the death glare she shot me at the recitation of her proper name. "Mab's daughter. If there's something you need to discuss…"

The soldier dropped to one knee and dipped his head. "Lady Fotoula," he said, oblivious to her twitching, "with your brother's death—and the deaths of your other siblings," he added with a glare for me, "the court is bereft of a leader, and the title flows to—"

"No."

His head shot up in consternation, but Toula stepped back and folded her arms. "No," she repeated, "it doesn't. Even if it did, I'm *way* too Arcanum to run a court, but…"

Her voice trailed off, and I caught the glance she shot across the circle to Val, who watched with concern from the rim of the gate. The two exchanged a silent, indecipherable look, and she turned back to Kiet. "I'm sorry, but no. Choose someone else."

"Return to Faerie and submit to my rule," I told him as he rose, "or take your chances in the mortal realm. The choice is yours."

Kiet's eyes were troubled, but he nodded. "My lords. We will not return to Faerie at this time."

"Suit yourself," said Oberon as Kiet walked away. He had the grace to wait until the soldier was out of earshot before murmuring, "Protecting someone, are we?"

"I have no idea what you're talking about," said Toula, and left us to rejoin her brother, Meggy, and Joey, who had somehow coaxed Georgie out of her feeding frenzy.

Seeing our knot break apart, Nath asked, "Is the matter resolved?"

"It is," I replied. "Mab's people may have safe passage to the mortal realm. I'll open a second gate from Faerie as soon as we take our leave."

"Very good. And as for them?"

I glanced at my sisters and brother, who said nothing and looked somewhat green, even in the dim light. "They will return with me. We have matters to discuss. And if that doesn't suit them," I continued, meeting their worried eyes, "then they can remain here, and you may do with them what you like."

Nath nodded and steepled her long fingers. "Then I suggest, for their continued well-being, that they accompany you."

"Thank you, my lady," I told her, and turned to find Moyna on the fringe of their group. "And as for you, young lady…"

When I wake in the early hours and replay my life in the still darkness, I often pause at that moment and rewind, trying to find the spot where I made the wrong decision, where I could have done something differently and rewritten the outcome. I've found several such moments through this retrospection, but even still, no matter how desperately I try to avoid re-watching it, my mind continues to show me the truth as it happened. There is no restarting in life, after all.

I see Moyna standing apart from the family, red-faced with anger and baring her teeth between lips the color of old port. The top of her corset heaves with her labored breathing, and her blue eyes dart toward the gate and her mother, who runs toward her with relief etched on her face, finally free to reclaim her lost child. Moyna's hands clench and ball into fists, and I remember—too late, always too late—that the magic flowing into the Gray Lands is hers for the taking.

I see the green fire spark between Moyna's fingers, and still Meggy runs to her, overjoyed and oblivious to the danger.

I see my own hands rise and flare in front of my face as my panic takes control. I hear myself yelling Meggy's name. And when that does nothing to change her course, I see the twin blue fireballs shoot from my hands, straight for Moyna.

But Meggy finally notices me. Meggy sees that I'm about to kill her baby.

And Meggy, who can't raise the shield she needs in the split-second she has left, jumps between us.

I started running for Meggy before she hit the ground, trying to somehow recall the power that had blasted holes through her chest and abdomen, but magic doesn't work that way. I can't turn back time. I can't raise the dead.

But as I knelt and cradled her head, begging her to hold on, to heal, to forgive me, I tried my damndest.

The last thing I remember from the Gray Lands is looking up to find Moyna staring down at us with a gloating smile. "How does it feel, Ironhand?" she asked. I stared at her, beginning to comprehend what had happened, and her smile resolved into a smirk. "Still love me?"

She vanished then, and I caught the flicker of motion

as she reappeared beside the gate. Helen was too preoccupied to offer her any resistance, and as Oberon had incapacitated the guards, there was no one around to stop Moyna as she opened a rip into the mortal realm and was gone—and I was left to clutch the body growing cold in my hands.

CHAPTER 24

Even now, I can't say with any certainty who dragged me back across the border, though I suspect Val had a hand in it. I do remember struggling by the barn in the twilight as he and Joey pried Meggy away from me. She had grown pale and stiff by then, but something in me that had snapped insisted that if I waited a little longer, held on a little tighter—hell, maybe tried clapping—she would revive. When they finally pulled her out of my arms, I never had an opportunity to reclaim her, as Toula, who had been standing by at the ready, moved in and punched the wind out of me before I could start sparking. Each time I managed to catch my breath, she hit me again, harder and faster, until I surrendered and stayed down, curling up to protect myself from the rain of blows. "Stupid," she muttered, but whether she'd directed that at me, Meggy, or herself, I suppose I'll never know.

When I hadn't moved from the dirt by full nightfall, a few of my aides ventured out to claim me and half-carried me back into the palace. I limped into my chambers alone, then erased the doors and windows from existence before collapsing onto my bed and letting the blackness take me.

I might have remained there indefinitely had a shaft of sunlight not roused me from sleep.

The light hurt, even with my eyes closed, and I first tried burying my head in the pillow to seal it out. But I could still feel it, a warm spot on my back that refused to leave me in peace. With the warmth came fuller arousal, which brought back once more the scenes I'd been reliving in dreams and trying to push from my mind.

I'd been sleeping for a reason, I remembered, and I'd removed the windows specifically to avoid this situation. Yet one had returned of its own accord...

Frustrated, I rolled over and forced my eyes to open— and in the daylight, I saw I was not alone.

She sat at the foot of my bed, petite and almost girlish in form, her blonde waves cascading over one shoulder and onto the coverlet. Her dress was unremarkable, a silvery sheath short enough to reveal the bare feet she'd tucked up beneath her, but her eyes...hazel and slightly upturned, faintly glowing, and ancient, they crinkled when I gasped in surprise to find myself with company. Her mouth twitched as I scrambled to right myself and scooted to the head of the bed, leaving a trail of dirt across the white sheets. "It's time to rise, child," she murmured, then laughed softly when I rolled off the bed and into a defensive stance. "Come now, don't tell me you don't know me. Are these measures truly necessary?"

My throat was too dry to produce more than a raw croak. "Who—"

"Listen," she said, pressing two fingers to the side of her head, and I heard her voice continue in my mind: *You don't know me, Coileán? You haven't completely ignored me this last year, have you?*

I felt my mouth open, then snapped it closed as recognition hit. "Moon and stars...you..."

She tilted her head and nodded. "Sit. I won't hurt you."

"But you..." I floundered, trying to drive the fog from my brain, and managed, "You have a *body*?"

At that, she laughed in earnest, high and trilling, as I stood beside the bed in my filthy clothes and stared at her. When the fit subsided, she patted the blanket in invitation and smiled. "This form is tiring to maintain, and I seldom find it necessary, but to answer your question, yes, I can be corporeal when I so choose. Now sit, child."

Struck dumb by the revelation that the voice of the realm had a face to match, I did as bidden.

She—Faerie, I supposed, having no other name for her—smoothed her skirt and regarded me with the sort of expression I'd not seen directed my way since Étaín had caught me setting the bushes on fire as a small boy. "You're shirking your duties, you realize," she began, and held up her hand when I tried to protest. "I know what happened, and I know the memory is fresh and agonizing to you. But hiding away isn't going to undo the past."

"I'm not hiding," I countered indignantly, "I just need—"

"Coileán, you've not left your bed in ten days."

That threw off my planned retort. "*Ten?*"

"Ten. They've carried on without you, but this can't continue." She sighed and reached across the covers to take my hand. "You have a duty. The world does not stop for one man's grief, does it?"

"You don't understand, I killed…" I couldn't bring myself to finish that sentence, but she nodded.

"You killed that child. And you tried to kill your own. I'm well aware. So what do you plan to do henceforth—sit here and mourn? Starve yourself? I know you're thirsty." She produced a glass of water and pressed it into my free hand, then waited as I chugged it down. "You know," she said once I'd come up for air, "you're not the first to lose a lover. The ache is there, child, but it passes."

"I *killed* her."

"And I don't mean to sound callous, but by anyone's reckoning, that's not the first life you've ended prematurely."

"You don't understand," I muttered, pulling free of her grasp as I refilled my cup and downed it. With one thirst slaked, I switched the water for bourbon and continued to drink, focusing on the familiar burn instead of the fresher pain.

She let me brood for a moment, then said, "You loved her. I know—"

"You *can't* know," I snapped, wheeling on her. "You have no comprehension of what that's like, so don't sit there and lecture me—"

"But I do." She sat silently, waiting while I pulled my temper under control, then murmured, "I was not always as I am now, child. My mother was mortal. And yes," she added, seeing my surprise, "I had a mother. A father, too. Sisters and brothers. Lovers. But that's not a story I care to revisit at this time." She stood and looked up at me with faint reproach. "We have matters to discuss if you can look beyond yourself."

It's embarrassing to be chastised by someone too small to look you in the face, especially when that person is in the right. "I'm listening," I mumbled.

"Moyna. What do you plan to do with her?"

I shook my head and shrugged, then began peeling my jacket off. The odor that assaulted me as soon as it fell away was far from pleasant, however, and I opened the window Faerie had replaced to let the stale air in the room circulate. "Has she been found?"

"Not to my knowledge, no. Do you intend to seek her out?"

"I should, shouldn't I?" I muttered, leaning on the windowsill. "Of course, I could wait for her to surface— she'll probably try to kill me soon enough. Oberon *did* just murder her boyfriend, but somehow, I'm sure I'm still to blame."

"Petulant, aren't we?" she remarked, joining me at the window.

"Paranoid. Could you at least take Moyna out of the succession? It'd give her one less reason to kill me."

"Well," she mused, propping her chin in her palms, "I *could*, technically speaking, but I'm bound by my word…" She looked at me, saw my blank expression, and said, "Ah. Your mother never gave you the terms, did she?"

"The terms of what?"

"Our treaty, you might call it." Faerie gazed out at the ever-blooming roses and let the breeze tousle her hair. "When Mab and Oberon and your mother stopped fighting, the four of us came to an arrangement to prevent further bloodshed: they would split governance of the realm three ways, I would provide them with the power they required to maintain the peace, and should something happen to one of them, that person's eldest living child would take the throne. This is unfamiliar to you?"

"Not exactly…"

She smiled to herself. "Titania is no longer a party to consider, and Mab broke our bargain. This leaves only Oberon, but as long as he lives, I will not change the terms. My word is my word."

We stood together silently, each contemplating the morning and our own thoughts.

"What did Mab ever do to you?" I finally asked her as I put my emptied bourbon glass aside. "Oberon said he and Mother drove her out in a power struggle—you didn't step in?"

Her delicate features hardened. "Oberon does not know the full truth."

"Which is?" She said nothing, and I pressed, "You had a deal with Mab, but you start shouting at me every time one of her people enters the realm. Come on, you still complain about *Toula*. What happened?"

She didn't turn away from the window, but her eyes slowly slid to meet mine. "You expect me to be content around Mab's daughter, the wizard?"

"You don't mind Val," I pointed out.

"The boy is no wizard, nor was he ever Mab's in any quality but blood. But that doesn't answer your question, does it?" With seeming reluctance, she pulled herself from the view to face me. "I could have stepped in when Titania and Oberon plotted against Mab, yes. I could have stopped them. But Mab had already betrayed me by that time, and I saw no need to come to her aid. When the others drove her out, I considered our bargain void."

"What happened?"

She paused, collecting her thoughts, then quietly said, "Mab had a love of power. Oh, the others did, too," she added, "but Mab was always the keenest of them to acquire it. She began to make forays into the Gray Lands," she continued, hoisting herself onto the windowsill. "And she became...*friendly*...with my counterpart there. He promised her dominion over both realms if she ousted me. I knew what she was planning, but Titania's greed swelled first, and Oberon, foolish boy that he was, sided with her against Mab. I simply withdrew the power I'd given her, and she could not stand against them. Her friend took her in, I see," she remarked dryly, "though I'm sure it pained her to rule in a land in which she was powerless."

"And...you never told Mother and Oberon about this?"

She chuckled. "Your mother wouldn't have cared, especially once Oberon moved out. And as for Oberon...well, he likes to imagine that he has full agency in his decisions. There's no sense in upsetting him. I do try to stay out of court matters," she added, "but sometimes I have to prod, even if it irks him."

"You sent him into the Gray Lands after us."

"He wouldn't have done it of his own choosing," she replied, swinging her legs against the stone wall. "By the way, if you were wondering, your siblings have been in custody since their return. The cells Titania designed have held up remarkably well."

I nodded and stepped away from her to strip off my shirt, then cringed as I caught another whiff of myself. "I suppose you'll give me hell if I throw them into an oubliette, hmm?"

"No."

I turned around, surprised, and she arched an eyebrow. "I have little pity for traitors," she said, "and they conspired to jeopardize the realm. Do with them what you will—you'll hear no complaint from me."

Deciding it would be rude to bathe while the soul of the realm was waiting in my bedroom, I simply willed myself clean and clothed. "If you're not partial to traitors," I muttered, sending my castoff clothing back into the ether, "you must have been overjoyed when I came back."

"Overjoyed?" she echoed. "No, not exactly, but I understood. Titania and I didn't always agree. I…" She hesitated, considering her words. "I knew what she did with your daughter, so no, I don't consider you a traitor for coming after her. And you did kill Mab," she added, almost as an afterthought, "which, as far as I'm concerned, counts in your favor."

"But you're not going to forgive Toula, are you?"

"Why do you insist so?" she replied, sounding annoyed. "You know what her mother did, the girl is pure Arcanum—"

"And she's risked her ass to help me twice. She's not the enemy."

Faerie's lips pursed in thought. "I'll consider that."

"Thank you. And Aiden?" I asked, suddenly realizing that I hadn't seen him on my return. "Is he—"

"He woke four days ago," she said, motioning for calm. "Sore and weakened but whole. His sister remains within the realm," she continued, and I detected a note of accusation in her tone.

"Helen also put her neck out on my accord," I replied. "If she wants to watch Aiden convalesce, I'm not going to expel her."

At that, she smirked and slid off the window. "I believe Helen is satisfied as to her brother's medical progress. Something intrigues her in the barn."

I could only imagine what Faerie had witnessed, but something told me Helen wasn't collecting dragonscale for Slim. "Is that so?"

"They are trying to pretend there's no attraction

between them. It's all rather amusing, really. Children," she sighed, and began to fade.

"Wait!" Faerie solidified and cocked her head, and I said, "You don't have a problem with Joey, correct? You're not going to nag me if he should, say, start coming and going between here and the Arcanum's hideout?"

"Of course not," she replied with a little smile. "I welcome my own."

"What does that—" I began, but she vanished before I could finish, leaving me with unanswered questions and a ravenous appetite. I sighed, seeing Meggy's face once more behind my eyes, then waved my door back into existence and stepped out to face my court.

At Toula's insistence, they had buried Meggy without me. Rather than keep the mangled corpse around and hope her spellcraft was up to halting decomposition, she selected an out-of-the way spot among my oaks, created a coffin, and asked Paul to say a few words. Meggy may have been a severely lapsed Catholic, but Paul didn't mind reading the proper prayers. While picking him up, Toula had also retrieved Mrs. Cooper, Stuart, and Slim from the Stowe compound, leaving poor Hal to face alone the prospect of surviving a holiday with his girlfriend's family.

I spent the afternoon in solitude at Meggy's grave, which Toula had marked with a white rosebush. Despite a few false starts, however, I couldn't find the right words for her. Apologies, declarations of love—she'd heard all of that before. I couldn't promise her that I'd bring Moyna home safely, not when Meggy's last action had been to save her from me. And so, as the shadows lengthened, I crouched beside the disturbed earth and whispered, "Rest well. I'm sorry I failed you, Meg. Maybe it wasn't what you needed," I said, resting my hand on the soil, "but for good or ill, I loved you."

With that, I rose and made my way home, knowing that

it was futile to ask her forgiveness.

There had been no one in the court to make decisions on my behalf during my absence. Even if my people would have listened to Oberon, he had returned to Florida almost immediately after loosing Mab's refugees on the mortal realm, explaining that my grief wasn't his problem. But while matters began to pile up on my desk, Val, who had sense, experience, and confidence that I would show myself again someday, took the liberty of incarcerating my wayward siblings as a security measure. They had complained bitterly about the mistreatment, he informed me, as had certain of their friends—he presented me with a list for later perusal—but he maintained that as long as he was overseeing my security, he had the right to act until I told him otherwise. I thanked him profusely, apologized for my behavior concerning Meggy's corpse, and gave him my instructions.

Late that evening, Syral, Huc, Ji, and Nanine were moved into a single, highly-warded cell. I told them what Mother had told me when I was in their position: the bonds on the room would allow them enough power to feed themselves and make themselves somewhat comfortable, but there was no escape. As they had been Mother's favorites, they knew well that I spoke the truth, and they tried to reason with me in the moment before I locked them in and walked away.

When the door was sealed and I could no longer hear their pleas for mercy, I left them to their own devices, confident that they would soon understand the unique hell that is forced companionship.

To my relief, Aiden made a full recovery. To my surprise, however, he made it clear that he wasn't leaving Faerie.

"I mean," he muttered at his oatmeal as he

backtracked, "unless you want me to go...I want to stay here, but if things are too, uh...tough right now..."

Before he could finish the thought, I rose, came around the table, and embraced him.

"I'm really sorry," he mumbled into my shirt as I crushed his ribs. "I should have cut the power, I didn't think—"

"You did only what I asked of you," I interrupted, pulling back to look him in the eye. "The fault is mine. Anyway, I understand you were barely conscious at the end."

Aiden shrugged under my hands. "That's what they tell me. I remember waking up in bed, and Hel was poking me in the shoulder until I hit her."

"Siblings," I said with a straight face.

"Tell me about it," he smirked. "One of them gives me the biggest migraine of my life, and the other's getting cozy with my friend. What am I supposed to do with you guys, huh?"

"I think I gave you more than a migraine," I said, returning to my breakfast. "And...Helen and Joey?"

"Yeah." He grunted and picked up his spoon. "They're basically dating."

"Dating? There's nowhere to date around here."

"Well, she spends all day with him and sleeps out at the barn. What would you call that?"

"Hmm...dating, perhaps," I replied, watching him eat with determination. "Still opposed, are we?"

He paused, laden spoon half-raised, and frowned at the table. "I guess I'm not opposed to it," he said after a moment's consideration, "but it's...*weird.*"

"If it's any consolation," I said, playing with my eggs, "I doubt it lasts long." Aiden's brow furrowed, and I explained, "She's going to be the grand magus, yes? How's she supposed to date a guy who's living with his platonic, draconic life partner in Faerie?"

"Hel *can* make her own gates," Aiden pointed out.

"This isn't about gates—this is about politics. Correct me if I'm mistaken, but wouldn't it be rather scandalous if the Arcanum's top wizard were caught sneaking around with the guy who lives in my backyard? Won't last more than another month."

Aiden mulled that over for a couple of bites, then put his spoon down again and cocked an eyebrow. "Want to bet on it? Five bucks says they make it to summer."

"Oh, a high roller!"

"Says the jerk who pulls money out of thin air. You in?"

We shook on it across the table, and Aiden sighed. "You know what this means, right? Now I've got to root for my sister to hook up with *Joey*."

"Or we could just not discuss this again until they call it off," I replied.

"Yeah," he said with a little grin, "that works, too."

The backlog of work I'd amassed tethered me to the realm for the next few days. As I sat through the usual complaints, a litany of grievances between neighbors and associates, I fought the urge to throttle the petitioners for wasting my time with trivialities. These were, by any definition, adults who appeared before me, yet they whined about minor trespasses—encroachments into shared spaces, missing invitations to parties, verbal slights—that somehow amounted to grave injustices in want of retribution. I did the best I could to sort through the claims and counter-claims, but in truth, I felt like I was dealing with a pack of oversized five-year-olds fighting over the same toys and crying to the nearest authority when someone pulled their hair.

But they were *my* five-year-olds, and if I didn't arbitrate, they were liable to fight each other to the death over name-calling. One aggrieved faerie is dangerous; two are a war waiting to begin. And so I dispensed justice, or at least a facsimile thereof, and slowly cleared the mess I'd acquired through my absence.

My siblings' supporters, who had been so vocal following our return, were noticeably absent from court. I kept Val's list close at hand and consulted it to make certain that I wasn't overlooking anyone, but word had spread of my dealings with my kin, and the rest of the realm suddenly decided to either disavow them or lay low. I asked my guards to keep an ear to the ground and inform me if something began to stir, but I couldn't say I was sorry to not have a pack of protesters crowding the throne room.

As the days dragged on, Val brought me periodic updates on the matters I actually cared about. Toula had returned to the Arcanum silo before I woke and explained to Greg what had transpired. He had posted a watch for signs of Moyna, but as yet, the nets had come up empty. Greg offered me the use of another compass—*and there are other methods*, his handwritten note informed me, *if you want to find her*—but I declined. I felt strongly that she was hiding in the mortal realm, and she couldn't stay in the shadows forever. More importantly, I didn't know what I would do if I found her, and I didn't trust myself not to kill her on sight.

Still, I would have asked Toula for more information on what tricks Greg had up his sleeve, had she been willing to speak with me. She was mourning in private, Val told me, and had made it clear that she wished no one's company but her own. Having no desire to wound Toula any more than I already had—and hearing the insistence in her brother's tone that I respect her wishes—I kept my distance and waited for her to drop in.

Helen had returned to school after her extended Thanksgiving break, but as the realm kept notifying me, she continued to make brief forays back across the border. Aiden had taken to babysitting Georgie whenever Joey mysteriously went missing—absences that, to no one's surprise, tended to coincide with Helen's goings and comings.

In early December, Vivi called from Alaska to check in. She had alerted the Fringe after Toula's visit, but they, like the Arcanum, could provide no clue to my daughter's whereabouts. "And this isn't a favor," she insisted while describing the spotters involved. "We've decided that this is self-preservation. No offense, but nobody wants her wandering around unsupervised over here, you got me?" Despite the lack of news of Moyna, I was pleased to hear that Hal had survived the visit, and Rufus had brought them back to Virginia in time for Rigby's last game of the season—which, as predicted, ended in another L. I enquired as to how the coach's unplanned absence had been explained, and Vivi snorted. "Half the buildings in town have FEMA tarps on the roofs, people have fled because they're worried about chemical fallout—hell, they had to hold the game in Richmond because the other team wouldn't come in," she replied. "Since he turned up alive, no one really cares where Hal was last week." Slim's, she noted, was doing good business with the returning refugee crowd, as the tiki bar on the beach was among the town's casualties.

But that still left the matter of my old shop to consider, and so, after several weeks' absence, I pulled myself away from work to see what remained of my life in Rigby.

We are, every one of us, the narrators and heroes of our own lives. As I stood at the base of my old building's outside staircase, however, shivering in the cold, damp wind rolling in from the Atlantic, I knew with complete conviction that I was not a hero—I was a monster. There is no redemption for monsters, no happy endings; no one roots for the monster to kill the hero and lay waste to the world. Monsters exist to be feared, to be fought, to be vanquished.

I had been the monster lurking on the edges of Meggy's life, and I had beaten her in the end without ever truly understanding that I was destroying her.

I didn't want to go back into that building. It might have been my building first, but it had been Meggy's in the end, and so much of her lingered in there to accuse me. Still, I knew I had to do *something* with the pieces left behind, and so I plodded up the stairs toward Meggy's last apartment, weaving a careful path around her dead ferns. I could only imagine what I'd find in there. Rotting trash and long-soured milk came to mind, but as I had yet to investigate how much damage the mantis creatures had done to the structure, I tried to prepare for stagnant puddles and nesting vermin as well.

The kitchen door was unlocked, as Toula and I had left it, but to my surprise, the first thing I smelled when I opened it was lemon furniture polish.

Perplexed and on alert, I shut the door behind me and took in the spotless kitchen—the chrome spigot polished to a shine, the counters clear of dishes and dust, the trash bin empty and tucked into its corner. I slid into the dining nook and found more of the same, professional-quality tidiness overlaid with the odors of citrus and ammonia. Even the rug bore the telltale stripes of a vacuum cleaner.

Before I investigated further, I picked up on the sound of running water coming from the master bathroom and held my position. "Hello?" I called, keeping one hand behind the kitchen wall and willing a fireball into being in case my janitorial-minded burglars came armed.

A second later, the water shut off, and a familiar voice called back down the hallway, "Mr. Leffee, dear? Is that you?"

I exhaled and extinguished my ammunition. "Mrs. Cooper? What are you doing here?"

She bustled out of the bathroom, her hair covered with a pink polka-dot scarf and her arms protected to the elbow with yellow gloves. "I do hope I'm not intruding," she said, adjusting her stretch pants, "but it didn't seem right to leave this place a mess."

Without warning, my eyes began to prick. "You didn't have to—"

"I wanted to. Thought it was the right thing to do. She was always kind to me," she said, tucking a stray lock of hair back under her scarf. "And...you know, there wasn't really a public funeral. I'd have brought a casserole or something, but...well." She paused, momentarily uncertain, then looked back at me. "You're a mess, dear."

I nodded.

"Sit down," she ordered, pointing to the table as she marched down the hallway. "I'll put the tea on."

"Oh, you don't—"

"*Sit*, Colin. You look like hell."

She was right, and so I pulled out a chair and watched her peel off her cleaning gloves and dig through Meggy's pantry for supplies. A few minutes later, she had come up with a half-empty box of Lipton and an assortment of sweetener packets stolen from local restaurants, and she set a chipped mug in front of each of us as she took a seat. "I'm so sorry, dear," she said, stirring pilfered sugar into her drink. "How're you holding up?"

I shook my head and wrapped my hands around my mug. "You know how it happened?"

"Toula filled us in when she picked us up."

"And I'm sorry about that, too," I mumbled.

"About what? Alaska? The Stowes were lovely, really. Couldn't have been nicer once Vivian and Mr. Matherson explained everything." She blew the steam off her cup and sipped. "And little Vivian's brother, Rufus—did you meet him? Such a sweetheart. Poor dear tried to show Stuart a thing or two, but I don't think it stuck. Rufus is a professor, you know," she added, smiling distantly. "American history. He's written books and everything. Such a *nice* fellow."

I stared at her, momentarily drawn from my funk by

the odd expression on her face. "Mrs. Cooper," I said slowly, "if I didn't know better, I'd say you were sweet on him."

She scoffed and waved the notion aside, but her cheeks flushed. "Nonsense, and even if it weren't, he's on the wrong side of the country." Her color flared and began to fade as she turned her attention to her tea. "There's only ever been one man for me," she continued, gazing into the mug. "Mr. Cooper was one in a million, and I don't plan on trying to replace him."

I smirked back at her over my drink. "Nothing wrong with admiring the scenery, though."

"Discreetly," she muttered. "But enough about that—I want to be sure you're okay. You hadn't been back, and I...well, I worry," she said, patting my hand. "Because while I know full well that you can take care of yourself, that's an awful lot to have on your mind."

Her eyes were as soft as ever behind her glasses, but they fixed on mine with an unusual intensity. "I'm not going to kill myself, if that's what you're worried about," I replied, and her face relaxed a degree. "Too much work waiting for me."

"Have you talked to someone?"

"Such as?"

"Well, Father Paul does come to mind. Y'all two are still friendly, right?"

I tried to imagine what Paul would say, knowing what I had done, and shelved the resulting unpleasant mental image. "We are, but I...need time."

"Of course." She sipped her tea and looked around at her lemony handiwork. "So, what's to be done with this place? It's a nice apartment, you know, you could rent it out."

"Or I could give it to you. Only if you want it, of course," I hastened to add, seeing her surprise. "There's no mortgage on the place, if you were concerned about that. Plumbing's solid, wiring's reliable...you could sell it, go on a cruise with the proceeds."

She pursed her lips as she mulled this over, then looked at me almost guiltily. "You know, dear, there was an awful lot of damage when those *things* came through."

"Oh, did your store—"

"No, no, I'm fine. But Stuart's building was ruined. Half the roof and a supporting wall—the landlord condemned the place. He's been staying with me ever since we got back."

I saw the question in her eyes and sighed. "Or you could give it to Stuart."

"How about I rent it to Stuart?"

"Do what pleases you. I'll take care of the title." I finished my tea, then frowned at Mrs. Cooper. "The furnishings here are somewhat on the feminine side."

"And that is *his* problem, isn't it?" She turned to look at the den, then murmured, "If you'd rather that he not use her things, I completely understand, but I'm not asking for a renovation."

I stood and surveyed the bits of Meggy left behind— cleaned and straightened, a sanitized version of her life— then closed my eyes. When I opened them again, the apartment was stripped to the hardwood floor, save the kitchen table and the tea things, and I struggled to make my throat unclench. "Thoughts?"

I heard her chair scrape across the floor as she pushed back, then felt her hand on my shoulder. "It's all right, dear," she said quietly. "We'll figure it out. You take your time, okay?"

"Okay."

"Good. Now, let's see what you might want to save from downstairs," she said, steering me toward the inner staircase. "I really haven't touched the shop, but the vandals have stayed away, so everything should be in order."

She opened the door and started down, but I caught her arm before we reached the floor, and she looked back at me inquisitively. "I'm going to miss you, Eunice," I said.

Her eyebrows rose. "You're not coming back to Rigby? Is this goodbye? I'm sure Mr. Matherson will be disappointed to hear—"

"No, not goodbye, just…thinking out loud."

"Ah." She hesitated, then murmured, "Down the line, you mean."

"You could come back with me," I heard myself say in a rush, quite before I knew I was going to say it. "I can't give you your youth, but I can make it all a little easier…"

But Mrs. Cooper smiled, and I knew what she was going to say before she began to shake her head. "I thank you, dear, I truly do, but Mr. Cooper…he's still waiting for me. Not today, not tomorrow, but someday, I want to see him again."

I nodded and released her, but when we reached the floor, she turned and hugged me. "It won't always feel like this," she whispered. "It gets a little duller every year, and someday, it's not going to hurt every time you say her name."

I didn't share Mrs. Cooper's confidence, but I stood there among the dusty bookshelves and hugged her back, hoping she was right.

Not until after the first of the year did Toula return to Faerie.

Twilight had fallen, and Joey, Aiden, and Georgie had yet to return. Joey had promised Aiden a long flight— Georgie liked the exercise, and Aiden loved the wind in his hair—but as the light faded from pink to deep blue, I stood by the barn and scanned the sky, wondering if I should look for them. Val, who had perched on a bale of straw with a set of blades and a whetstone to pass the time, looked up periodically and reminded me that Joey would call if he needed someone to fret over him.

Impatient but sensing that I was driving my captain

mad, I leaned against the fence and watched the sheep repopulate their enclosure. I had tweaked the settings several times at Joey's request, and the newest flock was fearless and insensate to pain. We had settled on a budding rate that seemed to keep their numbers stable, and Georgie remained content with a mutton-based diet, even if she occasionally lamented the fact that she couldn't char her own food in this realm. Despite her aggravation, I slept more soundly with the knowledge that the dragon, who at four months old was nearly fifty feet long, wasn't going to incinerate me in bed.

When my pocket began to buzz, I feared Joey had lost his way and hurriedly flipped my phone open. "Where are you?"

"Montana," said Toula. "You were expecting something more exotic?"

"*Toula!*" Val looked up from his work, and I pressed the phone more tightly to my ear. "Sorry, I thought you were Joey—"

"Caller ID isn't the enemy, Gramps." She paused to take a long breath, and Val joined me at the fence while I waited for her to resume. "All right if I come over?" she finally asked.

"You know you're welcome."

The line went dead, and as I glanced at the barn, a gate opened and Toula stepped across, sporting gray sweatpants and a lime-green sweater worn through at the elbows. For once, her hair lay flat against her scalp instead of teased into its usual spikes, and I noticed that she had opted for fuzzy pink slippers over legitimate footwear. "Hey," she mumbled, lifting a hand in greeting but staying close to the gate. "You came out of hiding."

"So did you."

"Yeah, well, I needed time."

"So did I."

Toula nodded, then marched across the yard and embraced her brother, who closed his eyes and pressed his chin against her shoulder. "Welcome back," he murmured. "Can you stay?"

She extricated herself after a moment and shrugged. "For a little while. Greg insisted on counseling, and if I miss too many appointments, he's going to get on to me."

"Counseling?" Val asked, holding her at arm's length.

"Therapist. We've got one in the silo for times like this," she explained. "No one wants a crazy wizard around, right?"

"You're not crazy—"

"No, but I haven't been myself recently, and Greg…keeps tabs. Can't say I blame him." Toula turned to look at me, even as Val tightened his grip on her. "I know why you did it," she said. "And I don't blame you. I'm almost to the point that I don't blame myself, but we're still working on that."

"Toula," I sighed, "you didn't do anything—"

"Exactly. I should have thrown Megs in stasis and locked her away somewhere until it was over, but I didn't do anything. And we see how well that turned out." She paused, letting Val hold her against him again, then muttered, "Are we cool?"

"We're cool," I told her.

"Good." After giving her brother's back a firm pat, she pulled loose and shuffled toward the fence to take a seat. "Where's Aiden?" she asked as she hoisted herself onto the top rung. "The announcement went out this morning—Carver's been officially tapped as Greg's successor. I thought he might want to know."

"They should be back soon," I replied, watching Val take a spot beside her. "Took Georgie out for a spin."

"Mm. Ever thought about getting those guys helmets? I mean, that's a long way to fall if something happens to Georgie."

"Actually, I've considered—" I began, but paused when an odd sensation suddenly came over me, like having an unscratchable itch all over my body. A glowing circle appeared in the grass at my feet, and I frowned at the others. "What's going on?"

Val had jumped off the fence at the first sign of an abnormality, but Toula stayed him with her arm. "I *think* that's the business end of a summoning spell," she said after a moment's contemplation, "but I can't say. Are you—"

"Fighting the compulsion to step into that thing," I said, bending for a closer inspection. "Any idea where it might lead?"

"Probably not the Gray Lands, but that's as close as I can get you."

"Sounds promising."

"*Coileán*," said Val, but I shook my head to silence his protest.

"If I'm not back by morning, I expect a search party," I told them, then glared at the ring and crossed into the light.

My skin flared with heat, then cold, and suddenly, I found myself standing in the center of a chalk circle studded with six white pillar candles. A sniff told me I was back in the mortal realm—and, tellingly, that the wizard who had summoned me was practicing his craft with honeysuckle-scented candles of the sort one might find at a better housewares shop. I blinked rapidly, letting my eyes adjust, then saw a familiar figure standing outside the circle, wearing a hooded white robe and several pounds of amulets about his neck.

"Stu," I sighed, folding my arms, "I hope for your sake that this is a legitimate emergency."

His eyes were saucers in the candlelight, and I spotted something in his right fist. "What are you holding?" I asked, then felt something brush against my leg and looked down to find one of Stuart's cats running through the circle—a circle, I realized, seeing more of my surroundings, that he'd drawn on the floor of my former bookstore. The place was no longer recognizably mine, aside from the heavy oak counter. I had removed most of the bookshelves when I cleaned it out, and Stuart had apparently salvaged his tables and wares from the rubble of his old shop. Even his fake ficus had found a home in the far corner of the store.

After a moment, the shock seemed to have worn off enough for Stuart's hand to unclench its death grip, and a carved metal ball fell to the floor and rolled toward a display of ceremonial drums. "It worked," he whispered. "I don't…I…it *worked*."

I had seen enough of the ball to realize what Stuart had been playing with. "Preloaded summoner? A single-use spell? Where'd you get it, kid?"

At that, Stuart finally remembered that I was standing several feet away from him, now being avoided by all of his cats. "Rufus Stowe. An old Arcanum artifact, he said to use it in case of emergency, but—"

"But you had to see if it worked." I spread my arms and let them flop to my sides. "Presto. Happy?"

He nodded slowly, not taking his eyes off of me. "So…you're trapped in there?"

"Should I be?"

"Well…yes. A circle is used to contain spirits until they agree to do the summoner's bidding…"

I let him ramble on for a minute, then held up my hand. "Stu, buddy, remember what I said about breaking circles?" I pointed to the fat candles in front of me, which completely covered the chalk beneath them. "And remember how you need to power up a circle first? Wards? Is any of this ringing a bell?"

"I did power the circle," he protested. "Drew it, lit the candles, cast the spell of protection—"

I stepped over the chalk line and smacked his head so hard his necklaces jingled. "For the last time, *you are not a wizard*. How much clearer can I make this?"

Stuart rubbed his head and pushed his hood off. "I'm *trying*."

"It's not a matter of trying—either you are or you aren't." I watched him as he crawled under the table to retrieve his summoner, then turned the lights back on with a flick of will and pointed to the café tables by the ficus when he reemerged. "Let's get a few things straight, shall we? What did this Rufus tell you, anyway?"

"Not much," he muttered, joining me at the nearest table. "I don't see why I can't be a wizard if I put my mind to it. I've got the books, I'm *certified*..."

His voice trailed off as a pair of glass tumblers and a bottle of scotch appeared on the table between us. "Do the honors," I offered, pushing the bottle toward him. "It's going to be a long night."

Stuart poured modest doubles, and as we drank in silence, I looked around the store, half-expecting to see Meggy grinning at me from behind the counter. But all I saw were shadows and my private ghosts, and even her jasmine smell had been supplanted by patchouli and sticks of incense. I listened for a footfall overhead that would never come, and I drank deeply, letting the burn in my throat soothe the creeping tightness there.

When my glass was empty, I pushed back from the table and stood. "Come on," I said, and headed for the street. "Let's take a walk."

He followed me into the night, still wearing his ridiculous robe, and traipsed after me down to the sea. And there we stood, conversing quietly while the stars wheeled overhead and the waves continued their eternal assault against the shore, with Meggy lingering always just out of my sight.

ACKNOWLEDGEMENTS

And we're back for round two…

Writing alone, in the comfort of your living room, is one thing. Putting your stories out into the world is another matter entirely, and it can be terrifying. A very special thank-you is due to all of you who read *Stranger Magics* and offered such lovely encouragement online and in person. I'm truly grateful for your support—thank you so much for reading (and for leaving reviews)!

For reasons unfathomable, the Novel Chicks continue to put up with me. Thank you, *thank you*, ladies, for your critique, your expertise, and your friendship.

And yes, once more, here's to you, Mom and Dad.

ABOUT THE AUTHOR

When not writing fiction, Ash Fitzsimmons is an appellate attorney and an unrepentant car singer.

Find her online:
www.ashfitzsimmons.com